THE LINGERING CLOUD

Dear Reader,
I hope you find this interesting,
entertaining and inspirational.
Hollis

THE LINGERING CLOUD

A Novel

Hollis Hughes

©TXu 1-878-16

ISBN-13: 9781496172488
ISBN-10: 1496172485

ACKNOWLEDGMENTS

To Lera, My Wife . . .

who took on the difficult task of typing this manuscript from my handwritten narrative, then helped me edit and proof the typed version. She wrote, at my request, a detailed description of a bride coming down the aisle as seen by a ninety-one-year-old bridesmaid. She tended to a host of other details that I could never have done.

and

To Agnes Owen Hughes, my long-deceased mother . . .

who read to me and my brothers each evening when the supper dishes were done. Those hours planted within my spirit a love for what the printed word could produce in the heart of a reader.

INTRODUCTION

Barely twenty-two years of age, the angelic young bride showed early symptoms of schizophrenia on the eve of their wedding. Yet Mack never allowed his wife's condition to deter him from becoming the most effective preacher that he could.

God had long ago forgiven Mack with the first prayer of repentance, but the difficulty lay in not forgiving himself for his sin when temptation blindsided him in the most unforeseen circumstances.

His deep love for and commitment to his God kept him heroically pressing on to rise above the odds against becoming the preacher that God had called him to be and that his supportive congregation believed he could be.

The Lingering Cloud was written during the author's eighty-fifth year. With twelve years of healing since his wife's death, he felt he had reached a level of maturity to write this narrative as it should be written.

CHAPTER ONE

As Mack Baldwin drove along the street, he glanced in his pickup's rear-view mirror, not once but several times. The Greek revival architecture on the front of the state's mental hospital, under other circumstances, might have given him pleasure. But the view on this day was gut-wrenching.

Lee and Anne Allen had been there to offer him all the support they could on the day their Rebecca was put away. They had left some twenty minutes earlier, assuring him he would not be abandoned to face this alone. In a manner he had never quite realized, he now knew what being alone was. Rebecca was probably already in one of the rooms on the second floor of the east wing—alone and scared.

Ten miles per hour was fast enough on this hospital street, going away. He glanced in the rearview mirror again and again, feeling the unrelenting hurt as the hospital slowly began to recede into the distance. He was leaving his "Angel" behind. That's how he thought of her and how she was until the illness hit. As the disease progressed, more of her angelic personality disappeared each time the madness took away more of her sanity.

Would their lives together ever start again? They had never actually been together, he realized as he had not quite as clearly seen before.

He reached an intersection, took a right turn, and the facility could no longer be seen; did that make him feel better? On the contrary, a bit more sadness was added to his burden because he could no longer feel the little comfort it had given him to see any part of the place that was to be her home now.

He considered turning around and driving back to the parking area and then walking 'til he arrived near her second floor room. But then he would have to leave as soon as an institutional guard spotted him loitering.

The sooner he began to learn how to live without her, that was going to have to be done. But what had been going on for well over a year had not been living, except for carpentry and preaching.

Turmoil had begun on their wedding night and had since hung heavily over his head, ready to be cut loose again at any time. What was done this day probably should have been done a year ago. Dr. Pickens had suggested it on the third visit when medication wasn't working well. Maybe . . . just maybe a better medication would come along someday.

A bright October day for the people on sidewalks, an occasional one entering or leaving a store. Their lives were apparently holding together, for there was a briskness in their steps that denied depression or a lack of interest in living. Just watching people could tell you a little of what was going on in their minds. The light changed to green and he drove on.

He had learned more about reading the signs of a person's emotional state after Rebecca's illness took over. Expressions in her eyes and on her face revealed an oncoming storm, many times just minutes before it hit. Even her body movements became less grace-ful, not as precise.

A major intersection came up. He had thought about driving to his parents' place. His dad was probably raking the last cut of hay, but his mother would have time for him. Deciding he had just as well face it alone, he took a right turn on to the road that would carry him home.

His dashboard clock showed 1:30, reminding him that his stom-ach needed attention. If things ever got too bad for food to be wel-come, just what in the world could he do for comfort?

In five minutes, that seemed like ten, he turned in at a short-order restaurant; there was only one other customer. He took a booth. The jukebox had not been recently fed any quarters; he hoped it would remain in that state for the time he was there.

A cute young woman came to take his order. "Coffee?"

"Black and a large cheeseburger with fries, please." The cof-fee came in seconds, it seemed. Rich tasting and hot. Carefully he sucked in plenty of cooling air with the coffee that made it just right, perfect.

The place hadn't looked like anything special, but the burger was mighty special. When the girl came back to refill his cup, he ordered another burger, "exactly like this one."

He was free and eating delightful food. Rebecca was in a place that offered no freedom . . . well, in time it might, if ever the right medication came along. There was hope that she might get out and be able to live an almost normal life. Lots of people lived with handi-caps. But as Dr. Pickens had pointed out early on, "Brain illnesses are gosh awful handicaps." He explained that it was the brain itself that was different from that of a normal brain. "Whether it would look different if we could look inside of it, I have no idea. But it surely acts differently. And the patient didn't choose to be sick. Rebecca is totally innocent of bringing on the illness. Don't you ever forget that, Mack."

He thought of this as he ate the second burger. Dr. Pickens was the most down-to-earth doctor he had ever met. Told you in a kind, but straight-forward manner what you were up against and what you had better prepare for. "How I wish I could honestly tell you better times are ahead." He had gone on to tell Mack to spend a little time each day doing something he liked to do.

A state park was about ten miles ahead on the road he pulled out on after finishing his meal. There were hiking trails. He'd take one for a half hour. The half hour hike was on a loop trail of four miles. Hilly land that offered grand views of gold hickories, intensely red black gum, red maples of every shade from yellow to flaming red, and a variety of other colorful species somewhat less spectacular. Remembering the doctor's advice, he completed the loop in an hour and a half. Ninety minutes of living where his feelings of loss and sadness were less acute. Tire the fellow out physically and emotions lose some of their cutting edge, was a lesson he began to learn that day. Hiking was going to be a part of his daily routine.

Mack realized that his life was going to have to be changed. Worrying and praying for Rebecca wasn't going to help; for more than a year he had burned most of his inner resources that way. Prayer had not healed her damaged brain. Worry could do nothing that helped. Maybe he should pray to God to give him the resolve and courage to face life as it is, since most of life brought things beyond his abilities to change. With God's help, he might be a better preacher and carpenter.

CHAPTER TWO

The world's most beautiful woman rode beside Mack in his pick-up. The ceremony at her family's church a couple of hours earlier had made her his bride.

Soft-spoken, demure, perhaps a little shy, a smile that was more about sweetness than dazzling sunshine, a heart that was soft and tender. It was no wonder that he had placed her on a pedestal as he had begun falling in love during their freshman year in college.

A preacher didn't need a wife who was so outgoing, she would tend to dominate conversations she took part in. She was the ideal wife for a preacher, an angelic helper.

At twenty-two, they both had their degrees, Rebecca's in elementary education, his in religion. Her personality was ideal for small children's mentor. Was his equally suited to helping people find the ways to spiritual tranquility at a time when the threat of a nuclear shootout was beginning to hang heavily over the heads of all?

Mack had been preaching for the past two years at a small church where Sunday morning attendance hovered around sixty.

About a mile from church he had rented a small house. This was to be the site of their honeymoon, until time to begin getting ready for church the next morning. A carpenter on week days since graduation a month earlier, Mack would be at work on Monday. There was nothing unusual about this sort of honeymoon in 1960. Rebecca had a teaching job that started in September.

Mack had read a short manual on sex in marriage. A born-again Christian at age eleven, and a certainty at age fourteen that he would be a preacher; he was an innocent. Compared to Rebecca, he knew the facts of life, a little knowledgeable on some aspects.

Her mother never shared her knowledge of the subject. Other girls sensed that Rebecca was far too nice to ever bring out "intimate girl talk" when in her presence.

Rebecca read novels, the kind where a young man might press his lips to his girl friend's lips, but no mention being made that this was anything other than an expression of tender sweetness. And the few times Mack had kissed her, it was just like in one of the church library's romantic novels.

But at a fundamental level in her stomach was the feeling that this was not quite how marriage was. Fear of something unknown? That's how it appeared to her.

Mack was no more at ease than she. Would any sort of physical intimacy tarnish the purity of his wife's image that existed in his heart? She was too pure and perfect for that aspect of marriage.

Before reaching their house, they stopped at a restaurant for supper. Rebecca ordered a fruit salad with cottage cheese. She had eaten lots of sweets at the reception and her appetite was almost non-existent for the time being. Mack ordered pork tenderloin with vegetables. They didn't hurry through the meal, putting off the time of arrival at their home.

"I've never been married before, Mack. I don't know how to act or what is expected of me. It will be so different. For twenty-two years I've been the me I grew up with. Now I'm going to be one-half of a couple, Mack and Rebecca or Rebecca and Mack. What a different way to live. I feel so uncertain. Actually scared."

"It may help that you and your mother moved your things to our little house a few days ago. I share some of the uncertainties with you. Life will never again be quite the same for either of us. We knew that months ago."

"Do you feel married, Mack? Did the preacher's going through the brief ceremony make you think in a different way about us? I don't feel married."

For the next few minutes they ate in silence. Rebecca remembering what a friend who got married the year before told her about being hardly able to wait to get into bed with that "hunk of a man." Well, Mack was the nicest young man she had ever known and she felt like waiting as long as she could get by with.

At home, there was an unfamiliar awkwardness in their behavior. No daily newspaper to read. TV was enough to distract their thoughts and anxieties, for ten minutes, at least. The inevitable hour was there and it was only a quarter past nine.

Without comment Rebecca made the first move. Then minutes later she left the bathroom and went to the bedroom. Not long afterward Mack came to the bedroom, dressed in pajamas.

When he had turned out the bedside lamp, he lay still for a minute or two. And then moved to her, taking one of her hands. Soon he had pulled her close; the room air conditioner added to his pleasure in snuggling. After a few minutes of close contact without her trying to pull away, he decided it was time for a bit more intimacy. One of his hands began to explore, not a lot but enough to create excitement in him. He stopped, giving her time to adjust to the feel of his hand on the lower part of her abdomen, almost too far, he thought. As he awaited her response, she lay still for maybe twenty seconds, and then slipped away as if she had second thoughts about the unfamiliar advance Mack had made.

Without a word, she eased out of bed and went to the bathroom. Soon Mack heard a familiar sound—water flowing into a bathtub.

He turned on the bedside light and got a book and began to read. A chapter later, she returned and sat on the edge of the bed, as if waiting . . . but waiting for what?

"I took a tub bath, Mack."

"I heard and wondered why."

"Because a shower wouldn't wash away the sin from the place you allowed your fingers to explore."

"Why, darling, my fingers didn't really do much of anything."

"Yet I lay there for close to half a minute. Not feeling shame as I should have, but a faint, subdued sort of pleasure. And that is where I sinned as much as you did."

"But we are married. There was no wrong done."

"Yes, there was. A preacher saying a few words over a couple doesn't turn what would have been a sin a week earlier into acceptable conduct a few hours later. The preacher didn't suddenly turn what was sin before into an act of purity. His words are not magic. You touched me where I'd not been touched before."

"But we are married; we made vows."

"A few words, and something that was evil becomes good?"

Unbelievable! But there it was, all too clear. Mack had a very sick wife. He turned off the light and lay straight as a broomstick, on his side of the bed.

Maybe this was a freakish sort of event. It might be related to the stress of the day. No, not this. It was too far from the normal way of thinking. Too far removed from what culture had repeatedly drilled into the heads of all. Marriage was the event that changed relationships, legally and morally. For thousands of years, this had been so.

"Are you displeased with me, Mack?" she asked in a soft voice.

"If you believed we had sinned, I understand your behavior."

"You didn't answer my question."

"I did as well as I could, sweetheart."

Nothing else was said.

Were the traits of personality he had thought of as ideal, actually precursors of the illness? Had she been too demure, too shy, too sweet, too quiet? Would it have been healthier if she had been something of a cut-up, laughing a little too much instead of not at all. That was something to bring up with the doctor on their first visit.

His marriage? Most likely, he'd never have one. Was that too pessimistic? Possibly. But if she is sick—as I am certain she is—it will soon show up in a different way.

On through the night he worried and prayed. Does God, as Jesus did, heal sick brains? He prayed that it might be so. Sleep, if it came, and he was not sure it did, did not leave any beneficial traces.

⇒⊹⊹⇐

Though he doubted he could deliver the sermon as he had planned, he must have, because he received an unusual number of congratulatory comments. Perhaps, that was because his audience combined the approval of his sermon with approval of the young beauty who stood beside him at the doorway at the morning service's end. How great this would have been had he not known what lay beneath the pleasant mask she wore. Mack turned down several invitations to Sunday dinner, but promised they'd come soon.

It was on the ten mile drive to a restaurant that offered a Sunday buffet that Rebecca's illness made itself apparent again. "That pretty young thing with the clinging handshake and cherry-red lips and dazzling white teeth is out to get you."

Mack continued driving. Another bomb had been dropped in the meadow of happiness he had expected to find in marriage. It had been expected—he just hadn't known before it was dropped what form it would take.

"I didn't notice anything special."

"Being a man, you wouldn't. You have blinders on. Men don't pick up on the little things like women do."

As she was saying this, Mack was wondering where the sweet, quiet angel had gone. She was right about one thing, he sure wore blinders during courtship. It was the first flare of anger toward Rebecca he had experienced. Instantly, he was ashamed. She was very ill now and its appearance had only surfaced hours ago.

Patience! Something he had better begin to cultivate. He had seen nothing yet! Only two symptoms of a mental disorder, but they were enough to recognize the seriousness of it.

Could schizophrenia come on this fast? Was it like other fast-developing illnesses? You have a nagging cough that's lasted two weeks and twenty-four hours later, you have pneumonia. You feel great and the next morning you wake up with strep throat.

Whatever is messing up the normal functioning of her brain could have quickly crossed the threshold separating sanity from insanity. It may be a narrow barrier separating the two for all the rest of us.

They arrived at the restaurant. Rebecca had no difficulty making her selections. Mack didn't know why she might suffer confusion, except he had wondered if her brain might malfunction in other areas.

His food—gravy on mashed potatoes, roast beef, and pole beans with yeast rolls was so good, his mind could focus on that as he ate. Rebecca didn't seem to notice the cute waitress who kept Mack's coffee cup filled and hot throughout the meal. If she did, she obviously didn't see these courtesies as designs on her man. She was so normal throughout the meal, he took the risk of believing the two episodes were no more than freak occurrences that might never show up again.

There had been times he'd had attacks that caused him to look at everything through a lens that magnified the many facets of depression, and the next morning for no discernible reason, his heart was filled with sunshine. Where did such attacks come from and why did they go away?

Rebecca came back to the table with a piece of pecan pie. "My favorite dessert and there are probably six others that are a close second," she commented as her brown eyes twinkled.

The touch of humor lifted Mack's spirit further. At that moment he had hope where there had been none. If she could do this once, she could do it again.

But on the short drive home, he reconsidered this. There are no limits to how far wishful thinking can take a fellow whose heart is filled with despair and there is no real reason for hope concerning my dearly loved one. What am I to do? Pray and wait on the Lord—that's what I advise from the pulpit when it seems a person has no hope. If there were a remedy for this kind of problem, the hospitals for mental illness would never have been so completely filled as they are now. But does this not make this preacher out as a man lacking in faith? Have I ever preached from the pulpit that there are some prayers that God is unlikely to answer regardless of the degree of faith? Of course I haven't. Should I? No doubt most of the patients at the hospitals for the mentally ill have family members who have prayed and continue to pray for cures.

Later at home, Mack's thoughts returned to faith and prayer. There were no clear answers to why all prayers are not answered no matter how strongly the person believes in prayer. A devout Christian's son suffers a spine-crippling accident. The parent convinced that prayer can heal, prays around the clock that her son will walk again, and he doesn't . . . ever.

He didn't have the answers. But shouldn't he? He was a preacher.

═╪═╪═

It was the first Monday of their marriage. Mack had left for the construction site of a house he was helping frame. Rebecca washed up in the kitchen. Still sleepy, she went back to bed for a few minutes. For a short while she took a nap and awoke to consider the past couple of days.

Was marriage anything like she had expected? Not really. She had expected bliss. Instead she got a heavy burden of guilt regarding Mack's unwelcome attentions that she permitted at first. Church had been like she had expected—Mack had preached a short, but very much to-the-point sermon. All was well until the hand-clinging witch got hold of Mack's hand. It wasn't nice to think of her in such ugly language, but that's what she was.

Her brief marriage did not live up to expectations. She had allowed Mack to go way too far before slipping out of bed. And she had thought of the young woman at church in a term she had never applied to anyone before.

Since she had never talked to anyone about what it might be like to be married, she could see that ignorance might be part of the reason for a bad start. Maybe she had been too much like the angel Mack had always said she was, at least on the surface. The few girls she had for friends did not feel free to discuss things in her presence that would have been casual talk had she not been present. Once a friend had made a pointed comment to this effect.

Her mother might have been a source of information, but Rebecca could never bring up the subject, and obviously the woman was uncomfortable with it herself. Once she had started, but soon gave it up as she began to stammer and blushes spread across her face.

Rebecca had read novels of romance checked out from the church library. Books that would never cause the faintest blush on the cheeks of an innocent girl—the kind where the boy might take a girl in his arms and press his lips tenderly to hers with nothing said about any strong emotions. Mack had kissed her like this on occasion and it had been just like the scenes depicted in her favorite romance novels. Gentleness, all sweetness, and no demands made.

And then there had been night before last when Mack had placed his hand where nice boys—in her novels—never placed theirs. She had *not* immediately stopped him. Contrary to what she should have felt, she felt a tiny bit of excitement like the forbidden fruit in Eden. Because she didn't instantly end that *touching* scene, she felt soiled—that she had participated in a sinful act.

It sounds like making excuses but I knew absolutely nothing about what is expected in the marriage bed. Nothing about what is permissible and proper. A week ago, what happened would have been terribly wrong. Mack hasn't exactly said the preacher's few words spoken suddenly changed sin into morally accepted, positive good, but he seems to believe it.

And in the midst of confusing thoughts and feelings came a strong voice. It could only be God, for never had she heard anyone who spoke so clearly, so commandingly, "Walk down to the church before the cool of the morning is gone. The door is unlocked. Go in, fall on your knees at the altar, and beg forgiveness for the evil act you took part in with your husband." That was all. It was more than enough.

Quickly she made preparations and left, walking alongside the road. Twice she was offered a ride, but declined. Walking might help the state of her nerves, and besides His voice had clearly commanded her to walk down to the church. Never before had she heard God speak and there was a sternness in His voice, a frightening experience for her.

The walk from the highway to the church was pleasant. The canopy of trees along the drive brought welcome coolness. Several acres of hardwoods free of underbrush gave the church foregrounds a park-like atmosphere. The parking area was immediately in front and to one side of the white clapboard siding building. A steeple made the building a picture-postcard scene. Beyond the side parking lot and behind the building was a cemetery. One car was parked in front.

It was an esthetically proper place to go to the Lord in prayer, giving her a little more confidence in the fruitfulness of prayer. The front door was unlocked as expected. There was no one else inside. Without pause, she went straight to the altar, eased down to her knees, and began to pray. Feeling no immediate relief, she continued to pray louder . . . feeling God had not heard her.

She heard steps on the wood floor of the aisle. Someone else had come . . . also in an act of penance? No better place than in church and no better time than on a Monday morning. Any prayer from the newcomer was in silence, for she heard nothing during a brief pause for breath. Still, she felt no forgiveness. Her prayer became more earnest and specific.

Soft footsteps now. A gentle touch and a hand rested on her shoulder. Rebecca was neither startled nor afraid. Here in God's sanctuary, no one with harmful intent would approach. She continued to pray.

"Rebecca," a soft voice interrupted, "You don't know me, but I know who you are, Brother Mack's wife. I was in church yesterday. I'm Fredda McDonald.

"I listened to your prayer before coming forward. Whatever you've done and asked God's forgiveness, God has heard your plea and knows what is in your heart. He knows yours is a repentant heart.

"Come let us sit on the front bench, something they are beginning to call pews nowadays."

Together they became seated, about three feet apart. Other than seeing Fredda was somewhere in middle age, Rebecca took no further notice of the woman's appearance. Kindness had already spoken to her and that was enough to create trust. She had felt no relief from the prayers she had prayed. In a minute or so, she would tell this woman. The sin was a fact and facts were not subject to be so simply erased. Without shedding a tear, she launched into her story from a memory that had every action, every emotion clearly etched in her mind. And she imitated—as well as a young woman could—God's loud voice directing her here. She left nothing out about what Mack had done in bed the first night and the tub bath she had taken in an effort to wash away the sin of it.

"And you saw what Mack did and the fact you didn't immediately stop him as being two sinful acts." Fredda had listened in a state of shock and even more in a state of horror as the story was unwrapped for her to see and assess its contents. The poor girl was sick, obviously terribly sick. Not many months had passed since she read a lengthy article in one of her magazines . . . the subject being schizophrenia. The symptoms were described and the hopes for a cure were dealt with. My God, neither had a chance to live first! Brother Mack knew on his wedding night what the score was, yet he preached to us as if the sermon was all he had on his mind. Poor woman. Is her life to be one of continued unfounded fears?

Rebecca was telling more of her story even as Fredda's mind was failing to be able to fully grasp what was already heard. "There was this witch at the church door following the morning service yesterday."

After what she had just heard, Fredda was only somewhat shocked by the ugly word that had just entered the story.

She had been right behind the girl just mentioned and had seen nothing unusual in her behavior. Fredda didn't have to prompt Rebecca to continue.

15

Rebecca said in a bitter voice, "Her handshake was so lingering, she held up the line behind. I was standing right there beside Mack. He's a tall man, you know. She was looking up into his face as though completely entranced, showing beautiful white teeth almost from ear to ear and cooed, 'Your sermon was so beautiful, so inspiring.'"

Fredda had heard a brief, routine compliment from the girl but nothing in such a voice and manner as Rebecca claimed, but knew better than to try to set the story straight. She allowed Rebecca to rant for a short while and then offered to drive her home.

On leaving her home alone, Fredda drove off with a feeling of unease. Maybe she'd not do anything that could endanger herself, like attempt suicide. Her condition was, as far as she knew, not akin to depression. It was around ten o'clock when she arrived at the worksite where she'd find Mack. Her brother was one of the fellows who had been placed on that job too.

"I didn't come to see you, Bobby. It's Brother Mack I came to talk to."

Mack knew it would be bad news of some sort. Fear sent his heart pounding. Was Rebecca hurt? Had she been in an accident? Had she attempted to end her life? Or was it some other kind of disaster? He walked with Fredda to the shade of the oak close by and stood with her awaiting the news. Bad news would be showing up every day from now on. The disease didn't reverse itself or fail to get worse. How long would this go on? . . . had been the question on his mind all morning.

"I don't know a good way to tell you this, Brother Mack, except to tell it plain and straight. You most likely know about it already. Your dear wife is—"

"Very sick, Fredda. What has she done that brought it to your attention?"

"Thanks for making it easier to tell you." And in as few words as possible, which was not few at all, she told him of the morning's

16

shocking event. "And I worried about leaving her there alone, but thought I must come let you know."

"I'll take time to drive to the nearest pay phone and call a psychiatrist in the city and try to get an appointment. I looked up a number yesterday."

"When did you find out, Brother Mack?"

"Our wedding night was the first time I suspected anything. And it was a certainty, not just a suspicion."

"I'm so sorry for you both." She didn't ask if there was a cure. "I will be praying for both of you."

He made an appointment for Monday of the next week.

Rebecca, on finding out they were to see a doctor a week later was worried that Mack might be suffering from an illness. "Have you been feeling bad, Mack? You have seemed worried, but not sick."

"We'll both see Dr. Larry Pickens on Monday at one o'clock next week."

"But I don't need to see a doctor at all. Never felt better. I'll go with you, but I won't see a doctor. I'll stay in the waiting room while Dr. Pickens examines you.

"Mother is coming tomorrow to take me to my dentist."

Mack paid little attention to this last remark. She went to her dentist several times during their courtship. He felt relief that her mother would be with her the next day, freeing him to work at the construction site.

"Aren't you going back to work after lunch? I appreciate your coming home for a bite. It doesn't take long to become lonely here. I saw Fredda McDonald at church this morning. We had a long talk there, and she brought me home. Such a sweet woman.

"Mack, isn't it about time you went back to work?"

"Got caught up on what I was doing." His first lie during their relationship and he felt guilt. Was he going to have to learn the art of evasion and lying?

Though he prayed almost without ceasing, he worried all his waking hours. Sleep had offered little relief because his hours of escape in sleep were few. And even in sleep came unaccustomed turmoil. Half awake . . . half asleep was the best he could do.

Around his eyes, he had a constant ache. Unshed tears he knew. Would he always be unable to cry and the pain never leave? A year later, five years later . . . would he still feel like crying? Would God leave him to his hopelessness? If so, how could God expect him to be a steadfast follower? Maybe he would be granted a measure of relief. Maybe the heartache would ease. Maybe the tears would flow—breaking the dammed up pain and worry. And he wondered again where is God when I need Him? I offer up prayers and they settle down around me like ground fog on a cold gloomy morning. And I worry and am even ashamed that I feel like this. It's been less than two days, and I feel the impatience that I might be justified in feeling, had it been two years of hopelessness.

He was pretending to read a book so Rebecca would think he might be preparing his next sermon. An act of dishonesty, when in reality, he was her sitter. He could not leave her alone as he had that morning. Would he have to always have someone with her if he wanted to work?Maybe he worried too much about the future, that being as futile as his prayers had been so far.

What if God became mad because he so quickly abandoned his belief that prayer would bring relief? Another worry.

But, how can I become worry-free? Just tell myself to be patient and if I do, it will somehow work out all right?

⟛⟛

On returning from work the following day, his mother-in-law was awaiting him. Anne Allen had Rebecca shelling English peas in the kitchen so she could have a few minutes of privacy with Mack . . . sitting in the lawn furniture under the back yard shade tree.

"Took her to her dentist today, Mack. As usual she had cavities—one old one that had to be drilled out and replaced, and one new one. As usual, the dentist lectured her about sweets." At this point Anne smiled, "He gave her the fillings as a wedding present.

"But of far more concern was the story she told me almost pridefully about hearing the voice of God directing her to the church altar to beg forgiveness for the sin of allowing her husband to touch her in an intimate place."

"I know, Mrs. Allen. She told one of the church ladies all about it, and the woman came to my work site yesterday. Actually, the woman who had just placed flowers on her mother's grave, heard Rebecca's loud voice and came into the building. After listening briefly, she said she knew Rebecca was suffering from some sort of mental illness.

"Had she ever shown signs of any unusual things in her mind before this?"

"In the past two weeks she has. Growing out of stress about the upcoming wedding, I thought. But then she did seem worried about what she was supposed to do in bed the first night. Would Mack try to do things to her or with her that would be terribly wrong if he had done them before marriage? Would they be free of sin if he did them after the wedding?

"And I wondered about what a poor job I'd done in rearing her. In one of the important things in bringing a daughter up, I had failed her. But had she learned nothing from her friends about the facts of life? When I was a teenager, we girls talked about such things a lot. Maybe some of the talk wasn't completely accurate, but lots of it was.

"Being the kind of girl she was made it awfully hard to prepare her for marriage."

"The uncommon degree of modesty. The unbelievable innocence. What appeared to be the soul of an angel?"

"Yes, Mack. Always there were those things making frank discussion next to impossible, or so it seemed to me over the years. She remained with the sweet innocence of a beautiful three or four-year-old girl who has not been to school where kids begin to be introduced to four letter words that we try to protect them from.

"For the parent, the years of the little child are all too fleeting. Maybe I tried too hard to shield her from the realities of life, thinking there was all too much of that to come in the future. Yes, Mack, she was an angelic child and I thought that was good. She was always respectful toward Lee and me. She was a quiet joy and we were proud of her. She was different and we were proud of that difference. She is very ill and we may have contributed to the illness."

"Mrs. Allen, I studied psychology in school—was especially interested in abnormal psychology. Right now, I'm pretty sure there was nothing in the rearing of Rebecca that contributed to her illness. Something in her brain changed—maybe chemistry, maybe brain cells themselves. Often the onset of the illness is in the late teens or early twenties.

"Freud led us down the wrong path. Analysis for countless months and even years—and patients with severe problems in the brain not being helped.

"There are drugs today that help some patients."

Rebecca had come out the back door and as she approached, she asked, "Are you talking about me? I looked out the window and y'all were hard at it.

"You probably don't believe God actually spoke to me. I doubt He does to many."

⚊✛⚊

It was a week later that Mack drove Rebecca to the city and the building where Larry Pickens had his office.

During the forty mile trip, Rebecca—feeling anxious about Mack, several times sought reassurance that Mack was not sick.

"We can't be going to a doctor about me, Mack. Never felt better. Not an ache or a pain.

"You look a bit preoccupied yourself, but you're all right, aren't you?" What if he is really sick and trying to cover up so I won't worry. I couldn't stand it if he gets sick. Now that I don't live with my parents, he's all I've got. Lord, please let my husband be well.

When Mack was checking in, she looked at him as he stood at the receptionist's window. At least six feet tall. Light brown eyes when he turned to glance where she was seated; apparently he's being asked something about me. A finely featured face. Hair so brown it would pass for black. Her man, she felt proud of him. It was no wonder that pretty woman at church . . . .

Mack came and sat beside her, taking her left hand in his right . . . a gentle squeeze and then held hers without further hand talk. A few minutes later, he was called and he entered what was a suite of rooms.

After a very brief wait in one of the rooms, a balding man with reddish hair entered. "I'm Larry Pickens, and you are Mack Baldwin?" He seated himself in an armchair and faced Mack, pale blue eyes sparkling with kindness. "How long has your wife had symptoms and what are they like?"

The man exuded the indescribable atmosphere that trust thrived in. Mack told all—everything.

"And you have made your own diagnosis?" There was no hint of criticism in the doctor's voice.

"Possibly schizophrenia?"

"We have to depend on family members for much of the information on which we base a tentative diagnosis."

"Could her almost too perfect, too quiet, too angelic personality have been a precursor of the illness to come, Dr. Pickens?"

"Mack, I don't know of any particular personality type in childhood and teen years that predict the onset of schizophrenia. It is my observation that pretty suddenly, brain function becomes abnormal. It is as though what separates in all of us sanity from insanity is not a wide and high barrier. A small change in the chemicals that brain cells depend on for communication with each other and interpretation of what goes on in the brain, and then it doesn't work dependably anymore.

"You go to bed at 10:00 pm feeling well and wake up at 4:30 am. Your throat is sore and burning. You go to look at your throat, open wide, look in the mirror. A small amount of bleeding is evident. Strep throat hit you as you slept. From feeling great, you've quickly crossed the threshold to feeling absolutely lousy.

"Dementia and other diseases seem to be like that. From wellness to illness in so brief a time.

"My guess is that changes in neurons caused by a virus that has lain dormant for years, may be the guilty party.

"Chicken pox may revisit you sixty years later as shingles. Such a latent virus might have revisited your wife.

"Since we don't know what causes it, we are badly handicapped in treating it. Psychotherapy seems to help some patients cope a bit with some of the worst fears and suspicions."

"What about drugs, Doctor?"

"Think of Rebecca's worst hallucinations, her symptoms, and her strong feelings that she has sinned. Think of these as exaggerated emotions that have sharp points sticking out making the rest of us aware she suffers an illness. Drugs tend to dull the sharp points, but not entirely remove them. The patient may live with the unwarranted guilt, suspicions, and hallucinations without as much discomfort. But there are usually side effects."

Mack devoted his attention totally to what he was told. Some of it he already knew, but not with the clarity of what he was hearing.

"Isn't alcohol used by many as a tranquilizer, Dr. Pickens?"

"It's a drug. A man has a very stressful job. He stops before going home and has a few drinks. His problems at work no longer have their sharp, emotional, cutting edges. He feels less inward turmoil and less worry about how he can face one more day. He's tranquilized as surely as the patient at the state hospital who has taken thorazine—a drug that often has side effects and serious ones in some cases.

"Now, I'll see Rebecca," Dr. Pickens said. "Then I'll talk with you again."

⇒⊦⊣⇐

On the ride home, "Was I the one who needed to see the doctor, Mack?"

"We both needed to see him."

"But me more than you. Did he show you pictures and ask you to tell what you saw?" she asked.

"No, we just talked."

"How was I to know what those pictures depicted. There were a number of them. I did as well as I could to tell him what they meant. Perhaps I gave him the wrong answers on some of them."

"I don't think there are right and wrong answers, Rebecca."

"If that's the case, what was the point in showing them to me?"

"See that cloud straight ahead. What does it suggest to you?"

"The head of a horse . . . and to you?"

"A shape like the blob of mud that I had to wash off the hood of the truck before leaving this morning. We both look at the same thing and see two different things. We are different and that may account for you being reminded of a horse's head and me a blob of mud."

"Do crazy people see things in a different way from sane people? Are there different patterns of interpreting for the mentally healthy and mentally ill? Do you think I have mental problems? Is that why you brought me to a doctor who neither listens to my chest nor shines a light in my throat? Instead, he asks me to talk and shows me pictures that look like a modern artist had blown a fuse or something."

"Rebecca, there were some things that bothered me about how you interpret certain things."

"Like hearing the voice of God? Like thinking I had sinned when I allowed you to touch me where you never had before?"

They had to stop at a railroad crossing while a train sped by. When the noise subsided as the guardrails were lifted, Mack could no longer delay answering, "Yes, that entered into my concerns about your health."

"The Bible said God frequently spoke to people in the Old Testament days. Do you doubt He spoke to me?"

Mack felt he was backed into a corner. "Maybe before Jesus came and showed us the way, God had to speak in a loud, clear manner, but doesn't have to speak aloud now. Just a gentle nudge or two seems to suffice."

"You mean God just gave you a gentle nudge to become a preacher, not telling you in a clear directing voice to go out into the fields that were ripe for harvest?"

"A pretty strong nudge in that direction.

"After seeing you, when I went back in, he gave me some pills he thought might help you."

"Help me in what way? Help me ignore your roaming hands inside my panties like you tried the first night? Will his pills take away the sinfulness of it after they have convinced me it's all right. Is that why you took me, thinking he'd take your side and then you'd have your way with me despite my knowing it is wrong for me?"

Was this manifestation of her illness a symptom that it was greater than he had thought? It was a good time to say no more about it and he didn't. He drove on for the remaining twenty miles in silence.

He hired a sitter—she lasted less than a week. "Brother Mack, I'm sorry, but this is not for me. If the medication is helping her, I can't see how. There is such a strangeness about her thoughts. No meeting of the minds between us, no meeting her in a conversation. Sometimes it gets to me in the stomach . . . almost causing nausea. I'm ashamed of feeling the way I do, but I can't help it."

Mack was more down than he had ever been before. What could he do? Pray! But prayer continued to be ineffective. Why, if God wants me to preach, does He not bring Rebecca out of this? Never should she have been afflicted with one of the very worst illnesses. Totally innocent and this happens to *her*. And a hell-raising sort of girl goes cruising through life without as much as a tiny glitch in her brain's activity. With these doubts, maybe I should quit preaching.

He didn't realize at the moments he suffered these doubts about God and injustice in life while on earth, how soon he'd be out of the ministry.

⊫ ⊨

At the end of a Sunday morning service when he stood at the church's exit with Rebecca standing beside him, she began to make accusations when the pretty girl took Mack's hand.

"I'll tell you one thing, bitch, you are not going to take my man away from me!"

Appalled, embarrassed, and a host of other negative emotions suddenly changed the girl's face into one showing pain and humiliation.

"Darling, I've not done one thing to try to take him away from you." The effort to respond like this took a lot out of the girl. Those waiting behind her must wonder how one so young could respond to such an unfair attack so calmly.

"No, Rebecca. No!" Never had he thought her illness could come to this. "Louise, please forgive. She is sick, very sick."

Louise made a quick exit. Mack had hands of restraint on both of his wife's upper arms, as she struggled to follow the girl outside.

"Turn me loose, Mack, so I can go give her what she deserves." She tore loose and Mack had to grab her around the waist. By the time he got her beyond the doorway, he had entered a world where all seemed unreal, not realizing that it was his only mode of escape when the real was far more than he could bear.

By the time he got his hellcat of a wife to the car—not having thought it could come to this—with great restraint, he was able to hold back the tongue lashing he felt like giving her.

Maybe he should be ashamed of thinking of her as a hellcat, but he was not. She was sick, but not that sick; no one could be that sick! How wrong he was to believe that. He'd later know it, but was very angry now. Such anger he'd not felt before. Preaching, his very life, was over! No church would ever want him!

Forgive her? He couldn't. The thing that mattered most, she has in a half minute taken away from me. What shall I do now? Bury my humiliation under ten feet of dirt if that could be done.

She can't be as demented as all that. Her illness is a spotty thing, not without periods when thoughts are lucid . . . times when she realizes that her suspicions and fears are greatly exaggerated. Then why do times come when she has no control? All of us sometimes have excessive fears or worries, but nothing on the scale she does.

Mack knew his fears were based on reality. He knew that the wife he thought he had married no longer existed. *She* was dead. He spent the afternoon mourning . . . hope no more than a dying ember underneath a layer of ashes inches thick.

Dr. Pickens had not predicted that her brain function would ever be quite the same as before, but neither had he indicated it could come to this!

He prayed for her, but he was too young to know that he should have been praying for himself, asking that he would be able to bear the unbearable.

God, do You just preside over us, knowing that my wife suffers terribly and do nothing about it? Do you not realize the most innocent of young women has been visited with the most terrifying of illnesses. That her's has become a life of fears and that there is nothing she can do to remedy it? And that her illness will always be with her to some degree. I married her believing that she would be the best of helpmates in my preaching. Now, I can't preach. That part of my life ended today. Was it not You who called me to preach? I assumed it was. Now I'm assuming maybe it was not Your call. For surely You would not have called if You knew illness would destroy my wife. Oh, how I have preached You are an all-knowing God. Have I been fooled? Have I been wrong?

Maybe instead of my questioning You, I should be begging forgiveness for allowing doubts to come raging in. Perhaps twenty years from now, I shall see this as a tempering process, making me the finest sort of sword in the war against evil. But can You not understand I can't see it that way now, that I'm all too human? I need help now . . . a sign of some kind.

The telephone rang. It was Fredda McDonald. "Brother Mack, six of us women will take turns in staying with Rebecca so you can continue to preach. All I've talked to understand she is very sick and parts of her life are beyond her ability to control. Your sermons are proof that you are truly called."

Silent sobs were shaking his body as tears streamed down his face.

"I'll be there at five," she added.

When he had composed himself a bit and washed his eyes and face in cold water, he went into the living room to sit with Rebecca

"Who was that on the phone, Mack?"

"Fredda McDonald."

"She's a good woman, Mack. She called about my conduct in church this noon."

"She's going to stay with you this evening so I can go preach."

"Mack, I know that what I did embarrassed and humiliated you. I'm sorry, but that girl wants you.

"I take pills and hope they will smooth out things, and I guess they do a little. I realize at times I'm a bit insane and wish I were not, but I can't control the appearance of things that get into my mind. I'm afraid, Mack. You can't wish all these things would go away any more than I do. Oh God, what am I to do?"

There she was, understanding she was terribly ill, but unable to do anything about it. Mack knew he had no words that could comfort. He took a seat beside her and took a hand in both of his. They sat thus for a half hour or more, saying nothing . . . Mack feeling so bad because he had become angry. In the future, he would at all times be understanding instead of angry. She was a helpless human and in greater need of understanding than anyone he knew. Holding her hand filled him with a warmth that had been absent since the onset of her illness.

He'd do better and knew he would. A prayer he'd not prayed very well, had in fact actually been answered. The warmth and sweetness of the small hand in his two explained that though sick, Rebecca still had needs. All too much he had concentrated on how her illness affected him. It was shredding her inside. She was in a living hell on earth.

"Thank you, Mack."

"For . . . ?"

"For sitting and holding my hand. I've felt so distant from you. Could we do this again? Could I trust you to go this far and refrain from putting your hands where you did on that first night? In a way, I have come to know that my reaction was a part of my affliction. Still the belief there was sin involved is something that will not go away—I can't help that."

Mack felt no sexual urge stir within. This fragile, beautiful woman was not to him an object to be felt that way about. Perhaps his sex drive was not as strong as some men's—a blessing in the present circumstances.

Could he maintain this attitude that left him feeling better about himself and a special tenderness toward Rebecca? He was all she had, except for brief visits from her mother. She lived in a world which he could understand only slightly, and his world appeared to her as a place of many threats. He prayed to God to give him patience and understanding.

What she had been, she no longer was, and it was unlikely she could fully return. She could still function as a housekeeper. And her presence offered him company and a barrier against complete loneliness.

So it was that he made his first adjustment. Not a great one, but a beginning.

Each day he took one of her hands in the two of his for a half hour or so . . . and felt better for doing so. His blessing was fully as great as hers, which she expressed by a faint smile appearing on her lovely, tragic face.

⚊⊹ ⊹⚊

Weeks went by when he could not go to work. He had tried another sitter who felt nauseated in Rebecca's presence. She explained that the things she had to listen to were far too much to bear. "Crazy" talk was something she knew she could never get used to.

Another one began having "regular migraines" and would call Mack around breakfast time that she had awakened with one . . . three times in five days.

The only bright spot was the frequent compliments on his sermons. "You are getting to be a better preacher and I don't see how you can under the circumstances," he had heard several times. He spent more time than before on preparation. Staying with Rebecca gave plenty of time to fine tune his sermon notes.

Then he found a lady who came five days a week. For seven months she came. An elderly woman, but completely dependable. A fall at home resulting a shattered hip, and Mack was back again—staying at home instead of being able to work.

There were times when self-pity tended to overflow his ability to deal with it. It was difficult to completely refrain from blaming Rebecca. Are schizophrenics ever free of exaggerating their emotions? Do they sometimes use their suspicions, their fears, and hallucinations to manipulate their family members? For even raising such unspoken questions, he felt shame and guilt.

They continued seeing Dr. Pickens. It was he who finally decided that the time had come to place Rebecca under the daily care and supervision of professionals. "I'll be the bad guy, Mack, and take the blame for placing her there. That's the way it has to be for several reasons that we've talked over before."

CHAPTER THREE

Living alone for the first time in sixteen months was harder than
he had expected. At times he had felt Rebecca was little, if any,
better than not having a wife at all. Each time a sign of her illness
had flared up, he found that experience had not prepared him for
this. Shock and despair swatted him almost as if he had not been
there before. Even when her illness was quieter, he lived in a state
of depression. Would things never get better? Enough improvement
so he would be able to live a half-normal life that would allow him
to experience an upbeat few hours here and there? Would his life
always to be mired in the desperate pits of despair?

In bed he had not touched nor snuggled after that first night
and not once did she come to his side of the bed. There was another
bedroom with a standard bed, but when he had suggested that he
sleep there, she had objected, saying she would feel so alone "with
you off in there." The center portion of the bed they slept on was an
undeclared no-man's land.

Yet she had been company. Knowing she was there and he could
talk to her a short while after going to bed was worth far more than

not having her at all. Now he could freely sleep in any position he happened to end up in—diagonally if he wished, and he sometimes did, but felt no satisfaction from it.

Holding one of her hands between the two of his in the safety of the living room had become a daily ritual, but he knew never to attempt such contact in bed. At times he had wanted to snuggle against her when the nights had grown cold. He had believed that most couples did. But it would have frightened her and might have stirred in him desire for closer contact. He had been able to keep his thoughts regarding Rebecca wholesome—partly because he had kept her on a pedestal before marriage, but mainly because he could not live with her if by day he allowed sex fantasies to dwell inside.

It had been a strange relationship that sixteen months—one that he would have found almost unbelievable had he heard of it happening within another couple's marriage. Now he knew loneliness as he had not known it before. He prayed asking God to lift the feeling and to fill his heart with His presence. It helped, but God had not intended that man live alone. He had preached sermons on the subject on a couple of occasions, basing his words on the Book of Genesis.

He was a carpenter five days a week now and looked forward to Saturdays. A seventy-five mile drive and he could hold her hand for half an hour or so. And this he did, while sometimes she talked and sometimes they just sat . . . finding a bit of joy in this simple contact.

"Mack," she said one day when they were thus occupied, "we inmates talk amongst ourselves at times about why we are here being doped up with stuff that may make us even crazier.

"I know my mind doesn't work right and that's why I'm here. The FBI is still investigating my past. I can't think of anything I've done that would cause them to investigate, but there is something they know against me. There is no reason for you to tell me they aren't doing it. I *know* they are and *that* is it!"

Mack had known from the beginning that trying to reassure her was worse than futile.

She talked on. "I'm scared that woman at church is working on you at every opportunity, enticing you with her female wiles while I rot in this nut house.

"No, don't try to tell me I've not been placed in an institution for crazy folks. Almost daily I hear some crazy carrying on about things I don't hear or things I don't see. And I figure I carry on about things they're not aware of.

"Something happened inside my brain that I wished hadn't. But it did. And I can't help it. I didn't ask for it and don't want it.

"This is one of my lucid moments, isn't it Mack?"

"Yes, sweetheart."

"Remember it and know that I do the best I can."

"Rebecca, I know you do. I treasure these few minutes when the fog of your illness clears.

"Your mother and father visit you earlier today?"

"Yes, Mack. I love them and I love you. I'm so sorry that things have turned out like they have. I still hear God's voice telling me what to do. Did you know that?"

"The nurse told me today that you do." He didn't tell her he had come on a week day recently and a doctor was on a rant about "jack-leg preachers who deliver hellfire and brimstone sermons about sin that pushes some into the pit of insanity where they believe they hear God's voice telling them they must do this or that to be forgiven." Mack hadn't told the doctor that he himself was a preacher and that the doctor was drunk on Freudian nonsense.

Following this interview with the doctor, he had visited Rebecca. She was not at all lucid that day. He left the hospital in a state of deep discouragement. The only positive thing to come out of that visit was the holding of her hand between his two for around thirty minutes. In this, there had been some communication and comfort.

CHAPTER FOUR

A year passed. On the late October drive to the hospital, he chose the route through a hilly stretch of backwoods in preference to the four-lane. It had been a year of no progress for Rebecca. On the day he had carried her there, he had thought she would be well enough to come home long before twelve months had gone by.

What had been accomplished? On the last visit, he had been told she was slowly becoming even less connected with reality. "And she complains of a headache every day," the nurse said.

"In the top of her head?" Mack asked.

"Always there. The doctor said that it's not the usual place for one, but it's nothing to worry about. We are to give her aspirin every morning and it works pretty well."

"She's had them since around age twenty that I know about. Could it be related to her dementia?"

"The doctor said there was no connection, but he did have some degree of concern. Her sinuses seemed fine. He was puzzled."

⚒

The autumn color was as good as it had ever been, even better than on the day she had been placed in the hospital. The steeper the hillside, the more intense the color. The narrow areas of bottom land had little to offer, but it seemed the highway had been engineered to give the grandest views of craggy hills and the glorious hardwoods. Blue sky and colors ranging from bright yellows to deepest crimson gave him a lift that he had seldom felt for more than two years. This aspect of life on earth made it almost worth enduring.

For the past long months, life had been something that had to be tolerated before reaching a better level. But on this morning, it came close to being worth all its psychic aches and pains.

On a particularly high point, there was a turnout. He stopped, got out of the truck, and took a deep breath that had been brought on by the scene's stealing his breath away. Blue hills in the distance. Color splashed hills closer by. Red and white cattle in a valley below where his feet were planted. In a more distant pasture, cattle all in black where a white horse came trotting through the heedless cattle that continued to graze. What a morning to be alive! What a morning to be right here.

For a minute and more, he stood. Living this moment in the most conscious possible way, the better to take it with him . . . to call back when circumstances made it most needed. The minute grew into five and more. If cars came by and they may have, he never knew. God's gift to him that morning and *that* he knew without thinking it through. Preparing him for what was to come? This was his shield against what was to come? It didn't occur to him to consider it that way. It was here and it was in the now to be experienced and no analysis was appropriate nor needed. Rare are such lingering moments in God's creation . . . in His presence.

In contrast, the rest of his drive was very ordinary. He thought of his wife and how her week might have been. And would she be somewhat lucid this day? Or would she be too concerned about the girl back at church, the girl who had been married at that church the evening before by Brother Mack? The groom, a young fellow he had not met until he had sat with the young couple two weeks earlier in his little church office.

Would it ease Rebecca's mind to learn she had no possible cause to worry about that girl now that the wedding knot had been tied to a fine young man? If Rebecca brought up the subject, he would tell her, but otherwise he would not.

After finding out that Rebecca had tried to run away a second time and that she had been out on the street trying to thumb a ride, it had been decided that from that time on, she would wear an anklet monitor she could not remove. And earlier she had not been long in setting off the alarm that sent a half dozen people after her. She had been in a hair-pulling fight with another girl. "Summed up, it has been a bad week for her and the staff," the nurse said.

The first thing Rebecca said to Mack was, "I guess the woman who clings to your hand before parting at the church door is still at her wily ways."

"She got married last evening at church by me to a fine young man from a neighboring church."

"I don't believe that's true. I used to see the look she gave you. She's never going to give you up. If she's married now, I bet it's to you. That you got a divorce so you two could marry." Tears appeared in her eyes and began to stream down her face.

Shaking with deep sobs and tears continuing, she blubbered, "While I, who was your wife, am imprisoned here and unable to fight your claim for divorce, you get one anyway and marry that sleaze who intended to have you regardless of everything. Is she now downstairs?"

A box of kleenex had been appropriately placed for such times such as this, Mack gathered a handful and offered it to her. Surprising him, she accepted the tissue and wiped her eyes and blew her nose.

Mack knew the futility beforehand if he tried to explain that the state did not grant divorces without cause, and a man's wife suffering from dementia was not a cause for divorce. If he told her this, she would turn it on him that he had considered such a step. He was in a lose-lose situation and that was the way it was and would continue to be. He was a preacher and his conscience told him it was wrong to feel resentment for the position he was in. Resentment stirred within anyway.

"Mack, my headaches have grown worse." She had regained enough composure to move on to something else. "And lately they started substituting placebos for aspirin. The shrink claims that the nurses haven't done so. He's checked my chart, but somebody's lying. You can't trust the staff here." Placing a hand on top of her head, she said, "Right here. It's killing me and sometimes I wish it would actually end it all for me. This place is a hell-hole and I don't know why Dr. Pickens put me in it. Wish I was out and had the power to put him in it in my place. Maybe you ought to try it. But you'd never let anyone take you away from that brand new wife of yours. I bet she doesn't mind when you try to put your hand in her panties. She doesn't mind sin, does she?"

He recalled the woman who worked two days as Rebecca's sitter. She couldn't take it anymore because his wife made her nauseated. That's exactly how Mack felt right then and should have felt shame for allowing her to upset him so. But that's how he felt in his very inside, and he got out of the visiting area as fast as he could after telling her he had to get back home and prepare tomorrow's sermon. This lie could hardly be called white, since it was not told to save her feelings, but was told to save his own.

How far would he sink if her illness continued as it was now? It was the most miserable drive home since the day he'd first brought her to the insane asylum. Usually, he steered clear of that word but not on this day when his stomach was so queasy, he had no urge to eat though lunchtime had come and gone.

He had learned something about himself that day and it was not pretty. Instead, it was ugly, the same ugliness that had long ago brought some to the point of beating the afflicted in order to send the demon on its way. They would then claim *that* was their motive for doing the dastardly deed.

He turned his truck around and drove back to the state park and the trailhead where he had walked the year before. At a fast pace, he did the four mile loop, not noticing or caring about the beauty that fell behind him with each step. Not quite as rapidly, he walked the loop again. That was enough to take his mind off his troubles for a bit and direct its attention to his aching feet. Darkness had begun to wrap around his truck before his painful last steps brought him to it.

When he finally came to a restaurant, his stomach had feelings other than how upset he was over Rebecca's condition. What a sad day it would be if sirloin steak lost its healing ability.

But *she* was not enjoying tender beef. A momentary feeling of guilt flickered in his conscience. But isn't that carrying sensitivity too far? Have I not tried in every way a man could have to put my wife first? Am I not deserving of the joy that comes from eating a good meal when I have been all a man can be? Does God expect me to wear a hair shirt at all times? Have I not been a dedicated servant? Do I not deserve a good appetite despite her illness?

Feeling a teeny bit defiant, he took a hot yeast roll, laid on the butter, and took a bite as his nose was taking in a whiff of rising fragrance unlike that of any other food—almost, but not quite as heavenly as the bite of sirloin that followed.

If my time to pass on is close, let it be stayed until I finish this meal, dear Lord.

As a preacher, he was supposed to wonder if such a prayer insulted God. As one of God's children, he believed God knew the depth of the sincerity of his prayer. Had his Son not known how keen an appetite could become and the joy that comes when such an appetite meets excellent food?

━┼┼━

His days became routine with a busy schedule with church, preaching on Sunday morning and evening services, and Wednesdays, carpentry on weekdays, and visiting Rebecca on Saturdays. Study and sermon preparation in the evenings. Being busy seemed to be life's biggest blessing. It was after he had turned off the lights and attempted to find sleep after his last prayer was over, that sadness and loneliness came visiting.

Strong coffee was necessary every morning to get him going for what faced him each day. But this was life for adults, he realized more with the passing of the weeks and months. In the foolish times of boyhood, he couldn't grow up fast enough to keep him happy. As a teenager, he had dreams of becoming a preacher first and then becoming a great evangelist whose sermons would lead sinners by the thousands to the Lord.

Unless a magic pill was invented, he had a young wife who would remain ill for the rest of her life. And he would continue to measure, saw, and paint wood. And through his preaching occasionally contribute to someone's salvation.

He was depressed and realized it as never before. He did what was expected of him and a great deal more—all the while he felt he was not doing nearly enough. In time, he mostly felt tired and wondered what he might do to feel rested.

━┼┼━

On an April evening as he sat in a rocker on his small front porch, a pickup entered his front yard on the gravel drive that came along one side of it. The sun was touching the tree tops in the distance.

An old man, whose greying hair had long ago lost all its suggestion of being sprinkled salt and pepper, got out and with a surprisingly smooth stride came up the porch steps . . . large right hand extended. As Mack stood up, he took Mack's hand and, as they say, squeezed the juice out of it.

"Brother Mack, I'm Fredda McDonald's father-in-law. I'm far from sure my son, Oscar, deserves such a good woman." Without giving Mack any more than time to say a quick, 'Pleased to meet you,' he took the porch's other rocker and continued talking. "Fredda is the best member of my very extended family and she's dang worried about you. And now that I'm looking at you, I can see why. There's a tiredness in and about your eyes that shouldn't be there in such a young man. She told me lots about your wife's illness. Your burden is one no young person ought to bear and there's no solution to it, is there?"

"No, Mr. MacDonald, and that isn't the worst of it. It's so little understood and no research in sight that offers a solution. No clinical trials that suggest hope for the future."

"I understand, Brother Mack. Fredda says there's nothing we can do for her, but there are things we can do for you. According to her, you have real talent, a gift for preaching which will eventually wither away if nothing is done for you. That's why I'm here.

"I don't go to your church. Mine is three miles beyond yours on the same road. One day years ago, I got to wondering why there were churches so close together, none of them with very large congregations. They were founded in a day when it was common for members to walk to church. Far less then every family had a surrey or buggy to ride in. Many couldn't afford one."

This man interested Mack. "And people had country stores within walking distance," he said.

"But that's slowly beginning to change, and churches aren't going to close down because most people are getting cars or pickups. I say all this to explain why I don't attend church where you are pastor.

"Obviously by now, I'm here because she told me I ought to come, and she's a woman worth listening to. Wish I could claim her as a blood relative.

"I talked today with the contractor who has several teams of workers including yours. Know him well enough to tell him what Fredda wanted him to hear. He agreed you were the best finish carpenter he has. He wants to keep you three days a week with an hourly raise.

"What will I do the other two days?"

"Try recreation for a change. Your boss said possibly work four days one week and two the next so you could occasionally drive to the Gulf Coast.

"You ever take time to fish?"

"Rarely."

"I have a boat and scads of fishing tackle.

"Another reason your boss wants to keep you, instead of losing you to poor health, is that you are a good influence on your team. Their talk is cleaner, they drink less, and are not as likely to fail to show for work because they're hung over.

"This is Friday. The weather for Tuesday looks good for fishing. If the forecast holds up, I'll be by at eight with boat and trailer. The first time out, I'll furnish you with sandwiches and cold sodas. Don't worry about tackle.

"I hope you won't feel guilty about having a day off. If you have the slightest twinge, Fredda said blame it on her.

"May I just call you Mack?" Not waiting for permission, he continued, "Call me Alf or Old MacDonald if that suits you.

"You have an old man . . . a preacher you can go to for counsel and advice?"

"The preacher who led me to my Christ is retired now. He and his wife live forty miles or so from here. Haven't talked to him in several years."

"On your next off day, you ought to go see him."

41

"I just call him up in advance and tell him I want to visit him soon?"

"You get Fredda's idea."

"What do I talk to him about?"

"Fredda predicted you'd come up with that question and said I'm to tell you that you'll know.

"You promise you won't back out on me Tuesday morning?"

"I promise."

Alf stayed a few more minutes talking about fishing ultra-light tackle.

Mack waited a half hour before leaving for his favorite restaurant. The first half of that time, tears poured, and his sobs shook him all over. For months he had known something had to change. Each time he had looked into the mirror, he saw what Alf had seen at a glance, but there had been no way out of any of it. When *his* health broke, then what was he to do? Rebecca would never be able to help him in any way. His mother and father lived sixty-five miles away and had problems enough of their own. They had been in their forties at the time of his birth.

Not knowing what kind of help he had needed, he had often prayed to God asking each time for some way out of at least some of the problems he endured. And God had used an ordinary looking middle-aged woman to respond to his prayers, and her seventy-something-year-old father-in-law of like mind and heart to set her plan and God's in motion.

It was only after he had gotten his emotions calmed, and his eyes and face back to normal with washcloth and cold water, that he went to supper.

⚬⟞⟝⚬

The lake was clear, the wind calm, and the motor fired on the first pull on the rope. Alf slowed it to idle speed. "A perfect day in the best part of the year," he commented before setting out up the lake.

A mile or so later, he stopped the motor and lowered an electric trolling motor that was mounted on the transom.

"Two identical light rods with small spinning reels . . . you ever use one of these things before?"

Mack shook his head.

"It helps if you don't depend on your right hand for everything. Makes it easier to crank left handed." He picked one of the rigs and cast the lure forty or fifty feet. Then let the small spinner bait sink for perhaps five seconds before starting a slow retrieve. "Now, you try yours. It looks so easy, but it's not really."

Mack imitated Alf's cast exactly, or so he thought. The lure might have traveled ten feet and the line was a tangled mess on the reel.

For maybe an hour, Mack learned the basics from a patient teacher. When he could get the lure out twenty feet or so without a tangled line on the reel, Alf announced him ready to fish.

"Feels like I ought to be working instead of loafing."

"That's to be expected. When you get to be as old as I am, you don't have those pangs of guilt because everybody thinks you are too doggoned old to work, and you can loaf five days in a row with a clear conscience. You fish often enough catching a few now and then, and you'll develop a few callouses on that clean conscience of yours, and you won't feel so driven to work all the time. You've been pushing yourself seven days a week, doing nothing about the daily emotional strain you've been under. You are young but you're not able to continue that on and on."

It was after lunch that Mack felt the first tug at the end of his line. It was time for further coaching.

"Keep your rod pointed up lots more or it'll break that four-pound line. When he makes a run like that, let the drag decide how much line he needs to be given. Crank in now while he's coming toward the boat."

And so it went for a few minutes. Alf got into position with a net ready and told Mack just how to guide the fish toward the net. A few seconds later, he held up the bass. "Sixteen inches if he's an inch—about as big as you could wish for on light tackle. Much nicer fish than the three or four I've caught today."

"What species is it?"

"A spotted bass," he said as he held the fish by the lower lip, lowered it into the water, and moved it back and forth a few times before releasing. "Just to make sure it was breathing okay. He's just done a fish's version of a hundred yard dash."

"You ever keep fish, Alf?"

"Sometimes. Crappie are my favorite fish when it comes to eating.

"Weather permitting, let's do this again next week. If you continue to improve in the basics, we might go try smallmouths one day soon."

"Are they harder to catch?"

"They are very different. If we go, you'll find out."

They fished another three hours or more. Mack caught three bass in the eleven to thirteen inch range, exciting Alf each time. Alf had one very good bass and a couple of smaller ones.

Toward the end, Alf asked, "You think you could learn to enjoy this, Mack?"

"So far today, I've enjoyed it much more than I could ever have thought possible. But I still have mixed feelings about being away from work."

"It bothers you that Fredda has you taking a day off?"

"Yes, I guess it does in a way."

"You've given of yourself to your church community for severals years now without a break. There are people who love you and want to give something back. In a gracious manner, allow them to do so."

To his surprise, Wednesday morning Mack was not so sleepy on awakening There was no thought of the problem of getting through

44

the day, and there was Thursday to be looked forward to. When was the last time he'd gotten out of bed feeling ready for the day? Rebecca was not likely to be better, but he was better and that was not something of little importance. Fredda and Alf were right. He had been on his way to being unable to serve if he had continued as he had for all too many months. Perhaps he was worthy of having his need for recreation met.

As he ate his breakfast of oatmeal with raisins, and sipped his coffee, he had enough common sense to realize he would not always feel this upbeat and have enough gumption not to allow the uncertain future to spoil what he had right now.

The following Tuesday, he and Alf were back at it again in a long slough enclosed by high rocky walls. Wild azaleas in varying shades of pink filled the still air with fragrance to remember. It seemed it was their nature to seek the most rugged of places to put down their roots.

"It seems they use land that's not fit for something else to grow, Mack. I always try to come to this same slough each April when the time is deemed right. They grow at other places, but nowhere else in such profusion. On a breezy day, their fragrance is blown out of here and you hardly notice it."

"Changing the subject on you, Alf, what size ball do you have for your trailer hitch?"

"One and a half inches. You thinking of pulling the boat and trailer some?"

"I don't always want to be a bum. Will tend to it before we go again. Where did you get your tackle?"

"Sounds like you are beginning to take recreation seriously. I have far more rods and reels than the two of us can use. Fredda will be pleased and so will I. Have or did have a good fishing buddy, but he turned seventy-five last year and his old lady allowed he had no business out 'til all hours. But he does make an exception, regardless of her harsh words, in mid-to-late June when the willow flies are hatching."

It turned out to be an average day of fishing according to Alf.

It was on the next day that Lowell Miller, the contractor came to the work site. Obviously skilled in observing the work of his crew and speaking a few cordial words, he was gone in thirty minutes.

On Sunday he visited Mack's church. Mack felt well prepared and was not bothered by the presence of the visitor. Lowell made it a point to be the last person leaving at the service's end.

"Great sermon, Mack. Be my guest for Sunday dinner at your favorite restaurant. You lead the way and I'll follow."

As he drove the ten miles to his regular eating place, Mack could not help but wonder what this was all about. But he was not nervous about eating with the big boss. Rather, he was pleased. The man, it was said, sometimes used more than fifty craftsmen at work sites scattered over a county-wide area.

The buffet looked especially good to both men and they heaped their plates. A waitress took orders for tea for Mack and black coffee for Miller. They had been able to get a table in a quiet corner. The first order of business was to eat and while they tended to this, the Sunday crowd began to thin.

"You may not have realized it, Mack, but Friday I paid special attention to your work while I pretended to be there for other reasons. I watched how quickly you measured, cut, and mounted trim. Never seen anyone better and that includes me. Did lots of it years ago before I had this crazy notion that keeps me awake too late at night. Never had the headaches in being a finish carpenter that there are in being a contractor. Lots of accounting and that kind of work is still foreign to my personality.

"Where did you learn the trade?"

"On a much smaller scale than you, my father contracts and does lots of carpentry still. I started working for him at twelve. I was big for my age and strong aplenty. He never drove only four nails where five were needed. At first he required that I measure and write it not once, but three times. Later when I was allowed to cut and make joints, the fit had to be close. If not, I had to tear out and replace. He wasn't ugly about it, but very insistent and persistent."

"Your sermon was like your carpentry. You showed how well prepared you were to be standing in the pulpit. As a preacher, you'll go far. Many people will become better people because of your influence.

"I'm aware of your wife's health problem and how much it's also your problem. So often illness strikes just as a person becomes ready to live, ready to contribute.

"Very much I want you to have the most successful life possible. You have so much you can contribute and I want to see you become a success.

"You may be wondering why the recent changes." His eyes began to twinkle. "An old man who was my father's best buddy and teammate on an amateur baseball team until they got too old to play, came to see me at his daughter-in-law's request. Said she was the best woman he knew, and that included his wife who was a close second. He soon let me know he was not going back to her with less than what she wanted—he couldn't face her. And if I didn't listen to reason, he would get my father's body exhumed and he'd tell *him* about it.

"So I learned right then about another woman besides my wife who could call the shots for me."

"Does that bother you?"

"The devil, no! Pardon the language, but I can't think of a better way to say it. Occasionally, a fellow needs to come across an opportunity to do something that rewards his soul in a way that getting ahead in life never does and never can.

"You like your new work schedule and hourly pay raise?"

Mack nodded his head.

"I'm going to pay Old MacDonald's daughter-in-law a visit and thank her for prodding me to do something really decent."

A few days later Mack learned he did just that. Fredda called him up and told of the visit.

"Thanks for everything, Fredda I hadn't realized how much I needed a break from the routine. There's no way for me to show how much it means."

"You just did . . . show me, that is." With a hint of laughter in her voice, she said, "Expecting to hear a sermon come Sunday that shows how much you appreciate it."

"I promise to do better."

CHAPTER FIVE

Rebecca grew so tired of the place. She sometimes wished she could shake off the last remnant of the affliction, but wishing wasn't getting it done. If that voice, a woman's, would just stop reminding me that I'd done something unlawful in the past, that otherwise the FBI wouldn't still be investigating me. I can't remember much about my past at times. Maybe I did lots of things I oughtn't. But what if they can pin a crime on me, they'd just put me in prison. In prison—that's where I am now, so things wouldn't be worse than they are. When I try to run away, they always come bring me back. Just as well if I give up on everything. If I could just be left alone. Nothing will leave me alone. Things keep coming after me. If it's nothing else, its headaches. At times I wish the top of my head would burst open freeing whatever it is to escape.

On another day, she was fuming about Mack and the woman he married after the divorce. And he lied to her about it a while back—maybe it was a year or two ago. I am confused about when it was but not confused about the fact that he married her. I wonder what they do when together in bed. How little I knew about that sort of carrying on when entering this prison, but some of the girls here have been educating me on the details of what they used to do with their men. I'm glad Mack and I never really did that bad stuff.

Rebecca slept a lot and was glad she did. Lately, she'd realized someone had wired her womb to a hot line in the Kremlin. An invisible wire but when the time came for a message that would stop the cold war in its tracks, she would know it was time to send it. She could be counted on to save the world from destruction. And she'd be whisked to Washington for a parade of honor down Pennsylvania Avenue right past the White House, and JFK would stand there beside the White House saluting as she passed in an open limousine.

And this is not the fantasy of a lunatic because it is beginning to happen right now. And there beside the president is that stately and beautiful Jackie—just as clear as the bright sunshine falling all about.

And Mack, as he and his wife watch it on the evening news on NBC, won't he be proud of the wife he dumped when he hears the roar of adulation from the millions who crowd the street along the way for miles? The cheers and applause went on and on. Off in the distance could be heard a band playing the national anthem.

Her headache and the daily fears returned after daylight to plague her through the hours. One day was much like the day before—the same old grind. The trip to Washington was over and only dimly remembered. She had hoped the freshness of it would linger, but like the rose in the vase on her dresser, its petals too had begun to drop off.

Her mother and daddy usually came on Saturday morning followed pretty soon by a visit from Mack. Was this a Saturday morning? She'd ask the first person she saw if this was the day. Her mother and daddy always were a beam of sunshine breaking through a hole in the dark and lingering clouds of fear and confusion. And Mack? Why did he leave his new wife to come visit the woman he had put away? It was a confusion that did not clear. As time went by, she resented the woman a bit less, not because she deserved it. She was just tired of it all, tired of feeling helpless about it all the time. After a time it just wore a person down. Everything else did too. Just wore a person completely out.

Why did what has happened to me not happen to one of those flirty bird-brains I was in class with instead of me? Just luck of the draw? That's as good a way to explain it as anything else.

⇒+⇒

Mack's new routine brought fresh energy to his sermons. His rec-reation was re-creation—just as his friends had hoped. He fished and he hiked long distances in the hills and on Alf's large farm of pasture, hayfields, and woodland.

From his visits with Rebecca, he gradually came to a very small degree of acceptance. From early in her illness he had begun to know what to expect, but knowing was not at all what was needed to live with the knowledge. Real living was so different from what the teenager thinks it will be . . . he thought for the hundredth time. I do the best I can or something very close to that to keep my con-science clean. Sure don't need a troubled conscience.

I remember the efforts of Fredda, Alf, and Lowell and how God answered prayers I had never clearly formed because I didn't know what to pray for. But a good woman understood I was a sinking ship, slowly going down. I was hardly aware of where I was headed. She prayed and through others my help came. God had mercy on me. Pity the man who knows not what God often does through others.

One Sunday morning he confidently stepped to the pulpit, his sermon well prepared and straight to the point. No more than five sentences into the sermon, he realized something was wrong. The audience was less attentive than he had expected. The light buzz of conversation— that sometimes existed as he opened his Bible, took a

51

sip of water, and looked over each section of his audience—persisted few seconds longer than usual. Sitting squarely in front of him—no back of a pew to obstruct the view was a young woman of a sort of beauty he was unfamiliar with. Quickly he looked away and directed his audience's attention to the 40th chapter of Isaiah and read the timeless poetry that began with Verse 31. He read the promise and majesty to the congregation, expecting the audience to respond with eyes riveted on the speaker and faces showing awed appreciation for the writer's expression of an eternal truth, ". . . for do not all men wish to mount up on wings as eagles?"

Believing that the visitor had in some way created a sensation—an expectancy in the audience—he glanced front and center as the woman uncrossed her legs, adjusted her skirt upward and thrust a magnificent bosom upward as she leaned back. In the days before pantyhose it was . . . bare flesh and frothy lace.

Mack's breath quickened and his heart hammered as his face felt on fire. For the first time ever, he felt crude, raw lust overpowering all else, except his imagination of what lay beyond what was obvious. He recognized the symptoms and the severity of them. All his suddenly befogged brain could manage was a silent prayer, "Lord, if you'll get that woman to close the gates of hell, I'll try to get on with my sermon."

And his prayer was immediately answered, for the woman recrossed her legs while lowering her skirt to such a modest level, she would have passed inspection by any other woman in the church.

But too much had been lost from his approach to his sermon for him to make a quick, orderly recovery. He sipped water after clearing his throat three times. And flipped pages in Matthew, large blocks of them while a puzzled audience awaited. And from the very top of a page he started to read, "If a man . . ." and he stopped short, not wanting to read about a man lusting after a woman. Many times he had read it without having fully understood what was meant. But this sudden flash of lightning made it all so clear—he had just sinned while standing in the pulpit, thus doubling or tripling the magnitude of the sin.

The home run he had planned to hit had suddenly become an easy pop fly to third. He turned in haste to find other scripture while taking yet another sip of water. One drop in his windpipe set off a genuine fit of coughing. Many in the congregation changed from puzzlement to sympathy, for had not they too had such an experience at an inappropriate time?

What was Mack going to do? He had a permanent bookmark located at the third chapter of Romans. Briefly he spoke about the background of Verse 23 and then spoke it from memory. The possibility of having a sermon fail for an unexpected reason had been in his mind for years causing him to place the bookmark that would never rest between any other two pages.

It was a short sermon he then delivered on the need for humility no matter how strongly we believe we are following God's will in all we do. Human nature being what it is, there is always a need for vigilance in combating the darker sides of what may be in our hearts.

It was his most polished sermon ever and it ought to be because he had practiced it every couple of months or so before the large mirror on his dresser, making sure his voice and movements of his hands, head, and eyes were what he had wanted them to be.

At the doorway at the service's end, he received several comments such as, "It took you a while to get on track, but when you did, you had everything going straight ahead." "A beautiful, polished sermon once you got into it." "You had a little trouble getting into it, but then, wow!"

And the last person to leave was the woman. A striking beauty in every way. Eyes twinkling with mischief, she said, "If you were a race horse, you could let the pack get out of the gates ten lengths faster and you'd come to the finish a full length ahead of any other. Amazing sermon!"

Mack spent the afternoon at home, mostly in prayer begging pardon for his sin of lust. He had not known 'til this day that he was capable of such a response. Since his early teens, he had fought a preventive war against such raw lust. His fortifications—inadequate for such as this—were quickly overwhelmed, completely. He had responded with a crude, unspeakable sin and was having difficulty in finding words to address to his God.

Finally he went to his bedroom, knelt beside his bed, and prayed aloud, "Father, how deeply I have offended You. If there is an excuse for what I did, I was totally ignorant of the possibility that such desire could have existed in me. What an ignorant fool I have been. Had the possibility of such a response even crossed my mind, I think I would have made better preparation to defend myself.

"I thought I was different from other men. I wanted to live a holy life. I found out on this day that I'm not half the Christian I thought I was . . . all pretense and nothing else. I thought that at age twelve I had dedicated my life to following in the steps of Jesus. Right now, I don't know what it was that happened to me.

"Has my life been a lie that I've been living? Has my every thought, my every action been one of hypocrisy? Am I one of those pretenders that Jesus blasted? I feel like flinging myself from the precipice of a high cliff. Would that be an act of sincerity? Perhaps a sin, but it would be my last sin."

He arose and went to his truck and after a twenty minute drive, he parked in sight of a tall vertical cliff where a free-flowing creek touched its base where slabs of rock lay partially exposed.

In ten minutes of rough hiking, he had climbed to the highest point on the rim and held onto a branch of mountain laurel. Right here at this place, he could commit his final sin. Millions in the last 2000 years over the world must have faced this moment of decision. Those who chose to end it . . . were they all roasting in hell because they decided to escape an unbearable life?

Later that evening he wished he had taken that leap. The woman was again at church. The feeling was instant and palpable. Her presence would in some way further damn him to an impossible life. Was the presence of his wife in a mental hospital not condemnation enough to a life of misery?

But the woman took a seat three rows back and was a model of decorum and an attentive listener. Relief! What a relief!

The audience was a little smaller than at the morning service. At sermon's end, he stood at the door as usual. When the last person had left, he went back inside to do a little tidying up of song books, making sure the church was ready to leave 'til Wednesday. He was in no great hurry to leave. Just being there gave him a sense of reassurance, something he had need of without knowing why except for the morning's revelation of himself.

The sound of footsteps . . . high heels on the wood floor broke into his awareness. A quick flicker of anxiety and he understood. It was that woman. Just he and she. "Help me to get out of this place whole," he prayed silently.

"Brother Mack, I came back to apologize for what I did this morning. It was deliberate. I'm a flirt and know I can use my body to excite a man. My respect for preachers has been at low ebb for some time. I was passing by this morning not thinking about church, but this one is in such a beautiful setting that I decided on the spur of the moment to stop.

"I messed up your first sermon, enjoying my power to do so. But you came right back with a beautiful sermon delivered with poise and an air of complete sincerity. And most important . . . convincing.

"So I came back this evening asking a lady about you before church started. I learned about your wife's illness and I felt shame greater than I ever have before.

"And tonight . . . another great sermon. You are a remarkable man!

"I go to my husband next week in Germany. He's in the army. When he's out of the military, I'll bring him to wherever you are preaching for at least one of your messages."

With that, she turned and walked out like a lady.

Mack's identity had been shattered. The man whose thoughts were always under control died that Sunday as he stood in the pulpit. Thinking good thoughts and encouraging his noble spirit had been paramount in developing his conception of who and what he was. But in a matter of seconds, a woman had lowered his estimation of who and what he was until he saw himself as being no better than the sinners he had hoped to preach to. What business did he have preaching against sin when a flirt and tease had in seconds turned him into someone as capable of sin as the next fellow.

On Monday evening, he phoned Ben Owen the preacher under whose preaching he had experienced his soul's salvation, and who had remained his mentor until time for college. Brother Ben had retired several years earlier.

On the following day, he drove back to the community—where he once had his roots—to a very warm reception. After seeing his favorite preacher, he'd drive the eight miles to see his parents.

Ben Owen's handshake was firm and strong as his left hand and arm drew Mack close. He then waved Mack to a comfortable armchair and seated himself beside a small desk. His grey eyes spoke of the warm heart that lived within the strong body.

"To what do I owe this welcome visit from one of my favorites that I have been too long in hearing from except in an occasional second hand manner?"

Mack's inner discomfort did not allow him to waste time, so he got to the point of the visit. In a few sentences he told it all.

"And you felt a need for an old preacher's advice?"

"Yes, sir."

"Mack, I watched you for about six years after you were saved, and had for three or four years earlier. As a kid, you were a little too good. As a teenager you became even more so."

Mack had not expected any such response as this.

"You are puzzled that your old preacher would make such a statement?"

Mack felt a nod of his head was a sufficient answer.

"You never got into any sort of mischief that I heard of—while some of the others were overdoing that sort of thing. Your attitude and behavior toward girls was always one of respect and reserve."

"Should I have been otherwise?"

"A bit of flirting and giggling with them wouldn't have hurt, but I never saw any of that going on between Sunday school and church as people sat and waited for latecomers to arrive.

"Your wife's illness preceded your marriage by only a brief time, so I've heard from the preachers' grapevine."

"That's true, Brother Owen."

"Was your marriage actually consummated?"

"No, it wasn't, not at all. On the first evening of our marriage, I recognized she was very ill."

"No doubt she never fired up real passion in you."

"During our years of dating, she was always so demure, so shy, so perfect."

"You put her along with the angels in your thoughts and feelings. Just the sort of thing you'd do."

"Was I wrong?"

"No, but not quite natural. Not as realistic as it ought to have been. No one is so good as to need a pedestal to stand on. If the human race is to survive, there is a necessity for sexual lust at times. It needs to be controlled, but its existence is essential."

For an hour they talked about what had happened . . . with Mack doing most of the talking. As he was preparing to leave, Ben Owen again reminded him his response had been natural, that he would never be the brittle, perfect person he had tried to be and thought he was successfully becoming.

"Are you suggesting if the opportunity arises, I should take advantage of it, that considering my circumstances, it wouldn't be such a terrible wrong?"

"What I'm saying is don't be too hard on yourself because you felt a rush of hormones. May God be extra merciful to you, Mack

Baldwin. I don't know of any other young person that I feel as much pity for as I do you. Even more than for your wife. That may seem strange but she receives medication that, to an extent, blunts her ability to feel emotional pain in the way that you do.

"What is she like when you visit her?"

"At times quite lucid. But she tells of living in fear she will be imprisoned after the FBI brings charges and gets a conviction.

"Does she say what they are investigating her for?"

"No, she's afraid there is something in her past that she can't recall.

"On her better days she knows she has problems within. She told me once that some of the women she knows at the hospital talk openly about sex with their husbands before they were put in the asylum and they never saw any wrong in it.

"But that had in no way changed her mind. Nothing exists which could change her mind about that. The fact that it is necessary to make babies is an argument that would be totally useless in convincing her it is normal in creating a family. I never try to change her thinking about that or anything else."

"There's no reaching her where suspicions, delusions, and illusions exist in her mind," Ben Owen said.

"And there is no need trying. I feel so completely helpless. What I'd love to do can't be done. How I'd love to be able to reason with her regarding the FBI. She's convinced that young woman at church has already stolen me. I performed the young woman's marriage ceremony to her boy friend recently and told Rebecca about it, but in her twisted thinking she didn't believe me but was convinced that I had married that girl after divorcing her."

"And you knew it was useless to tell her you could not divorce her without cause. Her illness was not something a court would buy as being a cause."

Mack's dad was a part-time farmer. Most days he was a carpenter, but when his cattle farm needed him, he left his small construction crew in charge of his most experienced man, one skilled in several trades.

Anita Baldwin's home cooking was beyond wonderful to a man who was used to cold cereal at breakfast, sandwiches at noon, and restaurants at suppertime.

She was twenty pounds heavier than the slender girl she's been when she married. As the years went by, she had worked at making her meals just a little better than they'd been the year before. A tiny bit more or less of seasoning and other things she'd learned to do, without realizing she was doing them. She measured less . . . estimating unthinkingly while her food became something even she thought was good. So a few pounds had been added over the years.

The company of his parents was as soul-warming as the cornbread, fresh field peas, and creamed corn not long off the stalk, mashed potatoes, sliced tomatoes, and cured ham. Mack passed over the ham. He could and did often eat it in the restaurant, but nowhere else could he eat vegetables that could half compare to his mother's cooking. Why not try to find a church nearby that needed a preacher and work for his father?

There was a hayfield not far from the house. After dinner his father had two large mules pulling a sickle-bar mower as Mack watched. Stalks of hay were falling as if by magic since the sickle bar couldn't be seen from his vantage point. His father stopped the team only feet away from Mack. "Would you like to mow for a while?"

Mack had done this many times before. The mules were a good experienced team and knew the routine well, requiring little of Mack's attention.

In a couple of days the hay would be dry and ready for raking into windrows. His father's neighbors had tractors and mowers and modern equipment for tossing hay into windrows, and hay balers to come along afterwards.

Mack would come back when the hay was ready and help load it on a wagon and to the barn they'd go where by pitchfork and straining, they'd get the hay unloaded and dragged back into the loft the old-fashioned way.

"The mules are only middle aged with years of good working ability ahead. I'm not going to send them off to be butchered for some undignified purpose I hate to even think about," was how he had explained his old-timey farming as he had hitched up the team a half hour earlier.

And Mack loved the tall rugged man who could still do a day's hard work.

"Is either of my two brothers going to be able to return to help get this into the barn loft?"

"They have wives, kids, and five-day-a-week jobs. I'm too independent to ask it of them."

"I take two days a week off from carpentry. I'll come back. Might get some of the grief and frustration worked out of me."

And now as he rode the mower watching with fascination as the cutter-bar smoothly laid hay to the ground, he could feel grief becoming more manageable.

How great it had been at dinner in the warmth of his parents' love and concern. He had come home again and he'd once heard a man say, "You can't go home again." The fellow had meant that a fellow would have changed and his parents would have changed in adjustment to his being gone. But at this dinner table, his parents were the same caring people they were before he had gone off to college. Perhaps they had never grieved over his being gone because they wanted for him a life of his own. It was as if the intervening years had never existed. Briefly, it was as if Rebecca and her illness had never come into his life.

And two days later, he drove back to the farm for a day of "recreation" in the stifling dusty heat of a barn loft. At times for minutes, Rebecca's illness was not on his mind. An uncomfortable routine he had known in boyhood now brought him comfort.

He did not blame his father for falling behind his neighbors. Some of them were in debt for having machinery that had more capacity than they needed. His father preferred to be conservative in all he did. The hayfield was not a really large one. His farming activities reflected his love of the land. His small construction business was where he made a living.

Before driving to his home, he ate another of his mother's meals. Troubles passed away as warm memories pushed them aside. For the second time that week he was home again. Somewhere a fragment of music stirred his memory—the music poignant and beautiful almost beyond bearing. Always he thought of it as the going home theme from a symphonic piece.

CHAPTER SIX

In June the next year, Alf McDonald and a crony of his, Ralph Nesbitt, had Mack on the front seat of an aluminum boat during a willow fly hatch. Three men with fly rods and popping bugs busily settling on the water.

Mack had fished with Alf several times before, but had never seen anything like this. Bluegill mostly, small to medium-sized ones striking and the large ones taking in the small poppers with a sucking sound much like a kiss.

Occasionally, a bass was on, accompanied by wild leaps and strong runs. What it was . . . was excitement! All of it!

Lines and leaders sometimes got tangled, but the old men would patiently clear them. Mack was impatient to get his back into the water. For the time being, he totally forgot he had a sick wife.

The two old men had experienced this many times and were excited, but even greater than this was the joy they took from seeing Mack completely absorbed in having a good time. They saw that for these hours nothing else was on his mind.

Large bluegills were put on ice in the cooler. Mack had agreed
to attend a fish fry if one of the others cleaned and did the frying.
This was beyond his skills, he had explained. To which Ralph had
commented, "Preacher, it's a simple sort of thing to do. Yours is not
a very excusable excuse." And Mack had come back with, "If I did
it, I bet you'd spend more time spitting out bones and scales than
eating crispy white flesh." So Alf said they might be wise to let a real
experienced hand do the cleaning and cooking since he's probably
done it at least ten times as many times as Ralph, who'd never seen
a day of fishing like this before.

"Preacher, Old MacDonald is a pretty good man with a fly rod,
but he's never seen an hour like I did once. Just me that day . . .
had a three-horse motor tightened to the transom of a little old
rental boat. Motored down the lake at maybe a mile an hour. If a
thunderstorm came up, I'd just have to stay where I was and take
it. But there was a heckuva hatch especially at two large trees no
more than a hundred feet apart. The water under their overhang-
ing branches was a mass of ripples and splashes. Dang! Just missed
a bass! Well anyway I already had a fly rod ready. Moved to the front
seat. Paddle in my left hand sculling the boat. Had out twenty . . .
twenty-five feet of line and leader. Bream couldn't get to my popper
fast enough. Looked at my watch . . . 1:15 pm. Decided I'd see how
many fish I could catch in sixty minutes.

"Maybe fifteen. Is that the tale you're going to come up with,
Ralph?"

"No doubt you'd be happy if I done no better than that, Old
Mac. But with a preacher in this boat, I'm going to have to stick
close to the truth.

"Doggone! This little rascal took the popper almost all the way
to his anus. Let me borrow your disgorger, Old Mac."

When the tedious job of removal had been completed without
destroying the small fish, Ralph continued his story. "Sculling my

boat with my left hand, with twenty to twenty-five feet of line and leader combined for a cast while pinning the line against the front of the reel seat with fingers on my right, I made casts. When a bream was on, I stripped line in, removed the fish, and repositioned my boat."

"Had to reposition every time you released a fish?" Alf said, "You don't mean them tiny bream was moving your boat around?"

"Actually they was and most were bigger than tiny."

"Now let's hear how many you caught in sixty minutes. Twenty? Twenty-five?"

"Hate to disappoint you. Doggone if I don't have a good one right now!" He played the fish, then held it up to be admired. "In the cooler you go, you handsome rascal!

"Back to how many I caught. It was sixty-four."

"Ralph, there's a preacher settin' in front of you and you tell something like that . . . ain't you got no sense of shame? And look at him. He's got the first smallmouth of the day on!"

The fish had just taken a wild leap. Advice was quick in coming. "Keep your rod pointed up more, Brother Mack, or he'll snap that leader!"

Already Alf and Ralph had flipped their lines back behind and out of the way. Mack continued to get advice and reassurance. The large fish came flying high and wide. Mack's heart pounded. An air of unreality was upon him . . . disbelief that such as this could be happening to him. The fish burst from the surface a third time and then came racing toward the boat. Mack worked hard to steer it to the other side and used the long rod to keep the smallmouth from getting underneath.

"That was done like you've done it before," Alf commented. He and Ralph had completely cranked in their lines and sat watching a young feller getting hooked . . . enjoying the preacher's baptism by a smallmouth bass.

Eventually Ralph netted it and held it out to Mack who took the fish by the lower lip and held it up. Ralph—without touching the fish—spanned it from tip of thumb to tip of the little finger. Twice he did this and reported, "He'll go over eighteen inches, probably a good nineteen. Now ease him back in the water and make sure he's breathing good before releasing. They don't eat as good as bream, but they are the most fun to catch of anything in this river."

For several minutes, Mack just sat watching the other men take bluegill bream, but not really watching. The air of unreality had not completely worn off. Neither had the weakness that had suddenly hit him in the knees as he had stood to keep the fish from taking the fight underneath the boat.

It had happened to him! The excitement of a willow fly hatch and fish in a wild frenzy of feeding! The smallmouth taken on a tiny popper and four-pound test leader. He sat, barely noticing the conversation of Ralph and Alf.

⚓

The fish fry was at the McDonald house out on the patio. Alf had connected a deep fat fryer to an outdoor base plug and fried small fillets for a brief period before removing them to drop in more. His wife Nell was lending an experienced hand indoors preparing the other fixings. Sarah Nesbitt had also come to lend a hand.

Later when the meal had been eaten, Nell and Sarah brought ice cream for anyone who cared for dessert. The three men did "after a hard day's work," as Alf had put it.

When the women had removed all signs that a feast had been held outdoors, the men talked about fishing. "Was fishing a good hatch like you had imagined it would be, Mack?"

"It was beyond anything I thought it could be. Until just minutes ago, I didn't think of Rebecca. Hadn't all day 'til just now. Once we started fishing, it was as though I had no sick wife. I was too excited to feel the pity for her that has been a constant companion for years. Also, the self-pity was off somewhere else in another world. Now I feel shame for having a joyful day of excitement while Rebecca is imprisoned by the fears that to us are unreal."

"Mack, don't feel guilt for having a day when you could be like the rest of us. Today was what my daughter-in-law hoped would occasionally come to you. It's good for your soul. God does not wish for you a life without an occasional day when joy overwhelms all your grief. I called Fredda a few minutes ago when I went inside while Ralph was telling one of his fishing stories. She thanked me for getting you away from yourself and hopes you go to sleep with visions of a smallmouth up in the air attached to your terminal tackle. One of her prayers has been answered."

CHAPTER SEVEN

How long had she been in this place? Years, she knew. Different medicines had been tried. There were times she thought one might be helping. There were times the voices returned more often than before, reporting that the FBI was about ready to end their investigation. She had watched a little TV news in one of the lobbies. It looked like a nuclear war was inevitable. Using her hot line to the Kremlin, she might be able to head it off if she just knew what message to send.

What day of the week is this? Will Mack come today? I hope he will. He doesn't seem as crazy like the doctors and nurses and attendants here. One of the other patients this morning was saying the real nuts in this place are the ones who supposedly are caring for us. They give us treatments that don't get us out of this nightmare of a prison. They want to keep us here, our souls rotting in this hell. If there was something I could do that would convince them I was ready to go home, I'd do it. But my confusion is everlasting and they make sure I stay this way so they can keep me here. Sometimes I pray that God will reveal what I need to do, but God has abandoned me. I believe He wants me to remain just like I am.

Not getting any better. Slowly sinking in this quagmire of the unreal. I know much of what I think is real is not what Mother, Daddy, and Mack see as being real. I might could believe that one of them is crazy, but not all three.

But still I remain as I am. My headaches get worse. Aspirin continues to lose its strength.

One of the other girls thinks I'm on the right track, that the people who claim to be here to help us are really trying to make us worse. So they'll have a job to do. Patients start getting well, and they'd soon be out of a job.

Later that day when no visitor had come, she had a great idea all of a sudden. She'd write a letter to the local newspaper telling the editor that she had a direct connection to the Kremlin and knew a way to stop the nuclear war before it started. It was her patriotic duty and the next time Mack or her parents came, she'd get one of them to take her out to get writing paper, envelops, and stamps. Then she'd start a letter-writing campaign to the larger newspapers. That's just what she'd do.

Two days later, Mack visited. Rebecca had not forgotten. She had already written three letters to newspaper editors informing them that she had access to the Soviets' inner circle of power and awaited the "proper time" to send a message that could ease cold war tensions.

Mack listened to her plan and offered no objections. He would take her out for lunch and then to the post office for stamped envelopes. Back at the hospital, he sat with her as she addressed three envelopes.

"Mack," she said when the letters were ready, "would you mail these for me?"

"Don't you have a drop for outgoing mail here at the hospital?"

"Yes. I'll go do that right now." She was a little surprised that he had not tried to talk her out of it. Some members of the staff would likely have tried to do so.

"I'll walk with you." There were times when he found it difficult to keep his mouth closed, but this was not one of them. News editors had, no doubt, seen out-of-touch letters before and would again and again.

This time Rebecca felt no sadness at his leaving. He had fully cooperated with her desire to save the world. It had been a welcome visit on a successful day—a far better one than usual.

⟞⟊⟝

Their sixth wedding anniversary arrived. Mack changed his work schedule so he could visit her.

"It's been six years today since we were wed, darling," he announced to her on arrival.

"And we are not living together and haven't for a long time. You may not be a faithful husband but you are a faithful visitor. How many years has it been since you and that woman from church got married? Four or five?"

Responding would have been worse than useless. It would have only fired up groundless suspicions into a hateful attack.

She said nothing further on any subject for a time, giving him time to think about their lives. The love that had brought them together was very immature, not much more than puppy love. Marriage in the true sense had never existed. Neither had real love. What had they had? She had the beginning of the most terrible of illnesses without a day's happiness. He? Burdensome responsibilities and grief for a love that never was. And no possibility of ever living as most men do. Who had been dealt the worse hand? Both had. What had happened was what most couples never thought of as a

69

possibility. He looked at her totally unresponsive face—a misfiring brain behind the forehead and eyes with seldom a spark of intelligent thought. For the thousandth time, he asked the question that had no answer. Why did God permit such a beautiful young woman who had not one flaw of character or behavior to be suddenly struck down as if punishment was being visited on the closest thing to an angel that any woman could be? And why did he continue to believe and preach that God loves His children? He did not have answers to any of it. Had the worst sinner he knew asked him why he remained blind to God's injustices raining down on the heads of the most innocent, what could he say? He could say nothing.

She had gone to sleep. Gently he patted a cheek of the one he had thought would stand beside him in the most difficult times that God's preacher-servant had to face. And reality hit him again.

"Mr. Baldwin," a man's voice in the hallway coming from behind him stopped him suddenly. Turning he saw one of the psychiatrists who tended to Rebecca's problems.

"Yes, Dr. Butler."

"A few minutes with you in my office down to the next floor." He lead the way and a couple of minutes later, he was seated behind his desk with Mack comfortably seated in an armchair facing him.

"Glad I caught you before you got away. Your wife's severe headaches up here," he said touching the top of his head. "They are indicative of something, but we don't know what. We have no knowledge that connects them with her mental disorder. She's being put on a stronger sedative.

"Then there is another problem. If she had her way, her diet would be 90% sweets. And poor thing, she has a mouthful of what dentists call "silver fillings." When a molar has been drilled out too many times, a cap becomes necessary. She has four of those. Of greater concern are the first signs of serious gum disease, especially around her molars, some at the base of a couple of bicuspids."

"What about her gums up front? When she smiles, the gums look pretty good there."

"She has fillings up front too, but they are not silver fillings. They are sometimes called porcelain . . . tooth colored because the other material would look bad when the person smiles."

"The dentist says the trouble began with her sweet tooth tendency and her poor habits of dental hygiene compound the problem."

"Is this something I need to be concerned about?"

"Probably not right now. Just wanted you to know we are watching everything," the doctor answered.

"As far as you can tell, is she making any progress?" Mack asked.

"If there is a magic pill for her case, we haven't found it. Shock treatment has been considered, but we ruled it out."

"Good. That's something that's now getting bad reviews."

As Mack drove home, he wondered about his silent outburst against God. Does God have a pencil and a tablet where He keeps a record of any disloyal thoughts that appear unbidden or come with full awareness and conscious intent?

The sixth anniversary of his wedding. What would the tenth and twenty-fifth bring in the way of a mood of celebration. How long could he go on living a pretense of sanity? Friends he owed so much to for his breaks from the monotony of work, study, and sermons along with respite from countless hours of loneliness, he appreciated more than ever. Without them? He'd not survive.

What if Rebecca slipped into a permanent catatonic stupor? Compared to that, her letter writing campaign he had lent a little assistance to was like a day at the state fair. Today might have been better than he would see again. Though symptomatic of her illness, her letter writing showed interest in something. So it was bad news *and* good news.

Her headaches grew worse. Her gum disease, especially around the roots of her twelve molars continued unabated. Would she lose her teeth? She was highly unlikely to be able to clean them three times a day like the dentist wanted.

That afternoon as he hiked around the outside of Alf McDonald's pasture fence—a mile each lap—he realized he needed to make adjustments in his thinking. Alf often joined him in these hikes as dusk approached, but he had it alone this day.

His thoughts remained on Rebecca. Her unexplainable headaches. They were not stress headaches. Not sinus headaches. He had experienced both and neither was confined to the top of his head. A brain tumor growing in size? The only possibility he could think of. Whatever brought on the pain could not be something good and she was so badly in need of something good, for a change.

He had been walking by the light of the moon as a small herd of cattle watched him when he came by in his final lap. Did they wonder at his unusual behavior?

CHAPTER EIGHT

A month went by. Even small churches had someone as an alternate pastor. He took his first vacation ever and drove his pickup to Jackson, Wyoming. Pictures of the Grand Tetons had drawn him in that direction for years.

Rebecca was not getting better and in despair, he believed that she never would. There had come a sudden inspiration to drive far away as if he could leave his problems behind. And to his great surprise, he did just that!

It was as if all that he left behind were distant memories that were no longer a part of his present life. Leaning his head so far back it tired his neck, there was just not enough of seeing the Cathedrals with their sharp spires and small glaciers that changed color as the sun all too quickly moved to hide behind what dominated all else.

With a guided group the next day, he hiked to Lake Solitude and back. The guide answered questions but said little else. Fortunately, awed silence soon settled on the group and there was no loudmouth to set on edge the nerves of those who came to experience the majestic moving peaks as walking gave way to slowly-changing vistas.

Before starting, the guide asked if anyone had ever done this before. No one had. Yet they were as free of *wows* and *oohs* and *never seen the likes* as if they had and had returned to again experience leaving the rest of their lives behind and forgotten. So overpowering were the sights that all other senses had graciously withdrawn so that sight had the day to itself.

On that day, Mack knew the true meaning and feeling of *getting away from it all*. And there came a passing fantasy of living in Jackson permanently.

At a western style outdoor barbeque that evening, he knew the joy of eating steak, corn-on-the-cob, salad with Italian dressing, and anything else that struck his fancy. And plenty did. At a table where five other people sat, it was almost like an instant family. From three different states they came, and they seemed to instantly know each other. They had come to eat supper on one of the last level places before the giant peaks so abruptly broke from the plain. Snow and ice on the almost sheer surfaces, steeples, and spires turned from deep orange to rosy hues as the sun was making final preparations for the night that was soon to come. A touch of melancholy settled on the six people as the time of parting was so inexorably closing in. Around twelve hours must pass before this most beautiful of places would light up again.

Mack was learning that on western vacations, friendships were quickly made and intensely enjoyed, and on the next day the experience came again, but each day differently.

With two he'd never seen before and likely never would again, he hiked alongside Lake Jenny and enjoyed the company of the two who were as spellbound as he by the mountains that overpowered their emotions. They were sisters from Alberta and told him that the Canadian Rockies were well worth going to see. At that moment he silently vowed that he would. "We won't tell you, sir, that they are more magnificent, but there are longer stretches that will turn your head, and there is more snow left for summer pleasure of those who do come."

The next day he went trout fishing with the guide he had been lucky enough to reserve on his arrival in Jackson.

From the upper Snake River, he combined the excitement of seeing yet different views of the Tetons with the joyous pleasure of trout taking tiny flies at the surface, barely dimpling the clear water. The cutthroat would take to the air in acrobatic leaps, not with quite the long jumps or the quick hard runs of a smallmouth bass. But there was a beauty in their response at the terminus of very light tackle, unlike he had ever experienced. Even as he watched the fish make their efforts to escape, he would take a quick look at the changing views of the mountains.

There was just too much joy to be completely absorbed. Without his realizing it, images were being stored that would be called up years later.

Doug asked as he was removing a fish from Mack's hook, "It's different from fishing down South, Mack?"

"Very. It's like fishing when you get to Heaven. Since I arrived here, I have several times wondered if the Teton Range is here to give us a taste of what might be in store for us."

"What would your congregation think if you made such a comparison from the pulpit?" his guide asked in a drawl.

"Some might think it amounted to sacrilege. Others might want to say, 'Amen!' but if they were out here, they might all feel as I do right now."

Mack worked out his line again with a few false casts, then let it shoot as far as the energy of his forward cast would power it. And almost instantly, the surface dimpled. A slight lifting motion by the rod tip, and the fight was on.

"A fine one, Mack. Don't get buck fever and do what you know you shouldn't. Stick to the basics. Don't let him get you in the position of having the whole rod pointing at him."

As this fish first broke the surface, Mack realized he would not be looking at the scenery until after this battle was won or lost.

Time stopped its passage. In a world almost dreamlike, it was just him and the fish. He heard Doug saying something in words of encouragement, but he didn't let his mind wander enough to interpret what was said.

When Doug had netted the fish and lifted it out for Mack to take, he exclaimed, "The largest trout I've seen in weeks, Mack! You kept your cool. A client I had last week, who claimed he's caught many fine trout back East, would have lost that fish. In fact, he had one a great deal smaller to break the leader after the first leap.

"You have what it takes. Fish as often back home as your work and your ministry allow."

Mack—more than he had ever before—felt mannish. During his teens when he was searching for an identity, people whom he associated with treated him with deference because of his behavior and his dedication to becoming a preacher. In college and since, men usually acted like he was a preacher and he knew they weren't completely natural in their conduct. Father-son relationship was not enough to prepare him to feel masculine. Alf McDonald made it clear that he was in no way going to allow Mack's ministry to make any difference in how he responded and acted toward him. If Alf had a nice-sized fish get off, he certainly did not say, "These things just happen sometimes. It's just part of the sport." Alf pointed out that as far as he was concerned Mack was, first of all, another man. And Mack appreciated and loved him for that. His occasional expletive when something unexpected or unpleasing happened let Mack know he was accepted as a man's man.

As the fishing went on, he proceeded to tell Doug about this man who accepted him as another man first and a preacher second.

"Mack, I've often wondered about preachers after they have been in the profession for thirty years or so. Do they not realize that they live in an artificial environment created by others who out of respect for the profession use a language that is different from what they use when the preacher isn't there. You apparently like Alf McDonald for, among other things, being himself when you fish or hike together or trade yarns."

"And you, Doug, appear to accept me as a man despite my being a preacher. You used one of Alf's favorite expletives when a better than average trout just became unglued from my hook about ten minutes ago.

Doug grinned. He'd forgotten he had used the word. "A customer's success, as I see it, is partly my success. I also identify almost completely with him or her."

"When it's a her, what do you do when either of you need to—" his voice just drifted off.

Again, he smiled. "About the same as I'll do with you pretty shortly. Pull in at a convenient place to tie up and get out. Separate as far as conveniently possible after I've promised the lady that my back will be turned until she gives the *all clear* signal."

Later, lunch was at a place where legs could be stretched a bit on a shore formed by rounded gravel. The boat was tied to a snag on the side of a large log that was firmly lying, for the most part, on the shore. The log was a comfortable change of seating as they relaxed while eating.

Mack told about Rebecca's illness and the near hopeless prognosis. "But out here, it all seems distant . . . almost as if it's not true. I can feel almost normal. I'm ashamed of it, but I've even thought about never going back. I'm a carpenter, as well as a preacher. Could probably find work."

Doug told of leaving the heat of West Texas thirty years ago and never going back except for brief visits. "This is an easy place to fall in love with. Was an experienced horseback rider. Found work on a dude ranch. Met a young woman tourist from Ohio. Before she had been out there five days, she had a job helping me show tourists how much fun it was to work on a real ranch including the joys of shoveling horse droppings out of stalls."

"You mean people paid money for the privilege of doing yucky work?"

"On a real western ranch, part of our job was to see that they had plenty of photographic evidence that they had been real cowboys or cowgirls. Back home they'd show friends and relatives proof they had roped a calf or got right into the spirit of things by working in barns or hayfields."

"I'm the idiot who came without a camera for you to use if I catch a nice trout."

"No problem. I've a thirty-five millimeter packed in my gear. With the great light of early and mid-afternoon, I'll shoot a twenty-shot roll of you, the scenery, and the fish you catch.

"The woman who dropped off my boat and me at the launch is my wife. She worked with me on that ranch my first summer out here. Married her before fall that year. The rancher kept us on that first year. He's eighty now and still likes to boast how he's responsible for bringing us together.

"Jan and I raised three kids who wanted to get away from this country as fast as they could. One in Dallas, one in Colorado, and one in the heat and humidity of New Orleans.

"My first winter here, I polished up my skills on skis. Had learned the basics in northern New Mexico. The following winter I became a ski patrol and still do that. Summer and Fall, I do what I'm doing today. I also work in leather, making all sorts of things . . . fancy belts, wallets, even saddles.

"My list of needs is pretty short. Jan sees things pretty much the same. She'll pick us and the boat up at day's end."

Soon they were back on the river with Doug at the oars making suggestions on where to let the dry fly settle on the surface.

A dimple appeared on the second cast and the fight was on. And when it was over, Doug took a shot of what was to be the largest fish of the day. Mack's excitement chased away any remnants of what he would face again back home. Rebecca existed as did preaching, but only in the dimness of the fuzzy boundary between the here and the there.

"Going up to Yellowstone while you are here, Mack?" Not waiting for an answer, Doug said, "It's so close by, later you'll wish you had gone if you don't."

"I'll decide in the morning. Probably will go. I'm so relaxed about what I decide to do and at the same time, so excited about this afternoon of fishing. If the fish weren't taking flies, this day would be well spent sightseeing and enjoying the company of a man who knows how he wants to spend his life. But they are biting and I have it all. It overwhelms me. This can't be happening to me! But it is!"

"I'm glad that I can be a part of your day."

At the day's end, Doug said, "That pickup you see with a trailer attached will have my wife, Jan, ready to pick us up when we've drifted the two hundred yards separating us. By the way, you've had the best day of fishing of anyone I've taken out this year."

"Today, He, who has at times seemed to have just left me hanging, has smiled on me."

"It's time that He did!"

Yellowstone won the next morning in the mental tossing of a coin.

At the entrance, he picked up literature with maps. Before driving far, he scanned this at a turnout beside a river. Much of the day he would spend in a volcanic crater unlike any preconceived notion of what a crater could be. Distant peaks with snowy tops were the jagged rim, but it didn't seem like they were.

A hundred bubbly, steaming places . . . many filling nearby air with stench. Groves of dead trees killed by heat from an earthquake of a few years earlier. The earth had been severely shaken and in places split.

And Old Faithful—greater and more exciting than he expected! Each time before the big blow came, it gave warnings as the buildup grew and grew. Excitement in the crowd of hundreds that gathered early also grew and grew during the buildup. When the big blow came, it shot up a hundred feet and more! As much as was his enjoyment of the geyser, was pleasure in being a part of a crowd having a good time. Too long before this vacation, there had been too little recreation. Oh, there had been good days here and there but not enough to make him feel like a new person.

His problems back home were something he was still aware of, but they intruded little on what he was living during this trip. This was reality too—the only reality of the day and week. There were adults and children at almost every stopping point. Excitement of things never before seen or felt, but exceeding all expectations.

A preacher of serious mind, he had been a husband who had never been a husband but a man of unanswered prayer, and maybe he shouldn't feel that way about the life back there. But in an atmosphere of people having a good time, especially the enthusiasm of children, he could not help but be caught up in the mood of people having a time of wonder and thrills, nor did he want to miss a bit of their happiness.

Twice, he watched Old Faithful. It was as good the second time as the first. That phenomenon of nature knew how to give a psychological buildup, and the letdown toward the end was a gentle one. And there was the good feeling left afterward. If you'd hang around about an hour, you could live it again. He stayed the extra hour, eating an early lunch while keeping up with the passage of time. Then it was back to a gathering crowd and growing excitement.

Afterward, he drove on to West Yellowstone and had good luck in finding a motel room for a couple of nights. With that taken care of, he yielded to the draw of Old Faithful and drove back, making a brief stop here and there at some of the countless attractions.

He lucked out again. The geyser was beginning to send up ten foot eruptions of condensing steam. And when the big blow came, it had all the excitement of the first. Supper he managed to work in before the next one blew. He witnessed it four times in all.

Along the way back to West Yellowstone, traffic was held up by a herd of bison making a slow crossing of the highway. By the time the last one made up its mind to cross and not go back as some had done, Mack hoped he'd seen the last one for the day.

Sleep didn't come as easily this night as before. He had experienced five days in an exciting world. Rebecca had probably sunken deeper into the world she lived in—a world only dimly seen and understood by others. Her revelations had no connections with what was seen by others. He wondered how she would interpret Yellowstone if she were here.

Was it wrong for him to be having some fun when she was so sick? He called the hospital each day from his motel room before setting out on a day so different—so interesting and exciting. Each time the staff member assured him she was glad he was taking a real break. One had said, "A break from that in which there is so little hope."

The next day, he explored places that in every instance exceeded all his expectations. The rainbow at Lower Yellowstone Falls was seen under perfect sunlight conditions.

He hiked, but not on trails that had bear warnings at trailheads. A herd of American elk in a river was his only sighting of those magnificent creatures.

The next morning, he began his trip toward home by way of Old Faithful and the Grand Tetons.

Before arriving home, he went by the hospital and soon learned that Dr. Butler wanted to see him on his return from his trip. Was there further bad news about Rebecca? . . . he wondered as he walked down the hallway,

"It's her teeth that I first wanted to discuss with you and close behind is another problem."

Mack felt the second stage of unease. "But her teeth have always been a problem. And the other development?"

"Except for up front, her gums are in bad need of treatment which could include bone grafts."

"The bony structure that anchors her teeth . . . has it deteriorated further?

"Yes," Dr. Butler said, "The dentist recommends extraction including her front teeth as the best route to take."

"Then she'd have to have a full set of dentures. At age twenty-nine, that seems terribly young."

"Mack, this is only the beginning. We've talked of her severe headaches. She doesn't talk much these days but still complains occasionally about pain in the top of her head.

"That has always puzzled me, but there are early signs of something more sinister. She's beginning to lose parts of her memory. Like not being able to get food off her plate with her fork. She just pushes it around on her plate."

"Somebody has to feed her?"

"Exactly . . . and she doesn't remember how to brush her teeth."

"Has this come on suddenly?"

"It appears that it has . . . to us, that is. But with her other problems, it could be that it has been coming on for some time and just went unnoticed. I think she suffers from two kinds of dementia, the second one now being called Alzheimer's disease. It used to be associated with old age. Recently, I read it could hit in the thirties. Rare, but possible and she is just twenty-nine."

"Is anything known about what causes it, Dr. Butler?"

"No. However, her dentist told me he knew a fellow dentist who could not treat a patient because he had forgotten what to do next after he had started treatment. And he was only fifty-two. Now, he is completely dependent on his wife."

"Rebecca can be expected to become even more dependent?"

"I'm afraid so. Already, she is on pureed food. She's fed with a spoon."

"If her teeth are extracted, will they be replaced with a set of dentures?" Mack realized all of this was going to require lots of adjustment on his part. Things were so much worse than he realized when he left on vacation. Now he wished he had not gone.

"She could get dentures, but she won't need them. With pureed food, there is no need for chewing. She's more likely to aspirate food into her lungs if it's solid enough to require mastication.

"Shall I have the dentist go ahead?"

Mack asked for a few days to think it over.

⇒┼┼⇐

Four weeks later, all of Rebecca's teeth had been removed. Dr. Butler had explained halfway through the process that a set of dentures would be something she would likely not allow to remain in her mouth anyway, and she had been way past caring about her looks for quite some time. Mack had been aware of this as she had grown quite obese and kept on eating all the sweets she had access to.

"Strange thing happened, Mack," Dr. Butler said. "Halfway through the extractions, her nurse asked how she felt and she said, 'I got a sore mouth, but my headaches are gone.' They didn't return.

"Daily for the next two weeks, someone asked about her headaches. They had been cured."

"Do you or anyone else having knowledge of this, have an explanation?" Mack asked.

"The dentist had heard of this happening once, maybe twice. In removing the teeth, any "silver" fillings the patient had are removed. He says this is not science, purely anecdotal.

"Those silver colored fillings are roughly fifty percent mercury.

"In the early 1930's, I was interning in a charity ward. There was a patient that was hospitalized with rheumatism. Such severe pain in hip and thigh, he couldn't walk without crutches. Even then, pain was excruciating. His physician started him on morphine. Back then, when doctors had a case they couldn't come up with a cause for the illness, it wasn't unusual to associate the problem with the teeth. This patient had no infected teeth or gums, but had lots of silver fillings."

"What could teeth have to do with illnesses located somewhere else in the body, Dr. Butler?"

"Teeth, it was believed by some, could be a locus of infection. So a dentist was called in and he removed that man's molars, leaving him handicapped in chewing. Surprising me, this fellow got better. Within a month, he was released. Was doing pretty well on crutches. That was around late January."

"Was he ever able to go back to work?" Mack wondered aloud.

"My interest in this was because I thought it was quack medicine. They might just as well have brought in a witch doctor. I got the man's address. That summer, I wrote a letter asking him how he was getting along. His wife wrote me that he was making a crop, walking behind his mule almost every day."

"Didn't it make you think that he might have been suffering from mercury poisoning?"

"That crossed my mind, but I couldn't find any science to back it up."

"Rebecca's new illness—what you believe is Alzheimer's—could be related to her schizophrenia?" Mack wondered aloud.

"Don't think so, Mack. Of course we don't know what brings on either.

"The farmer whose sciatic nerve problem began to clear after removal of his molars, and Rebecca's headaches located in an unusual place, vanishing upon a partial removal of her teeth causes me to wish for some solid science. And then there's the dentist who developed a severe memory disorder at age fifty-two and he had those same headaches.

"Sometimes I get so frustrated working in a state of ignorance. The country had the science to split the atom and harness its energy. And the science to send man to the moon and back. The search for answers to diseases of the brain has been almost totally neglected.

"People don't matter! Beating the Soviets to the moon does! People rot away in institutions like this one, but to the government they are out of sight and forgotten. Homeless people, many of them with mental problems, are noticed at Thanksgiving and Christmas by charitable organizations and mostly ignored otherwise. We are a shameful nation that doesn't care.

"Rebecca's dentist doesn't say he believes her gum disease was related to her fillings. He also can't say her new dementia was related to her dental fillings. Neither will he say that there can be no cause-effect relationship. However, he did say that he would never place another silver filling."

"Maybe I shouldn't have taken the vacation I just finished," Mack lamented.

"Nonsense, Mack. There is no reason two lives should be wasted.

"Come visit her as often as you wish, but get on with your life. Find pleasure and joy anywhere you can," the doctor advised. "Physicians not long ago would purge patients with calomel if they really didn't know how to treat them. A chloride of mercury—sometimes it was given to a patient who had undiagnosed appendicitis which could rupture the appendix. But the dead didn't complain and the relatives still had confidence in the family doctor."

The drive home was so different from the drive to the West. At that time, enthusiasm was a welcome companion. In the months before, he had worked out a life almost worth living. Rebecca's mental illness seemed to be stuck in a deep rut, but he'd become adjusted to that. Her headaches and gum problems had been a worry. He visited her less often than in the early years thinking there would always be problems of some kind coming up.

But he had hope. The magic drug always remained a possibility and she might improve enough to be released and live about ninety or ninety-five percent of a normal life. Though this had never been suggested to him as something to look forward to, he could hope for it. Now, there was nothing.

During the past year, he had read about Alzheimer's and thought at least she doesn't suffer from the dementia that kills. Maybe that was an incorrect diagnosis. But Dr. Butler said two other staff physicians thought it was correct. And the dentist had seen one case very much like Rebecca's. She might have been suffering from it for several years, but with her other mental problems, it may have been unnoticed. Twenty-nine and would not likely reach forty, possibly not even thirty-five. That miracle pill he had placed his faint hope in would make no difference now. A few years, in a near vegetative state, was as much as he could expect.

He took the long way home, too hurt to talk about it, too disappointed in God to do anything but silently ask, "Why me . . . and why a young woman who had never committed a small sin? Why could there be no justice in *this* life? Why do I believe in an afterlife when fate allows this? Would it not be better for . . . ?" and the questioning ended, for that too was futile.

The trailhead in the state park invited him to take a long, fast hike. Some of the disappointment and grief was blunted by keeping his legs in motion. Fast . . . the faster the better.

Twenty-nine and Alzheimer's. An old-timer's disease. He had done some reading on the subject two or three years earlier. Senile dementia as it had long been called was identified by Dr. Alois Alzheimer, a German psychiatrist for whom the disease is named.

He had found that it sometimes struck in middle age but rarely in the thirties. Rebecca was not quite thirty and yet was afflicted with it.

The little sliver of hope he had kept alive that she might almost become the young woman that age eighteen promised. At times, he fantasized that she might become able to support him in his ministry as other women did their preacher-husbands.

Where is God in all this? The questions were coming again and he couldn't stop them. Did He know as Rebecca and I were dating that mental illness awaited her? On occasion, I have taught my congregation that God is all-knowing. If I was correct in that, God knew it by the time she was in the first grade and before.

And I have dedicated myself to preaching that You are a God of love. How can I continue to preach that You are worthy of dedication and worship? God, I am serious in asking these questions. And yet it puzzles me that You don't send a lightning bolt out of this cloudless sky above and blast me for questioning You. I wish You would . . . for being the fool I've been.

If I had had the opportunity to decide whether I wanted to be conceived and born, would I have opted for being? Would Rebecca . . . if she had the choice offered to her as she still lived in her mother's womb?

The only source of comfort Mack could find in Rebecca's predicament was that the new dementia might already have numbed the emotional pain of a life lived in a schizophrenic world of fears. Lately, she had not mentioned the FBI's investigation, according to her nurse. Nor had she said any words of worry about Mack's intention to divorce her for another. There had been times when the divorce and remarriage were already an accomplished fact and at others, they were something she feared would happen.

As the brain was dying, was its ability to create illusions and baseless fears also passing? The nurse thought this had already started. "My grandmother had Alzheimer's and her worries of a lifetime went away. She seemed content. It was my mother, the primary caregiver, who then had the worries. Granny, before her illness struck, carried grudges against relatives and had a touch of bad temper at times, but that was all behind as the disease had a calming effect."

Hiking usually had a calming effect on his emotions, but not during the first forty minutes of this outing. Not until this day had he ever fully accepted Rebecca's schizophrenia as a permanent condition. It had taken the added dementia to make him fully accept the first one.

He now knew he had been living in a partial state of denial—a necessary state of mind because he could not bear the hopelessness of a full realization. Now she was fatally ill and all the lights in her brain were to end in total blackness. The nurse had said it was aspiration pneumonia that finally snuffed out the final spark of life in her granny's brain. Mack had asked how it had ended and on hearing the answer immediately wished he hadn't. To grief was added horror.

In a state of happiness at age twenty-one, he had slipped an engagement ring on her finger. It was a Saturday evening before taking her out to a favorite restaurant. No two had ever been as in love as they were. Theirs was so special, they believed it was unique. God smiled on their love for each other, on their purity, on their devotion to Him and each other.

Now all that had become cold, dead ashes. Though a three o'clock sun lighted the ridges in the far distance as well as where he walked, he was unaware of any light.

Mack realized he had made a mistake in reading all he could find on problems the brain might develop as the years passed. But Rebecca's did not wait 'til old age. There was no fairness in it, not in any aspect of it. Life was whatever came along, and that was all it was about. Maybe that was why God promised Heaven to those who believed and honored Him. There certainly was no justice this side of Heaven.

All of his prayers for Rebecca had just as well not have been said. He had believed that to ask was to be answered, if he had faith. His faith had not been weak. So why this?

Could he, in good conscience, continue to preach that prayers based in faith would be answered? Faith and moving mountains. Prayers not answered were the fault of the petitioner's faith coming up short—so it had been said—but his faith hadn't been weak.

Before going to sleep that night, he asked God for help in facing up to what was ahead. He pleaded for the fortitude to deal with whatever was to come. Rebecca is gone, but I am not, so I'd better start becoming what I can be. And I don't know why that is important, but it is.

⇒≑⇐

Rapidly, Rebecca lost language. When her parents visited her, she felt comforted and warm inside. Though she tried to find identifying words that would tell her who they were, she was unable to recall them. Mack was also familiar without her having available the words that would tell her who he was.

She responded to the routine of being cared for, causing no unusual problems for the people who saw to her basic needs.

For the most part, she lived in a fuzzy unemotional world. No longer were there signs that fear, love, anger or frustration lived within.

Dr. Butler was aware that with each passing month, the language center of her brain was either dying or being gummed up with abnormal tissue of some sort. She was only thirty years old. Why did he ever choose a medical career and the specialty he had chosen? Surgery was a specialty where many of your patients could be healed completely. Thank God for my wife. She reminds me often how horribly the mentally ill used to be treated, and that we and our staff members give comfort where none used to be offered.

CHAPTER NINE

When told of Rebecca's new dementia, Alf McDonald was completely attentive. He had heard of such an illness before, but not by name.

"People don't get over it, ever?"

"No, Alf. Some die in a few years after it's first been noticed; others may live ten years or even longer."

"And she no longer shows signs of suspicions and irrational fears, or hears voices? That could be seen as a plus."

"The hopes I had for a miracle pill healing her are gone," Mack commented in defeat. "There is nothing to do but wait for the inevitable.

"I'm beginning to think she doesn't even know who I am. If she doesn't at this stage, she never will again.

"Don't know why it seems so important that she be able to greet me by name, but it is. It's like *she* has already died and her body was left behind."

"Might be that she knows more than you think," Alf said.

"Language is so important, Alf. With it, we can know approximately what is going on in the mind of a loved one. Without it, we are terribly separated. We are alone even when in the same room.

"Most of what goes on in our minds does so in the words of our language. Words flicker through like distant lightening and as they do, there is at least some degree of emotional response. If the word *slime* dwells in our thoughts for a second, there is a momentary negative feeling," Mack said.

"Somebody says *love* and I think of my wife and have a warm, secure feeling. And you think Rebecca's inner experience is becoming almost empty of anything because she no longer talks, except saying a word or two on rare occasions."

"Yes, if she had the ability to call up words she needs, she could tell me what was going on inside. Her memory loss for words suggests that there is very little going on. The word *divorce* is gone, so she can no longer think that I'm going to divorce her and get another wife, one who is not sick."

"Has she ever thought you were divorcing her, or were going to?" Alf asked.

"Oh, yes, she has. And she'd get all worked up about it. But she shows no signs of anger about that or anything else anymore."

"Maybe she's just forgotten who you are, that she even has a husband," Alf wondered.

"I've been told by one of the staff that she eats better if her mother or I feed her. Maybe she *does* know who we are to a small degree.

"Her Alzheimer's may have been coming on for quite a while, but went unnoticed because the other dementia was so obvious.

"Emotionally, Alf, she's not in a continual state of turmoil and fear now. Is the schizophrenia gone? Dr. Butler thinks the symptoms would be obvious if her memory disorder suddenly cleared. He doesn't really know, he says. This is the first such case he has ever come across."

"If there is anything positive, it's that she does not suffer the horrors she had before," Alf commented.

CHAPTER TEN

Mack stepped forward and laid his open bible on the lectern and read John 3:16. Not the scripture he usually read at the opening of a funeral sermon, but appropriate in this case.

"David Lamar was far too young at age twenty to go to be with God." He didn't mention that a rock fall in a local coal mine took a life that need not have happened if the mine's operator had seen that high safety standards had been adhered to. Everyone in the congregation knew that. It had been thoroughly discussed, he guessed, at every coming together of two or more people over the past two days

"Only two months ago, he and his young bride came to live in our community. On arriving, they became a part of this congregation. In that short while, we came to know them as model citizens. His wife June told me his salvation experience took place two years ago. He heard this brief reading from the book of John at a revival meeting. Many times before he had heard it, but on this particular evening, he really heard what he already knew *by heart*, but had never taken it *to heart*. And the boyfriend—who had always been kind and considerate of everyone— became a mature young man who began storing up his treasures in Heaven. On that score, he had taken Jesus' admonition in Matthew 6:19-21 seriously."

Later at the graveside, he read the comforting words of Psalm 23. Beside June sat her mother, a brother, and a sister who had driven from out-of-state. David's family was represented by his parents and two sisters—they were also from out-of-state.

⟞⟝

Not that evening but the next, Mack received a phone call. It was June Lamar. "It's been my roughest day, Brother Mack. Could you come over? You've been here three times since David's death. You know the way." He did. It was at the end of a dead end road. He told her he'd be over in fifteen minutes or so. Her mother and sister were there, so there was nothing improper about going alone under the circumstances.

When he got to the door, he knocked loudly and waited for an invitation to come in. When no response came, he rapped hard on the door and waited again.

Then he tried the doorknob and found it unlocked. Opening the door a few inches, he called out in a loud voice, "Mrs. Williams! June!"

"Back here. Just come on in and back here." He assumed it was the mother's voice and went on through the living room. "Back here, Brother Mack."

Still thinking it was Mrs. Williams asking him to the bedroom to see her daughter, he proceeded. And to his shock and surprise, June was alone propped up in bed on a pillow.

"Isn't your mother staying over?" The first faint feeling that all may not be proper went over him with a feeling like a chill.

"Dad didn't come because, as you know, he's laid up in the hospital with a leg in traction. We received a phone call about an hour and a half ago from the hospital. He may be having a problem with his heart . . . scared Mother half to death. She called my brother Jackson at the home of one of your good Samaritans. He was over in minutes. My sister—who is Daddy's pet—wanted to rush off to be with him. My brother is driving the two of them.

"Jackson will borrow a neighbor's flat-bed, stake-sided truck tomorrow and return late to load up all my furniture and belongings and drive me back the next day. If Dad is in any kind of danger, he'll drive the car back after getting some rest. And we'll make the drive back home after dark and come back later to get my things.

"I insisted they go on . . . that I'd be all right. I thought I would. I had held up so well they said, and I thought I had."

"You could have called or asked me to call one of the church ladies to come spend the night with you."

"You counsel people, don't you? . . . as part of your responsibilities?"

"On occasion . . . here and there I do." He didn't feel comfortable alone with the young woman, especially in her bedroom. Why had she not awaited his arrival in the living room?

Without being asked, she answered that question. "I felt so down, I came back here after calling you. Pulling the sheet and soft comforter up to my chin might bring me some comfort. As soon as I did so, I realized as never before why these," she removed a hand from under underneath and patted the cover, "are called comforters.

"I wanted to talk to you. You're much of the reason David fell in love with the community. He frequently said there was something special about you and your messages from the pulpit. That you—a young man not much older than him—had insights and wisdom like a man forty or fifty years older. Before getting to more recent events, I want to tell you about my years in childhood.

"As you've noticed, I have a bit of a speech impediment, not a bad one, but enough to bring on an imitation of me and being made fun of by other kids.

"And in the ninth grade, there was an accident on our school bus. It rolled over and over down an embankment. I got this crooked nose from the wreck as it came back up on its wheels before taking a flying flop."

"And you got teasing about your nose?" Mack asked.

"A few times before David busted another's nose for being so mean.

"I could never see what David saw in me. To me, he was the most handsome boy in school. Played varsity football and baseball. And I'd wonder why me, Lord, why me?"

As she had been talking, Mack had studied her face and hair. Her hair was blonde and had just enough natural curl to let it fall about her face softly in a natural manner. Except for her nose, her face was all right. And her eyes were blue, very blue and clear, almost those of an innocent child.

Her voice was soft, but some words she spoke were not quite clear and there was a bit of a nasal sound. Maybe it was a matter of difficulty in sounding them and just as likely her tongue couldn't follow the brain's message correctly.

"Football and baseball came before his studies—that was obvious. His dream was that a baseball scout would invite him to try out as an infielder in a minor league. And a couple of years later, he'd move on up to the big leagues. But that's not what happened. He'd not prepared for college. Six months after he went to work in a coal mine against his daddy's advice, the mine closed and he moved on down to this part of the Southeast where he'd heard there were opportunities.

"It never dawned on me that I was anybody a guy would want for a girl friend and wife. But David did. Gave me his sweater with the school's initials in bold letters showing he had played varsity football. Almost the equivalent to announcing an engagement. Other girls took notice and I was shown a bit of respect.

"My home life was not bad like some of the other girls said theirs were. A little impersonal and cold, but that's nothing compared to some of the stories I heard from others.

"Home, now, is a five hour drive. This little house at the end of a country road so quickly became a real home."

Mack interrupted, "There are any number of people who would have come to take you for the night and the morrow while you awaited the return of your brother."

"I realize that, Brother Mack, and I may be too independent. I wanted to go it alone; there's going to be a lot of that in my future and I thought I had just as well get started. Fifteen minutes before I called you, I realized what a big baby I am. Thought if I talked to you a few minutes, I'd get back in control of my emotions."

At that point, she lost all control and sobs burst forth. Mack pulled several sheets of kleenex from a bedside box and placed them in an outstretched hand.

A feeling of unease had moved into Mack's spirit many minutes ago. A preacher sitting beside a bereaved young widow . . . in her house alone. Oh, for a chaperone. Where had his gumption been? He should have had two church ladies meet him there before entering. What if someone should, out of concern, drop in? Not likely since like himself, they would have assumed family members were staying with her.

"David! David, my beloved! The only person who thought I was worthy of love!" she exclaimed in a shaky voice that fell apart as violent sobs tore at her body. She had thrown back her covers. A nightgown covered her flesh modestly, but did little to conceal the remarkable womanhood above her waist.

A rising tide fast approaching—far faster arriving and far higher than that Sunday morning years earlier as he stood in the pulpit while he flipped pages in his Bible. The same sort of emotion, but ten times greater.

Get up, you fool of a preacher, and get out of here before it's too late! He had started rising from his chair when with arms upraised and eyes filled with the world's worst pain, she pleaded in a breaking voice, "Hold me, Brother Mack . . . please hold me."

And the tide swept through a narrow inlet with a roaring in his ears and spread out high, wide, and deep over virgin plain, where never had such been before. And later, it had quietly receded and the silence was broken, "Brother Mack, I'm so sorry, so very sorry for what I just did to you and to the memory of David. Until only a minute ago. I was faithful to him and his memory, and I made you unfaithful to your dear, helpless wife. Did you not realize that you should have got up and run?"

"Yes, but by the time I did, it was too late. You see . . . I was a virgin 'til minutes ago."

"You mean you and your wife never consummated your marriage?"

"She was already mentally ill on our wedding night and she believed it would have been a sin."

"I see, well I guess . . . you'd better leave now . . . and I'm so sorry."

He was on his way out.

⊰⊱

Sleep did not come at all that night. A conscience had been deeply scarred and a back had been lashed with a switch until it was on fire in the belief that harsh physical pain would put a damper on such carnal desire. And more than that, he deserved punishment.

When by using a hand mirror to reflect the image of the damage shown in the large mirror on his dresser, he was satisfied with the punishment he had inflicted on himself. He couldn't have endured more even if his conscience had called for it.

There had been no bleeding, but the skin was almost a solid mass of welts. After breakfast, he looked again. If there was any improvement in skin color, he didn't see it. Red was beginning to turn blue.

After a shower and a breakfast of cold cereal and milk, he phoned Ben Owen.

When he arrived at his former pastor's home, it was to a warm welcome. After a mid-morning coffee in the retired preacher's study, Ben began the conversation, "I've heard of Rebecca's additional illness. To the best, the worst things often happen. Obviously, this life is not always about justice. Convincing the non-believer is made doubly hard for the preacher because that is so. And I occasionally would have someone point it out to me that a certain practicing Christian was not escaping life's hard knocks and tragedies any better than the ordinary non-believer."

"And what brings you to see an old has-been?"

"Ben, last night, this preacher stepped on an unseen banana peel. Well, it was unseen until it was too late." At this point, Mack went straight into the story and told it all, making no excuses for what he had done. His counselor gave complete attention, not at any point breaking into the account. Only when Mack had finished and sat in silence for a couple of minutes, did the listener speak.

"Mack, you are an innocent. One phase of your education began last night. Whether you become a better preacher because of this experience depends on what you use this one for."

"There is no way such a sin can have any beneficial effects," he answered.

"First, you now know better than to visit a woman, especially one under eighty or so, unless someone else is present. Preferably a wife, but yours is unable to support and protect you from possible scandal. Just being there alone with her, had nothing happened, would have damaged your reputation had someone else known. You should have called a couple to come sit while you visited.

"Death or the possibility of death can turn on the sex urge. In crude biological terms, it's part of the reproductive order of things.

"At the intellectual level, she was unaware. But at the level where the sex drive ebbs and flows, it was different. And believe it or not, the death of her very young husband reminded her at that level. Death may steal in on us on any day. What if it does and we have left no progeny behind?"

"I never think of it that way, Brother Ben."

"It's not likely that many folks do consciously. But where the animal in us lives, it does.

"When I was a young man, the thought of death was very frightening even though I believed my soul was saved. It wasn't until I had three grownup children who could care for themselves that death lost its ability to almost terrify me. Now that I'm old and have grandchildren—wonderful ones—death has lost its ability to scare me. Except for the possibility that it might be a long drawn out affair with people having to take care of me.

"Mack, you have asked the Lord to forgive you?"

"All night long, but the magnitude of my transgression is so great, I can't see how He can have done so."

Ben wanted to shock the young preacher into a bit of common sense. "Then you ought to get out of preaching." He got what he wanted. Never had he seen a more pronounced look of disbelief on anyone's face. "I bet few Sunday mornings pass without your mentioning something to the effect that God does not hold grudges against the repentant sinner who admits wrong-doing and asks forgiveness."

"Yes, that's pretty much correct."

"That's for them, but not for you." A touch of sarcasm.

"A preacher has to live a model life for others to follow."

"And be something other than a human. If Joe Doe steps on a banana peel, as you did last night, and comes to you with his story, the first thing you do is ask him if he has been to God confessing his sin and pleading for forgiveness. He has. You tell him his sin is forgiven." Mack nodded his head in affirmation. "And, Mack, from the pulpit you proclaim the same thing loud and clear."

"But a true state of repentance must be present."

"I bet you truly repented all night long. You sit there and not once have you allowed your back to touch the chair's back. So filled with guilt and remorse, you scourged your back 'til I bet you've been on heavy does of aspirin for pain."

"You are right about that, but I've taken nothing for pain. I need to feel all the sharp edges of pain without the shielding effects of heavy doses of aspirin.

"When I've said every prayer over and over and begin to believe God has heard . . . it still starts to come back."

"Memories of how exciting it was and you'd like to have the experience again," Ben stated in a matter-of-fact tone. "Ah! There is the rub. Each time that memory comes back, you feel you have sinned again, that had you been truly repentant, those memories would have died. The innocence you lost! You indeed have a terrible enough life without this new burden.

"You came to me, an old man who has a special love for you. Apparently you have a degree of respect for me. Your's was a sin of the flesh. Our Creator must have known there must to be a strong sex drive or the human race would never survive. Greed and selfishness are far greater sins. And truly evil acts are the worst of all—consider what the Nazis did and compare that to your yielding to a built-in drive. My child! My child! Do you think God has not a lick of common sense? That it is beyond His capability to understand what you and Rebecca have been going through for about eight years now?

"When you stand in the pulpit this Sunday morning, tell your people that more and more you are understanding that being a Christian doesn't mean that your heart and theirs are always free of impurities. Tell them about the Man who lived amongst us and was less concerned about some of our weaknesses of the flesh than about hypocrisy. That He associated with people who were less than perfect, but had no tolerance for people who made sure the public knew of their good deeds.

"Your sin is behind you. Let it be a cause for growth. You hurt. Devote more of your time and thoughts to others who hurt—something you were doing when you responded to the young widow's plea for help. Perhaps your biggest sin was using incredibly bad judgement. What happened when you didn't call someone else, after finding her alone, is what I would have expected."

"Did you . . . ?" Mack started to ask but thought better of it.

"No. Nothing like that ever happened. I've been places where it might have, but I had a wife to go along."

⇒⊹⊹⇐

After leaving Ben, Mack drove to the mental hospital. Would Rebecca sense there was a difference in him? As for himself, he felt so very different that he wondered if everyone who knew him could see he was different.

She had changed in the four days since he last saw her. It appeared she had gained three or four pounds. Her face and eyes showed no expression, and a smile—that would have revealed toothless gums in front—never appeared. She was just there . . . sitting motionless in an arm chair, but he thought little of her condition. His thoughts were on what he had done the night before.

For a short while after greeting her, he was unable to confess his sin—his infidelity—to her. But it was something he felt compelled to do.

When an aide came by and greeted him and told him Rebecca seemed more withdrawn than ever, he expressed a desire to take her outside. The weather was perfect.

"Don't stay too long. We've had to put her in diapers. I changed her no more than thirty minutes ago."

Anne Allen had told Mack that Rebecca had "occasionally had accidents" as far back as a year ago. And at that moment, Mack knew for the first time another side of the horror that held Rebecca in its grasp.

And now as he sat with her on a comfortable seat in the shade of a live oak, he compared her to the memory of the young woman of their dating days. It hadn't taken a decade for the slim beauty to become a bulging figure where once only slight curves suggesting womanhood appeared. And the shy smile that occasionally revealed beautiful white teeth when she was really amused over something had now become a witless slit that occasionally fell open revealing bare gums. How can the state of the brain so change every pretty expression of eyes and face into the pointlessness of only being there?

Had she known ten years ago that she would wet and soil herself, the young woman of the highest standards of personal hygiene would no doubt have sought the highest cliff to fling herself from.

How much longer would she continue to live like this? For years? A miracle might appear. What sort of miracle? He had not the slightest idea of any sort of miracle that might happen. But he kept the hope, because hope was all he had.

He took one of her hands in both of his. She, as she had for years, did not try to pull away. Pleased that she did not, he began to review his last twenty hours.

"A young woman of our church lost her husband in a mining accident a few days ago. I visited her yesterday evening. It was such a sad case. What you and I could never do, she and I did as the moment spurred us to a very sinful act. Though I scourged myself severely and asked God all through the night to forgive me, I don't feel at all forgiven because I enjoyed the experience beyond belief. Though I feel absolutely terrible that it happened, my mind—against my will—returns to the ecstasy of that moment. Can't keep that side of it out of my consciousness anymore than I can the sin of it off my conscience. You, Rebecca, the wife I never knew . . . how I've wished a thousand times that illness had never struck you down. You'd have gone with me last night and my conscience would today not have been ripped a dozen ways. Do I use this as an excuse for a sin of the greatest magnitude? I think I may be trying to, but it won't work. Early in the visit I knew I should leave until I could return with chaperons. Why did I not, before unease and excitement came upon me simultaneously? Was it because I was from the beginning hoping that the moment would come that with so little resistance did come? It's strange that I can, while holding your hand, ask questions and make confessions that were difficult to say to Brother Ben Owen and to God, Himself. What a team we could have made had you not been struck down with so cruel an illness.

"Just holding your hand! It doesn't exactly give me comfort, but it does open my heart in ways not opened before. This, dear one, is why I don't want to lose you. So little of you left, but it beats not having you at all. Your hand is a hand of a living human being. It offers a tiny bit of hope, for what? I don't know, but it just does."

After a pause of several minutes, he said, "Sweetheart, the time I've been allotted with you has been used up." And he started back toward the entrance holding her hand and that was good. For that brief time until she was turned over to an aide, comfort outweighed the burden of his betrayal. Unbelievably, he felt she somehow knew and understood and forgave.

That feeling kept him company on the way home. Later, he would have to face God again and in two days, his congregation from the pulpit. But later. A sirloin steak, which he didn't deserve, awaited him twenty-something miles ahead, but on this day he ordered meat loaf.

⟞⟝

The Sunday sermon was about a forgiving God. Would He forgive a really big sin? St. Paul was an example of a really big time sinner and he was forgiven his persecution, even execution of early Christians. "Most of us," Mack told his congregation, "commit less serious sins.

Sins of the flesh, greed, questionable behavior to gain advantage, pleasure in seeing a disliked person get what he deserves. Mistakes in judgment that result in pain to ourselves and others." He touched on a wide variety of sins less than Paul's and made the point that if Paul could be forgiven, all we have to do if we are truly repentant is to take it to the Lord and confess our sins.

"God knows what man is like inside. His Son lived among us and saw human weakness first hand, and the man in him saw and understood what it is like to be a man. Did He understand that we are going to need, even require, lots of forgiving. Did He see that our free will was often a weak will in the face of all the temptations we might encounter. In teaching the parable of the prodigal son, He illustrated how far astray some of His sheep could be expected to go, and He showed how far the Father could and would go in forgiveness. The Father that Jesus introduced to mankind was one of love and understanding of what it is like to be one of His children. God understands. Bring a repentant heart and know the comfort of the erasing of your sin. And if you don't feel relief in your conscience, you may need to re-examine your core beliefs about the message of Christ."

At the exit, he heard, "Great sermon," several times. And one middle-aged man commented, "Today, you seemed a little more like us. You preached down at the level we sat rather than from the loftier platform where preachers often perch themselves before beginning."

That afternoon, it was to the nearest state park. At first, there were people in the popular places for recreation. But on this outing, solitude was what he sought. A thirty minute walk along a trail brought him to a place to leave the heights and seek a deep hollow, possibly with a small stream providing an undistracting musical accompaniment to his need for meditation.

A careless misstep sent him tumbling—sliding a distance that would have embarrassed him had he not been alone. At the bottom of the hollow, trees were mostly of large size. There was a small, narrow stream with soft, faint gurgles until it reached a tiny cascade where in all pleasantness, it made splashing sounds that delighted his heart. A place for brief enjoyment, but not exactly what he sought. Then it was downstream about fifty feet, he came to a quiet pool. A convenient log lay alongside and it was there he sat watching the barely perceptible swirl of the quiet stream. He could think here and he did.

Why could he not believe at the level that he needed, that his sin had been forgiven? For the other fellow, I'm convinced that going to God with regret for what he has done is the end of the matter. But being a preacher makes it a different matter. If Ben Owen committed the same sin I did and went to God in a repentant state of mind, I'd say in the instant I first knew of it, why of course he should put the matter behind and go ahead with his life as if it had not happened—except for exercising better judgement in the future. Why, that good man told me before I left him the other day to treat it as a learning experience, that God was probably tiring of my coming to Him whining about not feeling forgiven when I'd already begged Him to do so umpteen times.

God, I know one thing. If I get to feeling that my sin is still black as soot, I'm not going to insult what Jesus taught us by coming to You with it over and over.

May I have the gumption to get off this log and walk among these magnificent trees with appreciation, while looking forward to this evening's services.

Tulip poplars with furrowed trunks and tops stretching for a touch of the sky. And solid shorter beeches with no such ambition, content to offer trunks with the smoothest of barks. Mack preferred the feel of the beeches—they were older, many of them with hollow spaces for the little furry creatures in need of shelter and protection.

His appreciation of his uncommonly beautiful surroundings lasted only for a short while.

How large was the sin? A close second to murder? Not that, but it was the total disregard for one of the Ten Commandments. A living wife he betrayed—a helpless woman and that made it even worse. Claiming to be a man of God. Supposed to be setting an example for a congregation to follow. When a man answered the call to preach, he took upon himself a solemn though maybe silent vow to live an exemplary personal life—a model for his people to follow.

People expected more of a preacher, and they should, Mack believed. He just didn't measure up. What he had done once in deed, he now did several times daily in thought. There were times when these thoughts came briefly, but frequently. Unable to keep the memories away because of the almost incredible ecstasy of the moment, guilt episodes always accompanied the reappearance of the sinful memories. In no way could he feel complete forgiveness as long as the pleasure of memories continued to return again and again. If only he could recall the episode as being dull, he might could get on with the business of straightening out things with God. He lashed himself again, verbally this time.

⇒⼁⼁⇐

One day when Mack was feeling down again, Alf said, "You need to broaden your interests. Read at every opportunity, not just preacher stuff, but history, geology, etc. You like music, I know. The day after tomorrow, let's go to a good high fidelity sound system store. I've been in your house; you have a a table model TV and a little old radio. No decent sound could possibly escape from that kind of speaker.

"It's time you started really developing a life that doesn't rotate around thinking of your wife. And I don't believe God expects your every other thought and emotion to be about Him. He gave you a wide variety of talents and emotions, in addition to a rational mind. Wouldn't have given them to you without expecting you to use them.

"There is a life that you can have without your wife. Develop it. Oh, I know you have made some progress in that direction, but there's more to be done.

"I'm old . . . seventy-eight next year. Nell just a year behind me. Her health has grown fragile the last couple of years. If she passes on before I do, I'll grieve big-time, but then get on with whatever time I have left.

"In time, as my casket is being lowered into the grave, I want the five hundred or so mourners who stand watching in profound respect and deep sadness to say in unison with you leading one word ahead, "Old McDonald lived life as fully as a man could until his last breath had come and gone." As usual his eyes sparkled with humor.

And on the day after the next, Alf drove his four-door sedan into the city with Mack in the passenger seat. It was a heavy car he drove, a quiet car that encouraged conversation.

"Mack," he said as soon as they had departed his drive for the highway, "There is something else you might think about in your carpentry. I know you wear goggles to protect your eyes, but you don't protect your ears from the noise of electric saws, drills, hammers, and pieces of lumber falling with a loud crash.

"Before this day is over, you'll hear music with sparkle and brightness you are not accustomed to hearing. I'm still able to hear much of that at my age."

It was to a store that specialized in high fidelity sound equipment that Alf carried Mack. They looked and listened, not to a sales pitch, but to long playing records on two different systems. Alf had explained to a salesman before a pitch could be made that he had equipment from that store and had something in mind to show his young friend.

The result was that an hour later, they had the large car's trunk and back seat area filled up. It was then on to a record store.

"Mack, you listened to the Boston Pops Orchestra and to some hot jazz and then bluegrass music. Any preference?"

107

"Liked all of them, but the Pops best of all."

"Then you should have discs of all three types, doubling up on the light classical stuff maybe."

Alf advised on individual records (long-playing) and Mack accepted all suggestions, and then selected a record of waltz music. Of that last selection, he said, "I may be crazy for getting this one since there's no possibility of having someone to dance with, but I like the lilting rhythm and flow of pretty tunes."

"A good choice, Mack. I never heard an ugly waltz.

"Now, let's go to the Christian bookstore two doors down the street for some good recordings of hymns on pipe organ, piano, and by choral groups."

A week later, Mack was still getting to bed an hour later than had been his custom. The time he spent listening to music was not time spent in sadness and regret. Back to the city and record store he went before two days had passed for a table top storage cabinet.

Listening to music came only after he had done his studying and sermon preparation. This new line of activity occupied time formerly occupied by feelings of guilt, grief, and loneliness. Living in a world of negative emotions had been accomplishing nothing to help Rebecca. Of course, he had never thought it did, but he had at times felt guilt if he found for himself pleasure or joy in any of his life. Alf had figured this out and had sternly lectured him. "It's not going to help her even slightly if you turn your life into one of continuous mourning and passing episodes of guilt if you don't make yourself miserable enough." Alf had no idea where the greatest guilt lay.

With the advent of high fidelity music in his living room came times of relishing life instead of so many evenings of remorse and wondering why he had ever been born. Where there had been no pleasure, there were now hours of excitement for a spirit that soared as on wings of eagles while the world of conflicts and aggravations was far below and of no consequence.

A part of him which had once been dead now lived and thrived. What had been with him almost constantly was now only a part-time tenant. But Old MacDonald's work with him was unfinished. There were trips to the Gulf Coast with long hikes both early and late in the day. There needed to be more rather than less frequent trips like this and that point of view was hammered home, especially in the cool months when "beach bunnies" were hibernating, according to Alf. Hiking had been good but not enough for maximum benefit. Quick trips to the Great Smokies were just what were needed, Alf had advised.

"Work on Monday, Tuesday, and Wednesday. On Thursday, you, me, and Nell will drive to Gatlinburg. An evening hike to Laurel Falls will prepare us for the ten mile round trip to Mount LeConte."

"Do you plan to make the hike, or is this just for my pleasure?"

"Oh, I plan to make it with you. Been getting my legs in shape for it.

"I'll make your picture at the lodge entrance. It'll give you something to feel proud about. Not many have the mental and physical toughness it takes. Bragging a wee bit about that should not be unbecoming because you are a preacher."

"You are near eighty, Alf. Are you sure you want to go?"

"I ain't there yet by more'n two years. Fellers older'n me have done it."

And in late April, to East Tennessee they went with Alf and Nell doing the driving. Mack sat on the back seat finishing preparation for his two Sunday sermons.

The Thursday evening warm-up hike to Laurel Falls was no real challenge, but it made the supper that followed unusually tasty and satisfying. Nell had walked about half way with them before returning to the car.

At nine-thirty the following morning, they were parked close to the trailhead. With light shoulder packs with sandwiches and bottled water inside and sassafras hiking staffs in hand, they set out. Alf cautioned Mack that speed walking was *not* how it is done. "It'll still be there when we get there."

Creeks with rushing water over rounded large stones were constantly in their awareness. Before long, they passed on through a short tunnel in a huge rock formation.

Trees . . . large trees everywhere. It was almost beyond taking in. Mostly hardwoods and hemlocks, something that tree lovers who passed this way all took pleasure in. Mack thought of Rebecca who would never see this, but it was with light mourning instead of the usual. He was here now, and it would not benefit her for him to be walking through depths of despair.

He watched the back of the old man who was now leading the way. Warm love flooded his soul . . . for here was someone who cared about him and his predicament and cared greatly. Why were all people not like him and his sweet wife? And their daughter-in-law, Fredda? People who had learned the benefits of being concerned and acting out of concern for those who hurt and were in need. They were the kind of people who are wealthy of soul and have wealth to share. Such people were living reminders of how far he had yet to go. And he realized that he preached it and they lived it.

Breathing became deeper and harder. They arrived at a huge rock overhang, but climbing to its shelter was steep so they continued taking the slow, short steps that Alf said would eventually get them there. Steep stair-stepped places . . . and then there came a time when they started down hill along a narrow hogback ridge. When Mack expressed pleasure at this letup in the steep ascent, Alf said he ought to be saying otherwise for "we'll have to pay for every downward step we are now taking before we reach the top."

They paused to eat a bite and washed it down with water. "Did you watch the weather forecast on your room television, Mack?" He hadn't.

"Nell and I did. Supposed to snow up here tonight. I didn't mention it before. I hoped you hadn't watched the news, thinking you might back out on me if you had."

"You know me better than that."

At times they came to places where the trail was so narrow and the precipice to the left so steep, a steel cable had been anchored at intervals so the hiker could hold on with a sliding right hand while taking very cautious steps.

They had been in a virgin forest of giant spruce for some time. Mack was overwhelmed, thinking of little else except the careful steps he took and not forgetting to use his stabilizing staff.

"It'll be fir trees as we approach the top. We're now at an elevation approaching five thousand feet, I figure," Alf said. It was—under the circumstances—a long, labored statement.

Immediately Alf dropped to one knee and removed a water bottle from his shoulder bag. Mack followed suit gratefully for he had been wondering for some time when Alf was going to take the next break. Apparently, age has only toughened him.

"My legs, especially the calves, are hurting and have been for the past half hour," Mack said.

"It was a day much like this twenty years ago, when I did this. Nell made the hike too. I was proud of her. She would have tried it today, but she hasn't been walking lots like I have. She mentioned it, but I put a big foot down. A fall could easily shatter the bones of a woman in her seventies. Probably very foolish of me to come. A streak of cussedness and stubbornness runs through me, she likes to say.

"The views of the mountains we've been getting are so much greater than can be seen from the highway. Most folks leave the park, never realizing they saw so little of it!"

A long stretch through a fir forest and the final part was not quite as steep, but they were tired and this was not easy. At last Mount LeConte Lodge was reached.

People with large backpacks arrived occasionally. They would be staying in primitive cabins for a night or more. Mack and Alf saw them check in and receive instructions. A large water bucket was handed out as information was given on where the hand-powered well pump was located.

During an interval when no overnight visitor was present, Alf commented, "That's their drinking water and their water for brushing teeth and bathing. They pay for the privilege of living like I did as a child. I haven't completely recovered from my first experience with hot showers and flush toilets, and don't want to recover."

Before leaving, Alf took a picture of Mack at the lodge's sign. "Now, take one of me, Mack, so there will be no doubters about the story I'll be telling."

The trip back down offered many views not seen as they had been making the ascent.

Aching calves eventually became fronts of thighs under great stress of restraining the tendency to go too fast, When the time came for the narrowest parts of the trail, it was the left hand that slid along the anchored cable. Dizzying heights became even more scary. Rocks were steep steps going down with nothing to hold on to except the fragile staff of sassafras that steadied his descent, or seemed to. Mack was not sure, but he followed Alf's example.

Once when they paused to view a distant ridge, Mack said, "Aren't we a crazy pair? Why are we doing this?" He was more tired than he had expected.

"Because we have nerve and thrive on excitement. That's how I explained it to Nell many years ago. Or it may be curiosity to see what is beyond the nearest beyond. And the memories of this that we can call up and enjoy at least half as much as what we do on seeing what lies ahead of the next bend in the trail.

The last of the return was easy . . . a blessing at last. And Mack said, "This creek is a noisy one. Do you suppose during the last great ice age, it became sometimes silent?"

"Probably not, Mack. The water right here is not long out of the ground. I doubt there was ever permafrost here."

"Do you have feelings of wishing you could step into a time machine and see this terrain as it was a million years ago?"

"I hadn't until you brought it up, but yes, I wish we could. Fir trees probably grew at this elevation."

They were walking slowly now, not wanting the experience to end right then. When they reached the car, Alf handed the keys to Mack. "It's your drive back to the hotel and your drive home tomorrow. I made it okay today but to be honest about it, I'm doggoned tired."

Mack was tired too, and wondered how a man closing in on eighty could have averaged almost two miles an hour for that ten miles, including time for brief periods of rest. That he would do this in an effort to prove one old man still had it? That would be reason enough.

The trip to the Smokies and the hike didn't bring him happiness, but it did help blunt the worst of his guilt for his big sin. For days, it helped toward having something else to add to the things he could take satisfaction from. One more thing to live for, to occupy some of his memories and thoughts. The smaller ridges back home would remind him of this hike for years to come.

And on his return home, his evenings of music from his good high fidelity system were uplifting. Great church anthems sung by large choirs and accompanying pipe organs, pianos, tympani, brass, and full range of orchestral instruments. Praise—beautiful and magnificent—that carried his soul to places lofty and unfamiliar. Surely such glorious music greets us at our approach to Heaven.

Recordings of music originating on pioneer farms told of loved young wives that perished in childbirth, and of deaths of children who were denied the chance to live the fantastic experiences that had been awaiting them as they grew to adulthood.

Mack enjoyed a little jazz at times that revealed the moods and emotions of the black man more so than of the white man.

And the classical music that was pretty and delightful. And there was the kind that searched his soul, finding places that responded quickly to the profound message of hope and joy and beautiful pathos. It was a growing column of splendor forming one of the supports of his inner being as yet unfamiliar to him. How was it that something new was born in the heart of a man of thirty years? Had he not experienced to the full the depths of every possible emotion before this?

Filling his home with music in the evening took away some of the concern of his sin of adultery and the grief for the slow dying of his wife. Whether he was listening to music or preparing a sermon or delivering it, remorse and grief were always at the edges of consciousness, waiting to intrude on what he was trying to focus on.

The contents of his memory and awareness of what the future might be were not things he could put into separate compartments of his mind and go on with his life, as if memory and the future did not exist. Even as he cut a baseboard, prepared and delivered a sermon, hiked briskly or listened to music or ate good food, always at the fringes of his consciousness was the wasting away of what little of Rebecca was left. The memory of his infidelity to a hopelessly ill wife did not always pounce upon him, but it was always there lingering in the background awaiting its next opportunity.

How many more months . . . how many more years would the destruction of what was left of her extend into the future. Someone at the hospital had told him aspiration pneumonia would possibly be the end. He asked for no further information; he hadn't even wanted that much. As long as he didn't know how her life would end, he could and did hold on to glimmer of hope that a miracle could come along. He had read about denial and felt he wasn't in that state—a miracle might be granted.

He believed enough of what he preached to feel that any man or woman of his congregation who had sinned and begged God's forgiveness would have instantly had their conscience wiped clean. Did belief in forgiveness for sins not extend to their preacher also when he committed one? He knew it should but couldn't reach the point of feeling that it had.

Still, following Alf's suggestions for living a better life were helping. He saw humor where before he had seldom seen any.

On the Gulf Coast for a couple of days in November, he walked miles and miles on sugar-white beaches. Barefoot with old pants cut off at the knees, his feet and lower legs often were caught by an unexpectedly strong wave coming over the firmly packed sand that brought pleasure to his feet. Once, not far ahead, he saw two of what Alf had warned him against—beach bunnies!

The air was chill enough for the thick sweatshirt he wore to keep his body core warm. High enough on the beach to be on dry sand, they lay on colorful beach towels. Skin—except for tiny patches covered by sunglasses and what their bikinis masked—was very much exposed to the sun and the brisk onshore breeze.

And Mack had thought he was completely safe at this time of year. Careful to keep his eyes averted and face turned somewhat seaward, he thought he would in a few steps be safely by.

"Hey, mister," a rich alto voice demanded attention. "You got the time?"

Mack glanced at his watch and without stopping announced, "2:15." Hoping to escape another question, he took a couple more steps, but a small sweet voice exclaimed, "Been here since over two hours. Lord, I hope we are not like charbroiled beefsteak. Mister, would you take a look at us to see if you think we'd better get our fannies back inside?"

Within about fifteen feet, Mack glanced at their exposed flesh briefly and then averted his eyes, "You look fine." What if Alf could see me doing such a good job of not looking? I can see him shaking with silent laughter at my *exaggerated fear* of looking upon so much bare feminine flesh so closeup, and he'd be waiting to tell me later that Old McDonald could look upon such for an hour and not have one naughty thought flicker across his consciousness. And I'd tell him what an old liar he was becoming. That at his age, and not being a preacher, he'd not be guilty of very much lusting because he just wasn't able.

"Mister, we don't bite. Come close and take a good look. I'd like to stay out here a little longer, if you think it's safe."

Not for me, it ain't safe, he was thinking. He didn't want to commit the sin of lustful thinking. How did I ever get into this? How do I get out?

He didn't. A plaintive voice said, "Please."

"You could look at each other and ascertain whether or not you've been here too long."

"Don't know that I can trust her," the alto voice said. "She'd think it funny if I turned as red as a Maine lobster. She gets and keeps a good tan, and brags about it."

Mack stepped closer and briefly took a look at their tummies and then averted his eyes again as he stepped back. "I saw nothing suggesting sunburn, but I did see a few goose bumps."

At this, each picked up a beach towel and covered themselves except for their faces.

"What drove you to the beach on a day this cold?"

"We don't have classes on Friday. First year students at a community college not so far away, and what brought you here, sir?"

"The ocean. At a level and for reasons not understood, it draws me. I love to watch a boat as it heads out to sea, maybe because the earth's curve soon draws it into hiding beyond my vision, and where does it go after the sea has swallowed it? Will I ever see it again or was its visit within my sight only a passing reward for my gazing out to sea? And now, does it know to what port it will go since taking the one direction that I witnessed."

"Almost like a poet, you speak, sir."

"Kathie, maybe he is a poet here in search of inspiration."

"No, I'm not a poet. Far from it. Actually I'm a . . . ." his voice trailed off as he decided to end the conversation.

"My name is Cindy. Stay a little while now that we are covered and fit to be looked upon by even a clergyman. You wouldn't happen to be one of those, would you?"

"Actually, I am. My name is Mack and I need to be going."

"You seem a nice man, even if you are a preacher."

"Kathie, what a terrible thing to say. Most of them are very nice men."

"Did our almost nude condition offend you? We would not want to create even a hint of lust in your heart."

"Oh, you didn't," Mack replied.

"Well, that's disappointing," Cindy said as white teeth lit up a smile. At this, they both giggled—the sound of youth and delight. At their age, Rebecca had never released even a small outburst of pleasure at some light pretended offense in conversation. So little fun then, and years of illness ever since. If she could only have been a little light-hearted before disease set in, I might now be able to draw a little comfort from that. But she wasn't and I live with what I have.

"Since we are now modestly covered up, wouldn't it be permissible for you to sit a spell? Sometimes loneliness comes upon a person so easily, even in the presence of a good friend. And the comfort offered by three or four even more likely to warm loneliness out of the heart."

Mack could not turn this down. He sat and listened to the chatter of these two who had not had the joys of youth kicked out of them by adult realities, and he was not about to warn them that they had better enjoy it while they had it.

When they asked him about himself, he told of his wife's illness but did not dwell on it. Instead, he told them of his hike in the Great Smokies the past April and his trip to Wyoming and Montana a couple of years earlier.

"When you preach, do you usually come down hard on sin?"

"Not as much as I did in the beginning. I used to think I was pretty much sin-free and preached against the evil in mankind a lot, thinking of the evil that was rampant in other folks." He paused.

"But that existed hardly at all in yourself," Kathie finished the sentence for him.

He looked at the light brown eyes that were fixed on him as if she awaited confirmation. There was no hint of condemnation in the look, rather it was more like understanding.

"Life taught me I was as subject to sin as the people I was always preaching at. Now I try to stay more on the subject of God's love than in my earlier sermons."

"I bet they like you a lot better now," Cindy commented.

"They appear to, but getting my flock to like me was not why I changed. That came after I learned that love was what my faith was supposed to have been about from the beginning. Every few months or so I go back and read the parable of the prodigal son."

The girls talked of their high school experiences which had ended too soon. "We were two of those silly girls who cried our eyes out at the end of the graduation ceremony," Kathie said.

Cindy said, "For years we had known where we'd be in the fall and could count on being with people we already knew."

"There we were, Mack, for the first time in twelve years not knowing what life in the future held for us. No idea at all."

"Maybe we took the easy way out. Right there, we agreed we'd stay home and enroll at the local junior college come next September. That way, it wouldn't be such a strange world we'd face. You might say we weren't facing up to the world anymore than the girl who sticks her toe in the pool and doesn't plunge in and swim."

"So for two more years we could—" Kathie's voice stopped right there.

Mack understood. "It's enough to scare anyone. An unknown future. Unknowable future is a more appropriate description."

"You're an unusual man. Most people, including my parents, said I was postponing the inevitable, that I ought to go ahead and get a job or go to university," Kathie said.

"Mine didn't say that," Cindy commented. "I think they were pleased I'd be living with them two more years."

This conversation with two girls, something he was enjoying—a rather delightful and refreshing insight into the thinking of young ladies of today—was unlike anything he would have expected to encounter on the beach, especially at this time of the year,

"Mack, Cindy already knows the story I want to tell, if you are willing to stay a little longer."

"I want to finish my day's hiking, but there's more than enough time for that." He knew his heart was free of any lustful intent. He had prayed an often used prayer that God would protect him from that unwanted feeling. So he agreed to stay. Nothing in their conduct suggested flirtation in the slightest degree.

"This girl, who was in our class last year, decided to take the easy route. One of the brightest, she *borrowed* her brother's term paper that the same teacher had marked with an *A* five years earlier. Retyped it verbatim and added her name and turned it in. Dummies that we are, Cindy and I did our term papers entirely as we had been directed and received *B*'s. We had no complaints. This girl received a *B* also.

Mack thought he might see what was coming, but held back the laugh until Kathie revealed it.

"She was the maddest human I ever saw. After getting me to pledge I'd never tell our teacher, she told me she had carried her problem to our counselor, a very sweet lady. What she wanted Ms. Loggins to tell her was that something could be done about the injustice of it . . . an *A* for her brother five years earlier, but only a *B* for her.

"What would you have told her to do if you were her advisor, Mack?"

Mack stopped laughing. "That's an easy one, I would have told her to take her complaint to the English teacher, explaining why she knew she had an *A* paper."

"That's exactly what our counselor told her to do." When the giggling stopped, Cindy went on. "She reasoned if she did that, she'd be given an *F* and if she went to the principal, he would order the teacher to do just that and would likely add on suspension from school."

After more laughter, Kathie continued, "I never figured out why she told me or Mrs. Loggins the story. She couldn't have expected or wanted Mrs. Loggins to go to the teacher explaining why the grade should be raised. I asked her if she wanted me to go tell the teacher that she ought to raise the grade and why. I asked this with a solemn expression in my voice—how I managed that, I'll never know."

Cindy, when the laughter had fully subsided, said, "Kathie, it's time we went to our room."

"Mack, thank you for stopping and staying a while. Say a prayer for us because we still haven't faced the world and are so uncertain about being able to do it."

"You will be in my prayers. You can count on it. I haven't enjoyed a good laugh in years. Not until today. Thank you for letting a little sunshine into a mind far too serious in how it has perceived life."

"We didn't drive here in such apparel as you first saw us in. We have sweat suits and sandals in the car."

The goodbyes had been said and Mack was walking again, where never ending swells continually teased him, and occasionally a high-rising one chased him temporarily higher.

Though he had enjoyed the light-hearted conversation, it had also saddened him. The time these girls were in were times he had never known. At their age, he had already decided what he would do with his life and he had met a girl he wanted to share it with.

As adolescence was ending, he had not known what it was to be uncertain about the future, while at the same time enjoying freedom from worrying about what might await him. At eighteen, perhaps they were nineteen, they had a time that could have been freedom from adulthood—a time that had passed him by unnoticed. And now he felt sadness and regret, because he had missed out on an important step in growing up.

Rebecca had not experienced the time when seriousness of mind could be tossed aside while the years of a child becoming an adult could be experienced with a touch of joy in living. Even if illness had not struck her down, she would still have been less than she should have been.

At the time, I thought she and I were people to be admired because we were mature at nineteen and not at all sophomoric like the rest.

Now, I fear that I have become, at thirty, what I might not have become had I not missed the later years of childhood. That might be a bit of foolishness. Maybe I should have become more like an adult at an even earlier age, but I don't believe that for a second.

Knowing what I finally and fully realized today, I wish I had not taken on, at age fourteen, attitudes and objectives that should have awaited the passing of another six or eight years. I prided myself because I was so much more grown up than the others, feeling a bit superior to them. But those two girls showed me that I could still laugh, that there was something to be said for living as if one should *not* be burdened with the foreboding that troubles loom in the future.

As a preacher, was he supposed to think ill of them because of their skimpy attire? Perhaps, but he realized that what they were doing was not unusual. Their conversation had shown that they were not evil . . . just two young women enjoying the last years of being able to postpone the cares that being an adult would later bring. They are fortunate. Would he be feeling that he had missed out on an important stage in life had Rebecca remained whole? Probably not. As he walked, he prayed for her and then for himself.

CHAPTER ELEVEN

Mack visited Rebecca the next day. Dr. Butler had left word he wanted to meet with him. "*Mother* was the last word anyone had heard Rebecca utter, and that in Anne Allen's presence bringing a surge of excitement and hope in the mother's heart. Of course, she phoned Mack at the earliest opportunity. It had stirred false hope.

"Mack," Dr. Butler started the conversation, "We have done all we can for Rebecca. Her memory disorder has developed faster than anyone I've ever observed before and also began at a younger age."

"You don't see any hope she'll get better?" Mack found bringing out the words a tearing experience in his heart though he had known it for months. He had always held on to hope for a miracle drug for the schizophrenia. For Alzheimer's? Maybe a way could be found to inject something into the brain that would stimulate growth of millions of new neurons. Where that kind of solution appeared from, he had no idea at all, but he had it anyway.

"Dr. Butler, a desperate mind can deny anything that is too horrific to take in and fully realize, and seek solace from fanciful solutions when it knows better."

"You've done what you had to do."

"You see no chance for improvement?" The unshed tears were a dull ache around his eyes. A terrible emptiness in his stomach and a heart that truly ached. These had been there for many years—at times worse than other times, but never so totally as right then. *God, how can I make it through what I'm going to have to endure? For months . . . maybe years? It's been almost ten years now since our wedding.*

"When will she have to go to a nursing home?" He had dreaded that time and would put the thought out of his mind. He had seen it as a place to go to die. As a preacher, he had a church member in one, and visited him every couple of weeks—one who didn't know who he was.

"It should be done soon. We are crowded. I'm sorry."

"Why have so many bad things happened to a young woman who once appeared she would become an angel living among us? And why to me?"

"Mack, you are a man of God. How do you explain to your congregation that ghastly things may await or may have already arrived, for the good and the evil person alike . . . and as likely to one as the other?"

"I tell them that life on earth is the preliminary to life in the hereafter, that the hereafter is eternal, the important one."

"Exactly. No one has *ever* come up with a better response to a question that has plagued humanity for thousands of years. Every patient I attend has been one of those to whom a very bad thing has happened. It came upon them not because they deserved to have it happen to them, but rather for some reason that we are unable to discern.

"This is my life's work. I get so depressed because the best I can expect is that a patient here and there will become able to return to society and function at less than optimum as long as medication is regularly taken.

"Start praying more for yourself. Continue to pray for Rebecca, if you must, but don't—" It was a sentence that kindness didn't allow him to finish.

"Expect much," Mack finished for him. "I accept that right now, but tomorrow I may not."

Two consecutive Sundays, Mack's church had visitors, two men each time. Well dressed, not sitting together, but very attentive, Mack noticed. Other than that, he gave it no thought at all.

The audience had grown slowly and steadily over the years. A preacher cannot help but notice such things and hope that some of this sort of thing reflects his dedication to sermon preparation and delivery.

Lowell Miller made a visit to Mack's work site one day, not an uncommon thing to do. After chatting with individuals briefly, receiving and giving bits of information, he took Mack outside away from the distractions of construction noises.

"Mack, how goes it with your personal life?"

"My wife has been placed in a nursing home much closer than the state mental hospital. I can drop by and see her almost everyday."

"That's good, in a way. So bad about the memory disorder. Does her doctor have any explanation for it striking her down?"

"Not any hard science to back it up, he says."

"Then he has a theory?"

"He does. He got the idea from her dentist, who says he thinks there could be a link between her dental fillings and neurological problems. Most dentists would swear that the fillings release no mercury. But this fellow isn't so sure; he knows a dentist who had to quit work because he developed serious tremors in his hands, and heard about another who reached the point of not remembering how to treat a patient. This dentist told Rebecca's psychiatrist he has quit using it out of fear of what it might be doing to himself and his patients.

"The psychiatrist called the Centers for Disease Control and asked if there was any basis for such concerns and was told that dentists were medical professionals who were not subject to any sort of regulations about what they placed in and on patients' teeth—braces, fillings, etc. Further, he was told amalgam had been used for well over a century with apparent safety for dentists and patients alike."

"So the CDC hasn't sought evidence against a well-entrenched practice by a group with powerful political connections," Miller said. He went on, "Perhaps it's safe and perhaps it's not, but they don't want evidence that it's not."

"Lowell, doesn't politics end where health risks are involved?" Mack asked.

"Politics never ends; it doesn't even take off time for sleep.

"Now, what I came for today. A few weeks ago, our church's pastor announced he'd be retiring in six months. I've been asked by our search committee to speak to you about taking his place. You've recently had visitors, some you may have noticed. Two men and their wives the past two Sundays, sitting separately so as to be less likely to be noticed, and one fellow before that. They had already visited another church. It's unanimous. They want you."

"I'll need time to consider. Had never thought in terms of getting ahead. Your church has ten times, probably more, active members than we have. It's such a big jump."

"Bigger churches need good preachers too. I know you're not the kind of preacher who thinks in terms of getting ahead. If you were, you'd have moved to a larger church many years ago. I've heard you preach. I've seen your carpentry. I know what you are and like what I've seen."

Mack was momentarily silent. He doesn't know about the *sin*. He doesn't know the extent of my hypocrisy. I am unfit to serve in a small church and certainly not a city church of such size.

Mack asked for time.

"Of course. I didn't expect quick acceptance. If your answer is yes, tell your present congregation first and then it will be announced at ours. A guest appearance at our church would be needed. You'll be well accepted."

Mack needed time. But with Rebecca in a nursing home, he also needed the extra salary. That might be the deciding factor.

There was that one big stain—that lingering cloud repeatedly reminding him how unworthy he was to be standing in any church's pulpit. Would he be able to preach to a large audience? With many hundreds of eyes turned on him, would the guilt that was always ready to flare up turn into unbearable pain? At times before a much smaller audience, he would wonder what they would think of him if they knew. That question had accompanied him to the platform every time he had preached since.

That God had forgiven him, he had no doubt. What does God think of me because I have not forgiven myself completely? Perhaps I would have, Lord, if I didn't remember the experience itself. Why can I not remember it as being unpleasant? If only I could, I wouldn't feel that I sinned again each time I recalled the actual moments of its happening. Frankly, Lord, it was exciting and pleasurable beyond belief, and I've told You this countless times. But it accomplishes nothing. The next time I recall it, there will be no change. I wish it had never happened but now the hell of unmitigated guilt is upon me. You are probably displeased that I haven't forgiven myself; that in itself may be another sin that tacked on my record. Lord, I'm probably unfit to preach in any church. Why do I not hear from

You? Maybe telling me that my slate has been wiped clean and that it is quite natural that I can't forgive myself for what I did.

It was to Alf that he went for counsel. After Alf listened to what Lowell Miller proposed, he wasted no time in giving advice that Mack asked for.

"Since I'm not a member of your church, I feel free to express my opinion.

"You've been there for more than ten years. You first preached there when you were a sophomore in college?"

"Toward the end of that year."

"You may have accomplished about all you can at that one place. Accept Lowell's invitation to preach that sermon. See what it will be like to stand there. If it feels like a place you could do God's work, think of it as an opportunity to reach many more people.

"You are an unusual man. I have fished with you a number of times. When you catch a big one, you enjoy it as you should, but you are not boastful. You are patient those days when fish have lockjaw, and you never complain.

"We hike together frequently. You endure heat and cold with nary a complaint. You endure and persevere in the long, strenuous walks. I'm a tough old geezer who has walked thousands of miles holding on to plow handles, seeing far more than I wanted to of the rear end of a mule. And I didn't quit walking when I bought a tractor, but you know all that. I can't out-tough you.

"If you accept the position, get you an apartment on the side of the city closest to me and we'll continue on as we've been doing. Me and Ralph will take you fishing as before. Nell and I will visit Rebecca some at the nursing home; maybe that will take some pressure off you."

Tears begged to be loosed. With effort he kept them dammed as he responded, "Alf, you are the most remarkable man I know. If I thanked you a thousand times—"

"I'd tell you to knock it off," Alf interrupted. "You try to do God's will as you understand it to be. We do likewise. That's all."

⊯⊰⊱⊯

It would be a big change in his living routine. As difficult as life had been, he had made adjustments, even to visiting the nursing home instead of the state hospital. Rebecca wasn't going to get well; a brain scan had shown substantial shrinkage in the left temporal lobe. No more than an amputated arm was it going to grow back.

More than ever he needed to have a life that did not center around her. Not having one would not help Rebecca at all. Alf, Fredda, and others had shown him the necessity of living his life in ways open to him.

Did he need to move on to greater challenges? Should he ask God to help him accept as fact that his wife was already dead, except that her body would linger on for a while yet? Should he place the decision about moving on to Downtown Baptist in God's hands and go to the Great Smokies for another hike to Mount LeConte's summit? It was late April and the snow should be gone.

Hiking alone, he would be in solitude except for a brief exchange of words occasionally with another hiker. It would be a good time for him to be away from distractions other than those offered by crystal clear streams and trees and an occasional spell of wonder as vistas of distant ridges were suddenly opened.

On Thursday, it was on to Gatlinburg, checking in at a motel, and driving out to the trail head for Laurel Falls. It was a tuneup hike that would put him in the mood for the next day's challenge of a strenuous ten-mile one.

The next day, he awoke early. By eight-thirty, he had made all preparations for the trip. His shoulder bag was packed with bottled water, two sandwiches from a convenience store, and a lightweight poncho. Snowfall at higher elevations was a possibility by nightfall, according to the local weather forecast.

At nine, he was moving on at good speed where he could. The steep inclines would appear before much distance had been covered.

Before long, he came upon a group of fifteen or twenty who had stopped to listen as a park naturalist was making a talk about the variety of trees and shrubs that they had recently encountered and were now standing in the midst of. He squeezed through and continued on his way.

For a time, he was more aware of the careful steps he was taking and his heavy breathing than of what he came here for. Of course, what he had left back home came to him in flashes at times, but was as if that was of little importance; it was almost as if that was unreal. Here and now were the reality. If only he could walk and walk on into eternity, and that be the ending of the troubling world he would have to return to . . . a world that for now hardly existed.

He came to the first of the spruce forest and slowed, then stopped, spread his poncho on a bed of tiny conifer needles, laid his shoulder pack aside, and sat about three feet from the trail.

Coming up, a pair of hikers in animated, almost breathless conversation, greeted him and went on without pausing. Silence returned. Not even a bird chirped.

He released his mind . . . free of any sort of restraints, and it went no place in particular. Not even one memory disturbed its rest. It was content to float and drift without direction . . . without objectives. Content to just be. A new kind of experience, but it was to be later that he would know that he was waiting on God.

Twenty minutes passed or maybe it was thirty. A party of three coming down the trail were moving with ease though they had large back packs. Experienced hikers and campers, Mack surmised. Three women in rugged boots and flowing stride and obvious confidence in their ability to handle the rugged terrain, almost in unison wished him a "Good morning," and were soon out of his hearing. His quiet freedom from self now broken, he was quickly on his way again. Something had happened. What it was, he could not be sure. It would come if he would just await it without pursuing what he could not presently know.

Patience was one of life's hardest lessons to learn. And for once, he was patient.

The grade became gentler as he hiked through an almost pure stand of balsam fir. Soon he was at the junction of two trails as they became one, and before long he was at the lodge office. Inside, he as once before, wasted no time before dropping into a comfortable chair.

A female attendant was giving information to a man and woman who were going to stay overnight.

Mack talked with a woman who was sitting close by. She was young and a bit pudgy. Dressed for a spring day in pedal pushers, cotton blouse, lightweight jacket, and low-cut tennis shoes. Mack knew she was ill-prepared for the trip, but she had somehow been able to reach the summit.

"Have you heard," Mack asked her after he had eaten his first sandwich, "that it may start snowing by late afternoon?" He'd seen the forecast, but didn't take it seriously.

"Hadn't heard 'til I got here. Didn't turn on the room TV before my friend drove me to the trailhead. We came to see the wild flowers at the lower elevations. She was afraid to take this rugged hike. I decided to do it alone. She was going back to Cades Cove today and sketch a pioneer cabin and the gorgeous dogwood close by the front door." She checked her watch and said, "It's time I got going."

As he rested, Mack ate all the food he'd brought except for a package of nuts. He drank a second bottle of water, and chatted with the attendant a couple of minutes about the weather. She had listened to a radio advisory one hour before; the snow might arrive sooner than first predicted.

"But the sun is out right now, ma'am. Big cumulus clouds that look like summer."

"The forecast calls for snow showers possibly with lightning and thunder. Once in my life I've seen thunder with snow," the young attendant said.

"If that's how it comes, it will be my first experience with it."

"You probably need to start back soon. . . very soon, so you'll be at a lower elevation when it starts."

Mack was on his way before a couple of minutes had passed. Walking at a good speed brought him to the spruce forest in thirty minutes or so. For this, he slowed. The sense of urgency eased and his thoughts changed to the offer that Lowell Miller made for the church officers.

At times he had tried to imagine how being pastor of a large church would be. The change offered possibilities that he'd not had where he had been for so many years. He could reach out to more people. More souls could be saved. He thought of what he was doing as trying it on to see if it would be a good fit. Believing he was up to the challenge, he would make the change if he found it to be a good fit.

He walked on, but slowly now, soaking up for the days ahead the presence of old growth forest. Another presence was with him. A large congregation with many in need of personal advice and counseling. He knew there was more stress in even small cities of 20,000 to 25,0000, the size where he would be going. Houses so close together that a husband and wife couldn't indulge in a spat about the location of a new rosebush without a neighbor being aware of it. Kids without good raising coming in with your kids and getting on your nerves. He could have made a long list of irritants and stressors. Why had he even considered such a change? And it was at this point he knew. There was greater need there. Keeping marriages on sound footing and raising children were more challenging. A preacher's work offering many more opportunities to be of service.

He would go. Now that his mind was made up, he felt good about the decision—relieved that it had come so easily. Perhaps God was here more than other places. Perhaps He appreciated this place that shows no evidence—other than the trail—that man had changed what nature, God's caretaker on earth, had accomplished. It should not be surprising that I made a life-changing decision so easily in this sanctuary.

At an opening in the forest's canopy, he paused to observe a lone patch of blue sky in the massive cumulus clouds that were becoming darker. As much as safety would permit, he quickened his steps. The air was noticeably cooler and wet rocks underfoot were tricky. Icy rocks would be extremely hazardous.

With concern, he thought of the young woman. She could have taken the alternate route which may not be so steep.

The anchored cables at the most precipitous points were confidence builders that allowed him to move on without feeling his heart bouncing up into his throat. And steep declining steps that he would not have dared take in any sort of hurry without his light, but strong sassafras staff, a gift from Alf and his land.

When the spruce forest ended, he felt relief. The reduced altitude would not see snow accumulate as soon as where he'd been for the past hour. A soft rumble of thunder sounded above and giant snowflakes began falling.

Light conditions were good enough for him to see the trail. Hemlocks as well as hardwoods partially in leaf were collecting lots of snow before it could reach the ground. As the cloud moved on, the snow stopped as suddenly as it had arrived. Now thunder, muffled by distance, came again from ahead. For too brief a period, he walked in scattered rays of sun. Then back it was into a heavy snow shower.

With each step, the dread of accumulated snow eased slightly. Sounds of rushing streams became almost constant. The snow in large flakes swirled. Trees would soon be releasing large blobs of it. A sudden gusting of strong wind brought down lots of it. His waterproof poncho covered all of him except from the knees down.

Underneath it was a warm jacket. Going up, he had its sleeves tied in front around his waist so he wouldn't overheat.

Again, his concern for the young woman returned. He doubted she had any sort of warm clothing and not likely to have any sort of waterproof garment.

In places, snow had started building up on the trail, but had not started freezing. He noticed the first human footprints. Probably the young woman. Whomever they belong to could not be far ahead.

Alongside a stream that was hurrying to meet another, the grade was less and his steps fast. The rock tunnel and tight-fitting walls had been put behind. There was nothing to dread now. Snow was not accumulating. There just ahead was the young woman, limping badly each time her right foot came down. Her overall appearance was that of a young gosling whose mama goose was somewhere else when a rain shower had just been by.

On catching up with her, he could see her brown hair plastered to her head and neck. Her light-weight jacket clung in its total wet-ness to her body and arms.

She was shaking all over. He laid his poncho aside, took off his dry jacket, got her into it with difficulty, and then draped her in the poncho.

"But you'll freeze in just your shirt."

"We'll be at the trailhead before I get real cold. You going to be able to limp along another few minutes?"

"You can count on it."

"Let's get along then."

They talked little. Cold and fatigue had even worn Mack down as he concentrated on getting them to the warmth of his truck and her friend's car.

Minutes later, the trip was behind. A car was parked several yards from Mack's pickup. "Your friend's car?" Mack inquired even as he was realizing it was empty.

"She's not here!" she exclaimed in a voice filled with panic.

A park ranger was striding rapidly toward them. "Both of you come in the pickup?" After hearing Mack's answer, the ranger said that car belonged to a couple who used this trailhead. "I talked by radio to the lodge. Two other couples checked in today but they parked at a different trailhead. There may be someone camping where they shouldn't be.

"Traffic going toward the gap is completely blocked. Ma'am, your friend arrived at the road block below and was turned away. The road right here will soon be slippery.

"I told the fellows down there to inform your friend that I'd see you safely into town after you came off the mountain." He turned to Mack, "You headed into Gatlinburg?"

"Yes, sir."

"Could you take her to her hotel? There may be someone stranded on the highway up close to the gap who was between here and there when the road became impassable."

Mack got the girl inside the truck in a matter of seconds. He quickly got under the wheel. The engine started as soon as the key was turned. He shoved the temperature selector for maximum heating. Now it would be a very few minutes, two or three, before some warm air started. He backed, turned, and felt relief once the vehicle was on the road.

There was still snow in the air. With a dry wash cloth, he kept fog off the inside of the windshield. He had forgotten just how the road curved at every possible opportunity.

"My name is Mack," he introduced himself."

Between chattering teeth, she said hers was Joan.

"Glad to meet you, Joan."

"Not half as glad as I am to meet you, Mack."

"Ah, the temperature gauge is beginning to show signs of life." He increased heater fan speed and lowered his window a couple of inches so some of the air saturated by moisture from their wet clothes could escape. "Maybe the inside of the windshield won't fog up so badly now. You beginning to get warm?"

"Not really. What about you?"

"The same as you. As our wet clothes and wet skin dries a bit, the net effect is cooling as the water evaporates." He tapped the brakes lightly several times. "A skunk out on an evening like this and he doesn't have to be."

"If you and I had better sense, we'd not have been out either. But you came much better prepared than I did."

"A dear friend, Alf McDonald, about eighty, did the hike with me last year. His advice on learning I was coming back was that it is better to come over-prepared."

"And his advice led to the heavy jacket and poncho you placed me in. Never had been so glad to see another person as I was when you caught up with me. I could thank you and God a hundred times and that would not be enough."

"There are days, Joan, when it seems not one opportunity for an act of positive kindness comes along. Today one came and I feel that I have been blessed.

"Back up in the spruce forest thirty minutes or so before I caught up with you, a decision was made. One I could not make before coming to the mountains. Amongst trees I've come to love above all others, the decision came easily for the answer was at that place—quite obvious . . . almost compelling."

"Mind if I ask what it was?"

"Not at all. The small church where I've been pastor for over twelve years . . . I decided it was time to move on to where people have not been the beneficiaries of what little wisdom I have."

"Doesn't your decision have you excited, Mack?"

"Somewhat, and I hope humbled.

"My wife is in a nursing home. What started out as paranoid schizophrenia many years ago is now far worse. A separate, unrelated disease set in a year ago—a severe memory disorder that is said to always be fatal.

"I came to the mountains to make the hike I did this day, hoping it would take me into a high, quiet world that would be so different from what I face back home."

"So that you could briefly be rid of all you faced back there? And wasn't it sort of like that life back home did not exist? Just for a little while?"

"How did you know, Joan?" He slowed even more as a hairpin turn was suddenly upon him. "You can't be more than late teens?"

"Nineteen. But I've experienced lots in a short life.

"I came to the mountains with the intent of taking that long, rugged hike. My sweetheart since age sixteen recently dumped me. We had made plans to have a life together for the next fifty or sixty years. I was counting on it. It was my life. In the past six weeks I've gained ten pounds. My broken heart needed comfort and so I ate comfort foods, all of them fattening.

"Now I realize my problems are small compared to yours. You, I think, are coping far better than I. Right now, I'm making up my mind to go on a raw veggie and fruit diet, making myself more attractive. There's another guy out there somewhere."

"You are going on with life as though it has meaning—you didn't tell me that but you show you are."

Ten or maybe fifteen minutes later, Joan was removing Mack's poncho and jacket as he was pulling into the parking space at her motel's door. Her friend opened the door, ready to greet her.

"Thanks a million times a million, Mack." She kissed him on the cheek and then hurried toward a warm room and hot shower.

Mack drove toward his motel a few blocks away. What had been snow showers at higher elevations was but very light showers of droplets in the town. His first goal was a hot shower, then dry clothes, and a short walk to the restaurant where he had eaten breakfast earlier that day.

Saturday morning, he checked out as late as he could without paying for another night's lodging. His body needed extra time sleeping and just lying in bed. Though still young, a ten mile strenuous hike left him sore and lacking enthusiasm for getting up. He had not gone to bed until a little past midnight. Time was spent reviewing the next day's sermon. Then he had watched the late news.

He had walked alone with a young woman who had troubles far worse than the blistered toe she had picked up on the hike. Breaking up a relationship could be cause for serious emotional discomfort, especially for the very young. Her problem was not as incurable as the one that hit him at twenty-two, but still he had felt very sympathetic toward her. The start for her in the realities of life? And he had been alone with another young woman the first time in many years. There had, even under the circumstances, been a tiny thrill of excitement at sitting maybe twelve inches from her. And she had kissed his cheek, acknowledging his help. For him, it was so very much more; it reminded him of how desperate he was for the touch of a woman, and the company of one. There was no fire of sexual interest kindled, not even a hint of one. Instead he hurt because he had been a pauper in terms of female company for many years and there was no reason to see how his life could change

———

As he was driving a winding road that had to be where it was because a crooked creek had engineered its course, he dwelt on his chances for a life like other men had, if ever he had an opportunity. Hardly noticing the crystal clear creek or the constant turning of the steering wheel, he had relished the few minutes he had alone with the young woman. There was a sweetness about being able to help her, about the time shared shivering, and the time of pleasure together as the heater began to fill the cabin of the truck with warming air. The trip had been too short. Would Joan have understood if he had told her his feeling? Probably would, but there was nothing to do that would prolong the drive without making a fool of himself.

Nothing sensual about his feelings as he drove. He could be alone with Alf or his buddy Ralph, and it would be rewarding. But never alone with a woman and he understood and accepted that. Am I starved for the company of a woman? Indeed I am. Poor Rebecca, she in no way fills that need. Does she know me when I visit? No reason to believe she does.

He suddenly knew for the thousandth time that his lot was so much better than Rebecca's. She soiled herself and wet herself and had to be cleaned and dried by others' hands. And fed by others' hands. If she walked, it had to be with assistance. Only hours ago, he walked ten beautiful miles and enjoyed all aspects of it.

But if I get completely honest, I would probably admit that at times I resent her for messing up my life. So do I wish she would pass on and let me have a normal life? To that question, the answer is an absolute *no!* I still keep looking for something in science news that a way has been found to restore brain cells that have died as the disease has taken its toll. And then I daydream that a magic pill becomes available for schizophrenia.

For me, living this day that I have instead of foolishly trying to live the future is the hardest of all lessons. And a preacher of all people ought to know better. Will I ever learn, dear God?

If he believed what he preached, he ought to be handling the difficult aspects of his life far better than he was. A hypocrite and a believer at the same time? Is there such a thing as being both?

He was a bit upbeat because he had made a decision while on the trail. But not entirely upbeat, for anxiety was not completely conquered. For years he had faced a small congregation each time he preached, always feeling comfortable because most faces showed interest in what he was saying. At those times when interest appeared to flag, he always had in reserve a funny little story on a five by seven index card sitting on the lectern—this attention-getter right beside his sermon notes.

But a congregation ten times as large . . . could he cope with the bad moments with the same ease as he had done at Mount of Olives? But Mr. Miller had assured him he was ready, more than ready. God, who had a hand in the decision which came upon him as he had walked in wonder through the great forest of spruce, gave him assurance that he had no cause for anxiety.

Traffic lights and a change of highway signs soon occupied his attention. Shortly, he was free to drive at a comfortable speed. Pleasantly beautiful hills. Hayfields deep in grass and others with new mown hay drying and its fragrance filling the air, stirring memories from childhood that had been happy and free of cares.

Right in the middle of the welcome reverie, another memory interrupted without welcome or invitation . . . the night of the big sin. Not for long at a time would it leave him alone. He didn't leave her when he still could have. Did I stay because at one level of consciousness, I hoped what happened would happen? Oh, I knew there was risk of it early on. She was desperate for human comfort and I was aware of that.

She had told him that her nose had been shifted to one side in a bus accident when she was a ninth grader. Her parents had not been able to pay for corrective surgery. But her eyes were a shade of blue that lived in his memory. Some words were difficult for her to say. He would have still felt pity for her had she not just lost her husband.

But it was her eyes I remember above all. A tear or so in each, so that they had a sparkle even when she was not crying. They projected hurt and despair unlike any I had seen before. I was deeply moved. Her grief became my grief and I also needed comfort and companionship.

And that is how it happened, as I remember it. Once a mutual hug began, there was no backing up. It instantly became comforting, unbelievably so. And only the most naïve would not have known that a raging fire was being kindled. It was too late, too late! Now that is one way I recall that night.

The other is that I recognized danger signals in my pounding heart and my rapid breathing and the fire in the skin, especially my face. And I knew I'd better get out of there instantly or what happened would happen if I didn't. Was I hoping it would? I don't know. Over and over I've told God I'm so sorry. Still I don't feel forgiven.

I can't recall it without remembering how great and exciting it was, so I must not be as repentant as I ought to be. If I could just not remember the experience and what it was like, then I might be able to pray and feel the sin had been erased. Maybe I'm stuck with it because that is what I deserve.

Dear Lord, what do I do? Do the best I can from now on? I don't see how I can do better than that. Have mercy on me.

It was later that the other side of his sin had hit him. It was always awaiting him after a short respite from traveling the painful trail of guilt and remorse. Though he was expecting it, he was not prepared for it. Would it always be that way?

Infidelity was what it was. A lovely and sweet wife, through no fault of her own, in what amounted to a prison. Totally innocent of any wrong doing, she lived as if she were. For her "own good," she was taken there and he had been the person who did the taking. It was legal. He had become convinced that it was the way to go. But was it morally correct?

It was while Rebecca was locked away, completely unable to protect her interests, that I betrayed her. No woman could be betrayed more inexcusably.

Making it even more reprehensible, I enjoyed the sin as it was happening and the memory of how it was comes back all too clear, even exciting. After years I should have forgotten that aspect of it.

From the pulpit, how often I have preached that God is forgiving to the repentant sinner. For the congregation, I believe that is true. But for me, I can't bring myself to feel forgiven. One standard for the person I preach to, but a much different standard for me. Am I being irrational? Absolutely and completely, but knowing that doesn't help.

Lord, I might feel forgiven if I could destroy the part of my memory that recalls the excitement of it. But so far I've been unable to do that. I now fight off further temptation if the opportunity to experience it arises; I've done the best I can to avoid it. Have mercy on me.

Not every day did his conscience hound him as long and hard as it did on the long drive home. On the mountain trail yesterday, this barely crossed his mind. How good for me was the strenuous exercise. Steps and rocks and trees coming at me, often accompanied by the splashing of water as it raced toward calmer terrain. A forest ever-changing in sunshine and shading clouds. How could my thoughts dwell on the dark shadows that live in my soul? Shadows that await the monotony of pavement coming at me without letup come into the presence of my saddened mind. A restaurant for lunch and the welcome distraction of people sounds is what I need.

An eatery soon came into view. On entering it, he found it somewhat crowded though noon had passed seventy miles back. In a booth with coffee to warm his soul only five minutes later, he waited patiently for his grilled pork tenderloin and three sides. His long nights alone left him longing for sounds like this. Music came softly and no one at the other tables had to shout to be heard. The atmosphere was one of warmth and welcome. His coffee was not allowed to become tepid. The waitress was a frequent presence with warmups and a reassuring comment that his food was almost ready.

When it came, the tenderloin was indeed tender; its name had not lied. Lightly seasoned with something that spoke of its presence in soft tones—no shouting of whatever it was that had been applied by a light, caring touch. Green beans that had been cooked until lightly browned in a bit of oil. Whipped potatoes with just a wee touch of garlic and lots of butter. A large slice of garden-red tomato on a leaf of lettuce. What a pity this restaurant didn't move next door to him.

As if this was not enough, the waitress brought a yeast roll on a bread plate. "I waited a couple of minutes for your bread. This one is straight from the oven to you."

On opening the roll to apply some butter, the warm fragrance met his face. He almost swooned; something this good—why it's surprising it hasn't been outlawed.

Later the voice of the waitress interrupted the flowing of pleasure in his mind and body.

"Dessert, sir?"

"What do you have?"

"Horse apple cobbler and—"

"Enough said. I'll have a large serving."

"It'll be hot. You want vanilla ice cream on top, just to protect your tongue from the heat?" she teased as a smile lit up her face.

"Oh, absolutely. Hiked ten tough miles yesterday, so the calories don't matter."

As he ate the pie, his thoughts carried him back to his childhood. His parents had a large horse apple tree. Wonderful memories poured in as his brain's pleasure centers were tickled with every bite.

The glow from the meal lasted him for at least the next hundred miles of the highway. For the rest of the way home, the memories of yesterday returned with a small measure of excitement. At home, the decision he had made as he descended through giant spruce being decorated by large snowflakes, came back with the force of sudden newness. And again he prayed that it was purely God's will that had guided his decision. And when the short prayer had ended, there came a feeling of calm assurance that chased any brief doubts to some far place.

The man of no faith, if he had been reading my mind, would have thought me delusional. Does it never occur to the non-believer that those of us with faith in God find rewards, large and small, for our believing and asking for help and reassurance from the God we invite into our hearts? And instead of frightening emptiness, we feel a presence that helps us deal with loneliness that seems to always be waiting to take possession of our inner spirit. Thank you, Lord, for being there when I feel the aloneness that comes when I realize for the thousandth time that we only know—even a dearly loved one—as from a distance. You are the God who is there, filling my heart as no human can. You are not as from a distance.

Am I always this close to God? How I wish I could say that it is so. But there are times all too frequently when doubts assail me from some dark interior place of my soul. Will I ever outgrow such periods of spiritual weakness?

＝⸝⸜＝

The next time he met with the board of deacons, Mack had planned to announce his upcoming move to another church. Oscar MacDonald was chairman and it was he who opened the meeting with the statement that Brother Mack had been offered an opportunity to lead a much larger flock. It had not been a well-kept secret. The visitors had been noted and there had been speculation by a few that someone was interested in their preacher. Lowell Miller had dropped a few words to someone that confirmed that speculation.

"You may think you are the same preacher you were more than a decade ago when you first came to us. But we who have watched you grow in wisdom, understanding, and communication talent were amazed when we heard a tape recording of your third or fourth sermon that Fredda had saved all these years. At an unofficial meeting of deacons at my house, she played it recently.

"You were a good speaker then and had put together some good insights for our faith, but your growth would have been unnoticed had we not been able to compare what you were then to what you have become."

CHAPTER TWELVE

M oving day seemed to hurry upon him. Waiting had been almost as much a time of regret as it was a time of looking to the future.

Members of both churches made it into a joint effort—a short one. By noon of the chosen Saturday, it was complete. Mack's first regular sermon was prepared. He had as a visitor preached an introductory sermon three weeks earlier. And after the first few minutes he had begun to feel comfortable, and now tomorrow was seen as an opportunity to share insights. The afternoon was a time to visit Rebecca.

He sat with her longer than usual. No verbal communication was possible, and hadn't been for many months.

Her eyes were open but it was as if she didn't really see him. He moved a hand quickly within inches of her eyes. She blinked. Everything had not gone completely out yet.

A nurse's aide came in and told him that she had remained unchanged. Mack stepped outside and returned minutes later when the aide beckoned him. In an apparent effort to console him, she said, "You'll have all those good memories to live with."

Mack knew she meant after Rebecca was gone. It came to him again that everyone but him knew his wife was on a one-way path to death. Even Rebecca's mother had recently put behind any hope for a miracle.

"But, ma'm, I have little memory of her now except those of her since illness struck her down."

Intellectually, he could recall that she had been a very modest, quiet girl. But that was it. The memories of the feelings stirred by a sweet, delicate voice, was something he could not call back. But those feelings must have existed at one time, or they would not have married.

All I can clearly remember now are my experiences with delusional behavior, the sudden and absolute knowledge that her mind was sick. And Dr. Pickens making it so clear and certain that short of a positive response to medication, it was unlikely that she would ever recover good health. The improvement never came, and I had thought I would be happy if she became ninety percent normal. Later, I would have been happy to settle for eighty percent. If she could recover enough to allow me to work regularly and attend church . . . but she never did.

And then she slipped into Alzheimer's disease. No possible cure for that, her doctor said. In my state of denial, I first clung to a thread of hope that her physically damaged brain might be restored if a way could be found to get a growth hormone past the blood brain barrier. I read that there was a possibility that clinical trials might begin within four or five years. My hope amounted to no more than the light of one lone firefly on a hundred-acre of tract of land. But I held on to that because it was all I had.

By his watch, more than an hour passed after his summation of the realities of her illness. It was the entrance of an aide who came to get Rebecca up and walk her that brought Mack from wherever he had been. Unnoticed, unthought about, the time had passed. Where had he been? Not asleep. But not in emotional pain. This had become a way of escaping from life's hopeless reality. It was not the first time.

At such times I escape from myself. Completely . . . not partially like I do when I hike or listen to music. I escape consciousness of everything. While doing a duty by visiting her, I sometimes escape into a land I know nothing of and can't know where I was.

He continued thinking of it as he drove home. Taking away a large block of my obligatory time visiting her by not being fully aware of where I am or why I'm there. Perhaps a gift from God.

My life is like an old-time pigeonhole desk—compartmentalized. Place visiting Rebecca in one rectangular compartment. Separated from that, study and preaching in another. Hiking is separated on all sides from those two. And so it is throughout without realizing that there's a pigeonhole for music, and on and on. While doing carpentry, I'm not much aware of what's in the others. And there is one for eating, and fond memories of that lunch on the trip home from the Smokies.

In my youth, it now seems to me, life had no separate compartments. The boy studying chemistry would find his mind drifting to going fishing come Saturday morning and from that to playing touch football at P.E. and on and on . . . relaxed and unstressed.

Out of necessity, and perhaps due to growing up, he could now pretty much occupy himself with one thing at a time. He asked God to help him keep it that way. I'm not so blind, dear Lord, that I don't see that what's in one of the compartmentalized sections of my mind sometimes is interfered with by a spillover from another that competes for my attention.

But he was not as compartmentalized as he thought. Whenever working, studying, even preaching, there was awareness that he had a very sick wife. It was not a constant thing and on his frequent remembering, it was not with tearing up of the heart as it had been in the early days.

His sin defined his life almost to the extent Rebecca's illness did. Not for long could he get away from that inexcusable act. Oh, he had tried a number of excuses—he was young and ignorant of the strength of the sex drive. Other excuses he had tried as explanations. But none of them worked for long at a time.

Self-contempt and guilt hung heavily upon him. Despicable, he believed, was an even better fit. But these judgements that he had felt were deserved were not experienced with the same degree of condemnation or the intensity they had been

⇒╪╪⇒

On the third Sunday, he preached a very short sermon on honesty. And then told the congregation that he had been leading to the heart of his sermon which was about an honest man.

"A French scientist, Jacques Monod, had shared a Nobel prize with two fellow scientists. His book *Chance and Necessity* quickly became one of France's best sellers last year. English translations are available early this year. The book made a big splash right away. News media carried excerpts and quotations.

A March edition of the *New York Times* had a report of an interview of Dr. Monod by John Hess of the *Times*.

"It had been widely reported that Monod believed that there was no one up there nor out there who was aware of us or cared about us. According to Monod, millions of years of chance innovations accounted for mankind's existence.

"In the interview with John Hess, Monod got off on the subject of oughts or values. For centuries, man had tried to derive his *oughts* from the *is,* that is from what he knows, especially from philosophers.

"The scientist reasoned that man was a product of evolution that resulted from a series of chance events. And that we, like every other species, might just as well not have been.

"Since we might just as well not have appeared, shouldn't he have reasoned that it would be just as well if a nuclear shoot-out resulted in our total extinction. No creator to mourn our passing?

148

"No reason at all for our continued existence, I thought he should have said.

"How did the belief in *oughts* ever enter his mind? I wondered.

"The idea of value systems suggest that some things are more important or that they are more desirable than others. But if we might just as well not have appeared at all, it is absolutely absurd that there are things we ought to do.

"Did he take that next logical step? Not at all. What he did say was that since we are here by chance, then we are totally free to choose whatever value system we wish. He went on to say that we must choose a value system, that we can't live without it. That we can't live personally and can't deal with society without one.

"And choose one he did. From a friend he borrowed one that the friend had said was enough to 'fill the heart of man.'

"Heart of man? What did he mean? The world class scientist did not mean the organ that pumps blood. Like you or me, the friend meant his inner being, the inner spirit or soul of man.

"So what do we have? We have an honest man. He, like you, had to have something to give life meaning. Life isn't always easy to take; it can serve up the bitterest kinds of medicine. At some point, death awaits us all, and we are aware of this certainty even in childhood. If we see meaning in life, we can deal with that ultimate certainty.

"Monod, like the rest of us, had to have meaning if life is to be bearable. His absence of belief in God did not cause him to proclaim that man can live without faith in something.

"The world of evolutionary science, for the most part, sees people of faith in God as being less than intelligent. It wants to teach our children that a designer does not exist. They would have the public believe that a student is not educated unless he or she has been fully indoctrinated in their way of explaining how we came into being. They want your children to believe what they believe.

"Recently a scholar was heard to say, 'Chemistry and classical physics can be proven with certainty. The others, the soft sciences, are speculation to varying degrees.'

"By the way, the man Monod borrowed a value system from was a man who wished he could believe in God but said he could not."

⚊⚌⚊

It was in his church office that he met one Monday evening with three church ladies at their request. They were neatly dressed in casual clothes . . . ladies in their sixties, he guessed.

"Brother Mack," said one to give an idea of why they were there, "I bet it's been thirty years and three or four preachers ago that church ladies tried—"

"It was four preachers ago," interrupted a lady who had bluish tints in hair that was well styled.

"You're right, Sue Ann. Other church ladies have done what we are doing this evening."

When no one picked up on what was the reason for the meeting, Mack asked, "And what is it that others have had no success in accomplishing?"

"In getting Maude Dale to attend church," answered the third.

"Beginning four preachers and thirty years ago without any success, Maude Dale must be a very stubborn woman," Mack said.

"That she is for sure . . . and crabby. And a few other things, including being a tough nut to crack!"

Mack was interested and felt a small smile chase away any possible suggestion of not caring to hear more. Unconsciously, he leaned forward a couple of inches toward his desk. "She has been a tough nut to crack. Four sets of your predecessors have tried."

"Sue Ann, you shouldn't be telling Brother Mack she is a nut."

"Clarice, I used the term in a figurative manner, not meaning she is nutty."

"And you ladies want me to try my luck at bringing her back into the fold. I gather she was at one time a church regular."

"Oh, yes. She was our Sunday School teacher when we were kids. We looked up to her and loved her. She was a beautiful woman on the outside and inside."

"We don't know what or when it happened."

"But something changed her long ago. Would you go visit her?"

"We carry her cooked food and will try to set up a visit with her next Sunday afternoon."

"You know my wife is in the nursing home. I visit her at 2:00. See if you can set it up for 3:30."

"We think you can have success."

"Where others have not? Have you and other church ladies really tried?" Mack asked.

"Of course. Our last efforts were met with: 'Can't you busybodies leave me in peace regarding my soul's welfare? I appreciate the food, but that doesn't bribe me into coming to listen to what I don't want to hear.'"

"And how do you think you can gain me admission into her home?" Mack wondered.

Clarice said, "We'll tell her the truth. That you are over six feet. Dark brown eyes that tend to sparkle at times with mirth but always shine with kindness. Ears of delicate molding and a dimpled chin. And you are young."

By this time, Mack was chuckling. "I don't keep a shovel here but this evening I really need one. Why do you think such blarney will interest her?"

"She's a woman. She's eighty-seven, she says, with rheumatoid arthritis and a bad case of it. Some osteoporosis and bending of the spine."

"But she's still a female. My husband's father is a year older than Maude and his eyes light up at the sight of a pretty young girl," Sue Ann finished off any doubts that Maude would see Mack.

And so it was that on the next Sunday afternoon, he met the three ladies on the porch of a Victorian home that had seen better days but was still impressive. They had arrived before he had, "A couple of minutes before," Sue Ann said. "She knows we are here and is waiting for us in the living room. The sound of the door being unlocked came as soon as we got seated here on the porch."

Seconds later Mack was being introduced to a lady who looked as if her eighty-seven years had not been kind to her. The three church ladies kept the conversation with Mrs. Dale alive, giving Mack an opportunity to listen as they drew her out. The lady, to Mack's surprise had a clear alto voice. No roughness or shakiness as he had expected. How her voice had been that of a woman in early middle age was a whale of a surprise.

She had not risen as they entered. A walker was pulled up close before her. She was sitting in a wing-back chair, covered in substantial fabric with a floral design.

The ladies had told him they would keep the conversation going for at least five minutes, giving Mack a chance to become comfortable before they made an exit. One of them looked at her watch and then stood. "Mrs. Dale, we'll leave you in the company of our new pastor." And after a bit of talk as they were preparing to leave, they left with a final remark by one of them. As they went out the door, one of them said, "You two behave yourselves. We'll see you on Tuesday, Mrs. Dale."

For a moment, nothing was said. And then, "Mack, a young fellow like you . . . I'll not address as Mr. Baldwin and since I don't attend church, I'll not call you Brother Mack. You call me Maude if you will."

"I shall if that pleases you."

"It does. Those biddies want you to persuade me to come to church," the smooth voice announced as a statement of fact.

"That's about right. They told me you'd ask and I promised I'd not lie."

For a minute, or maybe it was two, no further words were spoken. Mack's gaze flicked across the face distorted by time and by pain and unhappiness too, he figured. Eyelids drooped, leaving her to view the world through slits. Outwardly, she showed all the major signs of old age. But when she spoke, her age was forgotten. Her voice was firm, smooth, and golden. How this miracle could happen was beyond belief, except he was here and had heard.

"You think you can talk this old bag of aching bones into attending church, Mack?"

"Hadn't planned on trying to," he said as he lightly chuckled.

"Then why are you here?"

"They asked me to come. I came to visit you. If after I have, you can decide if I'm allowed to call again."

"That's it? No tricks, no sneaky appeals?"

"That's right. No preaching. I do that in church.

"Did you sing when you were in good health?" he asked.

"Yes. Years ago, I was in the community choir. An ENT doctor was looking down my throat a couple of years ago when I had an inner ear infection. Said if he hadn't seen my vocal chords, he wouldn't have believed it possible."

"Still sing?"

"I have a recording of some songs from "Sound of Music." Sometimes I sing along just a little with Mary Martin.

"That's enough talking about me right now. I hear you have a helluva life, Mack. Pardon that little slip-up. It's that I think in such terms at times, and words like that just slip out."

"It's okay. Sometimes it's a hard battle for me to keep from releasing a few myself." And Mack told her in a few sentences what Rebecca's illnesses were.

"Does it make you feel better to talk about it? People are always telling me I'd feel better if I talked about my troubles."

"I don't feel better or worse for having told you, Maude. What helps is staying so busy at a variety of things that I almost forget myself and Rebecca. But it's as though the realities, hers and mine, lie in wait ready to pounce on me. I fight to keep the terrors away. Hiking at a good speed helps as much as anything. But there are other things that shield me.

"Sometimes my faith is insufficient to protect me, and I feel guilt. I'm a preacher, Maude, and am supposed to have faith that offers protection by day and by night. But at three in the morning when I awaken and have trouble going back to sleep—" He went no further. He didn't need to. He saw understanding beyond her glasses, through those narrow slits that revealed much of what she was thinking.

"Is there anybody you talk to about this?"

"Alf McDonald. He is close to eighty. We hike together often. Fish together occasionally. Sit and talk at times about all sorts of things. My mind bounces from one thing to another and on to something else."

"You still go see him often?"

"Two or three times a week," Mack answered.

"I guess it's my turn now," she stopped. Mack waited. When she said nothing further, he asked, "Your turn for what?"

"To tell you a little about me. Got married in my late teens, as much to get out of a house that held too many kids as for anything else. Had never gone to school anywhere except the one big room that served as a church and as a place to learn what today would be considered a basic education. It was a public school in a church building. I guess church and state weren't as separated as federal courts say they ought to be.

"Well, I'd been married a month and three days when it happened. My husband was working high up, riveting pieces of steel together. He misstepped somehow and died instantly, they said.

"I can't say it was a good marriage or a bad one since I never had another to compare it to."

"A lifetime of widowhood. How awful!" Mack exclaimed.

"I didn't really know the man. Had only known him three or four weeks before we married. Never anything resembling stories about romance like you see in books today. He did his duty by me and I did mine by him. He brought his pay home on Friday and I did his laundry and prepared meals that short time we were together. I guess we were both ignorant about what's called lovemaking but we each tried to see the other had satisfaction of sorts. Anyway he left me a gift in that short time.

"A little over a week after his burial, morning sickness hit and some days was darned stubborn about leaving.

"I knew that pregnancy often followed pretty close behind getting married. I was born ten months after my parents married and it seemed others kept coming along every year or so. Girls had childhood until big enough to help with the younger ones. And then got married and were soon in the baby business. It was what you expected out of life."

"Was it really that depressing?"

"You didn't think of it as depressing. You didn't know anybody who had a car. There were no movies. No radio or television. A kerosene lamp was the only light for reading at night, if you had anything to read.

"Families had lots of what people today claim they wish they had."

"Quality time together?"

"Yep. Dominoes, checkers, and rook. And arguments over whose time was next. Not much time for loneliness, except for maybe a little of the self-imposed kind."

Mack glanced at his wrist watch. It was past time to end the visit, but he stayed another ten minutes enjoying her conversation.

For a short while longer, she told how different those long ago times were. "But many of my memories are good. It was a time of optimism. I lived believing that the really good times were ahead. Surviving those early years was possible because the good things were yet to come.

"Is that how you saw your future, Mack?"

"Pretty much I saw things that way."

"I know you are going to have to go, but can you come back next week? I can think of lots of things I'd like to tell you."

At church that evening, he was asked by one of the ladies regarding how the visit turned out. To which he answered, "She invited me back next Sunday."

An excited voice exclaimed "Wonderful! But I'm not totally surprised." She hurried to tell the other two who had already taken seats with their husbands in a pew near the front.

⇥⇤

The next week went by in a hurry. Mack was too busy to count off the days. He still worked as a carpenter three days a week and three days he visited Rebecca. Time to do some pastoral counseling, but very little. Brother Wes, an assistant pastor who had not wanted the responsibility of conducting three services each week took much of the responsibility for counseling and visiting the sick and bereaved. He had once been a full-time preacher and never became quite comfortable with it. He wanted to serve in a role where he could minister to the needs of one person at a time. Standing before hundreds at a time without being a little nervous was something he had never become used to. Substituting for the pastor from the pulpit was something he could bear, if he knew that it would only be for a brief time. Brother Wes was warm and laid-back and liked by the membership, but they found his sermons less than inspiring and thought-provoking.

Mack needed the extra income from carpentry. Nursing home expenses, even in the early seventies, were burdensome. Rebecca's parents offered to help but retirement from their jobs was only a couple of years ahead and they had saved far less than they now thought they would need and only recently realized what their needs might be. Mack insisted that he take care of it all. If he outlived her, as was likely, he wanted to be able to look back and say with a clear conscience that he had done all he could.

Though she didn't appear to recognize him when he visited her, an aide told him Rebecca ate better when he or her mother fed her.

⇒⋅⇒

His daily planner was filled a week in advance. Working Maude in on Sunday at three in the afternoon filled that day. But after the second visit, he would have been disappointed if she did not suggest that he come back. She was sharp of mind and sometimes sharp of tongue. On that second visit, she gave him a bit of accounting for her ending church attendance twenty-eight years ago.

"Mack, she wasn't the first person to say something like this because I'd heard something similar at least three times before. Had a real short fuse on the subject. It was in a women's Sunday School class. Somebody brought up the subject of why men ought to be in church just as much as women. One woman said her husband was often so worn out from six whole days in his pharmacy that he needed to rest on Sunday. And up spoke another telling us all that it was important that her husband attend church and how much better his hardware store started doing because of contacts he made just by being here. The wife of a dentist said her husband's appointment book stayed filled after he had been coming regularly. And so it went on for about ten minutes. A plumber's wife had a similar story about how beneficial attending church had been for her husband's business.

"'Do you pass out business cards here at church,'" the woman, whose husband was at home resting, wanted to know.

"The lady who was our teacher kept her voice calm but explained she doubted the Lord appreciated people who came to church for reasons of success for their businesses or professions. And quickly directed attention back to the lesson."

157

"I bet I can guess what your thoughts were. Did you sit in silence while your blood pressure came to a boil?"

"It didn't reach the boiling point, but it came close. And surprisingly, I said nothing, but I started missing Sundays pretty frequently. Before long, I quit altogether."

Mack didn't realize it, but there was a twinkle in his eyes as he asked, "Didn't it worry you that the Lord might be displeased with you for not going to church anymore?"

"God is not stupid, Mack, and He is highly principled as is His Son.

"There were people in Jesus' time who used their religion and the high position they held in the Jewish hierarchy to acquire wealth. Jesus blasted them most of all. Eventually, it led to his crucifixion. Hypocrisy, He despised above all."

With a little amusement showing in his voice, Mack commented, "You couldn't bear to sit each Sunday with the Pharisees. Once heard a preacher claim that it was better to go to church where there were hypocrites than to stay at home and go to hell."

"That preacher didn't understand Jesus," Maude responded. She would have been miffed, except for the touch of humor in Mack's voice.

"You are an unusual preacher. This is your third time to visit me and so far, you have not suggested I'm a backslider.

"Oh, by the way, each month, I mail a check to the church, not a big one, but what I can afford. There are lots of good people there and the church has a hand in making them what they are. As much as the hypocrites, it was all those long years that I had been attending that same church. The early stages of arthritis had no small part in my decision to stay home."

It was during the fourth visit that Maude told about her life following her husband's death. The construction company her husband worked for had the decency to make a modestly good settlement for the loss of her husband. "Apparently, they took into consideration the fact that I was pregnant.

"At the time George was born, I was living in a boarding house in a city of fair size. A mile walk and I could reach the municipal library. I made that walk at least twice a week until a few days before George's arrival. My appetite for knowing things could not be satisfied."

"Do you still have that same appetite?"

"Who ever knows enough? I guess there are some who don't suffer that curse, but I'm happy I'm not one of them.

"There was a teachers' college in the town. I had moved into a rented apartment just after George's birth. A few months later, I hired a sitter and enrolled in school."

"And you prepared to become a teacher. Of what?"

"Science. Took heavy loads and by going to summer school, I had a bachelor's degree in two and a half calendar years. By that time, my nest egg was almost as spent as I was.

"To find a job, I had to look several counties away. I was lucky. Finished college in late August and began teaching in less than two weeks.

"My sitter moved with me. A widow in her late fifties, she had no income at all. Her three sons had scattered in order to find work.

"No social security in those days. It was in the first decade of this century that I began teaching. The high school was located in the county seat. Physics and chemistry were taught in alternate years and there was biology too—classes were quite small.

"To be hired, I had to agree that I would be a regular attender at one of the local churches. The superintendent said that was required of all teachers and principals."

"Federal courts would not permit such a requirement now, Maude."

"It wasn't as bad as it would sound sixty-five years later. More often than not, public schools used church buildings for classes. Except for the school where I taught, all public schools in the county used church buildings until times got better. It was in the early 20's that saw public school buildings being built and paid for by local taxpayers out in the county.

"Years later, George had already moved out on his own and Mary Lou had passed away. Then the Great Depression hit. I had moved to a coal mining town that prospered during the teens and twenties and offered better pay."

"Were you paid in script in the thirties?"

"Lots of times, Mack. Pay had shrunk with the coming of the Depression. Fifty dollars in script wasn't worth fifty dollars when you presented it to a store. The grocer didn't know how much the board of education would redeem it for; that depended on what taxes brought in."

"I've heard such stories before, Maude. And the coal miners, if they had only a couple days pay a week, could go to the company store and get groceries?"

"At higher prices. And if they needed a little cash, the store would advance that too, in what was called clacker. A dollar in clacker would buy less than a dollar's worth at regular stores.

"Mack, people today who were born after World War II can have no feeling for what it was like. Twenty-five or thirty kids in a class and not one as much as a pound overweight. I have pictures that will prove that.

"Hunger was real and chronic. After adjusting to it, children seemed to be not as aware as you might imagine. Kids from farms ate better but their clothes were just as ragged.

"World War II ended the Depression, but with it came scarcity and rationing of food."

As they had talked, one of the church ladies did laundry, washed dishes and cleaned up the kitchen. She was out of hearing and was not infringing on their privacy.

On a later visit, Maude asked Mack when he first knew Rebecca suffered from a serious illness. He told of the wedding night and the voice she heard a day and a half later.

"And your marriage was not consummated," she stated in a sub-dued manner, her voice expressing sympathy. "And you both were virgins."

He nodded.

"Two of God's finest.

"There must have been temptation since. You are uncommonly handsome; some woman must have offered herself to you at some point in the past ten years."

Mack could feel his face aflame with embarrassment, but offered no words to deny or confirm.

"And being the kind of man you are, you have paid for it ever since in fear you might do it again if temptation and opportunity arise. Remorse and guilt have been a daily companion ever since, never allowing you to enjoy one hour of unbroken joy from all you have accomplished."

Mack looked her in the eyes as she spoke. What he saw was loving understanding, contrasting the ugliness that age and pain had wrought upon what had been a handsome woman. She does not condemn me. Maybe God is as forgiving as this woman who could see me as a vile sinner, but chose not to.

"Mack, when George was a little fellow and his sitter was with him, a college classmate talked me into going on a picnic with him to a scenic spot on a free-flowing creek. I sensed there might be risk in going but I went anyway. Sometimes we can become so starved for companionship, so desperate for the touch of another. So I went and it was a place of beauty far beyond what I had ever seen before. The sound of cascading water was equally beautiful to my ears; it was as if the harp strings of my heart were being plucked. The small stream did to me what no thundering waterfall could. One moment so completely entranced by sight and sound and by the very human warmth of the man whose chest had become my backrest. And the sweet notes of a brown thrush's voice from high up in a tree. It was what I never had known. And there came a time, only moments in length, when neither bird nor stream was heard. And when awareness of realities returned, there was the sin that I had committed.

"Not being a preacher, mine did not haunt me with returning guilt by day and by night, year after year. Fear of pregnancy went away about a week later. For this woman, it had been sort of exciting, but nothing like it can be for a man. Frankly, it wasn't worth the few days of worry of a possible pregnancy without a husband. And I felt I had really let the Lord down, but knowing I was not going to do that again with a man I was not married to and having begged God's forgiveness, I put it behind me and went on with my life."

"Maude, each time I remember the unbelievable excitement and satisfaction of that moment, it is almost . . ." His voice faltered as he couldn't find the right words to express it to her. "It's like I shouldn't be enjoying the memory of it, but in a way I do and know that should the opportunity ever arise, I might be unable to control . . . ."

"You run scared. Of yourself," she commented and said nothing further.

In silence they sat. A piece of cookware hit the kitchen floor, and they talked of trivia for a minute or so before Mack left.

Following his departure, Maude felt tears begin, something her eyes had not released in years.

"Lord, why did you create us? For the thousandth time I ask you, and like always, You answer me not. You gave us free will and with it a conscience to make it possible for life to be a guilt-filled hell. That young man doing his best to please You, even as a teenager and how did You repay? A wife with paranoid schizophrenia. And if that was not trouble enough, she was not spared the onset of another brain disorder. But the second one might be a blessing if it takes her away in the next few years. But I bet Mack doesn't see it that way. The state of almost complete denial he lives in allows a wee bit of hope to break through his gloom, a baseless belief that her brain might become healed of both sicknesses is all he has left.

"What happens to me before my final days matters little one way or another. But Mack is the finest young man I've ever come across. He has a long time to suffer.

"I don't understand why You do to us what You do. And never have. Why don't You enlighten me?"

But she didn't expect God to do that. And she would continue as always—to try to make some sort of sense of it all.

⇒∔⇐

If Maude ever returned to church, Mack wanted it to be because she wanted to, not because of his visits.

He had seen in those eyes something he hadn't expected to ever see. *She understood me and my spiritual problems as I couldn't have believed possible. No condemnation nor syrupy sweet sympathy, but kind understanding. Lord, if I could only believe You felt the same. Did You not know when You created us that sexual desire could trample good intentions and make us feel a thousand times worse than anything short of murder could. That wizened old lady gave me a small measure of comfort. If she understood, Lord, maybe You do too.*

Though the next week was hectic with all his obligations and the additional things he had chosen to do, he had time to look forward to Sunday afternoon and his visit with Maude.

And it turned out that she wanted to talk to him about what she believed about God's understanding of us. On learning of this, Mack inquired, "What did God understand about man? At what point is it that you refer to, Maude?"

"Those many centuries before Jesus came is the period when I don't believe God knew man very well at all."

"But haven't all believers in God thought of Him as being omniscient . . . all knowing at all times? He knows what's in our hearts. I've preached a sermon or two to that effect, myself."

At this, she chuckled and said, "Consider yourself, Mack. If you've preached the omniscience of God, then you know that He knows how burdened down with guilt and remorse you've been and how many times you've begged that you be forgiven. But guilt never leaves you, except when you are too busy to remember it's there. But if you believe He is all-knowing, then you must believe that Jesus

163

died for nought, that the parable of the prodigal son was without
meaning.

"'Son,' said God in exasperation one day, 'I can't begin to
understand man though I created him. Over and over and over,
my chosen ones whom I've blessed continue to disobey me despite
my using heathens repeatedly to punish them to bring them in line
again. It gets their attention, but it doesn't last! Soon they return to
their wickedness. And I have to punish them again!'"

She had caught Mack's interest, but he decided not to interrupt
with a comment.

"And I believe for a while God kept talking and Jesus was a silent
listener. 'Son,' God said, 'I want you to go to the earth and be born
to a woman, a virgin. You'll grow up looking like one of them. You'll
have childhood diseases. You'll catch colds and blow your nose on
a piece of linen and develop deep seated coughs like ordinary kids.
In time, you'll have to work and sweat as they do. You'll feel temptations of various sorts; the human side of you wouldn't be human if
you didn't, but you are not to yield as they do.

"'You'll stay in touch with me often so that I can learn what it is
like to be man.'

"'Son, I'm tired of the stench of burnt offerings that have begun
to have little meaning and less effect in turning lives around.

"'After you have come to understand man, as I've never been
able to do, then I'll try to figure out what to do after you have
brought me to the point of fully knowing what makes them break
my laws and trample my wishes into the mud.'" Maude paused at
this point, being out of steam and out of words.

Mack said nothing about her unusual interpretation of the
Bible, about a theology different from any he had studied in divin-
ity school. He had no doubt as to her complete sincerity. But neither
did he doubt God's fairness; a just and merciful God would not
hold this unorthodox belief against this fragile old lady who had
endured so much for so long and still believed in God.

"Mack, it is the person of God I continue to search for. What is it like to be the Creator of the universe? That He even takes note of man and cares enough to want us to straighten out and become more than we are. How truly amazing!

"One of these years ere long, this heart will give up in fatigue, but until that day, my other heart will continue to seek to know the personality of God."

"Maude," Mack said in a voice shaken with emotion, "I know you will. And I pray that knowing the true personality of God will become the grandest of all your many treasures you have been laying up in Heaven."

After Mack had taken leave, he continued to be under the spell cast by Maude at the end to the revelations about herself. And he prayed that her remaining time on earth be one of fruitful search. And that his own remaining time, which could be fifty years, be fruitful, that he might also search 'til the end, learning a little more about the personhood of God.

For reasons he did not know, he thought of giant trees in California that were of great size even as Jesus walked on the shore of the Sea of Galilee. He vowed to go some day and touch a tree that shared time with Jesus. Wouldn't that make him feel a little more connected with Him? Maybe, maybe not. But he would experience that on one of the trips he loved to make.

How God had blessed him in having Maude and Alf in his life. Life is a mixture of tragedies and uplifting events. Of saints and near-saints like two old ones, Alf and Nell McDonald—several years younger than Maude—had been humbled and tempered by the Great Depression as she had been. Ralph Nesbitt, a natural story teller had been there too. People who lived those years with adult responsibilities knew things that the children of the current era would never know the same way. And the youth reaching adulthood in 1971 would never, ever understand what the 30's were.

Mack's mind rambled as he drove home to make final preparations for church, which included enjoying a toasted tomato and cheese sandwich. One of these days, he'd visit California and the big trees. More places to visit than ever he could get around to, but somehow he would make an effort every time an opportunity came his way. In the meantime, he had responsibilities that shoved aside those places so far away. The Gulf Coast and the Great Smokies were not too far, and they were always changing—always fresh and a new experience. What I should be is thankful for what I have and not fret for long over what I can't have.

Unknown to Mack, there were things going on that he was not aware of, things that would have an effect on his life. But they were things that he could not have changed if he had known.

A routine week passed. On Sunday morning he was sitting on the church stage as the choir filed in and the organist offered a pre-lude in music. The choir director sat across the stage from Mack. Eleven o'clock had just been chimed in at the end of the prelude.

Soft conversations among the audience suddenly ended. An unusual quietness settled in, a very brief one because an unex-pected event had arrived, and people in back were the first to know. An entourage had just entered, three middle-aged women accom-panying a thin old lady pushing a wheeled walker that had tennis balls on the tips of the two back legs.

Mack laid his sermon outline aside and gawked like everyone else. No one dared say a word that might cause her to turn around. For the unexpected had happened—no less than a small miracle. Maude Dale in a pretty dress, maybe a wee bit less than fashionable, but a sight to behold anyway. Hair whiter than gray, showing signs that a beautician had laid hands on her head the day before. Mack didn't know she could overlook pain enough to walk so erectly. There was something, something . . . regal in her bearing. And those who didn't think that adjective, felt just as impressed as those who did.

The parade of the four was long. There were obviously others who knew of it. Otherwise, the whole pew in the very front before the pulpit and lectern would not have been empty. With precision and elegance, the four simultaneously seated themselves.

Though the need to applaud was felt by most, not one set of hands came together. The choir director led choir and congregation in the Doxology. It was sung with unusual emotion and uplifting of voices.

Mack had been thinking that no one had let him know that she was coming. And he was glad he had been kept in the dark, for the surprise increased the lifting of his soul far more than beforehand knowledge could have.

As the morning service followed its usual pattern, Mack could not help but wonder if he had actually been an instigator of the event. It didn't matter. She was here! He had prepared to preach on his favorite parable, the prodigal son. Her favorite too. Had someone told her about the sermon . . . someone on the church staff who had seen the bulletin? He'd find out that afternoon.

When time arrived for him to step to the pulpit, he did that in five gliding steps. Barely glancing at his Bible from time to time, he read the story from memory. The changing positions of his head allowed his eyes to include people to the left and center and also to the right. As he was doing this, he saw those in the rear, the middle, and those sitting up front. This was not done consciously, thus not with deliberation. It was done out of habit learned years earlier. How else was he to know when he was in communication? Without this, he could not know when to take another approach to reach his people. He had learned early on.

Everyone knew the story, yet wanted to hear it again. Maude had told him during one of his visits "What an attention getter!" was the way she had described the parable . . . and told by a master story teller.

Mack was too intent on telling the story and its meaning to even think about himself and how it might apply to him.

The eyes of the eighty-seven-year-old woman never left his face. Each time he looked at her, her eyes showed encouragement, and he delivered a sermon as he had not before and sensed from other faces that there was something special going on. He was part of it. He was leading it. It was not pride that he felt. Strangely, it was humility as he observed the effects of the event. For he knew it was not his doing but rather that of the Holy Spirit. A frequent comment at the exit afterward was that, "I've never heard it quite like that before."

⸻

"Mack, I had been told you were a helluva speaker. There's that slip-up again. I'm sorry. Today proved to this cynical old woman who doubts much of what she hears, how wrong she can be. I plan to be back next Sunday. Does that suit you?" It was 3:00 pm and he was visiting.

"Did I ever try to get you to go back to church?" his dark eyes sparkled as if slightly amused by her naughty language, but that was Maude.

"No and if you had, I wouldn't have come," Her eyes projected definite amusement. "You had me figured out."

"Not really, Maude. Just tried to put myself in your place." Obviously teasing, he said, "If I had accused you of backsliding, you'd not have been there. Actually, you were not a backslider. You were protesting."

"So that's why you didn't preach at me."

"No, I wouldn't have ever considered talking to you about it on my first visit, which made me hope you'd invite me back, something you'd not have done if I started pressuring you. You held the upper-hand."

"But I didn't realize that. I kept thinking that one of these Sunday afternoons, the pressure would start. But you were a nice fellow and I hoped it would not come."

"Would you have been there this morning if I had?"

"No, and what a shame that would have been. Missing your sermon would have been another. I needed to act like a woman. Got my hair done. One of the ladies put a dash of make-up on. When I got that old, but always pretty dress on, and got my feet in a new pair of sensibly heeled, yet beautiful shoes . . . I looked at myself in a full-length mirror and you know what, Mack?" He didn't, so she continued, "Doggoned if there wasn't a thing or two that reminded me of what I had been, and still was enough of to stir memories that I had once been a right good-looking woman that could on occasion draw a wolf whistle. As I walked down the aisle of the church, I thought to heck with the pain. I still have a little of what I once had. Right there, as hundreds of pairs of eyes were on me—I didn't look but knew they were—I felt a woman's pride. Not as much as I once did, but enough to relish the small sinfulness of it.

"I'm glad I went. Even without the music and your sermon, it would have been worth it.

"Thank you, Mack. Because you had the smarts or decency to treat me as an equal and not someone to preach at, I went. To again experience a tiny sliver of what it's like to be a woman.

"I have a little money. My three special friends are taking me this coming week to assist me in selecting some new *rags*. How much and how long can I arise in spirit and be just a wee bit of what I'd given up on ever being again? I don't believe the Lord will hold it against me if I look a little less like a totally defective wreck of an old, old woman. Next Sunday, I think I can walk down the aisle of the sanctuary without the walker. One of the ladies has already offered to carry it, in case I suddenly decide I need it."

<hr />

On a Monday evening, after a long day of work, Mack arrived at the nursing home in time to feed Rebecca her supper. The TV he had placed in her room was on with an on-the-scene report of out-of-control fire somewhere. Rebecca's eyes were directed to one side of the TV. Though fully open, he felt they saw nothing. Strange. Something he had not noticed before.

She took all the food he spooned to her mouth while her eyes never wavered from whatever they were fixed on.

He watched her eyes as he got up to turn off the TV. They did not follow. When he walked slowly through her line of vision, her eyes remained fixed on the same spot. He approached her, then waved his hand quickly across her line of vision no more than four inches away from her face. Her blinking reflex was gone.

Oh, Lord, she no longer sees, not even a hand quickly fanning across her face. Has the vision center in the rear of her brain now been destroyed? Or is it in the lower part of her brain that operates reflexes that has been destroyed? Obviously the brain-destroying disease has suddenly taken away another important function.

Her ability to speak had been somewhat gradual in disappearing, but this was sudden. She either hears or senses when someone enters the room. Always she responds to feeding as if she is aware of the person and what is expected. Always she accepts food and water.

The scientific breakthrough that would make regenerating dead brain cells possible may not become a reality in time to save her now. Nothing of her that has been lost has ever reappeared. All has been a continuing one-way disaster that never pauses for long, if at all.

Is this how Alzheimer's always is? A little more of a loved one disappearing all the time, but going unnoticed until suddenly a big decline hits you right in the face? On an average day, do a 100,000 brain cells die? Or is it several million?

What exactly is it that finally takes the physical life away? Is it aspiration pneumonia as someone mentioned? I've been afraid to ask. After watching the evidence of a dying brain, you don't want to know the final step, and then all sign of life in the body is gone. Just to know I can come here at any hour and touch and see her physical body is a comfort of sorts; it's better than not having her at all. What will I do when I no longer have that? It's unthinkable.

An aide came in to take the tray. "Ma'am, do you know how long she's been like this?"

"You mean her eyes open but seeing nothing at all?" Mack nodded a yes. "The girl I relieved at three told me she first noticed at lunch today. Myself . . . I didn't notice at all yesterday; her eyes followed me when I went to adjust the blinds to keep out the lowering sun. Today she never took her eyes off whatever they were looking at."

"Is this a bad sign?" Mack asked not really wanting a truthful answer.

"Bad? I wouldn't know how to answer that. It's something that happens sometimes."

The girl was uncommonly beautiful. Her skin glowed with the triumph that often accompanies youth and good health. Her name was pinned to her blouse—Amy.

"Amy?"

"Yes, sir?"

"Are you happy?"

"Yes. Very. I love to help the elderly and that's mostly what we have. And people like your wife who need to be cared for, it is a blessing to serve them."

"Is that a lifetime goal?"

"It may be. Can you think of a better one?"

"No, Amy."

"The Lord came to earth to serve. I may train to be an LPN and later an RN. I'm only eighteen. Time to wait on God's will. I'll see."

She left the room. Mack felt a little better. He had just talked with a bit of the future. Not as discouraged about the direction young people were taking as he had so often been of late.

He sat with his wife until nine. He might not have even that for much longer. At eight, Amy returned to get Becky ready for the night. "Give me about five minutes," she said.

He walked down the long hallway and re-entered her room at the point Amy was giving Rebecca a love pat on the cheek. She stayed a couple of minutes.

"Took her for a long walk around four. Even outside for a few minutes."

"Thank you for your thoughtfulness," Mack said.

She smiled, "It's part of the war against bedsores. She never tries to go outside alone."

"You have some patients that do. She used to do that at the mental hospital sometimes."

"One especially. When the alarm sounds, we drop what we're doing like firemen at the fire station when they have an alarm."

Mack stayed 'til a few minutes past nine, realizing he might not have this privilege much longer. No teeth at all, something he'd never get used to. Any physical beauty she would have left, if she could have kept her teeth, was gone. It shouldn't bother him that his once beautiful, delicate-featured sweetheart had been so changed. He recalled a picture of a woman of the Great Depression fleeing the Dust Bowl on foot because the family's old car was broken down some distance behind. Her shoes were run over, worn out. An old dress bagged and sagged over a shapeless body. But somehow she had managed a toothless smile for the camera.

When Mack had seen the picture in a book that the WPA had put together, he broke down and cried. He now was looking at Rebecca, asleep with her mouth open and he recalled that Depression era picture of the poor woman and her five kids in clothes that couldn't last 'til they got to where they were going. There had been a defeated man in patched overalls and a long-sleeved very dirty shirt. An old felt hat warded off some of the desert sunshine. The woman wore an atrocious hat that years earlier might have been her Sunday best.

Mack had never forgotten the picture and never fully recovered from it. And it occurred to him that the picture of his wife at that moment might be as firmly etched into his memory for the future.

A sudden feeling of wanting to go screaming into the night hit him. Instead, he carefully covered Rebecca up to her chin with the sheet, bent over and kissed her on the forehead. There was not a flicker of a response.

In a state of deep melancholy and sadness, he started home to leftovers from the night before. Why hadn't he put them in the garbage so he could eat at a restaurant that stayed open 'til midnight?

Common sense won out. He stopped at the restaurant and had sirloin steak, medium with baked Idaho, and garden salad with Italian dressing. It was a night of wee miracles. The salad was crisp, and so were the crackers. The steak was perfectly cooked and he could see and smell that sauce could not improve it. The potato had an inside that was fresh, not stained from a long wait inside it's aluminum jacket following baking. French bread that was warm enough to soften butter. He'd rather have yeast rolls that still remembered the oven's heat, but he could forgive the kitchen; after all the hour was late. And they did have fresh decaf.

He had ordered a comfort meal and it turned out to be up to its task. Momentarily he felt shame. There were people who had a helpless loved one on a road to death and no money for nursing home care and probably no money for something special to cook for supper.

When he had finished, there was nothing left on his salad bowl or bread plate. The Idaho's peeling was gone along with the inside. One sliver of fat had been trimmed and left from the steak.

There was no horse apple cobbler as he had enjoyed on his way home from Gatlinburg months before. But they did have pecan pie, not right out of the fridge, for some thoughtful person had kept it warm.

What a fickle man I am! Completely down in the dumps. Inconsistent with my mood, I let the material world of delightful food lift me up. If only it will last 'til I can get home and in bed and sleep takes over my life until six in the morning.

On Thursday night around eight, Maude called him to tell him she had driven down to see Rebecca.

Surprised, he exclaimed, "You drove!"

"In my '57 Chevy Bel Air two-door hard top. Most beautiful car I ever saw when it was brand new and still is. Had power steering installed a few years ago. Rarely drove it the last couple of years. One of my friends drove.

"Your sweet wife doesn't respond much. She did let me feed her lunch. What I called you about was to go take a break down on the coast. The beach bunnies you told me about trying to avoid aren't likely to be out after this cold snap we are having. When is the first chance you might be able to go?"

"Thursday next week. Working Monday and Tuesday now for Lowell. Any special reason you think I should go so soon.

"Just a feeling I have." She had talked to an LPN who had suggested that the husband might be coming up on very hard times soon.

"I've decided to be getting out more, Mack. I live with pain. But staying at home all the time, I live with it whether I'm out or not, and it's no worse after light activity.

"Thanks."

"For what, Maude?"

"For not trying to talk me into going to church. My stubborn streak would have kept me staying at home if you had, as I've told you before. And now I get out on other occasions too, and I'm enjoying it.

Out of a different kind of unease than usual, he made the decision to take Maude's advice. The feeling that a breakthrough could happen anytime making it possible to treat a brain that had atrophied, now seemed like total denial. Nothing except wishful thinking could create such hope. Why don't I get smart and look at things squarely in the face?

Thursday morning at eight, he was on his way south. Running away? Of course I am. There are times when it is the only thing that helps.

Pavement coming harmlessly at me. Utility poles flashing by. They are a reality that I can experience as they fill my consciousness, crowding out the reality of what I flee from for a few hours. For a time, Rebecca's illness is left behind. The ocean calls and I answer. How different from other places it is. Hills and mountains just stand there. The ocean is always doing something—things you don't expect, likely as not.

On the beach that afternoon, he sat and let the breaking of large swells thunder almost at his feet. Nothing else was heard except the occasional scream of a gull cutting through the ocean's thundering.

Somewhere far out at sea, possibly near the Yucatan, an atmospheric disturbance brought the ocean to life, creating swell after swell to visit a coast hundreds of miles away. Each swell as it neared the coast piled water on itself higher and higher until it could no longer stand. And then in a torrent of physical excitement, it came curling and crashing forward.

In an altered state of consciousness, he gave himself to the ocean. And for a time, it became all there was. Maybe it was an hour, maybe it was two; he had no watch to mark time and disturb the spell that had been cast. This was what he came for. His watch was in the glove box of his pickup by design. His fascination by the ever-present frolicking of the ocean was not distracted by the turning of his wrist to get a look at the time.

Do the winds spiral at some point far out at sea sending their impetus equally in all directions? He imagined that to be how it was in that distant place, but that was of little importance. The beach, the crashing swells, the screening of the sun by a heavy blanket of cloud, and the gentle onshore breeze on his face were realities exceeding what he had expected. And for a time, that was enough. How much time? He had no notion of that, but it was time to walk.

Barefoot in pants cut off just above the knees and the top from a heavy sweatsuit, he felt prepared to allow his feet and lower legs to flirt with the incoming remnants of the great swells. Not nearly as quick afoot as the sandpipers, he tried to imitate them as they darted in and out.

The water was late-winter cold. Soon he was up to his knees in a surprisingly active swell that reached sugar-white sand that had almost completely dried. The raw edges of his pants lost dryness. He shouted with the excitement of it. Had he been a kid, he would have joined the gulls in a high-pitched squeal. What a fool he was! A man past thirty pretending he was twenty-five years younger.

The ocean does things to me that nothing else can accomplish in spite of the fact that my wife is as she is. Maybe I should be back there sitting with her when she can no longer talk, when her eyes no longer show awareness. In ways of great importance, she is gone, not to return. Back there, I could not accept that to the point of putting into words. But Maude, in her eighty-eight year old wisdom, wanted me to come here where maybe I could put false hope and denial aside long enough to put what was obvious to her in words of my own. Will denial ever set in again? In that environment, it probably will. That is Mack Baldwin, preacher, who is probably as weak as any member of his church congregation. But for right now, I'm going to live a bit with what the Lord has given me for an afternoon of relief.

He and the sandpipers and an occasional gull on the widening and then narrowing beach. He saw it coming and clambered to higher ground with all speed. But not fast enough, and the lower six inches of his cut-offs were soaked. He laughed and hurried on, staying higher up. But the dry sand provided almost zero traction, and it was to the wetness of the waves that he returned, prepared to be more vigilant in observing any particularly big one as it stood high and began its curl. But it is the big ones that add to the wild beauty of an ocean in turbulence as it comes racing at me from some point far, far out. Trying to catch me by surprise and occasionally I anticipate the jolly ocean's game as it plays with me. But I don't always want to come out a winner. So like the game of hide-and-seek when I was a child, being caught sometimes gave greater pleasure than remaining hidden until the seeker gave up and walked away. Crazy as a kid and crazy as a man; something to be said for being either way.

A long time later, he was walking with temporarily forgotten ease across blacktop to his truck. Seafood awaited him at some nearby restaurant. He went as he was, damp almost to the point where his pant legs joined. Soon he located a restaurant that did not require that shoes be worn. An occasional one did, including a shirt.

The next day was eleven hours to let his fancy of the moment guide him. Driving was what he wanted first. Breakfast could be out on the road somewhere. Thirty minutes later, he had just placed an order for bacon, scrambled eggs, grits, and toast. When it was served, he realized it was good but paid little attention to the meal. No road map to tell him where he had already been headed. Decisions would come when he came to intersections or forks of the road.

The sun told him a short while later that he was heading east. The clouds of yesterday had been blown off somewhere to the north, he guessed. Or maybe they had set sail to some point way out to sea.

Driving felt good. When had it not? On this day of absolute freedom, bridges appeared and were crossed as he glanced at a black water creek that had cut its way through white sand, cypress trees, and live oaks draped in Spanish moss. A world that was in complete contrast to the world of hills back home.

A sign at a crossroad proclaimed that to the right was Gulf Islands National Seashore, an exciting name, and the imagery that poured through his excited heart and soul drew him as few things ever had.

It was a highway to an earthly heaven on which he was soon driving. No subdivisions, no sign of commercial activity. Except for the pavement, it looked just as it had five centuries earlier. No doubt, the massive dune that only allowed an occasional glimpse of the ocean must have been relentlessly shaped and reshaped as storms of the ages worked and exercised their will on a coast that could only wait.

An access point to the beach appeared where parking was available. A protective board walk went up and over the dune. Soon he was up and over, walking a flawlessly clean beach.

He had stopped at a picnic table to apply a thick, gooey sunscreen to exposed skin. The fellow who had sold him the stuff told him water didn't remove it—paper towels would be of great help before he had a really warm shower with plenty of soap. It was the same formula that survivors in life rafts used during World War II, or so the fellow had told Mack. A cloth hat with a three-inch brim topped his six foot frame.

The ocean was as restless as it had been the day before. As the crashing waves went over feet and lower legs, he appreciated what the fellow assured him about the difficulty of washing off the fragrant screen. He had plenty left in the tube to reapply if he thought he needed to.

Occasionally, he encountered another person enjoying a beach that could not be believed unless it was experienced first-hand.

He met pelicans on the wing at high speed—thirty or forty miles per hour. He stopped and turned to follow with his eyes. On the wing, they were as handsome as any, but when seen on a pier as he had seen them yesterday, they were homely, comical, and highly entertaining when they walked.

Tomorrow would be different, the time of freedom gone and driving home to sadness because of what he would be driving back to. Never-ending grief. His wife was there but did not live. She wasn't there nor was she anywhere. Her body lived, but Rebecca was gone and had been for so many years.

Sandpipers scurried as water wrapped around his calves. The scene ahead was the same as it was thousands of years ago. People arrived and later on are no more on earth but the ocean neither notices their appearance nor is saddened by their passing. Tens of thousands of years from now, the waves will roll on this beach. It will be as we will not on this earth. Yet I do not envy its living on as land masses move an inch a year. All it can do is reflect what wind and water have done.

Man's transient nature is a blessing when he considers that oceans and land go on and on, changing so slowly that the only geological excitement is an occasional volcano or an earthquake. It was a strange feeling to experience such emotion and insights. He knew as never before that he did not want to live as long as a mountain. I've never thought this before and it seems I should have. On this day when I've been enjoying freedom from troubles back home, a new kind of freedom has come and found me. When God decided to make our lives on earth fleeting as compared to the life of Pike's Peak, what wisdom and thoughtfulness on His part. Am I just a little bit crazy to be thinking this way?

He had his watch this day. When he had walked an hour, he turned for the hour hike back to the truck. Then it would be to drive on to an exit point from this place that had the promise of the federal government that it would be preserved as it was this day.

That afternoon, his ramblings took him to a state park that had a forest of what was left of a magnolia plantation that dated back to the early 1800's. In the days of great sailing ships, the wood from the species was of great value in building strong interior parts. It had been in the interest of the federal government that young trees had been planted for the future. But when that future arrived and trees might have been ready, sailing ships were being displaced by steam-powered ones of iron and steel.

Left undisturbed for more than a century and a half in ideal soil and climate, they were giants compared to the ones he frequently saw in people's yards back in hill country. On the trip to the coast, he had occasionally seen them growing wild, but they were not particularly impressive except for foliage; most grew as understory for mature pines. These were the kings of the forest. They rose to be crowns of countless acres, their trunks like the foliage, impressive in size and handsomeness.

Having never seen the like before, he walked slowly along a trail, allowing the essence of peace and tranquility of this most unusual forest to soak in. The memory of it he wanted deeply embedded in his soul.

Three times he met another and swapped impressions of the rare and fine beauty of this wooded trail. Such a place, beyond belief for one who had never visited, was not to be enjoyed hurriedly and left behind. He found a place to sit and did for close to an hour.

But well before sundown and supper time, he was back to his lodging preparing to walk the beach by changing into a warmer jacket than he'd worn that day. He'd see about removing the heavy sunscreen after supper.

Compared to the day before, the ocean had calmed noticeably and could be experienced in a different way. His awareness of each breaker's potential to get him wet did not require as much attention. He could and did enjoy a relative peace and quiet, until for some reason only understood by the ocean, a whopper of a swell came silently and unnoticed until it built up a surprisingly high crest and came crashing down signaling it was going to push high up the beach. But Mack was not caught. He'd made the decision to walk in the soft, dry sand beyond the reach of a rogue swell. It was a slow go but he didn't mind. A time to think of his other life in an atmosphere that only an ocean can create. He was not alone, though no other walked. The ocean was his companion—the rise and fall of its voice constantly making its companionship known.

Rebecca . . . was she soon to be fed her evening meal? Does she feel the pangs of hunger, or does that like most everything else not come any more? I hope she no longer feels anything because if she could, there is not any possibility of pleasure or joy being any part of it. Maybe she is as unaware of everything else as she is of a swiftly moving hand coming close to her eyes.

Until a few days ago, he could hope that a cure for a destroyed brain might come along in time to restores hers. To a depth he had not before, he realized this was not going to happen.

His mind, he realized later, had at that point shut down. He walked without awareness of anything in his mind. The sounds of the ocean and sea birds no longer registered. Later he would turn to the west and see that the sun was touching the ocean. How long had it been? An hour or two? Where had he been when the passing of time had gone unnoticed? Wherever it was, it had been a place where the pain of having lost what he'd never really had did not crush his heart.

Once the sun touched the ocean, it all too quickly fled from sight, leaving a heart touched with melancholy, even a trace of irrational fear that it would not reappear on the morrow. Man had experienced these emotions as thousands of years passed by, and yet there remained some of what had been indelibly imprinted long ago. Nowhere was the passing of day into the night more beautiful nor more sweetly sad than when it sank into the ocean—so different than on land.

Mack hurried to his motel and was scouring sun screen from his skin with paper towels until he was suitably clean for a warm shower with lots of soap.

In the restaurant, there were plenty of people to chase away loneliness. That everyone else sat with people and he sat at a table alone did nothing to lift his spirits. The times he sat with others, especially at supper, were times enjoyed with inner warmth that knew him not on evenings such as this. Yet, being in a restaurant without a companion where others could be seen and heard, was far better than eating completely alone at home.

For himself, he felt pity. For Rebecca, he felt emotion that went far beyond. There are brief periods when I feel satisfaction and times when I feel joy beyond belief. At home when prayer has not completely lifted the variety of negative emotions I often feel, I can put on a recording of music that a composer penned a century or two ago and mount up on wings like a soaring eagle. And what has Rebecca had compared to the wealth of experiences I enjoy? Oh, God, it is enough to break a heart. People who have health and family, how often they complain but they ought to bury their faces in shame that they apparently don't feel. And I ought to quit such thinking and chase away all awareness, except this platter of the Gulf's finest shrimp, their crispness a delight often dreamed of but seldom realized, while their aroma and flavor overwhelm other senses in ways to be long remembered.

The food didn't completely chase away sadness and loneliness and make him like those he observed in twos, threes, and fours, but it helped. And he thanked God for the presence of others and the cheerful waitress who spread a little sunshine at every table she served.

To stretch out the time he could remain in the restaurant, he ordered a chocolate brownie with vanilla ice cream on the side. There are times when food is almost too delicious to bear. Such a time was this and he waited until there was only one bite left before his thoughts turned to Rebecca and her pureed food. Did she still smell and taste food? But it would not help her if he left the last of the desert on the dish, no more than it would help her if he ceased making any effort to live. Lord, is it wrong if I go on with life in the limited manner I can? Should I always grieve because my wife cannot live? Please make it up to her when she is in Heaven. Or is she already there, her soul having left her body when her brain ceased to function, except to the extent of keeping her senseless body alive? Unless by some miracle, she can become well, I hope she has already left.

As Mack drove home the next day, it came to him that the trip had been far from naught. The final step in accepting the inevitability of the course of Alzheimer's disease had been taken. There would likely be other steps, but he couldn't believe that there were.

Half way home, his mood had shifted again. Hope never dies as long as the heart still beats and the lungs continue to draw in air. At home he had a collection of news reports of people who even ceased breathing and without signs of a beating heart who had been brought back to life. Often these patients reported they had been to a place of peace and light, and later what seemed a normal life except for having lost the fear of dying that had always made happy days a little less than they might have been.

Baseball, an unlikely word to suddenly pop into his mind, but it did from having watched a game back in July. The local news had been finished when he switched channels to a game that was almost over. The Tigers were ahead of the Red Sox by a score of 9 to 1. Occasionally he watched a game. He liked the Sox for some reason he could not put into words. They were playing at home. It was the bottom of the ninth and they were at bat with two outs showing on the scoreboard. His team had lost, and he might just as well have turned off the TV but he didn't though he realized just one pop fly and the game was over.

The pitcher's fast ball was fast but his control was shaky. He walked the batter. The fans that had not left gave a half-hearted cheer. The next batter fell behind, one ball and two strikes and then was hit by the next pitch and trotted down to first base. The next batter sent back a fast ball high over the right field fence. At this point, Mack decided to see the game through. With the score at nine to four, there's no telling how the game might end.

The Tigers' manager made trips to the pitcher's mound. Mack's heart was now into the game because though the Sox didn't look sharp doing it, they whittled down the margin to three runs. Another change in pitchers and his warmup pitches were over.

The next batter hit a weak blow that barely cleared the short-stop's glove. The pitcher walked the next batter. The manager came to the pitcher's mound and chatted briefly, then left the pitcher in the game.

"The tying run is at the plate," the excited voice of the TV announcer made clear to fans who had stayed with the game. Inwardly, Mack smiled believing that only diehard fans were likely to be staying with this game. Ordinarily, he would have turned it off as soon as he saw the score. At this point he said aloud, as he got up to get a soda from the fridge, "In this game, you never know."

When he returned to his chair, a new pitcher was taking warmup pitches. "This fellow is really throwing smoke," the announcer said, referring to fast balls that were close to speeds of 100 mph.

Then the "winning run" as the announcer said, "had stepped to the plate."

Mack looked at his watch . . . 11:06 pm. Late and he planned to be up at six. He wished he'd never started watching, but decided he'd invested too much time in it to leave it now.

The pitcher "blew two fast balls by the hitter," for strikes according to the announcer. Then missed the outside corner with a change-up. A fast ball into the dirt that the catcher managed to stop. The next fast ball almost hit the batter. "The count is now 3 and 2; the next pitch could be it for the Red Sox. And here it comes. And there it goes over the left field wall by a mile! The Sox win! It's unbelievable!" Mack pushed the off button. It was the closest thing to a miracle win that he had ever seen. Once he had heard a wag say, "It ain't over 'til it's over," and though that had been said in another context, it was really possible in baseball.

And on his way back from the coast, he was thinking that in life, it's not over 'til it's over. Does this mean that I'm deciding to reenter a state of denial? Maybe, but maybe a miracle will come along. Events beyond science's ability to explain do happen. Except for that one slip-up, I've lived about as well as a man could. Rebecca, before her illness was as close to being an angel as a human can be. Dear God, don't we need a break?

And on that more promising state of mind, he preached the next day and worked the following week. And as fall became winter and winter brightened into daffodils and then came the greening of the ridges all around, he held on to that hope. Rebecca had a roommate now who loved to talk and watch television.

There had been no sign of further change in Rebecca. Often he visited her at the same time her parents did, and together in the nursing homes parlor, they talked. If mother and father were without hope, they concealed it completely.

On one occasion, Anne Allen spoke of seeing the earliest signs of illness the week before the wedding. "At times, I have wondered if I should have talked the two of you out of getting married until it could be determined if she was becoming seriously ill or was suffering from premarital stress."

Lee offered his view on the subject. "I saw the early signs too, but I didn't believe it was serious. Maybe a little counseling was needed. Was I wrong in not pushing Anne to get it postponed until we could see about it? Were we wrong in allowing the wedding to go on as planned? Were we fair to you? We've discussed this a thousand times."

"How could you have gone about it? Could you have said to me, 'Mack, Rebecca may be developing a serious mental illness. Let's postpone the wedding six months until it's been determined if she is seriously ill. You don't deserve to have the responsibility of caring for our sick daughter.'"

"Mack, can you see how we feel because we did nothing?" Anne asked.

"What would I have done if we postponed it? My church family knew of the wedding. Most were planning to be there. Should I have told them at the preceding Wednesday night service that the wedding was off for a few months because she had what could be early symptoms of a serious mental illness? Would I have told them if she was ill that there would be no wedding? There is no way I would have said, 'I'm bailing out.'"

They decided to continue the conversation on the east side of the nursing home, on a shaded porch that had comfortable outdoor furniture. A balmy day. When they had taken seats, they faced a woodland hinting of the greening of spring. Songbirds were active, their trilling voices from near and far. A most perfect day in the most perfect time of year. But this was little noticed by the troubled trio, beyond thinking how is it the world goes on free of troubles while we go through an endless hell. Lee expressed this thought aloud setting the stage for the continuation of the conversation.

"And we should have had this conversation with you many years ago, Mack," he said. "We could have postponed the marriage and later postponed it again. When the doctor's diagnosis obviously was correct, we could have let it be known that Rebecca's health made it necessary to postpone until she improved. In time the seriousness of her illness would have become generally known."

"But I loved her. I'd have wanted to do the right thing. It would have broken my heart. It would have been like I was breaking off with her because she was sick."

Anne spoke directly to Mack, "Hasn't this broken your heart a thousand times? It has ours.

"For you, it might have been one big episode of grief when you saw she wasn't going to come out of it. Before I married Lee, there had been another I had fallen madly in love with. It didn't work out. He tried to make the breaking off as easy as possible for me. It was his idea that we weren't for each other. No girl has ever cried more tears on the shoulders of people who would allow her to. After a few months of living in a state of feeling there would never be another man in my life, Lee asked me out. Before long I was thanking God that the other had lost interest in making me his wife. Actually he had never gotten as far as suggesting marriage.

"No, you could have recovered. And gone on with your life. Possibly had a couple of kids of school age by now."

"Rebecca was special in ways unique. Mrs. Allen, I doubt that I could have given up on her if we had postponed it a few months."

"But at six months, she wasn't responding to treatment." Anne said. "We could have seen about her and left you free to have a life."

"Yet she could have started at any point thereafter getting better. Had she become ninety percent okay, she would have been a blessing to me.

"Looking at it more than eleven years later, almost twelve actually, I couldn't have done other than I did. You do the things you got to do."

And Lee summed it up, "Character shines through if you have it, and you have it more than any man I know."

"Not always, Mr. Allen." Mack hesitated, clearing his throat three times and then told the story in the nicest way possible of the young widow and their sin, bearing down hard on himself. "The only time I've been unfaithful to Rebecca."

"And you felt terrible because of what you did," Lee told him.

"And begged God a thousand times to forgive me."

"Did you feel forgiven?" Lee came back with a question.

"No, never. Maybe I would have except Rebecca was in a mental hospital completely unable to tend to her affairs regarding me. The most defenseless person I knew."

"And in her sick mind, she would not let you consummate your marriage." Anne continued, "Mack, this is a terrible thing to say, but I'm glad, in a strange sort of way that you have had the satisfaction of knowing the fullness of passion. Death can inspire the bereaved to have desire more than it would ordinarily occur. The widow was not an evil woman, just a human one. And you were especially vulnerable at such a time for the same reason."

Lee lightened the conversation a bit with a question. "Now, how would you know about that, dear one?"

"The night after my father's burial fifteen years ago—" She didn't continue. Lee looked puzzled. At that point she went on, "I thought I gave you a night to remember." She turned toward Mack, "And husbands are always complaining. How could *he* forget?" Her eyes sparkled with a hint of mischief.

"Mack, you were forgiven by the Lord a thousand prayers ago. Believe it! It is you only who won't forgive yourself. How unfortunate with all the other problems you have." The blue of his mother-in-law's eyes shimmered now with tears that were kept from spilling over by sheer effort.

For barely short of a full minute, they sat in silence, then Lee said, "Life makes you wonder at times why a God of love, as you preachers refer to Him, would ever have created mankind. I've heard sermon after sermon explaining why He did, not all in complete agreement, but none of them make sense when I consider you and Rebecca."

Barely able to speak in a normal voice and holding back tears at the same time, Mack said, "How blessed I am having you two. Together we'll get through this.

"Like you, Lee, I have often asked the same question. Does He get mad at me for asking? I think not. He must have heard the same question a million times a million times. If He struck each person with a bolt of lightning for asking such, the earth would be littered with human skeletons.

"Thank you, thank you for sharing your thoughts so frankly. All of us, I think, needed this."

"We should have done this years ago, Mack," Anne concluded the conversation.

CHAPTER THIRTEEN

Every day can't be as bad as the worst one was, a lesson that had to be remembered, or else at times, he would lose what little sanity he had. The worst day was when he had carried Rebecca to the state hospital against her will. The second worst was his wedding night. Then, there was the day he learned she could no longer feed herself and Alzheimer's was the most likely culprit.

But there were better kinds of days. The smell of new lumber he measured and cut precisely and nailed it where ceiling met wall with no scarring left behind. Sermons as well reasoned out as the one about the atheist who believed man is a chance happening but that did not free him from the necessity of having a value system. The one about the prodigal son that was delivered the first day Maude showed up.

The evenings he hiked with Old MacDonald. What an inspiring man! And the occasional day when Alf's friend, Ralph, fished with them and the two old men's memories of the Great Depression were brought out, and maybe polished a little.

Music. Jazz revealing the souls of people who had lived hard. Great hymns played and sung in high cathedrals that had spires reaching for the heavens. Folk music that expressed the loneliness and isolation of people who experienced the valleys cut off from the outside world by ridges that had only rare notches to allow contacts with people beyond. And then there was what was loosely called classical music, some of the finest composed by geniuses and some composed by those lacking genius who got it like they wanted it by writing and rewriting and rewriting again.

Hiking that could take one to places never seen by those who remained tethered to their cars. The rhythm of long, quick strides and with it the relief of transferring the energy of negative emotions into his most powerful muscles which could move him on with ease. And he would realize that man had powerful leg muscles that were designed for use and their rhythmic motion gave almost spiritual relief to the most troubled souls.

Oh, there were so many ways to soothe the pain of having a wife who had, for years now, been somewhere in places he had not traveled, and was relieved he had not. Poor Rebecca. So long since he had been able to reach out and know that she knew even one of his feelings toward her. The loss of communication with a loved one was the loss of an important part of your life. Dear Lord, hang in here with me. So many times You and Jesus are the only light to guide me. Except for You, I could not face depression that descends on me with the coming of dark shadows of night. And I ask of myself if I am one worthy of preaching to others about how to conduct their innermost lives. Sometimes I even wonder why You let me live on. Then come memories of earlier that same day when purpose seemed clear and I could believe that my life might be of value to others. So, Lord, what I am one hour may slip away from me at another hour, and any positive feelings I had about myself have flown away. Am I living anything like the life you want me to live? How long must I live with the silence of Your voice? Would it be too big a burden to tell me I'm on the right track, if indeed I am?

What I've believed is Your truth, Your word, I've studied almost endlessly. People by the hundreds I've told it was truth. Alf's wife of almost sixty years, once told me she knows he loves her but "I'll be doggoned if I don't want him to put it in words every ten years or so." Even as he remembered her words, a tiny smile was felt in his heart and he said, "Lord, you are all too much like Old MacDonald, too stingy with words of reassurance. Who am I to criticize God? Because I just did and maybe I ought to leave the ministry. But I have taught that we are to just trust and obey."

Being a preacher is especially burdensome. One time I knew what it was to be a man with a woman . . . that time only for a very few minutes, maybe less than one whole minute. Had I been a layman, the sin would have been big, but because I'm a preacher, it was the size of a mountain. Four people have assured me God long ago forgave, but the problem remains because I haven't forgiven myself. I've tried to understand that I shouldn't blame myself for this any longer. Out of her grief, she called me and to her state of spiritual weakness I yielded. My wife in a hospital and I didn't pause to consider how absolutely lowdown such an act was. Once done, it couldn't be undone. Time and events travel one way and woe unto us if we don't get it right the first time.

It was a really bad hour between 2:30 and 3:30 one morning when sleep had deserted him and didn't want to return. Feeling yucky at five-thirty when he shut off the alarm a half hour early and got out of bed, deciding not to eat cold cereal followed by a glass of orange juice. For the next several weeks on work days, he'd be passing a store that offered water pumps, plastic pipes, and all sorts of supplies to chicken farmers and cattlemen.

But of importance to Mack was the breakfasts that he had heard they served. Premium bacon, Canadian bacon, eggs fried with edges as thin and delicate as lace on a lady's blouse, and centers that ran or stayed still, eggs scrambled to any degree of doneness you wished, sausage fat and juicy or lean that required a bit of pressure to cut, toast, grits, biscuits and coffee that could grow hair on a man's chest. The source of this delightful intelligence? His construction boss.

A wide porch that encircled the entire store displayed Depression Era farm tools and implements hanging from the unpainted exterior—among them a crosscut saw and a one-horse turning plough. His hunger led him through the doorway. Later, if he had time, he would tour the outdoor museum.

In the rear of the store was an area set aside for tables and chairs and several rockers off to one side on a raised platform.

At the tables, eating was in progress. A man Mack did not know signaled him to the table where he and two others were seated sipping coffee while awaiting their order to be served. All other chairs were occupied. "No need for you to stand 'til a table becomes available," the fellow said as Mack was seating himself.

"Thank you. I'm Mack Baldwin." Introductions were made, followed by Mack's comment that it was a most unusual farm supply and hardware store.

"Unusually good one, if you include the food and hospitality."

A waitress came and took Mack's order. He had counted the tables. Only ten and they were rustic like everything else. Barnwood exterior of the building as well as inside walls. Table tops were well-fitted material of the same attractive wood—large place mats of heavy fabric protected the wood from crumbs and light spills.

A sign hanging from the ceiling proclaimed, "A Retreat From Cold Cereal," and in smaller letters underneath had been added "For the Working Man and Loafer." The exterior sign said simply, "Men's Retreat."

The place had atmosphere, relaxed and warm. No one was wolfing down food and hurrying away. Before long, the three men were eating and conversation slowed not a great deal. Mack's Canadian bacon, scrambled eggs, grits and toast arrived. "What a break from corn flakes or oats that don't look like oats, right out of a box with a dash of milk," he said.

One of his companions said, "A break from a wife who belly-aches about having to get out of bed to cook something, She thinks I ought to be content with sugary Wheat Chex and milk poured over them and a cup of instant coffee." A good-natured complaint. "The actual reason I come here two or three times a week is that it's a retreat from the rest of the world."

"A retreat for men. Seldom does a woman join in for breakfast. They have hen parties that I'd not want to be a part of. The fact that they don't sit here for breakfast don't hurt my feelings."

The three men finished breakfast and after wishing Mack the best, went up front to pay. Two new men took seats after introducing themselves.

It was as if no serious problems could be discussed. Real complaints about anything at all did not appear at any time. Mack wondered if there was an informal agreement that the state of the nation and politics were not to be brought up. So far while he had been enjoying a leisurely breakfast, only the most light-hearted sort of things had been spoken of. Maybe everyone was so relieved at being away from what was believed to be the real world, they wouldn't have wanted to bring up anything that would remind them of how it was out there.

Maybe this was a retreat from reality. Perhaps breakfast should always be eaten as if no problems would be faced in the rest of the day. Mack didn't know such a place as this existed except in the fantasy world where all things are possible. If this is fantasy, what does it matter? The only realities that matter are those of the moment. All others are past events or will be in a future that cannot be accurately anticipated. After a fleeting moment for these reflections. Mack's attention rejoined the conversational trivia of the two men at his table.

"This your first visit to the Breakfast Retreat, Mack?" asked one of the men who had introduced himself as Ed three or four minutes earlier.

"Yes, and I made a resolution a few minutes ago that it won't be the last. Until you've been here, there is no way you can believe such a place exists. I was told by a man who sat where you now sit that history wraps around the entire building in the form of old-timey tools and implements.

"Yep, there's two examples of Hoover wagons. Did you ever see one?"

"No, Ed, but I've heard of them. Mule or horse-drawn sleds using whatever heavy lumber a fellow could find to make the runners."

"During the Depression, a farmer didn't go out and buy a wagon if he went back to the old family farm out of desperation after losing his job. My daddy had one. Had a plank floor and side-boards. Hauled corn to the crib in the fall as well as fertilizer to the field in the spring."

Another, Frank, spoke up. "I was a kid during those years and saw hard times as if they were regular times. Clothes might be patched, but we had plenty to eat and we made our toys. Enjoyed living, but papa and mamma worried plenty, I bet."

When the two men had finished eating, they invited Mack to share a table with them another morning and afterwards a checker game where the rocking chairs were up on the low platform. There he visited the same morning.

Mack took an empty rocker. After introductions were exchanged, he remained silent, not wishing to break into the teasing and self put-downs. That kind of conversation was going on over both checkerboards. The youngest of the four would have been at least seventy. These men had levels of skill—of seeing ahead—unlike any he had ever witnessed! When one game ended, he stood, "Gentlemen, I thought I was petty good at the game. Do y'all do this pretty often?"

"Most mornings," said the fellow who had just won.

"Could I return some day soon and learn something by watching you fellows who know how to set and close traps?"

The same man, who had just spoken said, "It's seldom that I can outfox any of these men. Mostly, I get clobbered. But you are welcome to play one of us." And Mack knew he was far from ready, but he liked the manner of these men—slow talking in soft tones, obviously enjoying the game.

It was time to pay up and leave for work. Behind the cashier prominently displayed was their health rating—ninety-eight, and he would have guessed it would have been around eighty. He complimented the rating. She thanked him and added, "We try. Our dishes and utensils are washed in very hot water and our fridge is kept just above freezing. The inspector will low-rate you in a second if you don't get those two right."

"This place has atmosphere unlike any I've ever experienced before."

At work he told his co-workers about the Retreat. They had all enjoyed breakfast there several times. "But you hadn't told me about such a place," Mack complained.

"Will try to do better in the future," one of them promised with a smile on his face and in his voice.

Off and on during the day, Mack thought about the store and restaurant. It would be another compartment in his life, another pigeonhole in the roll-top desk of his mind, making the tragedy of Rebecca's illness a little more bearable. One other facet of his life had now been cut, and it could now be enjoyed along with the others. Alf had seen the need years earlier for having additional things in his life so that not such a large share would be occupied with worry and grief over Rebecca's condition. He taught me to live with what I can have instead of barely living for what I can't have. He taught me that I had done and was doing all I can for her. Accepting that Rebecca is beyond help, other than the kind she receives in an institution, is something I've only recently been able to do. At times, I still have hope of a miracle. But in more rational moments, I know that her parents and I are just awaiting her taking her last breath. But the irrational moments keep coming back and hope has not died completely. Internally, my mind is a battlefield between what I know is false hope and the hope that lives despite facts that are obvious to all of us—doctors, nurses, her mother and father, and now to me.

I go on with life, most of the time finding joy and satisfaction with so much of it. How unfair that she has nothing except a body, that her mind long ago began leaving. Is she even just a little aware of me? Her eyes no longer follow what I do when I visit. And I know she is even further gone than I could have believed possible. How can she be so unaware and yet her body lives on? How much of her brain is left?

Did her spirit, her very soul leave her months ago, and is she already in Heaven? If that is so, why did God not take her body too? Lord, how can You . . . why do You keep her body alive when she's no longer alive? Why, Lord, do you do things that in my wildest imaginings I can make no sense of?

I've tried so hard to understand the things You do. Not once have I heard Your voice. Even before my big sin, I'd never heard You. How long do You expect me to go on as my wife dies and all I have are the small compartments of life that prevent me from sinking completely into the quicksands of despair. I don't fear that You'll take my life for blasphemy, but that You won't.

I complain that You don't speak to me. Knowing myself like I do, if You did say something to me in the English language, I'd panic because I'd think I was mentally ill. Lord, I bet You get tired of my bellyaching. I have my compartments where I can find satisfaction. Don't some people have even less? And he felt ashamed of himself for there were some who had a loved one who was in the advanced stages of dementia and were in dire financial straits and could not afford a nursing home.

I should be taking care of her, but I would have no income. Only the retired can be full-time caregivers, and maybe the rich.

The Sunday following his complaining to God, he preached a sermon on passive virtues that started with mention of some active ones that there is general agreement on. "His word is his bond. She is a hard worker. He takes pride in his craftsmanship. She gives a full day's work. Ambitious, but honest. Outgoing and friendly. There are more, but today is passive virtues turn.

"Without them, no nation can be called civilized. The flames of hatred will be continuously fanned. Warfare will be continuous except for breaks to prepare for further war. Thus, he preached from Jesus' sermon on the mount and the necessity of passive virtues if culture was not to shatter.

CHAPTER FOURTEEN

Hours ahead, the ocean awaited him. Never was it the same as the time before. Always changing even as he walked or sat and watched, flowing with its moods, letting it take him where it wished, never failing him, always able to surprise. Its call was with him; his right foot on the gas pedal impatient with him for not letting it have its way.

The ocean did not disappoint; it never did. He was standing after a thirty-minute walk, feet and lower legs experiencing splashes of dying breakers and the legs of his cut-offs flirting with a good wetting as the really massive ones found ways to steal in on him with little warning. The child that yet remained in the man sometimes squealed with glee and the man laughed at the fun the child was having.

But now seated, he turned his attention to the place where sky met the ocean. Between that and the shore, he saw for the first time ever, dolphins at play or feeding; he was unable to decide. Could they see him as clearly as he saw them and if they did, were they trying to entertain him? Were they having fun and wanting to share it with him? That they were smart had been proven over and over. Do dolphins try to communicate with us? Do they remember us when they are out cruising the seas?

For just a few minutes, would I want my mind to trade places with one of theirs and know what it is to be one of them? And bring back the memory and keep it as I return to what I already am?

The dolphins were soon gone. Mack still remained cast in the spell they had woven over him. As that slowly faded, his fantasies again became in the ocean's power again. He imagined himself a large chunk of wood floating on the surface of the east-bound current that had already traveled off the coasts of three other states and would visit the Florida Keys picking up warmth as it traveled on to just off the east coast of Florida. Subject to changing wind directions along the way, but now always being carried to the north by the river flowing in the ocean. And then at Cape Hatteras, the flow to Europe would begin. The winter storms of the North Atlantic would toy with the block of wood, but the river of water in the greater ocean would continue on. Landfall in one of the scenic masterpieces of Norway. Why not a quiet fjord when the long ocean journey was completed?

When the fantasy was over, he felt it was time to walk again. High clouds had moved in from the south, dimming the sun that had been flashing off swells and snow-white sand. He welcomed the change that eased the squinting of his eyes.

His thoughts of himself were now gone. Scurrying sandpipers. Spent breakers chasing him and the swirling screaming gulls were much in his awareness. Sea oats bending from the stiff breeze. The ocean itself as far as eyes could reach. And beyond where horizon made all a mystery, there could be ships or an occasional whale coming to the surface. And the things beyond view were whatever his imagination wished them to be.

Briefly, he thought of back home, but the magic of the ocean rushed that back to where it ought to be for this period of relaxation.

He was quite capable of being a number of things and the one that loved salt air and ever-crashing waves was one of his favorites. Always changing, always occupying different kinds of awareness, he could count on enjoying the man on the beach.

Occasionally, he saw another person, and once stopped to talk with a man walking in the opposite direction. They exchanged a few comments on their favorite things about the ocean experience. "It never disappoints," the man said, "except once in July when the air was so calm."

Thinking of nothing and walking only a little, he allowed the ocean to lift him from himself and become a part of its lively self. With rhythmic excitement, the water rushed in and upwards and little birds rushed back to just-exposed sand to examine it for food that had just arrived and then out of the way of the next on-rushing surge. How many thousands of years had passed since their first numbers had been conditioned to the incoming splash and the out-going rush. The small birds lived in a world he could only see the bold outlines of, but they survived in another that he could only guess the existence of.

He recalled his pain of the night before, of his doubts about God that at times ran deep, but this came and was gone as quickly and easily as it arrived. His doubt about being able to put together the sermon he wanted to deliver on Sunday came and went with the brevity of a visit by an incoming swell.

Rebecca and her illness came but that was something he'd get through; it was something else he was well-practiced in dealing with. In its place was the endless joy of being with the ocean. He thought of the people who came and never came back and wondered how they survived. He remembered how he stressed in sermons that the people could always take their cares and burdens to the Lord in prayer. What kind of looks would he receive if he instead, said to his congregation, just take it to the ocean, you might not have to take it to God in prayer.

Was it an insult to God that he even allowed such a thought to come fleetingly through his consciousness? Maybe he was wrong, and most preachers would say that sort of thing was a big no-no. Anyway, for this afternoon and the next day as well as Saturday morning, the ocean would be there for him, taking away some of the hurt of Rebecca's illness.

No small part of the reward for coming was the seafood. He lengthened his stride as he started the return to his motel, a quick shower, and then off to one of the fine seafood restaurants.

Pleasantly tired as he sat in a booth awaiting the preparation of his platter of five of his favorites. He sipped black coffee and let the restaurant's low-voiced background music take him along as it pleased. He had phoned the nursing home before coming; there was no change in her condition. For the time that he waited for his food, he thought of Rebecca. Whatever the next year brought, he felt he could endure and get through. His mini-vacation was succeeding to that extent.

His food that evening was almost enough to make the trip worthwhile. As the delightful food was being eaten, he turned his thoughts to his wife once again, and as usual when enjoying anything, he felt sad that he could and did find pleasure while his wife was unable to live in any way that mattered. Crispy crab cake . . . he'd never eaten a better one. What would his delight be if he had a completely healthy wife sitting across the table from him? There had only been one meal together as man and wife before he knew of her illness. What might have been . . . but it hadn't. Countless times he experienced this feeling of sadness that she could not know the satisfactions that life can offer, and he had known it so many times that the hurt had lost much of its ability to pierce his heart. He turned his attention to fried shrimp and the surges of pleasure flowed. Was any other food better?

If the joys of eating was muted by his sadness, then what could this food's delight level be? But perhaps its deliciousness was intensified as a compensation for what he missed as husband for a wife first struck down by non-responsive schizophrenia and later a fatal form of dementia added to her burden. In his thinking before this night, he had seldom thought of the second illness as fatal. Perhaps it was an afternoon on the beach and such a scrumptious meal that made possible the taking of one more small step toward accepting the horror of its inevitability. Lord, give the strength I must have.

Two more delicacies awaited him; the sight appealed to his robust appetite and the grouper's turn came with its perfection.

Because he wanted human company so badly, he ordered dessert—pecan pie of course. It would give time and a reason to stay another twenty or thirty minutes in the warmth of others' conversations. He didn't really try to understand what was being said, though he did catch a little of it, but the presence and voices of others was especially rewarding with even more importance than the pecan pie which was an exceptional dessert. On his way down, he had driven through large pecan groves. Likely, this pie was made with new-crop nuts from that grove adding something extra to the flavor.

A man who had eaten alone stopped beside his table . . . a fellow who appeared to be on the other side of fifty. "How does it go?" he asked.

"Better now that I've the company of this pie. Won't you join me in dessert?"

The man hesitated briefly, then accepted the invitation. There was about him an air of a fellow who was depressed. A rather handsome man, though somewhat small. Light blue eyes, hair pretty far along the route to becoming gray. A trim mustache.

When coffee and dessert, the same as Mack's, had been served, he took a sip of coffee and then said without introducing himself, "I've a sad story to tell and you look like you have time and patience to listen to it."

"Time, this evening I have plenty of."

"My wife had been visiting her sister who lived about fifty miles away. Yesterday I received a letter from a lawyer, the upper left corner of the thick envelope said." He paused unable to go on right then.

Mack waited as an idea started to take shape in his mind. A moment later he was pretty sure what was in the envelope, but he didn't crowd the man. He might need another minute to get the story ready to tell. He felt for the fellow and the bad news that had arrived by mail.

"It couldn't have been anything good. A letter from a lawyer you never heard of can't contain good news." He paused again.

"And . . ." Mack prompted, feeling the man was ready to go on.

"It was a claim for a divorce. And I had never had as much as a faint inkling that she was *that* unhappy with our marriage. Seldom did we have a spat—about anything. She had taken a job in a real estate office a year and a half ago. Our three kids are now out on their own. She wanted to work and have money of her own was the way she had put it. I didn't object. I don't understand it, where she's coming from. One day the marriage is okay and then three days later, what you thought is ideal you find out is busted. How long has she wanted out? How long has it all been a pretense that everything was fine? How long have I been a fool as she was—?" In tears now, the man stopped and took off his glasses and wiped his eyes as he was having difficulty holding back a full-blown case of sobbing.

Mack had gained experience enough in his limited role as church counselor to remain silent. There was nothing he could say to reassure the man. Damage had been done that is not subject to repair. He was willing to listen, making an effort to understand.

The waitress came to the table, saw, and eased away without interrupting.

"Even if she changed her mind, that wouldn't stop the hurt. If she came back and asked forgiveness, that wouldn't reestablish trust. The marriage is permanently busted. Can you see that?"

"Yes." Mack was wondering who the other man was. It did not occur to him, there might not be another. "Is your wife a pretty woman?"

"Beautiful until this happened." He took out his wallet and removed a picture.

Mack saw she was very pretty. "This was made—?"

"Only last year. After she started working, she bought lots of pretty outfits and started going to an excellent hair stylist who referred her to a store that had a couple of women who advised and assisted with makeup.

"I hired a private detective to find out if there has been another man in her life. Did that this morning after seeing an attorney who advised it. There have been times the last few months when she was out on weekends showing houses."

A few minutes later, the man was back to talking about the impossibility of the marriage ever being restored. "I don't know that I'd ever want her back, even if she came back begging."

"Do you think she might return, begging? I wish she would so I could tell her I'd lost interest and could watch her cry like I've been doing.

"You know why I came down here?"

Mack thought he did, but thought it wise to let the man explain it.

"There is something special about seeing and hearing the ocean. It is always changing in mood. Watch it and for a while it takes you away from real life and its problems. It can occupy all your attention and for the time being, all else becomes a little less important, less pressing. And what it doesn't do, the activities of the birds can. Watch a pelican walk a pier and it's hard not to be amused; I saw one late today trying to panhandle a fisherman for some of his bait, and I'll be doggoned if the man didn't reach in his bucket and drop him some— the only thing I've seen to cause a smile since that letter arrived.

"What do you think I should do?"

"Let your lawyer advise you. He . . . is it a man?" The fellow nodded his head. Mack continued, "Your best interests will be his main interest. There are times we have to put things in the hands of someone else.

"Years ago, I put my wife in the state mental hospital in the hands of someone who knew more than I did about helping her."

The man asked, "Did they heal her?"

"No, but through no fault of theirs. There is no complete cure and she responded less than others might to the same treatment.

"Now, she's in the stage of advanced Alzheimer's disease."

"No cure at all for that, is there?"

"It may take years, but it's a terminal disease. She's in a nursing home until . . .?"

"My God, and I felt no one else had problems of such magnitude as I have."

"I've had twelve years to make some sort of adjustment."

And the stranger, who was no longer a stranger said, "You still haven't adjusted?"

"There are times you think you have and then it comes back to the fact that you realize you have not. In a rational moment, I sometimes think it would be a blessing if she passed on, for her and for me." He paused.

"You could get on with your life if she did."

"Probably, and that bothers me. Do I want her to die so that I might live? What a terrible thing to wish for. I don't know that I wish for it, but I might and that possibility becomes another burden. I don't pray that God forgive me for a sin I don't know if I committed."

Mack saw understanding in the man's expression, "If you wanted her to die, you'd feel you had sinned, because you had felt that way so that you might have a chance at happiness. You have a finely tuned conscience. Are you a minister?"

"Yes," but Mack did not introduce himself beyond that. "I come to the ocean two or three times a year. Always it does something good for me. It helps me put my problems and my life in perspective. I don't know why or how, but I feel a bit less self-centered—a tiny bit of the cosmos. After I have been gone a thousand years, the swells will still become waves that crowd up on the shallows before curling over, and come racing up the beach.

"What a strange evening. You tell me of your problem and I come back with my own story, some of it I've never told before, a bit of it I've never thought before.

"As for you, pray to God that He will help you with your predicament. There comes a time in the lives of all, I guess, when they'd better pray for themselves. Pray for strength and ask Jesus to help you bear up."

They paid for their meals and walked out to the beach. The moon had just risen and showed itself briefly through a gap in the clouds. In silence they walked. As waves broke, they phosphoresced, adding a ghostly glow to their surroundings and themselves just for a few seconds and the next incoming wave repeated the process.

It was a strange meeting of two men, each somewhat better for it. After fifteen or twenty minutes without another word spoken, they parted on the beach and went to their respective motels. Later there would be times Mack would wonder if it had really happened. He had no name to help him remember the experience. If names had been exchanged, neither would have been as free to tell what was on their hearts.

It was to be somewhat like the long tubes of curling waves phosphorescing briefly, leaving you wondering where they had gone. It was there and then it wasn't! The man had been in the restaurant and they had bared their souls and understanding was apparent. Was it real? He sorta wished he's asked for a name and then was glad that he hadn't. He would never know how the man's life turned out, but expected the fellow to work it out if he was not too stubborn to go to God with it.

He took another turn of walking the beach before going to bed. Phosphorescing waves never ceased to attract him. The moon was fully obscured by clouds now. The walk was not for exercise nor was it for concentrating on the sights and sounds of the ocean. It was a time and place to consider himself. The ocean's presence and the white sand dunes rising above him were a good background for thinking. He knew more of himself than he had a couple of hours earlier. Accepting the inevitable about Rebecca was a little closer. For years, most of his life had not centered around her, yet his con- science had. When the time came, he would be able to meet it and cope.

It was a marriage that had not been a marriage. Not even for one night. Despair had been with him from the beginning and in all the years had not let up on him. I have found the ways of living with little . . . even with no hope that we'd ever have a marriage. The stranger who came to my table tonight had a marriage for many years. I hope he can appreciate that, and won't spend his life fearing what his future holds and dwelling on the past.

The only time I experienced one facet of what a marriage could possibly hold, it was a fleeting time of uncontrollable passion and betrayal resulting in countless hours of regret.

And yonder, far out at sea, are lights of a passing ship. Whether large or small, I cannot tell. Does it carry someone—as it passes through the night—with a soul as tortured as mine? What kind of hell do people all over the world carry in their breasts? My heart reaches out to them. If I only knew who they are . . . but people everywhere put on brave faces and hide their fears and aloneness from those they see. For to let others know the secrets of your heart makes you vulnerable to hurt from those who take hellish pleasure from inflicting further hurt.

He had stopped to watch the ship and remained there until it could be seen no more. A strange loneliness settled over him. Quick steps hastened him on now as if that might leave his discomfort behind in the sand.

Tears came, but with their flow came no understanding of why. Maybe it was the sadness of years of accumulation. Maybe it was living without a mate. He doubted he was so different from others who hurt. There were people who told of their terrible misfortunes and how the Lord had lifted them. And Mack wondered if they told the whole story. Did they not have their times of doubt and despair? He wondered.

Early the next day he left for reasons he couldn't understand, visiting Rebecca before finishing the drive home. Her mother was already there.

"Was worried about her in a way different from what I've been before. Took off from work a few minutes early to come. You go ahead and spend some time with her. I'll wait for you in the visitor's center."

Mack sat beside the bed, holding a hand. Though he never received any sort of verbal response, he told her about being on the beach the day before. As usual, she made no response. Her eyes were open, but unseeing, he felt certain. She seemed as she did two days earlier. Gone, but possibly even further gone. Surely, something of her remained. But where? Was there another land . . . another kind of reality filled with images and emotions that we were unable to be aware of?

Anne was awaiting him in a comfortable armchair in a quiet corner of the visitor center. He moved a straight chair close so they could talk without disturbing others.

"Mack, did you notice anything different?"

"No, but I felt a difference." She waited. He continued, "I guess over the past six or eight months, I'd reached the conclusion that her mind, her awareness, was a completely blank slate. She didn't talk because nothing was going on inside her brain, I thought."

"Did anything today change your mind?"

He explained the strange little journey in his own mind about the possibility of a demented person living in another world where our words were totally unsuitable for communicating whatever imagery might exist there.

"We don't know that such a possibility does not exist. Yet I'm of the opinion that very little goes on in her mind."

"Mack, for the past twelve years, I've studied the human brain from every possible article or book. Not the mind, but the actual physical organ itself. By sometime in the teens, the brain has all the cells it is to have. There are excess neurons to act as backups if some die of injury or from poisoning. What happens if the brain receives small doses of neurotoxic substances for decades? Do brain cells die?

"The wife of the dentist who used to do all Rebecca's fillings had not been to church for the past three months. I recently visited her and found her to be taking care of her husband. He didn't require constant care but she had become afraid he would leave the house and wander off to no telling where and not be able to find his way back. He'd done so once and she really had a scare.

"Fourteen months ago he had told her he had reached a point where he couldn't remember what he was to do next in treating a patient. At fifty-eight, he had to sell his practice. They had a nice nest egg, but his memory has continued to worsen. His neurologist told her it was very likely Alzheimer's.

"Mack, she told me this as he sat beside her on the living room sofa. When I tried to get her not to say these things in his presence, she told me his doctor had spoken very frankly about the disease in her husband's presence because 'he won't be able to remember what I'm telling you.'

"Mack, it gave me the strangest feeling, discussing his problem like he wasn't there, like he was already dead."

"Did you tell her about Rebecca's Alzheimer's?"

"She already knew.

"No, Mack, you have been kidding yourself. Her brain is not actively alive in another world. I've seen pictures of brains that looked like walnuts that were badly shriveled inside. You've cracked nuts that had kernels that were well filled out and occasionally you crack one that is faulty, mostly, it's an empty shell."

Tears came into her eyes. "I carried her for the biggest part of a year in my belly and then nursed her for months more. A bond was formed unlike any other kind in human experience. I can't accept what has been happening to her all these years, but I no longer have hope. All you and her father and I have left is waiting for the final end.

"Mack, the time cannot be far when she passes on. She *is* different from what she was a month ago. My feelings are mixed. I lack the cruelty of spirit to want her to continue like she has for years, and it would be something close to evil to want to see it prolonged. Down the hall four doors is a patient whose mind has been gone for months and months. Her life would have ended a week ago except her family wanted to have a feeding tube installed."

"You, not her daddy and I, have the authority to make that kind of decision."

"Mrs. Allen, as I was driving from the coast today, I was considering the possibilities that might have to be faced in a future that was obviously becoming closer. Decisions would have to be faced. I knew of the patient who had a feeding tube installed. Would I want something like that done to me if I were suffering what Rebecca has for a long time? Of course I would not. If possible, these decisions ought to be made in advance. I gather you would not want any extraordinary measures to be taken. They won't be."

Anne expressed relief. "It's been so long, Mack. And pretty hopeless from the beginning. You need an opportunity to have a life. And our family needs an opportunity to get on with ours. She needs to be released so she can go on to Heaven. There are times I have a feeling she did that years ago."

She turned the conversation in another direction. "You are still a young man. I hope that later on, you have an opportunity to marry a woman who wants children. Rebecca probably would have wanted children, but I really never quite understood her. We were not close, yet not distant. She had qualities that I thought almost too good to be true. It was like having an angel living in our house, or like I think that would be.

"I never thought the love between the two of you was realistic. You had her on a pedestal, it seemed to me."

"As she did me. She believed I was also special. Neither of us was realistic about what our relationship was. I can see that now. It was a fantasy. It was a romance that was—"

"Not robust," Anne finished for him. "Between a couple who planned to get married, there ought to be a touch of lust. From the Old Testament, read from the Song of Solomon. Do you ever preach from it? I bet you don't." At this point, she giggled. "You'd be afraid some might be influenced. If you have children, I'll consider them my grandchildren, sort of. Believe me, I hope you have a real marriage next time.

"What has happened to us is enough to question God's fairness. Also to increase our need for Him."

"Thank you for taking time to help me see what too often I've been blind to. You have helped me toward a maturity I have had all too little of. Facing up to life's realities has not been easy for me. I'm beginning to learn from counseling that it's not a rare problem for others.

"I'm to continue talking to my congregation on Sunday about the various traits of the blessed. Say a prayer for me. At the beginning I thought I had it all figured out."

"But now you feel uncertainty creeping back in. Perhaps Jesus was talking about the kinds of people God would like to share Heaven with. He didn't say blessed are the power-hungry and the ambitious or the go-getters. He did not say that the publicity-seekers are blessed. Consider the active virtues he did not say were blessed."

Mack added, "The hard workers, the early risers. I get the idea. And that will be the direction my sermon takes."

⇒‡‡⇐

Three weeks of the new year passed. Then the U.S. Supreme Court announced its decision in the case of Roe vs. Wade.

The Sunday following, Mack brought this up in the first part of his sermon. "It has been called a new direction for the country. Those who claim victory say that abortions will only take place in the first trimester or very early in the second. Those who are opposed say that we are on a *very slippery* slope. They don't think it will stop there.

"A popular physician/novelist a few years ago estimated that over one million abortions a year were already being done, many of them in hospitals by physicians who could face loss of license and prison time.

"Some have likened the decision to the repeal of prohibition. Legally recognizing what was illegally going on because laws prohibiting it weren't working.

"Proponents of legal abortion claimed it would make abortions safer.

"Today, the unborn is not protected by law. A month ago, there wasn't in fact a great deal of protection, but there was some degree of it under the law.

"It will be two years ago in March that Nobel Laureate Jacques Monod made it clear to a New York Times writer that he was positive that man was, like every other species, nothing more than the result of a chance event in the process of evolution, that man might just as well not have appeared.

"Put another way, he could have said that there is nothing special about man, that there is no such thing as sanctity of human life. Slowly, western culture has been moving this direction since Charles Darwin.

"Monod and his book *Chance and Necessity* had been a big deal in France in 1970 and a big journalistic fuss had been made over him and his book, with English translations available in 1971.

"Justices of the Supreme Court read: The question is, did the almost constant pressure of the biological science community to make man into nothing more special than a bright ape that evolution had spat out . . . did that heavily influence the court and the law? Did it, in effect, amend the fundamental law of the nation?

"Recently, I spoke to you about the counter-culture movement in this country, pushed by what some observers call the "me generation," focused and intent in what they say and what they do to destroy the culture of their parents. What did their parents do to cause so much venom to be injected into any attempt at sane discussion. The only sin their parents committed that might have affected their kids was the sin of being a bit indulgent. They were the first large middle class to be financially able to spoil their kids a little. Figuratively, what they get in the way of thanks is a kick in the teeth or spit in the eye.

"This country, going back to Presidents Kennedy and Johnson, attempted to stop the spread of communism in Southeast Asia. The Soviets had easily taken over much of Europe at the ending of World War II. Communists had won in China. The Soviet leader Khrushchev had boasted at the UN that they would bury us, but they showed during the Cuban missile crisis that they recognized our military superiority.

"How could Communists possibly defeat us in Viet Nam? How could they defeat us at home? If you were a communist in the U.S., what would you do to destroy the America that existed the first half of the twentieth century?

"Could it be accomplished with drugs and teaching hatred for the culture the kids grew up in? They took over the coming of age of a large segment of the baby boomers—a good start toward burying us."

⇌⇋

"Mack," Maude started as soon as he had arrived for a Sunday afternoon visit, "The first part of your sermon was appropriate. You could have stressed more that state governments no longer can protect the fetus. If the woman wants to get rid of it and has a physician who is willing, she can have an abortion."

"The court ruled the law does not protect in the first few months. That's my understanding."

"That's what the supporters now say, but what will they say in the year 2000 or 2010? A woman decides after six or eight months that she can't afford another child. Will it be legal that late?

"You don't remember it but I do. The income tax when it became legal by constitutional amendment was quite small, but the rates have become higher. Ninety percent, I believe it is now on the top part of earnings if you are in the top bracket."

"So you are saying eventually, an eight-month fetus might not have legal protection if the mother wants to get rid of it."

"Yes, but that's not what I wanted to talk to you about. You remember Senator Joseph McCarthy?"

"The one who believed Communists had infiltrated our government?"

"That's the one. In time, he became more reckless in his choices of whom to attack as being a communist or under the influence of communism!"

"Much of the public saw him as a patriot, didn't they?"

"Oh, yeah, but the communists in the '60s realized he had done them a favor," she added.

"By drawing attention to the possibility of a threat?" Mack didn't see what her point was.

"To speak out against suspected communist activity was to risk the McCarthyism label being attached to your reputation," Maude concluded.

"So members of the party felt they were pretty much free from attack."

"If they went at it with any cleverness, they could shape our politics," Maude explained.

"Khrushchev knew they couldn't bury us by military action. But he saw they could bring about the demise of the culture that saw us through the Depression and World War II."

Curious, but skeptical, Mack asked, "Are you ready to conclude that the Communist Party of the United States of America has been assisting the current generation of our youth to come of age?"

"I'll try to answer that with a question. If you were a member of the communist party in this country, wouldn't you be trying to create the distrust, dissatisfaction, even hatred for the values that had contributed to making the US the most powerful nation on earth?

"Can you think of anyone more likely to want the moral and economic decline than the people who have openly declared for more than a century their dedication to destroying capitalism and the environment of freedom that allowed it to thrive?"

"But Maude, you'd be the first to concede that capitalism has been guilty of some gosh awful sins."

"Yes, and I've seen child-labor laws passed, trust busting, and recognition of collective bargaining rights. This has been done, all the while keeping a high level of freedom.

"While communism everywhere has pushed a philosophy of materialism to the exclusion of the human soul, religion, and civil liberties. In the Soviet Union, even science must not, in its research, stray far from the party line. The same for newspapers, the arts, and music."

"And literature," Mack added.

"The baby boomers coming of age has been too tempting a target to pass up. And too naïve to recognize the thought control they are being subjected to.

"Earlier, departments or schools in the universities had been influenced by CPUSA, especially journalism and the various soft sciences, and Hollywood."

"Physics and chemistry being the hard sciences," Mack commented.

There was more from the old lady. Mack listened, unable to offer counter arguments. When it was almost time for him to leave, she thanked him for coming. Finally, she said, "I'm glad I won't be alive when the vanguard of that group starts holding important positions in government and business. It will be like nothing this country has seen before. More power shifting to Washington. Less individual freedom. Power over the people. Today's freedoms will worry this crowd. They'll say otherwise, but raw power is their goal."

Mack had lots to think about. Could it be that's where the promotion of the counter-culture was coming from? Or was it due to being raised by the Freudian psychology of a self-proclaimed expert. Always culture has been in a state of change but never as fast as in the past few years.

That night before going to bed, he escaped the gloom that Maude had brought him by listening to music from another time. What a treasure the composer had left for people he would never see. Only from a soul that was beautiful could such hauntingly sweet and memorable themes have flowed. It reminded Mack of highland pastures and forested streams flowing with muted sounds and the song of life. It was Beethoven at his best.

Why can't life be like this? Why must most of our lives be spent trying to make sense of it, trying to cope and persevere somehow in the midst of the violence and greed that pervades life? Why can't man settle for peace and quietude? For this short time, I'll make the best of what I have right now, and let the music take me to the places the composer wished for all who would but listen. How different from the music he penned that let us experience the pain in his soul and his excited triumph when he found a way through it. It was a memorable experience, but on this night, it could not totally ease the dread of what would result from the dying of the culture he knew.

With the last notes of the symphony, Mack realized his memory would be forever changed. He had listened to it before and would again, but he would save a place for this one. It had offered him hope on a night when his feelings of loss were great.

What kind of people would take away from young people all sense of right and wrong, he wondered. What goals could they have that were so important that they would want to turn a society into a bunch of pleasure seekers who had no belief in anything more important than selfish desires? The "me generation," social scientists were already calling them. Informal codes of conduct were already dying and legal codes could never take their place.

The most materialist political philosophy in history bragged of its materialism and suppressed freedom at every opportunity. Writers, poets, composers, and artists were forced to suppress their creative talent and stay within the limits set by the communist party.

Would they, the youth of our nation, be willing to swap freedom for extreme materialism? For guaranteed freedom from unmet basic material needs, would they allow government to kill one freedom and then another? The passage of Lyndon Johnson's War on Poverty . . . would that program lead to more and more dependence on the nation's rulers? What would happen to the old notion of pride in one's independence and freedom?

For several days, he let these thoughts ramble through his mind. Gloom became a daily burden. From the pulpit, he had always advocated going to God with worries. Trusting in Him with our problems, especially those you can't do anything about. It was thus that he went to God in prayer, ashamed that he had not done so earlier, and confessed his negligence to the Lord. He felt a lot better for having done so.

What I find most amazing about myself is my hard-headedness. Intellectually, I know praying brings relief. In the New Testament (1st Peter 5:7) ". . . casting all your care upon Him, for He cares for you," yet I continue ignoring that advice. What I don't understand is my reluctance to ask until I've worn myself out with worry about something that is entirely beyond my ability to change.

This coming June, it will be thirteen years since the onset of Rebecca's illness. It's hard to separate my feelings of grief from those of worry. All I can do is tell you this, Lord, and ask you to be my support in the days that are to come. Without You, it is far beyond my ability to cope with what lies ahead.

CHAPTER FIFTEEN

E ach time he visited the nursing home, he would take one of her
hands in the two of his. There was no sign that she responded
at all. No sign that her eyes saw, even though her eyes were open.
On the occasions he fed her, she still opened her mouth at the appropriate time and took food and swallowed. He hadn't asked the
nurse how much longer Rebecca was expected to live, but a rational
moment told him it likely wouldn't be long.

To God he prayed, "I still have hope of a miracle, a cure for the
memory disorder and then real progress in drug therapy for the
other. It makes no sense to You, I guess, but that's how it is."

One day the nurse said, "Just hang in there and keep hoping."
Then she went into the restroom and let the tears flow for the marriage she knew that never was. Her greatest grief was not for the
one who would pass in a couple of months at most. It was for the
man who had never had a marriage. She had learned the whole
story from the patient's mother. She, herself, was a church-goer and
devout Christian, but cases like this sometimes made it difficult to
remain steadfast in her faith.

It was her CNAs who were closest to the patients. They were dedicated to their work with their patients without exception, she believed. When a patient passed on, they showed signs of grief like a loved family member had passed on. Maybe other nursing homes had employees who didn't care, but all of hers did.

⚍⊹⊹⚎

There were two cats that had complete run of the facility and a mongrel dog who had shown up like the cats had and been fed. Any time one of these needed to go outside, they waited at a door until a passing employee came by. By scratching on an outside door, the pets could always gain entrance.

The dog was in and out of rooms but seldom stayed for long. Patients might pet and say a few words before he moved on. Somehow the dog knew when a patient was going to die and would enter the room and lie on the floor patiently. All employees knew this and the story was not a secret from a patient's family members.

The dog had a bed in the nursing home parlor and spent a lot of time sleeping there. His diet and lifestyle were not conducive to keeping a trim figure, but the once-stray dog had no concern about such matters. He had once known creeping starvation before coming here and never wanted to return to that style of living. He was home and never had a hankering to stay outside long, rambling the community that used to care nothing about his needs. His name was Joe-Joe, a name given him by a three-year-old visitor who had come with her mother to visit her great grandmother.

Joe-Joe had been a conversation-starter no telling how many times. He always raised his head when someone interrupted a nap by the speaking of his name when he was abed in the parlor.

One of the CNAs had explained about the dog's final visits sometime during the first week that Rebecca had come there to live. Mack never gave the story about Joe-Joe's ability to recognize the day a person was to pass very much thought.

On one visit in late February, he squatted in the hallway as Joe-Joe was making his leisurely way toward him. The dog paused, expecting some petting. Mack fondled the animal's ears, one badly scarred by a larger, more vicious animal? Most likely in the days before making his home here. Mack recalled the story of Joe-Joe and his prophetic abilities. Would he show up and lie on the floor as Rebecca reached the day of her passing? This got to him. What if the story was true?

One morning Mack felt different. A quick decision was made. He drove home from the retreat, packed a few clothes, made three telephone calls and carried his luggage and a warm jacket to his pickup. A couple of minutes later, he was on his way to the Gulf Coast. This might be his final opportunity before . . . he didn't want to form those words in his mind, knowing in advance that they would speak of a finality he didn't want to face. So he didn't think them.

The doctor at the mental hospital had told him that the Alzheimer's disease might be a blessing because she no longer showed any signs of the fears and suspicions that had ruled her mind in the early years of the first illness. "Her fears that the FBI would come arrest her had been real to her. Her pulse and blood pressure showed just how real. It worried her that she had not been getting any better and that in her absence from home, a sleazy woman had talked you into divorcing her to marry the other."

The doctor had once said that the public, for the most part, can't conceive of how absolutely real the world is as seen by a schizophrenic. "And many even believe the ill mind could, if it wanted to, begin taking control of itself and see reality as we see it. There's a wide range of realities the so-called sane members of society perceive when all are looking at the same thing, but for Rebecca, there is a vast difference."

At noon, Mack stopped at a fast-food restaurant. When he had been served, he immediately began eating, paying little attention to the food. His thoughts were on something else, something troubling.

What would he do when the time came? Would he be faced with a decision about whether to keep her on life-support that would extend her life extra weeks, that she would not live unless she was on such a system? He had said he would not allow life-support but that was at a different time. Would he be interfering with God's will if he had her put on life-support, as some might say? Or would it be interfering with His will if he decided to allow her to pass on at an earlier time by refusing to do anything that would extend her life?

Not doing all that could be done, would that be letting her die from neglect on his part? Would that be a moral wrong?

For a passing moment or two, he wished he could return to childhood where older people were there to make the hard decisions. Then a wry smile was felt on his face. As a child, he had spent countless hours wishing he was an adult and could do all the wonderful things they could do. But barely having entered that wished-for time in life, he had married. Maturity and responsibility had been forced on him before he felt he was ready. If he and Rebecca had been eighty-two instead of twenty-two, he might could have accepted her illness, but they'd never had a life together. He had never experienced this sort of tragedy and was not at all toughened for facing disaster. He had still remained a callow boy who saw life through the eyes of someone in their mid-teens. Clearly, he realized all of that as he finished wolfing down his food.

Back on the road in five minutes, he continued to think about his inadequacy for what was soon to come. Rebecca's early illness had left hope even as it slowly progressed, but finally even false hope no longer existed. Now he could only run away. That's all he had left. And that's exactly what I'm doing now. I wish there would be a boat awaiting me at the coast and I could sail away to Argentina. My carpenter's skills could make me a living. I took Spanish in high school and could learn the language pretty fast. But I can only fantasize about escaping my responsibility. I'll go back and do the right thing because that's how I am. I was living in a fantasy world when I dated and married Rebecca. She was no more mature than was I. We had no idea what life was like. Only a week or two before our wedding, our lives began to unravel. But we didn't know.

Would I have married her had I known the terrible illness had already entered her brain? I think I would. I hope I would. Being what I was and still am, there was no choice. A man of no principles, my dad used to say, is no man at all. He is a scoundrel and a threat to the society he lives in. That he had covered all this before didn't help much, as the *time* was surely closing in.

Mack recalled his big sin, and for the countless times realized he, as a matter of principle, shouldn't have done it, but as a matter of human nature, he had lingered in the woman's bedroom when he should have been getting out of there. During the first few minutes, he reached the point of no turning back. As far as God was concerned, the act no longer was of concern, but he, far from being over it, gave himself frequent mental kicks in the rear for what he had done.

As he had frequently done in the past, he wondered what had become of her. Had she married again? She was probably no more than twenty, if that, when it happened. Would he recognize her if he saw her again? Probably not. He had tried to forget her. She had not been a pretty woman. And her voice would have been irritating if heard frequently. A tragic woman and he had added to her tragedy.

Thousands of acres of commercial pine forest went by almost unnoticed. Rest stop signs had appeared and fallen behind. He finally pulled off the road to one of them.

A couple of camellia bushes near the entrance added an almost breathtaking beauty to the utilitarian place. In full bloom, there was the gentle humming of honey bees that sought the golden pollen and unseen nectar at the base of the pollen-tipped filaments. Rosy-red petals, fluted and highly visible for both man and the busy insects.

"Really beautiful, aren't they?"

"Yes, ma'am. I love coming by here at this time of year. They add so much to the trip to the coast."

She was a well-dressed woman in a suit that must have been tailored just for her. Her voice was softer and more gentle than that of women no more than 150 miles to the north. A woman in her mid-forties. He wondered if she was as beautiful in her mid-twenties.

When he had used the facility and was back on the road again, he thought of the lady and her manner of speech, so soothing and pleasant. Would television, as he heard one speaker say, eventually erase and blur the distinctive manner of speech that each region of the country had before 1950? Probably would in fifty years, as the speaker had predicted.

The thrill the camellia blooms had created lingered. This time, while on the coast, he would visit a nursery or two and ask if cold-hardy ones were available.

West winds were up. It was a wild ocean he viewed on his arrival at the beach. A cold front was going to blow through during the night according to a report he had heard on his way down.

The noise of the ocean was greater than any he had experienced. High up on the beach he walked, almost to the point where sea oats began. Obviously, the tide was in and high. Walking barefoot was a struggle in the soft sand. Trying to hurry was an exercise in futility, so mostly he was content to let the sand set his pace. Stopping and gazing out at the white-capping sea took away his thoughts of what he'd left back home. It was as he had hoped. The ocean always awaited him with a new experience. The unpredictable beauty and the balm it brings to the soul can be almost more than emotions can bear without the release of tears to wash the eyes that behold such beauty. It was a wild shout of blubbery joy he released to fly along with the sounds of the sea birds whose expressed joy of the ocean also flew with the wind.

He had no reason to believe there would be any change in Rebecca's condition in the next few days, so his mind settled down to take in the sights and sounds of the ocean. At the end, clouds broke enough to let the sun peek at him with its last rays of the day as the top of its disc followed the rest into the sea.

Taped to the door was a message to come to the office on his return. With almost complete certainty, he expected it was to receive bad news.

From the young woman at the counter, he learned his mother-in-law had called about thirty minutes earlier. "Your wife has been taken to the hospital with pneumonia. When I asked her if you should return tonight, she said she wished you would."

"Ma'am, I'll get my luggage and be on my way in ten minutes."

"You did no more than set your luggage inside before going to the beach?" On seeing his head nod a couple of times, she said, "Turn in your key to me as you leave. There'll be no charge."

As he did that three or four minutes later, she said, "I hope you find your wife feeling lots better."

"May God bless you, ma'am."

And me too, and her poor mother. A blessing for Rebecca? What would that be, Lord? The unthinkable?

The tires of his old pickup were soon rolling beyond the small area where traffic lights interrupted their turning. Their droning sound at this time did nothing to mask his emotions from his awareness. This was it. A CNA had one day, on being asked, explained that very advanced cases of Alzheimer's sometimes developed pneumonia when they became unable to cough up food that started down the wrong way. "Loss of reflex," he had thought out loud, and she had nodded her head.

Immediately, he had steeled himself against the worst of the attack of his emotions on his innermost being. His first time to ever do this was the night of his wedding. It was not accomplished by turning his thoughts to more pleasant things. It was more like just shutting himself down and being aware of only the things he actually had to do. It's not at all like making myself a zombie or sleeping a dreamless sleep. When hunger comes, I'll answer its call at the first fast food place I see.

At times like this, food was especially good. It was all there was to feel good about, and he was sorry he only had time for one burger and coffee. This restaurant was old-timey; it had a waitress who took his order and topped off his cooling coffee with a smile when his sandwich was served. Overly vulnerable to any little act of kindness when he was steeling himself against the emotions that he knew were always there awaiting a chance to tear at his tender being. He asked God for help for himself and a noticeable measure of relief came.

How negligent I am about going to God. I wonder if some of the people who hear me on Sunday morning are too busy—worrying about the things that may lie in wait—to stop and ask the Lord to help out.

And the non-believers who poke fun at us who believe in God, does it never occur to them that we might have something that they don't, that our time is not wasted when we pray a believer's prayer?

As he came closer to the hospital, he had not allowed himself to remember how Rebecca looked the last time he saw her fifteen hours ago. A few months, three short of her thirty-fourth birthday. Somewhat obese, toothless, and hair that had no shine and worst of all no expression of anything in her face or eyes. Propped up in bed . . . waiting?

Before her illness she had been great to look at, but he had no real memory of what she was like. All his memories that he could call up were of her after she became ill. In an effort to comfort him, an aide would tell him that he would have "all those memories of her." And he would not tell her he was unable to recall how she was before, realizing that would be unkind.

A few minutes later, he was walking down the hospital corridor to room 202. Anne and Lee were there. Rebecca looked much as she had in the nursing home.

For quite some time they and Mack had talked in her presence as if she were not there. Mack couldn't remember when that had started . . . when they realized she was not there and hadn't been for a long time. Mack knew that he had fought recognizing that longer than her parents.

"Looks like we're about to the end of the road, Mack," Lee said.

"I tried to feed her some supper," Anne commented. She didn't exactly cough, but there were signs she sort of attempted to. Lee pushed the call button and a nurse came in, took a look. "Get a device to suction food from the upper end of her trachea," she called, "and hurry!"

Mack apologized for being five or six hours away when she was carried to the hospital.

"You couldn't have done anything to help. Lee and I came right on up as soon as they called. You've had a long period of responsibility. You needed a break from it.

"Mack, I thought I was as ready for this as a person could get" Tears came without sobbing.

Lee said, "In our minds, we imagine how it will be if we face losing a loved one. But our imagining never prepares us for the shock that comes. My mother suffered long with cancer and toward the last, I'd think it would be better if the Lord carried her on to Heaven so the suffering would not continue. But I could tell at the end that my mental preparations had done very little toward getting my emotions under control. The time of denial and wishful thinking had run into a brick wall of reality. My heart pounded, my breathing speeded up. That was more than twenty years ago. I've not lost the memory of it, but the sharp pain of it has been dulled by time."

Mack had been looking at his father-in-saw, seeing a side of the handsome gray-headed man he'd not known was there.

"I'm beginning to see what you mean, sir. This is my first experience at losing a loved one. And I finally am beginning to know.

"Have they considered installing a feeding tube?"

"We talked to her doctor about that," Anne said, then stopped. "And?"

Soft spoken words came from his father-in-law. "The doctor said aspiration would still be possible. He asked me if I sometimes had a little bit of food come up when it had been a half hour or more after I'd eaten. Of course, that sometimes happens. A bit of throat clearing or coughing and a swallow or two of water gives relief. He explained Rebecca had lost any such ability to clear up things.

"Anne, it's time we go home and get a little rest before coming back tomorrow. We'll try to relieve you by 8:00, Mack."

And the routine was set for the next few days. One of them would try to be there. Later, Mack might have slept thirty minutes; if he did, it left him feeling worse than ever. A doctor came in to check on Rebecca and then asked, "Are you the husband?" On being told he was, the man continued, "You've had her illness to cope with a long time. You understand what we are up against?"

"Yes. She has pneumonia and it's not the kind you treat with antibiotics. A feeding tube might keep her alive a little longer. And it might not. Been sitting here for hours thinking.

"In my mind, I traded places with her. If I were in her shape and she in mine, what would I want her to do if I had a couple of minutes when I suddenly could think rationally before returning to sickness that would equal hers?"

The doctor said nothing for a moment before asking, "Do either of you have a living will?"

"No, maybe we should have taken care of that before our wedding. It might help me make a decision."

"But who thinks of such things in their twenties. I'm fifty-three and I don't have one. Keep putting it off, I'm ashamed to admit.

"Will see you tomorrow, if you'll be here around seven."

—⟨+⟩—

Two weeks later, Rebecca's funeral was held at her home church. Mack was to deliver her eulogy. There was music . . . a fine old hymn, "In the Sweet Bye and Bye" was sung by a young tenor. Mack's memories flickered through the last ten days. The oxygen concentrator had been hooked up beside her nursing home bed since the hospital had released her back to the nursing home. Her breathing on the last day had slowed and slowed until early afternoon and finally stopped and didn't return. Her mother was holding her daughter's head and he and Lee each were holding a hand. They wanted physical contact in the hopes that somehow Rebecca would be aware that they were there as she passed from one existence to another. She had given no sign that she knew.

Minutes later, his mind turned to the eulogy that would be coming up in seconds.

"Yesterday, a kind and well-meaning man told me what a pity Rebecca never had a chance to live. He meant not being a homemaker and raising kids, and in that, he was right.

"It was my freshman year in college when I first noticed one of the most unusual young women who graced the campus—consistently and at all times—with her many passive virtues. Absent was the kind of behavior designed just to draw attention. Modest in dress and speech.

Gentle, a giver rather than a taker. Always unselfish. Considerate of others' feelings before she opened her mouth to speak. She especially loved babies and small children. Her life stream, not bubbly and cascading, was a quiet one flowing between mossy banks with a beauty that calmed rather than excited the soul of those who knew her.

"In her thoughts, she was not easily upset or angered. In her presence, you felt as if life was something that tended to bring peace.

"From the time she had a genuine salvation experience at twelve until illness sought her out ten years later, she had a positive influence on others to seek the Lord if they did not know Him. For so obviously, she had something that many did not have. By example in behavior and by example of attitude, her life was her testimony.

"When illness hit, she experienced new kinds of realities. Her suspicions were as real as her love for others had been. Her fears were as real as her trust in God had been. Her delusions became as real as the quiet soul that had always been before. It was not, as people used to think, just in her mind, but in the physical changes that had occurred in the brain cells. Telling her that her new realities were not real would have been no help at all.

"After several years of schizophrenia, a memory disorder set in and as it progressed, she was no longer bothered with the fears, suspicions, and delusions of the first disease. Her brain was quietening down and eventually shut down. Brain cells that had once held countless memories no longer could function, perhaps because they had died. Her dentist from childhood 'til after we were married now has every appearance of the same disease. Had something in their environments brought on their illnesses? Was there some factor that they had in common? Pray that someday, those two questions will be answered. Pray for all people who suffer from brain disease—the most devastating of all illnesses."

CHAPTER SIXTEEN

Though Rebecca had not lived with him in twelve years, he missed her. When he went to bed at night, he lay awake for a while, experiencing a painful sadness. As long as she was in the mental hospital, he had the feeling of knowing he had a wife; she was just not with him but might be someday. Even when she was in the nursing home, he drew a tiny bit of comfort from knowing that he had a wife. Even though she was not with him, who knows . . . maybe a miracle might happen. No longer did he have a wife and there was absolutely no comfort to be had from that. For close to thirteen years, he was a husband.

She was in Heaven but he wasn't and he felt more alone than ever. How could it be that he did? It ought to be impossible, but it wasn't.

On awaking in the morning, he would lay an arm across the bed and feel a new emptiness, though that space had not been filled in all the years of their marriage. This was something he had not been prepared for and had not steeled himself against. He knew with painful certainty that grief could be postponed, but would at some point in the future overtake him.

As quickly as he could, he made preparations to leave for the Men's Retreat. *Am I again running away from what I can't face? Of course I am. Isn't it one of those days I'm supposed to just turn it over to the Lord? No, there comes a time when God wants you to look at sadness straight on and recognize it for what it is, and realize that you've got some hurting to do before you get well. Mack, you ain't going to be whole until you suffer through the pain and sadness of getting well. It's time for denial to stop. Jesus never said He would bear all your burdens, but that He would lighten them to where you could cope and heal some from the experience. You never completely get over such tragedy. You'll keep enough of it to be humble and to keep her in your memory.*

A young man took his order. Coffee came with his arrival. Cream was on the side and packets of sugar were already on the table. Mack sipped it without either.

As he awaited his food, he looked around the dining room. All males. A hint of a smile lifted a corner of his mouth. *What would women's lib think of this? Probably raise Cain if someone told them such a restaurant existed.* But on a few occasions, he had seen a woman or two . . . once with two of them sitting together.

"May I sit with you," a man's voice interrupted his musings about women customers. "I'm Bill."

"Of course, glad to have some company." He extended a hand and introduced himself.

"I'm William but everyone calls me Bill. Aren't you the man who lost your wife a few days ago?" he asked after he had been served coffee and the waiter had taken his order.

"After an illness of almost thirteen years."

"That had to have been really tough. I read about it in the paper. I've been married thirty-one years. Would be lost without mine. She keeps all of our records in addition to being cook, housekeeper, and companion," Bill said in complete sincerity.

"I had a long time to prepare myself to lose Rebecca. And I *was* prepared to some degree."

"But some things you can't prepare for fully. I wasn't when either of my parents died . . . hasn't been a year since Mom passed away."

Bill wore the clothes of a farmer. His handshake had been as strong as his thick fingers and hands suggested it would be.

"You farm?"

"Cattle and broilers. It's been a hard winter. My chicken houses require lots of propane to keep my chickens warm enough to meet our weight goals."

"You get paid for weight added to the little biddies that the processor brings out?" Mack liked the man's company. His breakfast had been served. Bill had insisted he begin eating immediately. He took a bite of crispy bacon at Bill's suggestion.

"That's how it works. I didn't have quite enough hay to get my cattle through in good shape—thought we didn't. Searched for sources to buy, but the warm-up in March greened our pastures as fast as I hoped it might."

Bill's food was served. Mack had been eating slowly and now settled down to serious eating. Mack, after what he'd been through, thought the conversation had been mundane. And sane. Just what he needed. Does anyone who grew up on a farm ever get it so completely out of his system that he does not enjoy talking about it? Even the hard times, in retrospect, can be pleasurable subjects for conversation.

They talked of home-cured bacon, sausage, and fluffy biscuits and eggs, as they ate the Retreat's excellent food and enjoyed fresh coffee.

"For years on Saturday mornings, Bill, I knew what I was supposed to do. Go to the hospital to visit my wife and for the past severals years, it's been to the nursing home."

"And you miss it on this first Saturday morning?"

"Visiting her at those places was hard. Seeing her in the shape she was in, and the other patients in various stages of serious mental problems would always leave me feeling down. I should be glad it's over; she's out of it. Had not had a life for years."

"You do feel some relief then?"

"Yes, I'd have to have a sick mind if I didn't feel a subdued sort of joy that God has finally taken her home, but I miss her."

"Within the past year, my mother passed on after a slow, painful death. She is better off now in Heaven, but I'm not. At least once or twice a day, something will come up that I don't know or have forgotten. 'I'll ask Mother the next time I talk to her,' I say to myself and then realize that she's gone.

"I'd better be getting on. I come here once or twice a week to give my wife a break from cooking. Milk and cold cereal gets her by."

Mack had a day without plans. His mother and dad might welcome a visit.

There was an emptiness in his house that was not there before Rebecca's death. How could that be? She never was there. It's an emptiness that goes with me wherever I am, unless I'm unusually busy. It's like something of me is gone. It's responsibility for Rebecca that is gone.

Her last days kept returning. Times came when the last hours of her last day came back in memories he could not turn away. At 6:15, he had received a call from the nursing home that there had been a change and he ought to come on in. That morning he had left the place at 2:30 after an LPN had told him it looked like he'd better go home for some rest. "You'll be called at any time we see she is different." And now he had the call.

Mack felt he could not get ready and make the drive. More than anything, he wanted to sleep. This could go on for weeks more. If only I could sleep just a little longer.

He felt like he'd rather be dead, but this could be the day she was to go and he did not want her to go alone. Lee and Anne will want to be there. I hate to wake them up. Rebecca will not be aware that we are there. But then again, she might come out of it enough to know.

He called. Anne answered. "I could not go to sleep, Mack. Kept feeling this would be the day."

By 7:23, they had all made it to Rebecca's room. "The beginning of our third day here," Lee said.

"The dog never has come by," Mack remembered.

"You think there is anything to that tale?" Anne asked.

"They say there is," Mack answered.

The oxygen concentrator was running as it had been for days. Time went slowly by. Rebecca's breathing had slowed some more, according to the CNA who came in to check. She dipped a small cube of sponge in water and holding the tooth pick that it was speared by, she swabbed Rebecca's dried lips and the interior of her mouth. "Be back in a short while, folks. If she gets restless, push the call button and we'll administer a sedative."

The dog came in and lay on the hard floor, right beside the bed. "So, there may be something to it after all, Mack," the father said.

And Mack now felt *this* was the day. He tried to steel himself further. It seemed he had foreseen the time was very near—he didn't know how long, but for weeks and more. Never had he been through anything like this. How well would he bear up?

Rebecca's roommate had been placed in a wheelchair and rolled out into the hallway, some distance away. This had not been done before. No one needed an explanation that the dear old lady shouldn't have to endure the stress of being in the room as her roommate died. This day was different from the others—the staff all knew. It was chilling.

Around eleven, the dog silently left the room. Nothing was said. The time for talk was past. It was just being there at the time of her passing; she might know. Her breathing was noticeably slowing.

A nurse came in, observed, and then said, "One of you might want to hold her head and the others one of her hands. You don't know what she might be able to know." She left.

Anne took and held the head of her daughter in two hands. Mack took her left hand and Lee her right. "This is how it will be," Lee said. Later, Mack said of her slower breathing, "I thought that would be her last." But it wasn't. And around 12:30, the next breath didn't come even though they waited for what seemed a full minute, and then more. . . . Finally, Lee pressed the call button.

Mack didn't know why he let the memory of that last day revisit him, but guessed it was another part of his journey through the dark valley of grief. Though they had not shared the same bed in twelve years, he sometimes felt himself reach out as to touch her face or arm when he would awaken briefly in the earliest hours of the morning, something he didn't do those months they shared the bed.

Sometimes he would find himself driving toward the nursing home without remembering making a decision to start out. He could remember a heavy sadness had been on him; he must have started out seeking a bit of relief from it. It was to Rebecca's room he would go. Her roommate was still there. The lady had a sharp mind but had the worst case of arthritis Mack had ever seen. She loved to talk and had looked forward to Mack's visits.

"Every day, Brother Mack, I awaken to the hope that it will be one of the days you visit."

"You remind me of my friend, Maude. She has joint trouble, but not quite as bad as you, Marie."

"If I had a phone, I'd love to talk to her."

Before leaving, Mack stopped by the business office to see if a patient could have a phone. He received a positive answer. If Maude would accept a telephone friend, he'd have one installed. Calls would not be subject to long distance charges. Maude told him she'd be glad to have a phone buddy. Mack had the phone installed and would pick up the monthly charges.

Both elderly women said they were indebted to him. "Though I don't like feeling indebted to anyone." Maude said with a tinge of sarcasm. "Will try to pay you back by searching for a good-looking young lady for you."

"Might ask you for such assistance in a year or so. Will let you know if the time comes when I'm looking for one. Right now, I'm far from ready."

"Keep in mind that I'm an old, old lady and I want to see you married to a good woman before I take a notion to go on to that pain-free world. But I'm willing to hang on for a while yet and help you pick out one worthy of you."

"No way I can tell you how much I appreciate your willingness to suffer on for my benefit. You know you are my favorite old lady," he teased.

"You better not let that other old bag take my place, Preacher Boy. Having found out I'm your favorite old bag, I'm going to end this phone conversation while I'm ahead."

CHAPTER SEVENTEEN

Mack visited the sick more than before. He helped more with counseling people who desired help, who needed to talk with someone who would really listen. Wes, his assistant pastor, had been doing most of that. "Mack," he said, "I've as much of that to do as before. Apparently, there was greater need than I realized."

The extra duties he had taken on helped, but still he felt that his troubled mind was as messed up as before. He prayed that would change, that he would not continue having the emptiness, and that filling up extra hours of his life helping others would remove it completely. He had expected that it would, but it didn't.

He did what he had known for days he should do . . . visit Alf. Spring was in its early stages. Peach trees were in bloom. Tulip poplars were ready to burst their buds any day. Oaks and hickories were preparing to give everything else a dusting of light gold.

It was to the woods they hiked alongside a pasture fence until the fence made a right angle turn instead of taking off through heavily wooded land. They had hiked here many times across a small wet-weather stream and up a steep incline and on to a fallen tree that offered a good seat. They always sat there a while. Light chatter it had been as they walked, but now it was silence for a few minutes.

Alf became uncomfortable with the silence before Mack. "So you came because you wanted to talk, but here we sit as silent as two tombstones."

"How did you know I wanted to vent my feelings?"

"'Cause if anybody has reason to have pent up emotions, that fellow is you. You been through more hell than any other person I know. In years past, you have expressed a little of it.

"Have you realized that her Alzheimer's was a blessing . . . in a way?"

"I've thought of that, but it's hard to see it that way. Her schizophrenia wasn't going to cut her life off just a little short of her thirty-fifth birthday. What if in four or five years a real cure is found. Would I feel good that Alzheimer's had come along and ended a life that could have turned out to be normal later on?"

"You have a point, Mack. Has any psychiatrist said there was real cause to believe that cure is just a few years off? You have always told me that no one anticipates such a cure in say the next ten, twenty, or even thirty years."

"True, Alf, but I always had hope until a few weeks before her passing, even though I had read and been told that the memory disorder would end her life."

"That the failure of the coughing reflex would come and end it."

"You knew that several years ago, Alf?"

"Yes, I did that by visiting a large nursing home three or four years ago and asking how people with that disorder reached the end. Aspiration pneumonia was given as one way life could end. Pureed food was prepared to delay the aspiration of food for a while.

"Didn't you inquire, Mack?" he asked in the gentle manner he nearly always spoke.

"No, I never did ask. An aide once mentioned that. But I didn't pursue the matter with questions. To be honest, I didn't want to know what could end her life.

"Didn't want to think about it. Couldn't bear to think about it."

"That was okay. Denial serves a good purpose when reality is as gosh awful as what you were up against.

"This log felt fine at first, but now my backside is paralyzed. Let's walk and talk. Not like we're on a cardiovascular sprint, but more like we're a couple of snails."

After about five minutes of leisurely walking, Mack restarted the conversation. "Alf, it's been almost twelve years since she went off to the hospital. All those years, I lived alone. This is going to sound crazy but my house seems empty, more so than several years ago, and she was never in my present home—not one time. Even when I am other places, there is a new emptiness. This is totally unexpected. What do you think causes this?"

"Mack, there is nothing I can think of right this moment." They walked on for a short while, then Alf said, "I've had enough stress dealing with loss of a loved one. I knew I would lose my mother and my father. I lived those months hardening myself against the emotions that were sure to attack me if I didn't sort of prepare myself against the loss that was sure to come. Didn't you do something like that?"

"I had to. I couldn't preach or do carpenter work or any of the other things I had to do if I wept for thirteen years. Of course I had the empty house feeling for a while after I was first alone."

"But you couldn't keep on doing that. So you postponed the terribleness of the empty feeling, the grief of all those years. You couldn't live with full-blown loneliness of it for so many years."

Mack said, "And now I can sort of deal with what I have to?"

"I think that's about right."

"Alf, you should have been a clinical psychologist or a psychiatrist. How can you know so many things I don't?"

"Because I never went to college? I read a lot, I think a lot. It's not that it comes easy; I put a lot into trying to understand things that interest me. And almost everything interests me."

"Changing the subject, Alf, pasture, woods, fields, and homestead . . . in all, how many acres do you own?" Mack asked.

"Two hundred and fifty."

Mack whistled in astonishment. "Have we walked only on your land today?"

"Did you think we had? If so, you were right."

"Thought what you had was more like one hundred. You've something to be proud of."

"Wouldn't say I'm proud, but I'm glad to have it except at tax time. The newspaper in the city is always complaining that timber land owners don't pay enough tax. It buys newsprint that's made from pine trees, mostly.

"Land in timber, especially if there's substantial acreage, should be looked at like it was being preserved for future generations."

"Like it is a fine resource in a natural bank." Mack added thoughtfully. "And what a place to walk all your emotions away, without damaging the natural resources.

"You have a big and generous soul, Alf, and you need room to let it live and grow.

"I rent a small house as I did when I was pastor at Mount of Olives Church. What does it do for me? Maybe in the next year or so, I'll try to locate a few acres with a few great oaks and maybe a beech or two. You ever feel like hugging as much of a large tree as your arms can wrap around?"

"What lover of forested hills and hollows does not? Tree huggers, I understand, are beginning to come out of their protective shells and admit they suffer from this weakness."

They had reached a place covered by moss and it was there they sat as this conversation was taking place.

"We may be more alike than we are different, Alf."

"No doubt, people are. Otherwise, a social group would have a devil of a time getting along with each other.

As Mack was eating supper in his favorite restaurant an hour later, the realization of what that afternoon at Alf's had done for him continued to grow. It was something he'd been in sore need of. The empty place was not now quite as empty. God had not intended that man be so out of touch with others as he had been.

Would he ever marry again? This was the first time he had allowed such a question to enter his mind. To have done so earlier would have seemed like a moment of disloyalty to Rebecca. And then, maybe there had been the briefest of times when such a question would stealthily slip into his consciousness. He couldn't be sure there hadn't.

He had slowly reached a point of feeling quite certain that God had forgiven him for the big sin. Now he was beginning to be a little less harsh on himself. Under the circumstances with such poor judgement at the time, he was beginning to understand how it might have been almost inevitable. Perhaps it was a price he paid for being so inexperienced. But he was in his mid-twenties . . . a very young man to have lived a quarter of a century.

At the time of the wedding, he and Rebecca had been living in a fantasy world, knowing almost nothing about what most young adults had a smattering of common sense about. Thirteen years had passed. No young woman should be placed on a pedestal as he had done with Rebecca. When reality suddenly hit as mental illness, he was totally unprepared to cope. When the preacher read the vow including "in sickness and in health," he gave it without even a passing thought regarding what he had just agreed to. She was a perfect example of a perfect young woman. Theirs had not been a starry-eyed courtship. It had been somewhat emotionless, he realized later. Maybe it would have been better if there had been a bit of passion between them like some of the other couples he had known. How could he have been so unaware that something was missing, that their marriage would never have been robust even if illness had not been in her future.

As for marrying again, the risks were too great. He had adjusted during those years to being alone. Made a life for himself even as Rebecca's Alzheimer's had progressed, eventually destroying her brain completely. Would he put at risk the life he had put together, despite Rebecca's illness? If he married again, there was no guarantee that the second time would be better than the first. What if the second wife became ill? Far from ready to seriously consider such a life, he turned his thoughts to fishing with Alf the following Thursday.

When the day of anticipated fishing arrived, he awakened from a dreary dream. It was from a time when Rebecca's illness first seemed hopeless. They were returning from a visit to Dr. Pickens and he was recalling not the exact words, but the contents of the doctor's prediction that there was no real reason to believe she would get better. As he had done on several mornings lately, he laid an arm across the other side of the bed. It was empty. He wondered why he had done that and wished he hadn't. It caused him to experience another bout of hurt for the marriage he never had and for the loss of an angelic wife. He knew she had been beautiful, but it was only a mental thing. He could not recall her face as it had been during their courtship. The mental picture he did have was one of an overweight, toothless woman; he wished he could remember her as she was before.

He got out of bed quickly and busied himself with the early routine of preparing for another day. At the moment he opened the refrigerator to get out milk for cereal, he recalled what this day was to be. The old saying that a day spent fishing does not count against your allotted time on earth and with that he felt a smile's slight shifting of his facial muscles. His spirit lifted. It was not so much the fishing as it was a day to be spent with a good friend who was a master teacher of the art of living.

His thoughts of Alf continued through breakfast and a second cup of coffee afterwards. Though the man was close to eighty, he claimed that the time of passing on wasn't something he often gave much thought to. There was too much living to be done to waste any of his allotted time worrying about that. Time had to be taken out to experience God, knowing His presence and the peace that always accompanies such a time. And cattle needed to know the touch of a hand that showed appreciation for them. A wife, bless her soul, needed time spent listening to her. There was a horse who presented a head with eyes so beautiful, you had to take time to rub her ears. And fall's last warm breeze was calling for an appreciative response for coming from the Gulf of Mexico to caress his face. And in his woods, a large willow oak always beckoned with spreading limbs. "And Mack," Alf had once said, "these are but a few of the things that fill my heart."

Mack loved to listen to a man who knew and experienced the fine art of living. It was to this man's house he drove after all preparations for a day on the lake had been completed. He found the farmer with boat and trailer already hitched to his pickup and engaged in the final chore of keeping a rocker in motion on his porch. He beckoned to Mack and for a few minutes, they sat while the "old lady" was putting the finishing touches on ham sandwiches.

"But I brought some peanut butter and jam sandwiches," Mack said.

"You've eaten her ham sandwiches a couple of time before . . . and?"

"I'm pleased to wait.

"I couldn't help but notice you have a brand new boat."

"Hadn't told you, Mack. Wanted to make it a surprise when you got here. It has a fishing seat toward the front and a bow mounted trolling motor. When I brought it home the other day, my wife said, 'You're living proof that there's no fool like an old fool.' Didn't have an argument to offer on that, but I did tell her I'd wanted one a long time and had a little money ahead and it'd be a little less for the kids to argue over when I'm gone to the other side."

"Four kids, and they are all on the other side of fifty. How long 'til they are grown up?" Mack teased.

"They'll always be kids in my thinking. Recently, I was telling someone who asked about them that they were all doing well and how hard it was to realize *the baby* had his fifty-first birthday just before last Christmas."

⊱–⊰

It was early spring on the lake. It should have improved Mack's spirit, riding in a new boat, but he was afflicted with a case of emotional blahs.

Obviously, Alf was enjoying his ride up the lake to his favorite point. The boat had a steering wheel as he had pointed out earlier, "Just like a car."

Fishing with ultralight tackle got under way. Alf caught three before Mack, who was fishing from the back seat, caught his first . . . a very small one. The pattern of Alf catching good- sized fish and Mack catching far fewer, and small ones at that, continued. "Going to have to swap seats before long so you can have first shot at 'em, Mack."

"Would take me a half day to get the hang of operating the trolling motor like you do. I'm okay for now." But he wasn't. Rebecca's illness and recent death was weighing heavy on his heart. At times, for a short while, he would feel he was making progress. The grief, because she had never had an adult life, would become almost too much. He believed she was in Heaven now, but even though he was a minister, sometimes he had found he was capable of doubts

246

about all things spiritual. It was petty, but that he was being badly beaten in trying to catch fish . . . that would be released anyway—was beginning to bother him.

"Time to try another place, Mack." Seconds later they were on their way to one of Alf's favorite spots. Mack had lost interest, almost completely, until suddenly he felt Rebecca's presence! Overpowering and totally convincing him that she was with him. He saw her clearly, not in front with his physical eyes, but in the back of his head to the right. It would be something to wonder about later but right then he shouted at a level far greater than the sound of the boat motor, "Rebecca is here, Alf, and she's well!" The image in the back of his head was Rebecca in all her beauty as she had been before their marriage!

As Alf eased the boat in to a small cove where he wanted to stop, he told of a man he knew whose wife visited him numerous times after she had passed.

For the next forty-five minutes, Mack caught considerably more fish and mostly larger ones than Alf did. "Wish I was having your kind of help, Mack. Maybe I need the back seat."

To a degree he never had before, Mack knew! She had been resurrected! She cared, she loved the sad man that had been left behind! The sick Rebecca of all those years was no more.

Alf didn't ask if she was still with him. He knew she was while he was being soundly thrashed despite his fishing just ahead with an identical lure. He hadn't changed the way he cast nor how he retrieved his lure; he didn't want to wonder later if he might be easing up, and in effect, improving Mack's chances.

Mack's initial joy became greater as fish continued to bite in what could only be a miracle! Nothing less could account for the change in the behavior of the fish. Rebecca was here and she was well! It had been many years since she had communicated her love for him. There were times when he wondered if she ever had. Either she or God or Jesus or the Holy Spirit had been aware that this was an especially difficult time for him. But it was Rebecca's presence he felt.

Even as this was going on, he and Alf occasionally remarked about it. After about forty to fifty minutes, the presence of Rebecca gradually diminished though his vision of her face had only lasted for a minute. [*See Author's Notes at the end*]

When her presence was no longer felt, Mack, instead of feeling regrets that his help was gone, experienced quiet joy that she was resurrected. His faith in God and the resurrection of Jesus were stronger than ever, and he had thought it had already reached an absolute limit of belief.

Alf noticed that Mack was no longer out-fishing him two to one. "She's no longer with you," he stated. "How blessed I am, an old man, to witness proof that Heaven is awaiting me when this old body can no longer serve to keep me here."

"I no longer feel her presence as I did for a while, and she may not come back another time but today's visit should last me a lifetime."

"It's what they call a life-changing event," Alf said. "I feel blessed that I was here to witness it.

"Right up here in the next little cut in the shoreline is a good place to tie up and have ham sandwiches.

In his worst hours of grief and depression, food had sometimes seemed his best friend. But five minutes later, when his soul still glowed from Rebecca's visit, he was eating a sandwich that was incredibly pleasing. "What a day, Alf! Food like this and a healed wife's visit from Heaven! Thousands of times, I prayed that God would heal her."

"And in His own time, He did. And His own time is not always at our convenience. There may be reasons we can't understand that God does not do things the way we wish or as soon as we wish."

Running the trolling motor and keeping the boat in position wasn't as easy as Alf had made it appear to be. His buddy had insisted that he be the one to cast first into undisturbed waters for the next hour after lunch.

"Alf, I'm a bit of a bookish sort, and maybe pretty good at it, but when practical smarts were being passed out, I must have been behind the door."

"Your boss says you are his best finish carpenter."

"That's nice to hear, but if he saw what a crooked line this boat is making in places where the shore is straight, his high opinion of me would take a fast drop." Mack had noticed that Alf had paused in fishing and was studying the sky.

"Pull up the trolling motor, Mack. I've been watching a fast-developing cloud while you were getting fretted with what you are trying to do. Maybe a quarter of a mile from here is a place we are going to soon be in bad need of."

It was only seconds later that Alf was at the wheel and Mack was in the passenger seat. The motor fired on the first turn of the key. The twenty-five horsepower motor was at top speed almost instantly. A sudden down burst of air hit the lake before them creating acres of instant wavelets. It was quickly becoming an interesting ride. Alf needed to be ready to make small, but fast corrections as wind hit without warning. Because the gusts were almost vertical, no large waves were piling up. The cloud continued to darken. A massive bolt of lightning hit less than a mile ahead lighting up the sky before them!

Fortunately Alf had overestimated the distance to the shelter under a large overhang in the face of a vertical cliff of rock. At the end, he eased the throttle before shifting into reverse at idle speed. As the boat entered the shelter, both men reached up with short boat paddles and brought it to a stop long enough to grasp one of the very small bushes that had somehow managed to cling on to life between the ragged layers of sandstone that formed the back wall of the shelter. They were at least ten feet from the edge of the over-head stone that formed a roof. Horizontal winds were now blowing the beginning rain in the most favorable direction possible; they would remain dry.

"Room for another boat in this place," Mack said in a loud voice between blasts of heavy thunder.

"One heckuva cloud. It's almost as dark as night. Uh oh! Here comes the hail!" Likely from thirty or forty thousand feet, Mack was thinking. "Could this produce a tornado?" he shouted.

"We are covered it it does!" Alf shouted in return. This was not his first time to ride out a storm in this shelter.

A blinding flash, cracking, and booming thunder came together. Some poor tree out there must have taken the hit. Before, the storm had been exciting, but now Mack felt real danger. What if the next one came running along the ground and underneath the roof of their shelter. An aluminum boat sitting in water would be an attractive target. He would never be able to tell of the miracle that had visited him in such a overwhelmingly convincing manner.

Miracles were rare and to be treasured. He had thought he had believed in the resurrection of those who believed in Jesus and the Father, but now he believed at a level of absolute certainty.

Another close lighting strike took his mind off that miracle for the time being. The storm grew more intense. The next strike was across the lake. They remained dry but had to constantly be attentive to holding the boat in place. No rain was blown in on them, but storm-created swells tended to push the boat against the rough wall and holding on to the small bushes was not enough. The occasional pushing off with the boat paddles evened out their position. All the lightning strikes were now on the far side of the lake.

From left to right, the storm cloud reached as far as they could see. Not all the lightning sought the ground. Now they could catch glimpses of horizontal lightning zig-zagging from one part of the cloud to another. Mack had seen many thunderstorms but never one so spectacular and from such a grandstand seat!

Though heavy rain continued and water poured off the edge of their shelter, they still remained dry. It was a noisy cloud that slowly moved away.

"Mac, this is becoming a little boring. If you laid the jam on heavy enough on the peanut butter, this is a good time to find out." Mack had, and they both had a finger licking experience.

"You didn't live in the Great Depression, did you, Mack?"

"Was born in thirty-eight. I lived one year of it."

They had finished eating and the storm had quietened where they were, but was of astonishing size and intensity a few miles away. A light rain still fell.

"This country is seeing the greatest prosperity right now it has ever seen but the thirties are beyond the ability of young people of today to imagine. I knew one or two people who were fat. Today we are beginning to see quite a few who need to lose weight. You see ads in the newspapers about weight loss plans and exercise equipment for losing weight."

"Maude says she was teaching back then and saw plenty of hungry kids in ragged clothes. She added that apparently they got used to having too little to eat."

⫸⫷ ⫸⫷

He stood behind the lectern, the outline of his sermon and an open Bible before him. His opportunity to open his sermon with a different kind of message should be made *now*; he had already stood there in silence for four or five seconds.

"Your pastor has periods in his life when belief in God and the Savior are not felt as strongly as at other times. I wonder if some of you are sometimes like that too. By your presence here, you strongly profess your belief. Are there times you wish that God would do something in your life that would send you the message that He is very much aware of you? I mean something loud and clear. Something that could not be confused with something else as to its meaning. Something that could only be from God or his Son. Perhaps we feel that our God experiences would be met with silent expressions of disbelief or brushed off as something of little significance by others.

251

"How much better if we sat down in twos or threes or more, and talked openly of our inner lives. I teach a Sunday school class here and we study and discuss, for the most part, verses, half chapters, and even whole chapters. It's a lot like what those of you who are in school study in a class on American history.

"It's like regular school and properly called school. Afterward the preacher often reads to you additional passages from some other part of the Bible and presents a commentary.

"When my father was a boy, at the beginning of a church service . . . especially at a revival, there were times that were called experience meetings before the preacher started his sermon. A number of people would stand, one after another, and give testimony concerning experiences that held great meaning for them. Sometimes a testimony had little meaning for others, but occasionally something very profound and full of meaning for others was spoken of.

"Thursday, Alf McDonald, known by many of you, and I were fishing." Mack smiled good-naturedly. "Yes, this is going to contain a story about catching fish but don't totally discount the truth of it before I get started. Alf is a fine old man, a Christian to the core and he will vouch for this as a true story.

"He had this brand new fishing boat and offered to take me out on its maiden voyage.

"While fishing, he operated the boat from a front seat by using a small propellor-driven electric motor, he was out-fishing me by three to one. I was feeling low and had been for about thirteen years, over the slow loss of Rebecca and finally her recent funeral. Being out-fished so badly didn't make me feel any better. Now the guy fishing up front is expected to catch more, but not by the wide margin I was being clobbered.

"Then he started on up the lake using his regular gasoline motor. Suddenly I felt Rebecca's presence as strongly as I did years ago when she was riding in the car with me. I saw her in the back of my head to the right . . . her face appeared briefly. She looked just as she did before her illness struck. Fine featured . . . beautiful. An expression of sweetness graced her face. So very different from those years of illness when she lost her teeth and her body and face ballooned and her eyes lost all ability to express anything going on in her mind. It had ripped me apart to realize that was because nothing was going on in the brain behind the eyes that had once radiated the mind and feelings of an intelligent, angelic person.

"In the early years of paranoid schizophrenia, those eyes could and often did become windows to a soul that lived in real and gripping fear. And then Alzheimer's hit and the terrors no longer showed in her eyes, as the parts of the brain where those fears arose were destroyed by the second disease.

"Well, I shouted above the droning sound of the boat motor, 'Alf, Rebecca's here!' And as tears came, I shouted with even greater emotion, 'And she's well!' In the back of my head, the image of a young and healed Rebecca appeared momentarily.

"We came to a stretch of vertical cliff. My heart filled almost to bursting with relief and joy. I automatically cast my small lure toward the place where rock and water met, places where Alf had fished less than a minute before. And I caught fish on the lure that had earlier failed me. By at least two or three to one, I began out-fishing Alf, and mine were bigger than his.

"Did I take pleasure in the finest bass fishing I'd ever experienced? You bet I did. It was proof that the woman who had visited me on this miraculous day loved me and had become tired of Old MacDonald beating me. Alf told me he was doing his best to catch fish, because if he had broken his rhythm in any way, my beating him wouldn't definitely prove to him that Rebecca was there. For forty-five minutes or so, the pattern persisted. When no longer I felt her presence, fishing returned to normal, but that caused no regrets on my part.

"If there is a doubter in this sanctuary, call Alf." He had covered every section of the congregation with unceasing eye movement throughout the story. Never before had he received such close, even rapt attention as he had this Sunday!

"How many times did I ask God to heal her? How often did I feel disappointed that He didn't? Perhaps thousands would be an appropriate answer to both questions. But now I know with certainty that He healed her. Why not before, I do not understand. But this I have learned—those who enter the kingdom of Heaven will leave behind all ailments, all disabilities, and leave less than handsome and less than beautiful faces behind.

"This is what I learned when I took off a day for some loafing out on the lake. Why did God reward me with such a visitation? Not because I'm such a devout Christian because I haven't always been. Maybe because He felt sorry for me. I have borne what I thought was far more than my share of bad luck or misfortune. The Son seemed to favor men who fished. Perhaps the Father does also."

He smiled at what he was to say next. "If I find that the air has been let out of the tires of my old pickup during one of our evening services, I'll suspect one of you fine ladies did it because husbands want to fish more than sweet wives think they should, and I'll be the one to blame for encouraging such loafing."

Later, without looking at his watch, he knew it was time to ask for a hymn of invitation, giving anyone who wished to be baptized, move their membership from another church or just to have a few moments to speak to the pastor an opportunity to come forward while the congregation sang stanzas of a moving hymn.

When the prayer of benediction had ended the service, Mack had already made his way to the doorway. He had wondered as he preached, how his story would be received. The general consensus was that all had been blessed and this was one fisherman's story that was true. One man said, "I know Alf MacDonald, but there is no need to verify your story by calling him. I have heard truth from the pulpit many times, but none more convincing than today."

Maude and the lady who brought her were the last. Maude's usually smooth voice broke as she said, "If ever a young man deserved such a visit, you are that young man. This sometimes skeptical old bag of arthritic bones is completely convinced a miracle was visited on her favorite preacher the other day."

Mack teased, "Don't you start getting all mushy on me, Maude." She had planted a gentle kiss on his cheek.

"You're the first man I've bestowed a kiss on in many decades, and the first who deserved one.

"I tend to be skeptical when I hear stories of miracles, but not yours. You are such an innocent, I doubt you know how to spin a web of untruth."

⇒⋮⇐

Mack had thought he believed in Heaven as much as a fellow could. Before, he would have told anyone who asked that Rebecca was in Heaven, but now he was certain of it and just as certain that God had healed her. She had not come to give him an emotional lift because he felt down about poor luck fishing, but to assure him where she was and that she was well. Had it been she or the Holy Spirit that caused the bass to ignore Alf's lure and await his? One thing he knew for certain, the lovely face that for so long he could no longer remember, that day he saw clearly restored to her former beauty.

He chided himself for allowing the light of happiness to dim after a little more than three days. Why, he could find something to worry about—to feel empty about with hardly any effort at all. Only an hour ago, his third grandmother had planted a kiss on his cheek because she loved him like a grandson. Later, he sat in his favorite restaurant with a refill of coffee and a slice of pie considering whether to take a small bite or the one his greed urged. He felt down compared to earlier when he stood before his folks letting them rejoice with him in the visit from Rebecca.

He took the large first bite and felt the sweet and crisp flavor of roasted pecans mingled with the delightful goo of the filling and was immediately ashamed of his lack of self-discipline. Rebecca couldn't be siting beside him enjoying one of her favorites. What was he thinking? In heaven, she was enjoying far more luscious delicacies than was available to him anywhere on earth and that without the worry of cavities.

That set him to wondering if Heaven's residents still had some of the personality traits they had on earth. Those who had always wanted a little more than what they had . . . when in Heaven, would all of such little imperfections be left behind? He felt sure they would.

As a child, he had taken the preacher's word that in Heaven, there would be everlasting joy and peace. Worry and sorrow were earthly things never to be encountered there. But what if we carried some of our earthly traits with us? Would some of us become a little bored by the constant joy? Now, why in the world would a preacher allow such thoughts to enter his mind? What would his people think if they knew he even allowed such a thought to emerge?

The waitress asked if he wanted more coffee. He did. Sipping slowly he let his thoughts return to the nature of Heaven. If it is eternal, there would be no awareness of passage of time. On earth, we are reminded frequently that time is going too fast, or it drags. We would not suffer from the emotions we do on earth that are related to time. No worry about becoming infirm and awaiting death. All would be different. Rebecca's visiting him on the lake was not imagination on his part. There was a reliable witness to one of the tangible results of her visit . He had heard of others who felt and believed deceased loved ones had visited, but none of these had such strong evidence for someone else to witness. He was blessed as no other grieving person had been that he knew of.

He began to wonder if Rebecca's illness could have been a message from God that He did not really want him to be a preacher. That her illness might have been intended as a roadblock to being a minister, casting doubt on his life's work. Should he take this as a sign that God never intended for him to be a minister? That question had often come to mind, casting doubt that had to be fought, over and over. Out of that doubt grew feelings of inadequacy. He phoned Maude one evening and expressed to her what was bothering him.

"Sometimes, Mack, I feel like giving you a hard lick on the head. Maybe it would increase your gumption a bit." During his next visit with Maude, she told him, "Mack, you turned the life of a sour old woman around by ministering to her spiritual needs in a way her skeptical mind could accept. No one else had been able to. You were and are the genuine article. Instead of preaching at me, you allowed me to share my inner doubts, without trying to convince me how wrong I was on some points. Never had I experienced such acceptance. I'm a bit strange; I've known that for many decades, and never had shared some of my strange feelings and beliefs with anyone, especially a preacher who would likely imply that my soul was in peril of being condemned to eternal doom for entertaining such unusual and unorthodox ideas.

"I saw myself as a bit of a heretic, and it had only been a few hundred years since people, who did not completely accept the official church/state version of faith, could expect to be burned at the stake or face some other horrific way of execution. This was not some rare occurrence in those days.

"You didn't as much as lift an eyebrow when I expressed my version of why God sent His Son to earth. You didn't lecture me for stopping church attendance years before. You didn't even one time suggest what I needed to do was get off my rear and get on down to church. You came to see me because I invited you, following your first visit. Eventually, I went to church and continued to go. It helps my arthritis to get out.

"Fishermen have what may be a deserved reputation for stretching the truth. Old MacDonald is not one of those. Called him. He backs up your story completely. No reason for him to stretch a story about how he got beaten badly for the better part of an hour.

"Are you such a ninny that you are beginning to wonder if God really allowed you to receive such a blessing? Alf, a devout believer, told me he felt blessed because he was there when it happened . . . that his faith received a strong boost, at an age when his passing cannot be many years in the future. He felt greatly reassured. And you know what, Mack? It removed any residual dread I had about the ending of this life.

"Yeah, I tend to be skeptical about the very unusual in matters of faith even when you tell it, but Alf called and confirmed it."

"I knew you'd tell me exactly how you saw what I had doubts about. That's why I phoned you," Mack said.

"Mack, you grieved over her illness. Now that she has escaped its clutches, you can take joy in that. But you may still have grief, a sense of loss ahead of you. I doubt you could fully complete grief while she still lived. If you feel sadness, it is natural and it can be healing. My guess is it will have to be dealt with before you are fully whole. Don't get down in the dumps if you go through such times of regret and loss. If you have a rotten head cold, you get antihistamine and a large box of Kleenex, knowing you have a few days of sneezing and blowing your nose before you get well. You have already experienced grief enough to teach you some routines about taking care of yourself when it threatens to get you down. Colds in the past have taught you to rest more than usual. Grief, when it comes on, has taught you to hike more, go to the ocean or the mountains, listen to music more than usual. These are but a short list of things you've told me in the past that have helped.

"Perhaps you've been postponing some of what you may have to deal with. But on the other hand, you may have gone through most of it," she said.

"I need to be patient," And with that the conversation ended.

More than usual, he walked and he thought. He spent a day in a state park where trees had thrived unmolested by timber cutters for decades.

Had her memory disorder been a blessing in any way at all? When it became pronounced, it seemed that her fears and delusions went away. Isn't she better off in Heaven than she would be in a mental hospital awaiting some new drug while delusions and fears and hallucinations ran rampant through her mind? To wonder if a one-way trip to death is better than a longer life plagued with fearful unrealities is not much of a choice, but once the first illness set in, she had no choice in any matter anyway and neither did I. Why do I keep experiencing the feeling I allowed something to go undone? Is that because until almost the very end, I had faith and hope that a cure for each illness would arrive in time for me to take a healed wife home? Do I feel that if I had prayed harder with all possible faith, she might have recovered from both? I don't know. The feeling that I was inadequate in some way walks with me along this trail.

The marriage that never was. Poor Rebecca. She never had a life. And I've often felt sorry for myself because of my loss. But I've worked and preached—two things that gave life some meaning. Instead of meaning, she could only wait helplessly for whatever horror might be visited on her. I know of no other person who existed and suffered so long for nothing. After her visiting me, knowing she was completely healed, I should be rejoicing, but I am so alone and have been for so many years. She is well now. Why have I been left to continue life on earth where no telling what bad thing awaits its turn to get at me? How I wish my life would be over. When I walk through a cemetery, I look at a stone and read the name and date and wish that I had been so lucky. For that person, all earthly suffering is behind.

Mack had arrived at a rocky point, high on the side of one of the park's tallest peaks. Virginia pines gnarled and twisted, three of them had fought a long tough battle against winds that came with speed and during droughts with air so dry that the short needles were helpless in trying to hold on to what little moisture they had. Postcard picturesque, but he felt greater pity for them than the pleasure they gave. Nothing should have to endure such life as these. But they had clung to it for a century, and more, as if it was worth living. Was he doing the same thing and would he be imitating the trees forty years in the future, holding to life as if it was worth all its troubles?

A young man and woman arrived from a direction that he had not taken. They said they not seen anything else so beautiful in the park as those trees.

Mack wandered on. Two people can look at the same thing and not see the same thing at all, he realized anew. They might be happier and that could account for seeing things differently, for seeing the trees with unmixed pleasure. Had there been a time this day when he saw sights through lenses clear and bright? Briefly, yes . . . before his mind went back to his wife and himself. Perhaps those short spans of time were even more dear because he would soon be returning to memories of Rebecca and his own predicament. A few hours at the beach or in the mountains stolen from the sadness that always awaited his return to reality.

From the mountainside, he descended into a deep hollow. Before reaching the bottom, there came the sounds of a small stream splashing and gurgling The sounds were as music. Music . . . is there anything else like it, whether a violin or an alto or soprano voice? As he drew closer, he moved quietly, slowly, letting the sounds of a lively little stream shape his emotions into a mixture of merriment and light joy. He thought of Kilmer's poem about trees and he formed a line of poetry about small streams that never overwhelmed the delicate emotions of delight they gave. A mossy spot on a rock at water's edge brought him to his knees, and then to sitting. There was no tinge of melancholy that fall colors would bring. The bursting buds of beech and tulip poplar told him there were months to go before the most beautiful of days arrived . . . before the forest was to again slumber through the cold days ahead.

The comfortable contour of the rock did not soon remind him that it was time to move on. Peace had the opportunity to take possession of him and peace never irritates; it never calls for the mind to move on. How many years since he had possessed it? He realized its value and treasured it and gave no thought to the sadness and self-pity that might soon be with him again. So real and so lasting it could be—a memory to form a bridge from this day to whatever might be ahead. It would be a bit of hope to cling to when life returned to gloom again tomorrow or the next tomorrow. How little life he had lived the past thirteen years. There had been exciting times and hours of gloom and despair. He would take this for now, and store its essence where it could easily be recalled when needed. He had made a short step of progress and would call up its blessing when needed most.

He knew he was not totally free from all guilt, all sadness. But he had this moment of a peaceful soul and the knowledge that it would not always be so, but that did not have the frightening aspect it would have had a day earlier. Quiet joy even when he was aware that unsettling thoughts might reappear. It was something new. It had come unbidden and he thanked God.

A little longer he sat where he was, content to experience the sound of the stream. Then a large woodpecker started making a lot of noise as its sharp beak started slowly hammering a dead pine a hundred feet or so up the slope from his tiny creek. A sound often heard in the happy days of his childhood from the small area of forest not far behind the family's farmhouse. The noisy bird soon flew off, sounding its mating call. He wondered, as he had often done before, how they ever found enough to feed themselves and their young who needed large quantities of the insects that inhabited deadwood.

Mack arose and moved on. The afternoon had been rewarding. It would take time, but he could now see how he might become less absorbed in himself and more of his thoughts turned toward other things.

Rebecca had been gone a long time. He realized that more fully than ever. Her mother had once said that a year or more before and he had been upset with her.

Will I always live in denial when life's saddest events are approaching with certainty—the death of Mom and Dad. I need to go see them more often while I can. There are other things I need to do that I have been neglecting because of Rebecca's illness. Was I helping Rebecca when I went to the nursing home each day? Could not some of that time have been used better? But I'm glad I went. I could not have not gone. A man has responsibilities and if he is what he ought to be, he lives up to them. My parents didn't love me less for what I did. They would have loved me less if I hadn't.

He carried that thought and the mood it induced to the state park boundary where his truck had been left and drove off, a somewhat different man than the one who had arrived several hours before.

CHAPTER EIGHTEEN

The church seemed to need him more. Counseling was in greater demand. Culture was moving on to where it was going, creating anxiety in people that they only recognized as wanting to talk to someone. And when they talked, it was likely they wanted to talk of the possibility of the President being impeached for crime. The hearings droned on in the heat of the summer. War in the Middle East could lead to they didn't know what, but it was an unsettling possibility. And the country's oil supply could be threatened. Depending on some distant nation's good will for access to an energy supply was something that was going to take some getting used to. Things had been and were continuing to change too fast for comfort.

Few of the people who came for counseling would have been able to recognize and articulate what was bothering them. One told Mack of visiting the lighthouse at Cape Hatteras recently and halfway up the enclosed spiraled staircase, she and her husband met two girls, maybe eighteen or twenty, dressed in dirty, tight jeans and t-shirts that had to have been worn at least three weeks without being washed. "Their stench had been so terrible, I must have climbed fifteen or twenty steps before their foul odor began to abate one iota. Brother Mack, I thought I would throw up. Taking pride in being offensive! What kind of freaks did they have for parents?" Mack didn't try to answer the question. He thought of Freud and Spock, not that those two ever encouraged parents to allow their kids to be so dirty and smelly.

The woman continued, "Brother Mack, it wasn't really their filth, though that too was bad, it was frightening that the country has come so far from where it was twenty years ago. Instead of trying to look nice, they and several million others like them are in rebellion . . . against what?"

"Maybe the country has been fighting wars too long. With hardly a break and they feel it's the generation before that's to blame."

And that caused the woman to say, "Lord, yes! They are scared of nuclear war. They have had no chance to live their lives and doubt they'll ever have a chance to. Maybe they are not doing as bad as we think. Still, they scare me half to death.

"My husband says I'm just a worry wart, and this is not the kind of problem to bring to pastoral counseling.

"Others might come because a spouse threatened to leave or because their kid might have joined the counter-culture movement you spoke of from the pulpit. I'm here because people are changing too fast and culture is way out of control. What weird thing will become popular next? We don't have a fallout shelter and don't know that I'd go into one if there was a need to do so. What would we come out to later? It's not just our youth that are badly frightened."

She thanked Mack for listening. When he left the office minutes later, he carried her fears with him. A nuclear war could wipe out most of the human race. Not until fifteen or twenty years ago had two potential enemies had the power to destroy all human life. It was a horrific threat, one that people had never had a chance to develop emotional defenses against.

What a bad time to have this hanging over society's head. The *God is dead* movement left its participants with no system of beliefs to undergird their defenses against such a possibility.

He had stopped at a small restaurant for a late supper. For a change, his mind was hardly on the food. His order was just for something to fill an empty stomach.

He recalled a novel he had read years earlier set in Australia. As the fallout from a nuclear shootout in the northern hemisphere slowly made its way south, the Aussies kept up with the news of their ultimate demise, their government-approved suicide kits to be used when lethal levels of radioactive dust arrived. Mack had read it the second year of his and Rebecca's marriage. Far from the kind of book he needed to read, he read it all. With the memory of the fears that he had experienced, the actual emotion reappeared. He almost wished the lady who had come for counseling had stayed home. As pastor/counselor, he didn't feel up to the job. Before taking a bite of his spaghetti with meat sauce, he asked God to give him the insight and spiritual strength to deal with the mess the counter-culture leaders had made of the lives of others. And then prayed that the nuclear shootout would never happen. He forgot to offer thanks for the food.

Paying little attention to twirling his fork properly, he managed to get spaghetti and sauce into his mouth and all around it. His thoughtful waitress had left extra paper napkins. He was able to notice the sauce was extremely good, otherwise his mind was busy. His sermons were going to remain biblically-based but a bit more relevant to modern problems.

Kids in college were raising Cain, demanding that their classes have more relevance. Many had used extreme methods of trying to bring change, methods that had in the past been associated with revolution. Mack realized that he didn't know where this was coming from; he had suspicions, and Maude had certainties.

There would be no great amount of change in his sermons, but enough to give his flock a better way to deal with a culture so greatly different than what preachers used to have to prepare their people for. He would listen more, allowing his people to express their needs and from that become a more informed pastor, and hopefully a more effective one.

Society's problems were different and also the same. Once he had read a clipping from a mine worker's journal . . . and right on target, he had thought. Then the friend told him to unfold the very bottom of the one-column clipping and read. It was a quotation from an ancient Greek observer on the youth of that day.

That spring and on into the summer, he did use scripture to start sermons on things that were about the people's concerns as were noted in news sources and what he learned by a little more listening to what his people were saying. He was a little less of a Sunday school teacher and a little more of a developer of values; at least that is what he hoped he was doing. He talked more of active values, bravery, and courage based on brief passages of the Bible. He looked at Isaiah 40:31 for example, and Psalm 91:4, and from these, he preached a two-pronged sermon. He got so carried away by "They shall mount up on wings as eagles," that his eyes misted and his voice became slightly hoarse with emotion. The beauty of it, the poetry of it, the promise of the complete verse. Mack's soul responded. His words became touched as with poetry. He was inspired. He didn't know he had such eloquence. Where did it come from? And suddenly, he knew the Source. Again, he read the complete verse and it was remarkably different, every gilded word he read in a voice rich and silky this time, instead of emotionally hoarse. From the rear of the audience came a loud "Amen!" immediately joined by several others. Then came a request from the first person who had spoken, "Brother Mack, would you please read that again?"

"But they that wait upon the Lord shall renew their strength, they shall mount up with wings as eagles; they shall run and not be weary; and they shall walk, and not faint."

This time, the spell was not broken by an amen. In silence they sat. Mack realized they were more blessed than he. Better to be the listener to than to be the reader and for once in his life, he had read something as the writer had intended it to be.

And then Mack read again from Psalm 91. "For those of you who worry about a nuclear war, and wonder if you should build a fallout shelter. 'He shall cover thee with His feathers and under His wings shalt thou trust; His truth shall be thy shield and buckler. Thou shalt not be afraid for the terror by night; nor for the arrow that fliest by day; nor for the pestilence that walketh in darkness, nor for the destruction that wasteth at noonday.'"

Mack explained briefly that the psalmist did not mean that "nothing bad" will ever come your way, but that you have the Lord to rely on for strength to face whatever comes in the depth of the night or in the brightness of the sun. With His help under the shelter of His wings, you will be able to bear up. For the Lord's help, it would be good to ask often.

"God designed and operates the universe which is more vast than we could imagine if we started trying to conceive at sunup and were still trying as the sun touches down at the western horizon. If He can be aware of and in touch with every star, with every planet at all times, He could hear millions of prayers simultaneously. One of our biggest problems is that we do not express our concerns often enough. God has the ability to hear all of us at the same time.

"You trust in God? Do you trust Him enough to pray often throughout the day. Or do you think that your little old worrisome thoughts are too insignificant to bother Him with? Your pastor doesn't pray half enough but he's working on it.

"If you suffer the terror by night, you may not be asking the Lord for help as much as you should. Under His wings you will know comfort and peace unlike any you have experienced before, but you've got to be under His wings. It's your choice.

"He doesn't expect you to sail through life without asking for help. We don't live in a Garden of Eden . . . as far from it as things could possibly be. SNAFU came home with the GI's of World War II. *Situation normal, all fouled up,* was what those letters stand for. Not an optimistic way to look at life, but pretty realistic.

"How often we feel that life is one big foulup, and we believe that's to be expected. 'But those who wait upon the Lord shall mount up with wings as eagles.'"

Later, as Mack stood at the exit, the comments from members of his flock revealed that many had been deeply moved. People waited in a long, slow-moving line, most feeling compelled to express appreciation for a sermon that had affected them so deeply.

Maude had waited until the line was short before she arose and slowly made her way to the church door. "You didn't surprise me having it in you. Just didn't know why you waited so long before allowing us to share it."

Mack took a gnarled hand in both of his and applied the gentlest possible pressure. "Will try to do better than I have in the past." And the vow he had made a few days earlier would stay in place. The pattern had been set. Short and straight to the point passages of scripture would be the basis of his sermons.

The following Sunday, He read Matthew 6:19-21. His opening comment was to the effect that Christ had an uncommon amount of common sense. "The *only* thing we can take with us is what lives in our hearts; the rest of us will be left in the grave. Our material possessions will remain behind. Will God be impressed by the ambition to get ahead because of our discontent with what we had in this life. Imagine, if you will, that you could change places with the Lord, would you want to be associated throughout eternity with a person like you have been?"

Mack, in the kindest of tones elaborated on the theme that what we treasure becomes what our soul is. Would the listener want to endure eternity in the condition of the soul that was cultivated and nourished to run in a race to become as well off as the neighbor.

Mack explained that he was not calling for everyone to live as though in poverty, but rather to create an inner environment that would allow the soul to grow robustly, preparing for a life that would be eternal.

Another point he dwelt on was that we will carry our identities with us, including memories of who we were here, but with no memories of our sins. Otherwise what would be the purposes of wanting to be there, if we became someone we had never known. The Rebecca I knew before her illness was the Rebecca who visited me the time I'd been having a bad day of fishing.

"Begin becoming what you want to be in Heaven. Are you completely satisfied with who you are now? Do you want to enter eternity as you are now?" he asked. "How much treasure do you want to lay up for eternity?"

Mack elaborated on this theme in the sermon because he wanted every listener to understand the message and how important this life is to the next, that we are becoming what we are to be throughout eternity. Rebecca had slipped away from Heaven for a little while and showed her love for him that still existed in a manner that was beyond doubt as to the certainty of its meaning.

He was to feel good about the sermon and about himself until Tuesday morning on waking from a troubling dream that the alarm clock ended at 6:00 am. With no memory of the dream's actual contents, he knew it was bad.

It was not a morning for milk and corn flakes and instant coffee before making ready for a day of work. It was the sort of day when the comfort of Men's Retreat was called for.

Fluffy hot biscuits, lean bacon, grits with butter and scrambled eggs and black coffee should give him the life he needed to be at work by 8:00 o'clock.

Carefully sipping scalding hot coffee while he waited for his food, giving him time to consider the change from the past two days. Maybe the dream started it all, but maybe whatever was mood-changing had set in earlier in his sleep and from that grew the unpleasant dream.

"And why is my favorite preacher here at Men's Retreat instead of at home shoveling in cornflakes with milk?" the good-natured bass voice of his boss asked as a warm hand from behind clasped the top of his right shoulder.

Mack looked up into the twinkling brown eyes of Lowell Miller, then at his soft rubber soled Hush Puppies. "You wear those so you can slip up on a feller?"

"Bought them so I could slip silently into the house if I was late getting in at night," he teased.

"Susie would scalp you if you came in late. You wouldn't dare."

"You have that right, Mack," he said as he took a chair opposite Mack's. "Did you notice the new sign hanging from the bottom of the *Men's Retreat* sign?" Mack shook his head. *Wife's Relief,* Lowell informed him and went on to comment that he had never expected the women's lib movement to reach way out into the country to poke a bit of fun at male chauvinism.

"No telling where that is going to lead the country to," Mack added after the waiter had taken Lowell's order and poured fresh coffee for Mack. He filled a cup for the late comer and suggested that he hold Mack's meal in a warm oven for a couple of minutes while the second order was readied.

"I woke up from a bad dream at six. It set the tone for the morning and I ended up here, Lowell."

"After the way you preached Sunday and the week before, I figured you'd still be up on a cloud."

"Clouds have little substance and sometimes you fall right out the bottom. Praise for a sermon is great. Right then. But what if I fall flat on my face next Sunday?"

"Do preachers worry about such things as that? If you do, it never shows. You are confident when I see you in the pulpit. Not arrogant ... ever. But always like you came well prepared. Your eyes make sure that all know your attention is on them as your voice reaches out with a message especially prepared for them. You are God's servant and it shows."

"Sometimes I wonder if I really am. Doubt can creep in despite all my prayers for God's wisdom and assistance. It's not doubt in God, but in my ability to carry out His will."

Their food arrived and their coffee was topped off. They ate with relish and deep enjoyment. Unfinished talk could wait. This was too good to be interrupted by talk of Mack's blahs.

When the meal was finished and drinking their last cup of coffee was ahead, Lowell said, "Grief is an unpredictable thing. It lies in wait and you may think it's over until it slips up on you in a dream while you sleep and your defenses are down. Completely down. It seems to me that it's grief that caused you to wake up hurting this morning. It had brought the bad dream with it before you awakened. You can't live sixty years as I have without becoming acquainted with grief." He paused so Mack could comment if he wished. The very early wave of customers was long gone. Three vacant tables awaited any late comers. Lowell looked at his watch. "Ten past seven. You are no more than fifteen minutes from your job today. Another cup of coffee?" The waiter brought a fresh cup for each and poured from a "fresh brew."

"Lowell," he said after taking an exploratory sip of very hot coffee, "even when she was in the nursing home, I had someone. She was in bad shape but she was still a human being and I could go visit her at three in the morning if I woke up and couldn't go back to sleep. The outside door was never locked. A ten minute drive and I was sitting beside her bed. I could hug her if I liked. Maybe placing a hand on her shoulder would give me the satisfaction of knowing this warm person was mine. My parents live two hours away and I couldn't go wake them up when I couldn't get back to sleep.

"It may not seem like much. But it was to me. It was all I had of her and it was better than now when I no longer have that."

Lowell said softly, "But you know she's in Heaven now and that she is no longer ill. Aren't there times when you feel relief that she's out of those long, terrible years. And that she loves you and came to let you know that she cares?"

"Of course, I feel all of that most of the time. But then I get so lonely and she's not there to go see. And I tell myself that I'm selfish because I miss having her to go see and place a hand on a warm shoulder, and I ought to be celebrating because she has those terrible years behind.

"It sounds crazy, I know, but that's how it is at times."

"You are a young man. There's time for another woman. You're a very eligible bachelor as you will soon find out."

"That has occurred to me. But I'd be afraid to try again. What if I married and she became very ill?"

Lowell grinned and said, "Sometime in the next few months a match-making woman will tolerate the freedom of your bachelorhood as long as she can stand it and will make a big effort to fix you up with the perfect mate.

"Grieve because you must, but I advise you to treasure this time when you are as free as a breeze."

Mack was enough better to see there was a shred or two of truth in the last part of his friend's advice. A smile could no longer be kept harnessed. "Thank you, Lowell. Breakfast is on me."

"For my sage advice, I will allow that including the tip."

⚞✦⚟

"How human was He?" This was listed in the Sunday bulletin as the sermon.

When it was time, Mack stepped into the pulpit and laid an open Bible on the lectern.

"Most emphasis on the Christian message is and will continue to be on how divine He was. But let us consider how human He was, for a change.

"We have read how Satan tempted Him. You have heard it said over and over that He never sinned, not once. He was without sin. You were taught that early on. But consider this question. Could He have sinned?" For twenty or thirty seconds perhaps, Mack paused. He scanned all parts of the audience. Some looked a bit puzzled Some had a faint smile—was it one of expectancy for the answer they expected him to give? Perhaps they expected an unusual answer from the man they had come to expect the unusual from.

"The fourth chapter of Matthew makes it clear the devil tempted Him. Had it not been possible for Him to yield to one of Satan's attractive offers, there would have been no temptation involved. The human side of Him could have yielded, but the divine side had important work to do. There are rare humans who live saintly lives, but most of us don't come close.

"Did Jesus suffer childhood illnesses? No doubt He did. Did He sometimes overeat fruit that was not quite ripe and get sick? Probably. What boy doesn't?

"In my youth, I did not realize that facing crucifixion would be as difficult for Jesus as it might be for us. He was the Christ, God on earth. Knowing that after a few hours of agony, He would be in Heaven with His Father in joy everlasting, He ought to be able to face anything to get His time on earth behind. I felt and believed that even a weak-courage fellow like me could brace up and endure any ordeal if Heaven and its eternal rewards were just a few hours away.

"We see in Luke 22:42 that Jesus said, 'Father, if it is Your will; take this cup away from Me; nevertheless, not My will but Your will be done.' If God had said, 'Son, We'll go to a different plan that doesn't require this,' would Jesus have felt great relief?"

Mack saw some who nodded their heads in agreement that Jesus would have been relieved.

"And an angel came and strengthened Him. And being in agony, He prayed more earnestly. Then His sweat became like great drops of blood falling down to the ground.

"Sweating blood under great stress is very rare, but it has been noted in medicine. Sweat glands, as other parts of the skin, have a blood supply; tiny capillaries bring blood. A man in shaving barely nicks his chin and out comes the blood. It's as if blood is there just waiting for a chance to pop out.

"Jesus was not impatient to go to the cross. Maybe not quite as scared as you or I would be, but probably pretty close. Don't dismiss even the one tiny part of the painful sacrifice He made for us by thinking, but He was God on earth . . . He wouldn't have to fear it like I would. I must confess that at one stage of my life, I felt somewhat that way.

"As the time approached, He at one point made it clear He would like it if it had not been required of Him. Though He said He wanted His Father's will to be done instead of His own, an angel's visit and praying to the point of sweating blood tell us it was difficult almost beyond belief.

"What should you take from this sermon? I hope a greater and deeper appreciation of the sacrifice He made."

Mack went on to talk about martyrs who had been executed for their steadfastness in keeping the message alive.

He was receiving more compliments on his sermons than ever. It was something to feel good about, but also something to make him feel humble to an even greater degree. Was he as inspired as Maude and Lowell said? Probably so, and more. He prayed more than ever for direction and guidance. Decisions on topics to preach about came easier than ever. Once he got into planning and making notes, thoughts came flowing in rather than appearing in bits and pieces that used to require three times as much effort. Either he was benefitting from years of experience or the Lord was lending a hand more than ever. And he knew which and thanked the Lord. On a rare day when he forgot to thank God, on the next day he would offer a prayer of apology.

It helped that he was too busy to think much about himself. There was music to be listened to. Every evening before going to bed, he let the hard work and inspiration of the world's most appreciated composers come from his two good loudspeakers. He came to know many and appreciate the growth of his inner being they instilled within him.

He didn't read the critically acclaimed novels that people occasionally urged him to read. Once was enough. He didn't get the point; if there was one, he couldn't find it It was the escape novel he turned to, even if some thought it was the low-brow thing to do.

He placed Beethoven's Fifth on the turntable and turned the system on. The opening movement said much to Mack's state of mind. Later when the finale's first excitement burst forth, he could hardly restrain himself from shouting. Not always did he respond with this much grand emotion, but the composer had created tension that on being released was bound to change something in the heart of the listener. Mack thanked God for the composer, the orchestra members, and the conductor who had spent so much of their lives preparing to bless this listener. He had been deeply moved. It might be months, even years, before he had such an experience again, but he had this one and his memory would keep it on and on.

When the spell cast by the music eased, he sat considering his future. It would be greatly different from the past thirteen years? Would he continue preaching? Of course he would; he could not envision himself ten years from now doing anything else. Carpentry? It gave a different kind of satisfaction, an escape from the responsibilities and duties of being a pastor and had its own rewards, but often left him dwelling on feeling that he was not as effective as he should have been at either. Compliments from his audience were pleasant to receive, but he knew himself far better than they. His carpentry was tangible. The quality of his work was there for anyone to see and he turned out his work at a faster rate than others—Lowell had told him that, as had a couple of the guys he had worked with. But his ministry and its effectiveness were not tangible, except for increases in church membership. Did the members carry something from his counseling and his sermons that changed their lives during their time in school, at work and in their family relationships? A fragile marriage that held together, was it because of something he had said or done? A young person who went off to college and did not join the trendy counter-culture movement. Did my efforts influence their behavior? It would be gratifying to know that he played an important role in the student's decision, but there was no way of knowing. As a preacher, would he always be subject to doubts about his effectiveness? Probably, but that was an occupational hazard, he thought. To be honest about all this, he doubted that his listeners knew to what degree he affected their lives. But they keep coming, ever in slowly increasing numbers, so I must be keeping them thinking I'm worthwhile. And on this note he smiled and changed into pajamas and got in bed. Sleep was not long in coming for his uncertainties were not so troubling as at the beginning of his self-exploration in his world of intangibles.

By the day, the sun came brighter and higher and roses bloomed in the park where he walked in late afternoon. He could not do otherwise; he often stopped long enough to fill his lungs with the delicate aroma. It was the roses that invited and he didn't want them to feel slighted.

Often he found himself personifying flowers and trees and also a house-size boulder on very rare occasions when he came upon one in one of the two state parks within an hour's drive. What would his congregation think about him if they knew this side of him? No reason to tell them and destroy what respect they might have for his limited ability to think rationally. Alf knew and thought it was okay, but Alf was a different kind of bird from the rest of the flock.

These days and weeks were an interim of recovery and giving thought to the future. His past had been so unlike most other people's. He had the present and had not the foggiest notion of what his future was to be. Was there something out there never experienced and awaiting him? His grief over what was past no longer maintained the intensity it had during those years, and he was not completely comfortable with that. Ever so slightly, he was getting over the tragedy that had been visited on Rebecca and on himself. Was this less than loyal to her? But she is no longer of the earth and I am blessed with the certainty of where she is and that even there, she has not ceased to love me. The promise she showed and the person she was died years ago and what remained was not even a shell of herself. Was there a time years ago when she went on to Heaven and left a meaningless body behind? To some, it might not seem reasonable that God would wait for the death of the body before bringing the soul to Heaven. There was no suggestion at all that she was still within the body that could make no response except to accept a spoon of food or a drink of water. So much I've been through and so little I understand.

Not because of fatigue, he took a seat on a park bench and watched the strollers and hikers come by. All spoke and the few that were from his church wished him a good evening, but didn't stop to talk for they saw him in the park rather frequently.

Supper usually followed pretty soon. He was beginning to feel better about life and very little guilt because of that. Rebecca was having it better than he was, and he thanked God for allowing her to come back and make sure he knew she was healed.

Change would come. Would he welcome it? A bit of unease walked across his back. He hoped it wouldn't hurry up in coming.

CHAPTER NINETEEN

A few days later, he was back in the state park that had a stream-side rock to sit on comfortably as he listened to the voice of the small stream. Tiny gurgles and splashes that were just the right background for thoughts and daydreams that were beginning to return at times.

Once he had seen on TV a program that carried the viewer to places of uncommon beauty. Scenes from Washington State had awakened his heart and now returned from some pigeon hole of his memory. Mount Rainier, Mount St. Helens, and Olympic National Park with its elk.

This was a time when his future was impossible to imagine. There were some things to daydream about while he was awaiting the first signs of what his future was to be. His memories of the Grand Tetons and Yellowstone were treasures to be relived at times as were his fond memories of hiking in the Great Smokies, and the frequent trips to the Gulf Coast.

There was no thought of leaving the ministry, nor carpentry as long as Lowell wanted him. But he would need a new life for the coming decades. Maude would insist on it and Alf would encourage it, he knew.

Would the change bring marriage? That thought had begun popping up the past two weeks. It was scary, but loneliness was too, and he had just finished living through too many years of that. Genesis 2:18 came to mind. He wasn't going to hurry the process of arriving at that point, but neither was he going to fight and delay it year after year. She would have to be someone special. Maude would insist on it; inwardly he smiled.

There were women at church who would be glad to assist him in selecting. He felt the smile once more at that realization. The marriage he'd not had didn't have to a prevent a future. Rebecca would not begrudge it; neither would her parents. He felt things were moving a bit fast, to be this far along in adjusting for the future.

There were things he wanted to do while he had this new freedom. Travel at every opportunity seemed very important. The future was not likely to leave him as free as the mocking bird that had been singing him awake each morning since spring had come. He prayed for guidance. It would be wise to depend on the Lord.

For what seemed a strange sort of reason, his thoughts shifted to Jacques Monod, probably the most talked about atheist of the past couple of years. The fellow had stated plainly that you couldn't live without a value system, that you couldn't live personally, that you couldn't deal with society without one. Mack knew he meant himself and everyone else. Had he tried to live without one and failed? Mack would have loved to have had an hour with the scientist to learn the answer. He admired the fellow's honesty. The man he had borrowed a value system from a friend who said he wished he could believe in God, but was saddened because he couldn't.

Mack was as certain of God's existence and concern for man as he was that the little stream added beauty to his life. In advance, he had known the flowing water and its small sounds of life would add to the emotions that flowed through his heart in response. His love of the sights and sounds of God's creation brought a joy he continued to seek.

In the worst of times, he could tell God what his needs were and know a partial solution. Rebecca's illness would have been worse than any nightmare had he not been able to pray, "Lord, please be with her and me," and he would feel better, not happy, but better. A simple prayer, but effective. Do people of no faith not realize the man who trusts in God fares far better when problems come? I never heard the voice of God as Rebecca said she did, but hundreds and hundreds of times I call on Him and things are less terrible. When I simply ask for His company, I feel not so alone. And I sometimes realize I don't call on Him enough, thinking I shouldn't bother Him with things I might be able to handle myself. If the Creator of the universe can keep trillions and trillions of stars shining, He can easily listen to my every plea. I had prayed this morning for help with decision-making that I knew I would face, and less than an hour later came the urge to come to this place. What a blessing that I followed the nudge. I know again that whatever troubles come, I can face them better with the help of the Lord. The facing of the next stage of my life will go far better if I am humble enough to depend on Him for help. He knows the fears and doubts that tend to invade our hearts. It seems I have to relearn each day that He is concerned and wishes that I'd come to Him with my worries. How easy it is to forget that the things we worry about are not usually what happens. How quickly a new and growing fear can take the place of the lesson of Psalm 23.

The next day, when it arrived, he might not be as upbeat about God. That was the way he was. Some day he might confess to his congregation that there were still times when his faith in God faltered briefly, that he would probably always have his spiritual ups and downs. There were times his faith was so overwhelming, he believed that he would always remain as he was then. But it would later be diminished by concerns that were of his everyday life. Would it be a wise thing to do if he confessed that he was often not as dependent on God as he urged from the pulpit? They might lose respect for him. But it could be that they would feel relief to hear that he was sometimes prone to be assailed with doubts just as they were. Didn't St. Paul confess that he did not always do as he knew he should?

⊰⊹⊱

The counter-culture movement continued to be a cause for concern. He prayed about it, but that didn't cause it to go away. Should he pray that he would change enough to have no problem with it? But how could he become something that he wasn't? He included some of these worries in his sermons. He would take an issue or two at a time.

"*Just do your own thing,* we are advised by the counter-culture movement because *God is dead,* and there is no one up there who cares if we cheat, steal, release unbridled sex urges, lie, and feel free to be as corrupt as we desire in all things. According to these people, God is not all that is dead. Sin died with along with God. That being so, we can't be held accountable for our actions because sin is no longer is a valid concept. There is no longer a conscience to guide us; that died along with free will. Our heredity and our environment determines all that we are and do. If we are among those who think we have a free will to chose our behavior, we are among the unenlightened. *If it feels good, do it.* That's all you need to know to guide you in choosing what to spend your money and time on. There are no absolutes that would interfere with *doing your own thing.* Right or wrong? It's all relative . . . depending on the situation you are in.

"What will the country be in twenty-five or thirty years when people who've bought into this value system are running it?

"Will churches make changes to try to accommodate and attract these people? Will religion become irrelevant?

281

"As of January of this year, sanctity of human life was ignored by the Supreme Court. In Germany in the thirties and forties, it was ignored if you were a Jew or old or infirm or mentally retarded. God had been declared dead in that country a half century earlier. Fifty years from now, will it mean we'll not be as protected as we are today? No longer would human life be special. Will the day not come when the old and very ill are seen as not being worth the expense of treatment?

"Will you be as free to practice and express your religious beliefs as you are today? Will Christians be allowed to freely preach that some kinds of behavior are a sin? Will the new culture blast you as bigoted and narrow-minded? Today, that is already beginning.

"As Christians have less impact on where the nation is headed, will we hear a great deal more about the separation of church and state? Some of you older folks attended a school in the same building as you went to church. A public school in a church that didn't have to remove any sort of symbols before school on Monday. Churches allowed the use of Sunday school rooms as classrooms in the fifties to help with overcrowding in public schools and the separation of state advocacy groups weren't screaming.

"You are beginning to see that what was once wrong is now right. And the people who are living by the new code do not and will not want to hear or read that what they are doing is morally wrong. And they are already developing a new language to make what they are doing sound like it is harmless.

"We will continue to have freedom of expression of our faith for the foreseeable future as long as it is kept inside the walls of the church and probably over radio and on TV.

"Can a biology professor in a state university teach that the earth had no creator, that we—like any other species—got here by chance? Not only can the professor do this, but professors all over the country *are* doing it. If a professor expressed an opposite view, that there had to be a creator or designer, he or she would face disciplinary action, even if no reference had been made to the story of creation in the Bible. It is already happening.

"Karl Marx's view of religion has become the official policy of United States courts. And at the time of Marx, Darwin explained man's origins without the need of a creator at all. The U.S. Supreme Court has bought into the belief that religion is a hindrance to progress. And we get it's decision in Roe v. Wade that had been the position of what is sometimes called the intelligentsia for at least a century. Who says they are the intelligent ones? They do!"

CHAPTER TWENTY

When Mack had finished a series of sermons on the counter-culture and religion, he knew he needed a change. Emotionally and spiritually, he needed it. In late June, he boarded a flight to Denver and then caught a flight to Seattle. He had never flown before, but had no anxiety about flying. If the plane crashed and he perished, he was certain where it would all end for him. Anyway, his excitement was far greater than what little anxiety he might have felt.

It was a day filled with new experiences. Clouds seen from the top. A bumpy ride as the plane flew near the edge of a huge thunderstorm. Snow-capped mountains were seen from above as they crossed the Rockies and later as Seattle was approached. The engines eased up and ten minutes later, there was obvious excitement and anticipation amongst the passengers.

After Mack had collected his luggage, he rented a car. All went smoothly and an hour later, he had left the city behind and sought a place to spend the night. For the rest of that day, there was nothing that would be particularly memorable.

He would have loved having a traveling companion. Now that would have been an almost new and memorable experience in itself. It wasn't that he felt self-pity because he had traveled alone except for going to the Smokies once with Alf and Nell. At supper that evening, he thought how warm and cozy it would be to have a wife seated across the table. Never having had a wife on an overnight trip, it could be that a year from now, he might have experienced that. But he couldn't very well imagine that now. There was not one woman he could think of that might attract him, that he could day-dream about. But he hadn't gotten far enough along in adjusting to single-hood yet to begin considering who might be available from church. Would he start looking at single women from that stand-point? Maude had told him when the time came when he might be interested, the good matchmakers would have someone suitable in their sights; he could count on it!! He would want to do his own picking, but then he might welcome the judgement of someone else.

Did he come twenty-five hundred miles to think about getting married? Not that he knew beforehand, but here he was—as his salmon was being cooked—doing just that.

As usual, the sounds of others in conversation in a restaurant were a pleasure to his ear. It was the next best thing to having some-one of his own. It had always seemed a bit strange that this was so. He had experienced it so often, and it seemed it would have caused him to feel even more alone than he was. But it never did.

The salmon was grilled and the seasoning showed signs of being prepared by an expert. Instead of a strong fish taste, there was a blending of delicate flavors. The baked Idaho was lightly buttered and care had been taken to fluff it a bit, a touch he'd appreciated. He had saved some of his salad to be eaten with his main meal.

The young waitress had a smile that would brighten anyone's day. There's something special about a woman, Mack thought, some-thing he had not been so aware of before. There was a sweet long-ing in his heart, not for this woman, but for what she represented.

Though Rebecca had never held his head and comforted him, he sensed there were some women who took a man's face between soft hands that spoke of a kind of love that melted and then healed a man's heart.

The waitress returned to pour hot coffee in a half-empty cup. Also she brought fresh warm bread, crusty on the outside, soft on the inside. Herb-seasoned dipping oil had been there from the beginning. There ought to be a law against serving food this good, for what man can resist the temptation to turn to gluttony?

With that thought came the sensation that a big smile had broken out to replace the doleful look he too often saw when he looked in a mirror.

Despite his deep faith, there were times when he needed more than that. Even the company of people he didn't know and the opportunity to engage in just the briefest sort of conversation could give respite from the emotional coldness that he had lived with for years. It might be that this coldness was the worst aspect of being alone.

When he had sipped the last of his coffee, he picked up his bill, looked at it, and left a forty-percent tip. He would not see her again, but he hoped she'd remember him for a couple of days. On sudden impulse, he doubled that.

The next day, he entered Olympic National Park. As he drove the steep climb to the first high ridge top, he recalled ". . . they shall mount up with wings as eagles." It was exhilarating . . . uplifting! Though in an automobile, he was seeing God's creation almost as eagles did when they soar over these mountains. Mack felt a freedom that did not come to him often.

When he came to the point where the road ended, he parked and looked for trail information posted on a board.

The air was cold. Clouds had blotted out the sun, and at that altitude the wind was active. He added a jacket to his light sweater and began walking briskly through dense forest. He had once seen a nature film on TV about Olympic elk in high grassy meadows. Maybe that lay ahead somewhere. Should have gotten information about just where and how he might find such a meadow, but his anticipation of just getting there as soon as possible had overwhelmed his common sense. But soon he discovered that his mistake made no difference; snow blocked the trail before he had taken a hundred steps. He went back to the trail-head and tried another; it too had snow up to a couple of feet deep. There were few bare places, but where there was snow, there was lots of it.

There was a souvenir shop that sold sandwiches. He bought a couple of hotdogs and a soda. The car sheltered him from the wind while he ate his early lunch. Clouds, big and fluffy, came boiling across the sky almost touching ridge tops while allowing short bursts of sunshine to intensely color the forest in deepest greens. A scene to be stored in his memory for days less inspiring than this one.

Somewhere along the road, not far from the ocean, he walked amongst Sitka spruce, tall specimens reaching for the sky and the light that could be found there for growth. Skeletons from fallen limbs and old trees were draped heavily in moss that had withstood winds that had come unbroken for thousands of miles before making landfall. Ferns, giant ones, were everywhere except for the wide trail he walked on, and close by was a salmon stream, not the Columbia by any means, but beautiful in a place unlike he had ever dared to fancy in his daydreams.

This was a place he wanted to stay until approaching darkness would send him on his way. Three times he met other hikers and exchanged information for a few minutes. In a place like this, he decided, you never meet a stranger. There was a common bond that brought people to places in wilderness areas of the Great Smokies, or on a raw cold day on the white beaches of the Gulf Coast, and the West Coast was no different.

Five minutes of living here was worth an hour of living most places. A light shower came and was soon gone, leaving him pleasantly damp, a refreshing breath of moisture for him and the plant life.

He started his journey of exploration along the highway again. When rustic lodging was found, he registered for a room with at least two hours of daylight left. A restaurant was nearby.

The sound of the ocean poured through an open window of the room he was to sleep in. He left his luggage and walked over to the nearby restaurant to check the evening's menu. Then he hiked along the coast, not for exercise but for viewing. At his pace, a snail would not have been left behind. So different it was from Gulf Shores or Destin. Rocky and completely unlike those sugar-white beaches.

A dead salmon was repeatedly tossed up on the rocky beach for a moment, and then lifted by another surge of sea water. Over and over this went on. On top of a nearby sea stack, a bald eagle appeared to be watching. His eyes on the fish? That's how it appeared. Mack heard the scream of another eagle from high in the sky; it was coming inland from out over the sea. The one he had been watching was quick to fly down and pluck the fish from the frothing water and back to the top of the tall sea stack with his catch. The second eagle wasn't about to allow that without a fight. It turned out that the first one knew well the art of keeping a prize. The second one, after a good effort, gave up and flew off down the shoreline. Mack had watched something he never imagined seeing, a most unusual and rare sight—how a large fish-eating bird could easily rip and tear a foot and a half long fish into swallowing-size pieces with great efficiency. His first bald eagle ever to see, and what a demonstration put on by a creature of real skill!

The sun broke out of hiding from behind the clouds that had been present for an hour or more. Mack made his way back toward the lodge and restaurant. A crowd was gathering on the shore of rocks that had been tumbled for ages until all had rounded edges, none more than a few inches across.

Tripods were being set up and cameras mounted in preparation for the approaching sunset. Many had hand-held cameras of all descriptions. Forty or fifty people? Probably no more than forty. Mack didn't bother to try to count. It was obvious why they gathered.

There were two very tall sea stacks covered with moss and shrubs and even very small trees that were hanging on to life. The sun was obviously going to set between these two that were separated at an ideal distance for picture-taking of the scene.

Broken swells came between the rocky giants and crashed ashore, tumbling broken chunks of rocks underneath. Rocks grinding on rocks added to the noisy sea. The vibrations from the grinding could be felt through one's shoes. How many centuries did it take to form the rounded surfaces? Was there ever a time in the past millennium that the coast was not being pounded by incoming swells shattering themselves against a hard coastline? Was it true that the sea stacks were very hard remnants of what used to be the seashore?

There was some talking going on when he first arrived. A hush was descending over the crowd as the sun was only minutes away from touchdown. A narrow band of dark blue-gray clouds crossed the sun's face, and then the disc was shining in its completely flawless ball of intense red as breaths were held and the bottom of the disc kissed the water far out to sea, at its very horizon. The western sky was aflame and then all too quickly, the sun was moving into the ocean. When its burial was complete, the awe-struck crowd slipped wordlessly away.

The sun now gone. Would it arise again? There was in Mack, and he suspected in all others, a touch of fear that it might remain where it had now gone. Or was it just sadness or melancholy that another day had gone, never to be back? In any case, it was a silent group that made its way toward wherever they were going.

Mack had seen many sunsets, but none to match this. What did the first man feel on witnessing one? Terror that the sun would not return?

At the restaurant, there were three empty tables. A number of people were halfway through eating. How could they have sat here when just outside, the glorious brilliance of the sun's fiery descent into the ocean was there for all to see? People are more different than Mack could get used to. Even before he seated himself, a man beckoned him. He stood as Mack approached.

"Won't you sit with my wife, Joan, and me? I'm Bill Rice," he said as a strong right hand was extended. "We saw you at the sunset. That makes you our kind of people. We live at Port Angeles."

"I stayed in a motel there last night," Mack told the couple after introducing himself and taking a seat.

Coffee was ordered and served. The couple, Mack guessed, were in their early fifties, a really handsome pair that showed no signs of aging that wear and tear of careless living could bring on.

"We noticed you had no camera with you, making you an exception out there," Joan said.

"Left a disposable one in my room." Mack explained that it would not do nearly the job that his eyes and memory could do. "The higher the emotional level of an experience, the more vivid and permanent the memory becomes. I've seen the sun sink into the Gulf of Mexico, but this was so different. Framed between two magnificent sea stacks, accompanied by the sounds and feeling of the tumbling and grinding stones underfoot.

"What do you suggest I order from the menu, Bill? By an oceanside, I usually order seafood."

"The halibut here is exceptional. We always order it."

While they ate, Mack asked questions about Mount Rainier, his destination for the next day.

"You haven't seen it yet?" Joan inquired.

Mack smiled, "Only from the Space Needle. Like any good tourist, I took time for that after arriving yesterday before driving to Port Angeles."

"Pray that it will be cloud-free tomorrow. Some come out from the East and wait around close by and never see it after staying a week. Others see it their first day. Pray that you do," Bill said.

"I'll do just that," Mack commented. "It had better work." He grinned. "I'm a preacher on a short vacation. How could I return and report to my congregation that I came twenty-five hundred miles to see the Olympic elk and Mount Rainier, and that snow-blocked trails resulted in no sightings of those animals and that three days of clouds had the mighty mountain all wrapped up in a fog?"

At another point in the meal, Mack asked if they were staying the night at the roadside inn.

Bill said, "If the road is free of ground fog, we can be home in two hours. The weather forecast is that it should be clear We come here two or three times each summer."

"Just to see the sunset?"

"Primarily," Joan answered. "Each time, it's a little different Today, it appeared the clouds might not lift in time. We're teachers and on the long summer break. If we don't get up 'til nine tomorrow, it's okay. After living through a drippy winter, there is something very special about summer out here.

"We have a son who finished at Washington State and has been a civil engineer for about a year now. And another son who is currently taking courses at a local community college. Will probably decide to become a science teacher." She apologized for not having asked Mack about his family.

Mack summed up his story of the past thirteen years in a few sentences.

"And you kept your faith through all of that," Bill said in a tone of disbelief.

"Looking back, it's hard to believe that I could. But if I discarded faith in God . . . it took awhile, but eventually I learned to pray a different kind of prayer."

"Which at first was that God would heal your wife?" Joan asked. "And eventually you learned to ask that God would help you bear up under your grief?"

"Yes, ma'am. It took longer than it should have, but eventually I arrived at such a place.

"Coming out here was supposed to help me get ready for the next stage of my life. This evening's sunset was a spiritual experience that will help me on my way. I don't know just how, but I believe my spirit will be richer for the remainder of my life."

Bill said "That crowd of people probably had folks from several states and maybe another country or two. People wouldn't have stood there waiting a half hour unless they wanted their souls to experience the awe that they knew would come. I can't speak for those who could have watched but didn't," he said in a low voice, since at a table close by sat four people who had passed up the opportunity.

"The cameras were to help remember the experience, not just to make pictures to show the people back home. I bet most already have pictures of other sunsets in their photo albums," Joan added.

When the time came to part, Mack walked them to their car and thanked them again for the invitation to share a table. "And especially for your understanding and well-wishes for my future."

A few minutes later, after reading the 13th chapter of Corinthians, he turned off his bedside lamp and pulled up the covers. The sound of the ocean came through an open window which he would close in the morning before taking a shower . . . after turning on some heat. But what was entering the room now was super special, to be long remembered and treasured.

Instead of feeling lonely on this night before sleep came, he reviewed the warmth of companionship at supper and the experience of the sunset that would forever live in his heart. He thanked God for placing in his soul the ability to feel the overwhelming emotion and wonder that came to him those few minutes when the sun touched the water and all too soon was gone. He appreciated nature's job of stage-setting and carrying out the act with a glory that could not have been conceived of without actually witnessing it.

Each time he awakened during the night—several times briefly—he was aware of the breaking surf. After remembering where he was, he drifted quickly back into deep sleep.

⚒⚒

He found just the kind of place to park he had been looking for. Stepping out of the car as his face tilted back . . . then far back, he took it in—the jagged icy beauty of it all. He had known for more than three hours that it was to be a blessed day unless a shifting of wind direction brought in moist air. Each time he had a good view of the mountain as he drove, it had remained free of clouds. And at last, it was there above—it's blinding beauty in bright sunshine! He thanked God.

Along a trail through wildflowers, there were plaques here and there identifying the different species that thrived with snow only feet away. He stopped more than he walked, for quite awhile. The mountain that he had come to see stole most of his gazing time. Then off in another direction were ridges and more ridges with lots of snow adding to their tree-covered beauty. Too much to take in. It took his breath away! His ever-moving eyes tried to store it all, but that was an impossible task. His disposable camera lent him some assistance. Back home, its pictures would be permanent memories of scenes he only took in for fifteen to twenty seconds. There was far, far too much for one man in one afternoon. He could not count on coming back the next day and felt so blessed to have the whole afternoon.

With the giant mountain of ice towering above and endless ridges that would have been more than outstanding back in the Southeast, small flowers of such intense colors were able to capture his attention and his heart. That they lived and thrived was no small miracle.

But then his attention was drawn back to what he came to see . . . Mount Rainier itself. Its cap was not the perfect cone seen in pictures of volcanic mountains in some places. It was an old mountain and a few thousand years ago, it had erupted blowing its top off and had never regained its perfect shape.

At a turnout on the trail, he stood imagining what would happen if the hot molten rock ever so slowly rose close enough to the surface to cause all the ice to start melting, but not fast enough to cause an eruption. From his readings on volcanos, he knew that the hardened cap of rock under the ice would not give way slowly enough for a gradual melting of the ice sheet. When it came, it would be explosive. Would Tacoma and Seattle escape its rage?

To get changing views, he picked up his slow pace. Even as his eyes took in more than his soul could appreciate, his mind returned to the hill country of the Southeast and its subdued topography, far older than this land of almost vertical landscape. This was stupendously exciting at every turning of his head! Yet a touch of longing for the soft, rounded hills back home intruded on his thoughts.

At one point he followed a trail that led into heavily wooded ridges and hollows, and he walked at a good speed, enjoying the flowing of muscles in his legs, the freedom to move uninhibited, and by sights almost too astonishing for soul to bear.

Later, he discovered he had picked up a trail that led him back to the tree line and a new perspective of Mount Rainer's broken crown. An extremely short bridge spanned a miniature canyon with completely vertical sides. Water almost as white as milk cascaded along the bottom, carrying a glacier's grindings at the beginning of its journey to the sea.

At another place, he found a rock awaiting a hiker to come sit at a vantage point where his eyes could easily take in the grandeur of the mountain. After a while, from behind, a pleasant voice announced, "Ah, I let you beat me to it."

Mack turned to see what went with the nice voice and teasing manner. He was looking up into the face of a young woman of maybe twenty-five. Blond and eyes of a color that some of the wild flowers would envy. He quickly tried to yield the seat to her, but a firm hand on his shoulder pushed him back.

"Sir, I sat here earlier for a long while. Now, it's your turn. I was teasing." She paused to smile and definitely had a dimple in her left cheek. "Or maybe I was flirting a bit." The dark blue eyes sparkling with humor caused Mack's heart to skip a beat or two, or maybe it was three or even more.

Where it came from, Mack didn't know, but here's what he said: "No one has ever flirted with me before."

"You would have been so absorbed inside your head with too many great thoughts to have noticed if someone had. I came upon you and stood close behind you for about five minutes and you never sensed my presence." She wished him good viewing and moved on. And he thought she said "Poor man," as she left.

Mack felt a lingering excitement from the presence and manner of the woman. It came to him that he had missed so much in life. Maybe there would yet be a woman in his life that would be lively and full of fun. His heart hurt at what he had missed.

Even before her illness began, Rebecca was different. Was it that she lived in a world of youthful dreams, that she was ill-prepared for the realities that most others saw all too well? So much human evil was all about, that one could not afford to live as if most people had invisible wings of angels. And when the illness struck, she began to see evil where there was none intended. Dr. Pickens didn't think her youthful innocence and purity were precursors of the illness that awaited her in some dark recess of her brain.

Had she been more of a social animal like the woman who had just left, would it have kept the illness at bay? Maybe not, but anyway, if there is another in my future, I pray it will be one who laughs easily and worries little. Concerned about others, but not too concerned about what others think about her, and that she has fun along the way. It's not that I didn't love the shy, demure person Rebecca was, it's just that I wish . . . oh, Lord, I wish both of us had been more mature emotionally and socially.

In my mind, I made her what I wanted her to be. I was so young, seeing the world as from a fairy tale point of view.

Soon Mack was up, walking back along the trail seeing more uplifting sights than could be taken in. Absorbing and appreciating all that he could. It could not but change the soul of this man who had lived through the hell of life's ugly side. Back home, there was to be a man different from the one who came. Nature's finest scenes had called; he came and knew God had brought him here. He thought of the so many who would see such beliefs as nonsense, and his heart was momentarily burdened with pity, for the multitudes made their choices and would never connect nature with the Creator. But he thanked God for what was before him, and the conservationists who had placed such jewels as this in special preserves for the uplifting of souls who came to see and treasure.

Mack's thoughts quickly moved on to his experiences of the unequalled magnificence ahead and on all sides. For not any of his experiences should be spoiled by pity for those who came but could only appreciate it at a physical level. They had decided to be what they were. They could have taken a different route and even at the worst of times have had the comfort of knowing that there was far more to our existence than chaos and chance.

⊨⊨

Mount Rainier was cloud-capped on his third day in Washington though it's lower elevations were visible. Perhaps Mount St. Helens would have clear visibility. Before driving far, he got a view, and its peak was below the deck of clouds. He thanked God.

The mountain was not nearly so high as Mount Rainier, and from a distance, the peak had appeared a far more perfect cone. Someone had told him the day before that it had not erupted in a long time, but that it would again since it was an active volcano.

There were trails, streams, and trees. As he walked, he took in the sights and the general atmosphere of nearly perfect places for a person to explore nature and himself. As usual, there was a feeling of being back home; he didn't quite understand how that was but felt it was not necessary that he do so. There was something so very special about forests,

The night before, he had stood before a large mirror on the low dresser in the motel bedroom and did something unusual; he studied the man who looked back at him. Perhaps it had been because a young woman that day had given him a good looking over, and apparently liked what she saw. So, maybe he was trying to see himself as he appeared to others. Or perhaps, he was not as completely untouched by vanity as he had thought he was. And it could be that he was in a state of changing his attitude about the possibility of a woman in his future.

The brown eyes, with darker brown speckles were warm and friendly. There was a trace of that even as he examined himself. His features were rather regular, not resembling a Halloween mask at all, he thought. That brought a ghost of a smile and a bit of twinkle to his eyes. No permanent lines of sadness were to be seen in the face he examined. Usually he looked at himself no more than required to shave or comb his hair after a shower.

His hair was, he admitted to himself, a rich brown and free of even one grey hair that he could see. Oh, he already knew the color of his eyes and hair; that was on his driver's license. His height at six feet and one inch could be found there too. But this was the first time he had wondered, since perhaps age sixteen, how he might appear to a young woman. Rebecca had seemed to think he passed her inspection on meeting him their first year in college. And that had been enough. Was he going to hurry when he arrived back home and start primping and using a men's fragrance that "a woman could not ignore" as an ad would say. Had four months and this trip effected such a turnaround?

While he stood there examining himself, he wondered if there might be an extension of self beyond the cranium that enclosed his brain and the mind that lived there. He had never been able to find scientific evidence that there was an aura that extended ten feet beyond or even one inch beyond. With a momentary sadness, he realized that he was confined to living within that bony structure. Perhaps mankind's desire to travel to distant and really far away places was something growing out of his feeling of imprisonment within that hard structure. That there came times when touch and the other many ways of communication were not enough. And the desire to leave the everyday mind behind, and have a vacation from the self inside became something he longed for.

An unusual frame of mind for Mack for a few minutes and not one he was likely to repeat on a regular basis.

On this day, he stood at the timber line and let the limitless wonder take over as the nearly perfect cone of white filled and overflowed his field of vision. He knew that something of what was inside him was projected to meet the summit of this most shapely of mountains.

Where Mount Rainier overwhelmed with its rugged and shattered size, Mount St. Helens was of a size and shape to allow one to love it from the beginning. Hot, bubbling liquid rock eons ago becoming a shape like this one was almost beyond belief.

Mack walked on a trail that thousands of feet had visited. He was not alone in his admiration as he lifted his face to take in all that eyes could see. Ahead and behind, he could hear soft-spoken words of others. He could not imagine anyone being noisy in the presence of such a marvel.

Mack had read of plate tectonics and how the edge of the Pacific plate was slowly being forced under the rock of the heavier continental plate, and that it became molten as a result of friction and pressure. In time something had to come up as more of the ocean's floor kept coming underneath. But science didn't affect his belief that the Creator gained satisfaction from His earthly children coming to enjoy the thrill of seeing what had been created for their wonder.

Was pressure being exerted from underneath at this very moment? Would the almost perfect shape of the mountain someday be blown sky-high? Could it come at any time? Like right now?

There were woodland trails and lakes to be explored. For as much as a half hour at a time, he would have a fine stand of old conifers to himself. There were tiny streams and small streams of ice-cold water to place a hand in up to the wrist, and that was far enough. A fantasy came visiting . . . one of living in such a place in a small log cabin, studying the Bible and a fine book of masterpiece sermons. Uninterrupted except by the comings and goings of the Holy Spirit. Tall and Heaven-pointed trees forming the grandest cathedral.

It was a stop and go hike, stopping to take it in . . . letting it soak deeply into his memory. If he lived to be ninety, he wanted this all to remain. The brain, he knew, could store an almost infinite number of images and memories if they were of great importance.

He thought of an old saying, "This is the first day of the rest of my life." That day is not this day nor yesterday, but the day of the sun setting into the Pacific, while it was framed by two ancient sea stacks, and awe settled in as the last of it was buried for the night.

He now realized that as the sun itself became buried, he had buried part of the sadness and loneliness of the past thirteen years. It would, a part of it, come again and then again, each time a little less hurtful. From the evening of the day before yesterday, real healing had made a definite beginning. The images of the sun would remain one of his most treasured memories.

And he knew why he had come to the majestic West. God had sent him. It could have been no one else. Not one person had said "Mack, old fella, you need to pack up a piece of luggage and get yourself away from here, but he had come as if Alf or Maude or Lowell had insisted. It had been a gentle, but insistent urging and before long, he made flight reservations.

He came from hiking the forest to take an unobstructed view of Mount St. Helens, a mountain that had been love at first sight, not too big to inspire a comfortable emotion. The next time he came to the West, he would include this mountain again. With a smile and hope in his heart that next time there might be a wife and kids. It was the first time he had actually formed the word *wife*, meaning for himself, since Rebecca's passing. And kids? Well, mid-thirties was not too old to consider such a possibility. The big question was, would a woman consider him good husband material? He would want to date for a pretty long while. He and Rebecca had never, when dating, done the kind of goofy fun things that other couples did—like going to an amusement park and taking a ride on a roller coaster or some other scary ride. They had never eaten cotton candy from the same cone or shared a popsicle or hiked to the top of a high hill and had a yodeling, laughing contest. They had never been kids. They had never been unserious. They had not been kids at twenty, nor even at eighteen on their first date, "supervised," of course, by an older couple. No one else knew, but they did at that tender age, that no kind of supervision was needed.

At these thoughts and memories, Mack felt a big smile crack the solemn expression on his face. An unfamiliar feeling, but that was something he hoped in the future, to correct by multiplying by ten.

I'm not going to become wild, but I'll be darned if I'm going to be the prim misfit I used to be. Maybe it's wrong to be thinking that living should include some fun, with my wife so recently buried, but I postponed happiness for years and never enjoyed a bit of harmless fun before that. Did God require that of me because I was going to be a preacher? Does piety mean a solemn face and attitude? Can a good man on smashing his thumb with a hammer think, "Dammit!" and still be a good man. I've thought it a few times but out of fear someone would hear me if I exclaimed it, would bite my lips instead. Did holding it back make me a finer servant for the Lord? I don't know, I really don't.

These were some of his thoughts as he drove toward a reserved room near Seattle. He didn't know how different he was going to be back home, but he'd be at least a shade different.

He thought again of the woman who came upon him on the trail at Mount Rainier— someone he had instantly liked and was a bit saddened because he'd not see her again. Maybe there'd be someone like her back in the Southeast. How often he'd heard that everyone has a double. He could hope.

CHAPTER TWENTY-ONE

Maude was the first to comment. He had dropped by on Sunday afternoon. "You are different, Mack. You've been back from the West two Sundays. Didn't pick up on it last week. But today, it shows."

"What shows?"

"You look a tiny bit different in the pulpit. More confident? I think so."

"Haven't I always appeared self-assured? You told me once that I did. I hope you don't mean I'm beginning to appear cocky. Actually, I feel quite humble—I know so much less than I wish I did. I spend lots of time preparing and praying before I deliver a sermon. If the congregation knew how little I do know—"

"They'd love you anyway. Maybe you are not more self-confident. It's hard to put a finger on it, but you're different."

He had been looking carefully at the wrinkled face and the hazel eyes that sparkled with affection. She had never tried to hide the fact that he was her hero.

"I do feel different. I saw sights and felt emotions that would leave anyone changed. In a manner and to a degree I'd not imagined, I saw God's message in nature more than I ever had before. Long before man was to arrive on earth, He caused natural changes in the earth's interior and its surface that would speak to us of His desire to let us know that He is God and one way He speaks to us is through the environment He created that can thrill our souls with its splendor. I saw the sun sink into the ocean framed between two magnificent sea stacks. I saw and walked along the sides of two volcanic mountains. Could they have been as uplifting to an atheist as they were to me? I feel sure they could not. To a non-believer, they could not speak of anything except the physics of geological change."

"Are you saying that a non-believer could not appreciate snow-covered peaks that reached for the sky toward infinite space?"

"But the believer can and does feel that this is one way God speaks to us. Surely that gives an added dimension to the experience. Can the atheist say that a long series of chance events plus Darwinian evolution somehow placed in us the ability to thrill and love the beauty of nature? Such an ability serves not at all to help with survival."

"Maybe you've made progress in putting your sorrow behind. That may be what I sense."

"I've made a start. You can't live if you are going to stay in the past. What I have are memories and what's in the future. The present is like a distant flicker of lightning, then gone."

"You haven't wanted to feel you're *completely* over Rebecca?"

"No, I don't want to feel disloyal to her memory, but I have accepted that I'm only due her a limited amount of time spent in grief. There are souls to be saved and my future to be lived. Up until recently, much of my life has been dedicated to seeing that I did all I could for her and—"

"And now, it's time you see to your own needs while dedicating much of your life to others. That is not in any way unfaithful to her memory. Quite the opposite."

≈✠≈

It didn't start with a bad dream and after-awakening effects. Milk had been poured on cold cereal and a cup of instant coffee sat beside it, hot and awaiting him.

It started with tears flowing from a source that had been a dull ache since awakening. A bright, sunny summer morning greeted him, but was unappreciated and hardly noticed.

The tears matched the mood that had suddenly fallen upon him. It was Thursday. No obligations until the evening when he had duties as a counselor. The breakfast could sit as it was. It was a time to eat at the Men's Retreat. Taking time to shave and wash up, so no signs of tears would remain, he dressed and left as soon as possible. At a time when he had believed he was fast recovering from the past, this! There was no accounting for it. It was real and it was here, and he feared it might be a companion for a long while.

Temporarily, the restaurant worked its magic. The smells of bacon and sausage and biscuits and coffee and the pleasing sounds of conversation by people, who were apparently having lives, took his mind off himself.

He could await the cooking of his food comfortably in this environment. The people sounds were even more enjoyable than his coffee. His mind touched briefly on what he'd left behind on the kitchen table and he thought, "Yuk!"

Where was the happiness he knew in the West? Would it return as suddenly and as unexpectedly as this present mood had hit him?

What if food lost its usual ability to offer comfort in the worst of hours? It was at this moment of anxiety that his food arrived. One bite of crispy bacon reassured him that in the worst of gloom, good food could still be counted on as a friend. He was a preacher and believed that God could be depended on for help in his time of need. But with a quick thought of apology to God, he appreciated the quick answer to an unspoken prayer that the hot food brought. Even as his spirit glowed in appreciation of fluffy scrambled eggs and hot buttered biscuits and grits, it was the bacon that stood out. And I had thought the days when good food and the company of others at nearby tables as the high points in life were times I'd not have to seek as before. Times that almost meant more than my belief in God. And me being a preacher, I'm ashamed of my shallowness. But am I expected to never live a human moment, here and there? Does God expect me to live in my loneliness with a disdain for food such as this and a love for Him only? Here I sit with food not only for me, but for my soul, wondering if I'm being displeasing to God by enjoying the food so much. And quickly I wonder—and just as quickly regret it—if God doesn't sometimes feel like giving me a kick in the seat of my pants for thinking of Him as possibly begrudging me the simple pleasure of a fine meal. Must I always feel that I haven't done enough for Him?

Another serving of hot biscuits was brought and real wild blackberry jelly in a small bowl. More butter too, and a refill of coffee. He thought maybe he wasn't being too displeasing to God.

⸎

Eight days later, he drove to the city to arrive for a ten o'clock appointment with Dr. Pickens. The spells of crying or feeling like he would burst into tears at any time had not abated. He had preached on Sunday and received compliments as pleasing as usual; it had taken unusual concentration to deliver his sermon from notes prepared a month earlier.

Mack arrived shortly after 7:30, giving him ample time to review how he would tell Rebecca's psychiatrist that the husband now had unexplained problems of a mental nature. He reviewed possible approaches, but had not come to one he liked. About ten minutes before the appointed time, he decided the best approach was just to respond to Dr. Pickens' first question. The man was good at what he did, knowing just how to get a person started.

Dr. Pickens' warm handshake welcomed him as it did those years ago.

"Does Rebecca still live?" he asked in a soft voice.

"She passed back in March in a nursing home," Mack said in a voice calmer than he expected.

"Alzheimer's, wasn't it?" Not waiting for an answer, he went on, "Her doctor at the hospital informed me that the transfer had been made and how much the additional illness was disturbing to him.

"And you are here today because?"

"Because eight mornings ago, I awoke with a case of dammed up tears. The dam was not long in bursting and today I still feel pretty much the same. A bit of dull pain around my eyes. Each day it comes and stays. I've almost quit letting the tears flow. The dull pain stays.

"Did you cry when she died? Did tears come when you first learned she had Alzheimer's?"

"No, sir."

"When did you first cry? Last week?" He asked before Mack could answer the first question.

"Thursday of last week. There have been episodes since, but I hold it in when others might see."

"It's not uncommon to respond to grief in the manner you have. You were already bereaving Rebecca when you first brought her to me years ago. I pulled her file which had been put into Inactive Files years ago. I talked with you at length that first day and noted that you were bearing up well, knowing what you did about the disease. Today, I'd tell you that you were bearing up too well each time you brought her."

"You mean I've been hiding the grief from myself all these years?"

"You did it to keep her from realizing in the early days of her illness that her condition was as bad as it was. You did it so you could have hope that the magic pill might soon be forthcoming. You had your job as a carpenter; there were other guys around and you couldn't let it show that you were having a hard time by getting all choked up and teary eyed when they asked of her welfare on a Monday morning. I wasn't there, but I'm a man and I know how we demand of ourselves that we not bawl like we say women do."

At this point, Mack told of his recent trip to Washington State and how much he had believed real healing was underway.

"Did you feel that, in a way, you were being somewhat disloyal to Rebecca by starting to get over her so soon?" the soft voice inquired.

"How did you know?"

"Because I'm an old man and through my patients, I've experienced grief in a number of forms. I've experienced it myself.

"Your Christian faith does not exempt you from the pains of living. It helps, but your salvation did not change you into an unfeeling robot who by repeating a few of your special Bible verses, feels all is now okay."

"You mean I'm not over it, that I still have to go through the steps of bereavement. That's all that's wrong with me."

"That's enough to take you a while yet. You've been patient for more than thirteen years. I'm betting you can make it a little longer. Try praying more for yourself and a little less for the hundreds of millions in far away lands. You, a servant of God, need to ask your Christ to be your servant and healer.

"When He was on earth those years, He preached. He made it clear He was a servant and wanted us to call on Him in times of real need. He was not too high and mighty to wash his disciples' feet.

"Have you considered you are free to marry if the right one comes along? You never had a marriage my record shows."

"I did have sex once. That was with a very young woman whose husband's funeral I'd preached one day earlier." He had suddenly decided to tell this man who understood him better than he, himself, did. "Her mother and brother had hurried back home suddenly on learning her father had suffered a setback in the hospital that afternoon. The brother would be back by late afternoon the next day in a truck to take her and her small amount of furniture back to her old home."

"And church ladies didn't—?"

"Realize she had no family member with her."

Mack was impressed at the doctor's perceptiveness. "Neither did I when she called and asked me to come over to see her."

"And after being alone for a while, I bet she wanted to be held a little. And the inevitable happened. As if more was needed, a recent death can have that sort of effect."

"You mean on her?"

"Yes. And somewhat on you. A matter of biology, I think."

"But I sinned the big sin. I prayed for forgiveness. Over and over I asked God to forgive. I'd been unfaithful to Rebecca and to my calling. I prayed a thousand times and more."

"He forgives on the first prayer of repentance, yet you have never completely forgiven yourself." Again, Mack appreciated his perceptiveness.

"I might could have except for the—"

"Memories of how good it was," Dr. Pickens finished the sentence for him. "And you never had sex with another?"

"No, I love to go to the Gulf Coast when the weather is a bit cold and walk the beaches and absorb the moods of the ocean."

"You go from November though February when the beach bunnies are in hibernation . . . because you don't want to feel you lust after a woman; you avoid sin that way. If some hardy female braves the cold in her bikini—"

"I avert my eyes, but few of them ever do."

"You are a good man, Mack. I can't come this Sunday but maybe the next one. Your church's name and address?"

He wrote this down and then asked if Mack felt a need to come back.

"Could I?"

"Two weeks from today at the same time, I think I can see you. Check with the receptionist on your way out." He arose, took Mack's hand in both of his, and wished him better days ahead.

Mack accepted the doctor's diagnosis completely. The next few days when tears came, he accepted them as a normal form of behavior, but he controlled them when in the presence of others. When alone, he let the silent tears flow at times and at others in body-wracking sobs. He had been through far worse ordeals than most others ever knew in a lifetime and now that it should all be behind, it wasn't. What he experienced now was worse than the other had been, or so it now seemed.

When I was out West, I thought I was pretty much through with all this. Now it has hit me harder than I ever dreamed possible. What I had put off dealing with all those years because I just couldn't deal with it then, has been dumped on me all of a sudden.

These days were a time to be honest with himself, to let all his pent up feelings surface and be recognized. At one point, Dr. Pickens had advised doing that.

His efforts to assist others by trying to become a more effective listener was a source of deep gratification to him. If only he had the ability to understand others with the skill Dr. Pickens showed. That became a goal and took his mind off himself some of the time. How many times would he have to learn that long, regular hours in thinking of self was a straight road to depression and dissatisfaction. But a hard head has to learn and relearn life's most helpful lessons. By the time he returned to the psychiatrist, he felt he was making some progress toward keeping his mind on doing what was best for himself by doing for others. Next year? Well, he'd probably be learning this again. Is that due to man's nature, or due to Mack's nature? For some reason, he hoped it was due to human proclivity and realized that wasn't a good failing to wish on anyone.

Dr. Pickens was in his usual good form, cordial and warm. "And how is my preacher of the day?"

"Is it terrible of me that one day last week, I let it cross my mind that it was Rebecca's Alzheimer's disease that ended up making me a free man?"

"I bet you thought it was a terrible thing to let that reality occur to you. I thought of that on hearing that disease had started. But I was in a far different position. No guilty feelings growing out of that reality in my case."

"Had that disease not happened, was there any chance she could ever have recovered from the schizophrenia?"

"Without something coming along that I don't foresee, I doubt it seriously."

After further discussion, Dr. Pickens said, "Mack, you're in pretty good shape. I've not even decided on a name for your problem, except for the old-fashioned one of *grief.* Now I'm giving you a prescription, verbally. Go back and live; you never have. Marry the right woman and raise a couple or three kids.

"I'll surprise you before long and see you in your church." And he did just over two weeks later.

⤜⤛

Mack often thought about the possibility of marriage in the future, and could do that now without feeling disloyal to Rebecca. It wasn't that he looked at each young woman at church, who was not with a male companion, and asked himself if she was the one. But sometimes when shaking the right hand of an attractive one, he would glance at her left hand. Without his realizing it at first, young women at church and other places were becoming more attractive. And he noticed that there seemed to be more pretty ones than before. Without thinking about it, he was not quickly averting his eyes on seeing one.

More of them had curves, nice ones that caused a bit of a tug on his heart. He was not lusting, but he *was noticing*. And he did not wonder what Rebecca would think. She was in Heaven now and if she thought about it, she would want him to have someone to love.

Rebecca's traits of being demure, quiet, always courteous and deferring to others . . . were these her natural personality? Or did she become this in order to be what would please me? I was many things I thought a young aspiring preacher ought to be. Seldom laughing when I'd see humor, when something funny was there . . . if I'd just have looked. While others laughed, sometimes gleefully, I might have a hint of a smile. Now I can see as I did not then, that as Readers' Digest says, "Laughter is the best medicine." The first time I went to the Men's Retreat, I chuckled on seeing the board over the entrance suggesting it was a place to get away from women for a little while. And later, a sign board hanging to the bottom of the first one, at *Men's Retreat* proclaimed in bold letters *Wives' Relief,* and I laughed outright. *Gonna Wash That Man Right Outta My Hair* from South Pacific ran through my mind.

Did I project the image in my college days that religion was a necessary burden and your demeanor and attitude and conduct at all times must reflect that? What a horse's rear end I must have been. I doubt I drove her to paranoid schizophrenia, but I do wish I could have been more optimistic and fun-loving; maybe our days of courtship could have been happier ones for her. If I were doing those days over, I'd carry her to the county fair and we'd ride the ones that wouldn't make you wet your pants. We'd watch a clown perform and join the crowd that laughed in appreciation.

But I didn't. I was what I was and wish I had been a lot less of. Dear God, in the future, may I have a little common sense when it comes to a lady friend, if I'm ever so graced to have one that would give me the time of day. I know I have to be more of what I've been so slowly becoming, if I ever have a great relationship with a woman.

CHAPTER TWENTY-TWO

Mack was beginning to approach his duties with less of a frantic urge. No longer did he have to be busy, busy, so he wouldn't have time or opportunity to dwell on his life and its problems. Almost effortlessly, he could now prepare his sermons which were becoming more thoughtful. The mind works more rationally when it doesn't have to occupy itself with activity that seems necessary to preserve sanity, he realized.

More than two years earlier, he had told his people of Jacques Monod and the scientist's absolute certainty that man—just as any other species—appeared on earth purely by a long series of chance events. Rather than seeing the scientist as some kind of threat to Judeo-Christian belief, as he had initially done, he now saw Monod's conclusion about the need for a value system as strong support for his next sermon entitled, "Living Without a Value System."

He reminded the audience that he had spoken of Jacques Monod, a world-class scientist, more than two years ago. And on another occasion, he had talked of Monod's dependence on a value system. And now for a third time, he referred to the man.

"Dr. Monod was also a world-class atheist who made it clear in his book, "Chance and Necessity," that there was no one in the universe who was aware of us or would be concerned about our problems. He said that mankind, like any other species, was a product of chance events and might just as well not have appeared. Perhaps he should have gone on to say that it would be just as well if man disappeared in a nuclear shootout, since there was no reason for man's being here.

"Seemingly contrary to this line of thinking, the scientist expressed elsewhere that he was deeply concerned about the buildup and stockpiling of nuclear arms. You see, he was concerned about the possibility that man—who had come from nothing more than a long series of chance events over millions of years—might perish worldwide from the effects of atom bomb explosions. You'd think that wouldn't concern him, but it did!

"Almost as puzzling was how the atheist ever came to think on why a value system was important to a species who might just as well not have appeared. Are we not like a twelve inch strand of seaweed that a storm far out in the Atlantic broke off from a huge blob? And somehow, after many weeks of drifting, washed upon the beach at Gulf Shores? Of no greater importance than that, are we?

"But he said you cannot live without a value system. You cannot live personally. You cannot deal with society without it.

"Being a product of pure, blind chance left him free—he reasoned—to pick out anything he wished to guide him through life. But he didn't pick out a value system by chance. He borrowed a friend's who said his was enough to fill the heart of man.

"Not only was Monod a world-class scientist in a biology-related specialty, he was a world-class atheist as well. He is completely convinced the universe and all that is in it did not require a designer for its origin.

"What does the scientist mean by the word *heart* when he was talking to John Hess of the New York Times? Not the organ that pumps blood. The only thing left is the inner being that he makes no claim that chance events created in mankind. Did he mean that the value system he selected filled his inner being, his soul? I'm certain that he did because that is all that is left.

"In Matthew 6:21, Jesus used heart to mean soul. It is also referred to as spirit, as all of you know.

"Think of it. An evolutionist—and not your run-of-the-mill evolutionist—talking about the need for a value system to fill the heart of man. When he said you cannot live without a value system, did he mean not just himself, but all others? Obviously that's just what he meant!!

"People who consider themselves a part of the intelligentsia, the elite, look down on Christians as being simple-minded. The term Bible Belt is not intended to mean something good or admirable, but is intended as a term of contempt. You know it, and don't need me to remind you of it.

"You are here in church this morning because you need a value system. If Monod couldn't live without one, hopefully, the people who have nominated themselves as intellectually our superiors will take note that even a Nobel Laureate has stated frankly that he couldn't live without it."

A woman worked her way to a microphone that had been placed on the floor for questions related to the sermon. "Brother Mack, why did people latch on to evolution almost as soon as Darwin proposed it over one hundred years ago?"

Mack thanked her and responded, "It freed the sinners from feelings of guilt when they lie, cheat, steal, commit adultery, or whatever their favorite sin might be." He looked at his watch and said, "We have time for a couple more."

A man came to another mike, "Many were tired of the restraints that religion places on the kind of conduct they were interested in."

Mack said, "Exactly. Sin without guilt, and it became no longer sin."

The next question came from a lady. "You really think we can take the atheist's core message on values and use it to further Christianity?"

"Yes, I do. Monod gave respectability in the community of science to the need for a value system. I hope it has caused all of you to appreciate a little more the One who came and in a message of love gave all who would accept, a value system for the best and worst of times.

"Who had the greatest scientific mind of this century?" Mack asked.

There came an almost chorus of answers in unison, "Albert Einstein."

"And he flatly rejected the chance explanations of origin of the universe in favor of God as a Creator. Not a Christian was he, but a believer in God," Mack concluded.

⋖⋗

At the doorway that Sunday noon was a woman he had not noticed before. He took her hand as she said it was a sermon unlike any she'd heard before. As the next person was greeting him, it flickered through his mind that the young woman was unlike any he had seen before.

As he was driving to his favorite Sunday restaurant, his thoughts were interrupted by the memory of that woman. And to his mind came the Mount Rainier trail and the woman with a dimple in her left cheek, the woman who teased and admitted the possibility that she might be flirting a bit.

Then his thoughts returned to the unusual sermon of a few minutes earlier. He liked taking time for the questions from the audience, something he might try again when it seemed appropriate. It would have to be done when there was only a little time left before normal closing because of the possibility of someone long-winded getting up and asking a long list of questions. That wasn't something he felt proud of letting enter his mind, but there it was. The sermon itself, he believed was something to feel good about. Responses at the exit had been unusually positive.

The next week at the end of the Sunday morning service, the young lady came forward to join the congregation. What young lady? The one who had the previous week reminded him of the one at the hiking trail on Mount Rainier. She filled out a card that would be used in requesting a transfer of membership from a church about fifteen miles away. Mack took his eyes off the congregation as he awaited the possibility of another coming forward. The ring finger of her left hand was free of jewelry. He was pleased and wondered if that might not be premature. Was he looking for wife material?

When the time of invitation had ended, he stepped back onto the platform, and announced that Crystal Nolan had come forward to transfer her membership by letter from a nearby church. Acceptance into the membership was a brief formality.

On Tuesday evening around eight, he received a phone call from one of the deacons. "We met at 7:00, Brother Mack. Sunday school classes came up, among other things. Two of the fellows said it's time you joined the Young Singles class, that their wives had said there was talk of it in their class. I just finished talking with Wes. He'd be glad to take over the large class you've been teaching in the sanctuary."

Mack found this unsettling. Not once had he considered such a change. It might appear that he was looking for a wife . It would be too obvious. His wife had been dead only six months. He explained this to the deacon, Maxwell Brown, who came right back with, "Mack, everybody in the church knows your wife has been gone for years. I hope that it doesn't upset you that I'm being so frank."

"No, you don't upset me by stating the obvious, but still . . . what does Lowell say?"

"He's the one who first brought it up. You may not know it, but that man loves you as he does his two sons. I recall that on two occasions before your recent sermon on Monod that you've preached on Matthew 6:19-21. I've known Lowell for thirty years. He runs his business according to that passage of the Bible.

"If you go to singles, there may not be a match for you there. Could be that you'll find just the right one from another place."

Mack was trying to think of excuses not to change. "I'd hate to face my class on Sunday and tell them it it is my last day. And use what to explain to them why I was leaving them? That I was leaving them to search for a wife? Wouldn't that sound terrible?"

Max said, "Brother Mack, you can be as dumb as a clod of dirt. Don't you know that your people love you?" Mack could imagine the twinkle in the eyes of the man who was talking. Max continued, "There's not a person in that class who doesn't want you to have an opportunity to live the kind of life you never had a chance to live."

"But it's so soon after my wife was buried, some folks will say," Mack said, as a final argument for continuing on as things were.

"Oh, I can't believe I'm still hearing this," Max protested. I'll get Wes to announce that the Board of Deacons promoted you to Singles effective this Sunday and he's to be their teacher 'til they find someone else.

"To make things easier for you, I'll escort you to Singles and introduce you as a new member who was a wee bit bashful to just walk in and take a seat."

To his surprise, that had some appeal; he realized he was too shy about entering the class. Max was a charmer in his mid-fifties, and Mack welcomed his support in what he knew would be an awkward moment for him. Some people wouldn't understand his reluctance, but Max did. He thanked God for him and Lowell Miller. "Thank you, Max, for understanding," was the way he accepted the change. Mack hung the phone up with a trace of a puzzled smile on his face.

———

Max was a keeper of his word and did meet and escort Mack to the Single's classroom.

"May I have your attention, please," he said loudly from just inside the doorway. The hum of voices ended as all turned. "I want to introduce you to a newly recruited member of your class. He has requested that you call him by his given name, Mack."

He walked on up to the front after indicating that Mack take a seat in an empty chair, one of three empty ones in the large circle of chairs.

"It took a little arm twisting to get him to leave his sanctuary class. Would you believe he was even shy about coming in with a new group, even though he knows each of you to some degree?

"Since his wife's death, he has become more active in helping Brother Wes with counseling. Following Jesus in his trade, he is a carpenter two days a week. Our church is growing and his responsibilities here keep growing. The deacons agreed that its time he not have that class, that he needs to be relieved of preparation for teaching it. We could have talked Lowell into relieving him of his work, but actually we didn't try to talk him into ending Mack's employment after Lowell said that he was the best finish carpenter he'd ever seen, including himself.

"Typically, a Sunday school class covers the lesson with ten, maybe fifteen minutes left. A little time for socializing with people of similar age and circumstances. I don't think Mack had ever had even one time for that in the past thirteen years." He directed his next remarks to the teacher, Percy Cleburne, who sat as a part of the circle. With a smile on his face and in his voice, he said, "Percy, be sure the socializing time doesn't get infringed on."

Mack sat as Percy opened the class with a short prayer. Hardly listening to the teaching of the lesson at first, a familiar emotion grew within that at first he couldn't identify. And then, there it was—his first day in school almost thirty years earlier. Though he had shaken the hands of all these people and exchanged a word or two many times with most, this was so different. He had never known any one of them in circumstances like this. In this setting, they were as much strangers as those kids so long ago in first grade had been. They had known and accepted him as their religious leader. Now it was as a stranger to them, and they as strangers to him. The musing on the similarities of this day and the one so long ago—also in September—was suddenly shattered by Percy's clear voice, "Mack, it puts me on a bit of a spot trying to teach this lesson with a far greater expert in the audience."

At this Mack chuckled, "If you only knew how inept I feel on many a Sunday morning. Notes prepared thoroughly I had thought, and all of a sudden wondering how I could ever have been such an idiot to have put such an interpretation on a verse of scripture. Momentarily with all confidence gone, I'd take a sip of water as I recalled what it was I had intended to say. A time when a lack of self-confidence stalls me for a few seconds.

"Believe me, I won't second guess you in your teaching. I am not an expert, but very much, I am a learner."

"Are you serious in what you've just said," a feminine voice inquired. "I always thought you were very close to being the ultimate expert."

Mack, feeling relaxed burst out with a short laugh. "If you could only know how humbled I often feel when I come very close to making a sad mess of a sermon that was so carefully and prayerfully prepared."

"And always," someone else said, "we had thought you didn't have any feelings of inadequacy that the rest of us feel sometimes. Now, consider yourself a full-fledged member of this class." Immediately there came an outburst of *Amens* from the nearly thirty members.

Mack felt he was in the right place for the first time and was able to be a listener. Others had insights that were fresh, and some very inspiring. He appreciated those men who knew he needed a change.

When he later took his position in the pulpit, it was with a renewal of enthusiasm. Had he lost a bit of it in those years of sameness of routine week after week?

⇒⊹⇐

It was a new day in yet another important way. Two of his classmates had told him of a restaurant that was a favorite of some for after-church dinner and suggested he might wish to meet with them. He explained he would run a little late as he made it a habit to remain on duty 'til the last person had left.

When he arrived, three tables were occupied by class members. There was an empty chair at one. On seeing Mack, one of the men waved him to that place.

To his right sat a man of thirty or a year or two past. "Mack, I'm Greg," the fellow said. "And the lady facing you is Crystal, who came to us two weeks ago, and to your left is Suzanne. We waited to order 'til you got here. You'll soon have names of all other class members at the tip of your tongue."

As the introductions had been made, Mack looked at each of the two women. Crystal would be in mid to late twenties—eyes noticeably green, honey blonde hair done up on her head, regular features—a handsome or was it beautiful woman? Suzanne was a brunette of maybe twenty-five or a young-looking thirty, a cute face and dark twinkly eyes.

The waitress came and orders were placed. Chicken tenders with two vegetables was the special for the day. Crystal and Suzanne appeared to be resuming a conversation that had been started before Mack arrived. A local store that primarily carried

321

ladies' fashions had a sale going with prices cut 30% to 50%. Susie, as she was called, was bubbly with enthusiasm. Crystal was interested, but not just carried away at saving all that money. Greg shrugged his shoulders slightly and asked Mack if he'd seen the Georgia-Tennessee game the day before on TV. To everyone's surprise but himself, Mack had watched the second half. Susie paused in speculating on the savings at the store to ask if Mack had a favorite team. Not really and that had made the game enjoyable; he didn't have to get nervous about the possibility of a favorite team losing the game.

"Did you ever play the game?" Greg asked.

"Went out for the team in the tenth grade. Stayed at practice three days. Told the coach I was too slow afoot and uncoordinated to be of any use to the team. He didn't twist my arm at all, trying to get me to continue practice."

When all had been served, Greg said, "We each say our own silent blessing giving thanks to the Lord for what we feel are our special blessings. Ten seconds, estimated, and then say our own Amen softly. Does that suit you, Mack?"

"I hadn't thought of doing it that way, but it has an advantage over one prayer fits all."

During the meal, conversation was pleasant and touched on several subjects of interest to Mack. He said no more than was necessary to keep talk from stalling. Lately he had become more of a listener than ever. His increased counseling duties had brought about that change. Wes, who had more experience, had told him more than once that good counseling requires good listening and most of your comments should reflect an understanding of where the person is coming from. "If they ask for advice, go over the choices they have. If they ask for spiritual advice, you of course share with them, but in a little different way from preaching from the pulpit. It's time for a little softer touch, for after all, you aren't having to get their attention."

His eyes fell on Crystal more easily than on his other companions. Though she was without a dimpled cheek, something about her brought to mind the woman that he'd met on Mount Rainier. Her eyes held just a hint of fun. To him, it seemed there might be real happiness inside the mind and heart of the woman. Was she one who saw humor in situations that others might see as aggravating? Did she laugh more than she moaned? Was she a person he would love to be more like? Her voice was rich, her words clearly spoken and easy on the ears, the kind that would wear well on the listener. Susie's voice was cute and delightful at first, but would it wear well if listened to frequently? As he was making the comparisons, inwardly he laughed at himself. Was he comparing to see which might be better wife material? Of course he was, and inwardly was amused.

Three more Sunday school classes went by. Associating with people close to his own age was a new experience. His two closest friends were senior citizens. And Sunday dinner, he found was a time of lighthearted fun. He sat at a table with different people each Sunday—their way of letting him get to know everyone gradually at a time that was predictably pleasant.

Despite his inward protestations that he was not interested in finding a sweetie, his emotions on the subject were of a different mind. To him, all the women had appeal when he chatted with them. Something about the soft flesh on cheek and neck and a swelling bosom covered by a pretty blouse—he knew that he, a preacher, was not supposed to be dwelling on that, but trying as he did to keep his eyes and attention moving so as to be not especially noticing was difficult. Sometimes his heart skipped a beat as he looked upon what he would have tried to avert his eyes from a year ago. No doubt he was changing. Could the budding character remain the same preacher, the one who often drew praise for his "thoughtful to-the-point sermons? The purity of heart that accompanied him almost one hundred percent of the time, would it be distracted and carnal enough to change the nature of the man he presented to his people? Was he willing to pay the price of loss of some of his goodness in order to be more like other men?

⇌

A week later on entering the classroom, he saw Crystal make a first move. She removed her purse from the chair to her immediate left and placed it underneath her chair as she looked up, her face breaking into a smile. She twice lightly patted the now empty chair. That was all. That was enough. So much like the girl on the trail on Mount Rainier, except she had no dimple.

"So good to have the preacher sitting beside me. Do I have to behave extra special?" she asked in a rich alto voice with every word so clearly enunciated. It was the first move one of the ladies had made. Mack was glad she was the one. Had it really had its start twenty-five hundred miles away? At that time, he had almost wished there was some way he could have established a relationship with that one. He recalled thinking then that such a woman might appear in his life back in the Southeast.

As the rest of the members were arriving, they had a brief opportunity to chat. Not more than two or three sentences that were uninterrupted by greetings and acknowledgements. It wasn't much, or wouldn't have been for most, but for Mack, it was of large consequence. Not one time in all those years had he sat beside a young woman who had indicated interest in him like Crystal had just done. It was intentional, a bit of a flirty move and he had not realized the full extent of his desperation until now. She wore a delicate fragrance that struck just the right note.

Was she a fast woman? But that question left in a greater hurry than it had come. Once Mack's mother confessed that she had made the first move with his father. "Sometimes a good man, an other-wise smart man, can be so doggoned dense in that way." When had he first sensed that Crystal might be the one? The minute she came forward to join the church, but he had chided himself for trying to hurry up something that should come about naturally. But there is nothing unnatural about a young Christian woman wearing a faint fragrance and indicating a man is welcome to sit beside her. I've been so out of circulation with how regular people live. Perhaps I never was in circulation with other young people. Despite all her wonderful qualities, Rebecca could not be called a regular young woman. At the time I thought she was like all others should be. But now, more mature, I can see that a person can live a life that pleases God and still be jolly and have clean fun.

A little later when he stepped to the pulpit and laid his open Bible on the lectern, all thoughts of what had happened in the Sunday school class were shoved into temporary oblivion. Barely glancing at St. John 8:2-11, he read it with clarity and conviction as his eyes, ever moving, made contact with all parts of the audience. He spoke of the harshness of what the Scribes and Pharisees described as the law of Moses, and it was their test of what and who He was. But Jesus put them to a test that they could not answer with the old law.

Mack spent about fifteen minutes posing questions and leaving many of them for the audience to come to their own conclusions. How different was the day Jesus began teaching. Forgiveness and love were in Jesus for those who sought a very different value system from the old. Much of the past history of the Jews had been of disobedience and harsh punishment.

He asked three questions for his audience to write down in their bulletins in the space provided for note-taking. "Turning in homework won't be asked of you, but if you put a bit of time into working out answers, it may make next Sunday's sermon more interesting.

The next Sunday, he was late in arriving for class. She might not be saving a seat for him, but she was. Someone had held him up to ask a question as he had left his office. He hoped he had not showed any sign of impatience. Several times during the past week, he had thought of Crystal, not just as a member of the class, but as a woman. As an eligible woman? A couple of times, he had consciously done so. The delicate fragrance she had worn was remembered and as he took the seat she had reserved for him, he recognized the same one. He was doubly touched. Was this how it started? Maude could advise him. Why Maude? She had very limited experience in matters of the heart. But the elderly lady was wise in so many ways, though he could not always agree with her theology.

But Maude was just a passing thought. It was Crystal and the awareness of a sweet woman who wanted to sit beside him. If any other woman had thought of him as a man who might be a desirable companion even to the extent of wanting to sit beside him, he had not noticed. Crystal was not too forward, he thought. Tentative interest until she got to know him as other than his role as a pastor was how he saw it.

To be honest about it, he had been interested in her from the beginning. She reminded him of the girl from the trail. Each time he saw Crystal, he relived the moments he thought that meeting the other girl had been something of a glad foreshadowing of meeting Crystal. It had been one of the great moments on Mount Rainier, just as this was one of the best Sunday mornings as he sat beside Crystal. It was time he turned his attention to the lesson to be discussed and in this, he was moderately successful, but never to the extent that he was unaware of the woman who wanted him to know she had an interest in knowing him better.

But as usual, when he stepped up to the lectern, all else except for the sermon and the attentive people before him were completely outside his awareness. Martyrs were the subject of his sermon. Early martyrs had been stoned or crucified. Knowing their faith would eventually cost them their lives, they taught and preached about Christ and His teaching. More than a thousand years later, there were those who were burned at the stake for disagreeing with corrupt practices within the official church. Christians burning other Christians at the stake? How could that be possible? The Christians who did the burning were a part of the church/state apparatus that would not tolerate any disagreement with the church/state version of Christianity at that time.

On that Sunday morning, Mack stressed that the later martyrs saved Christianity from the official church. And lessons learned from the persecutions of fifteenth, sixteenth, and seventeenth century Christians led to this country's founders putting into the Constitution the first amendment that guarantees that our government will not create an official religion that outlawed all other religions.

Jesus paid the price for our redemption, thereby establishing the Christian faith. Over and over a price was paid down through the centuries to preserve what Jesus had paid to establish with His own life. Mack concluded his sermon with, "Thank God for the first Christian martyr, and then thank Him for all the others who followed in making the ultimate sacrifice to preserve Christianity from persecutors."

Not so many minutes later, he was sitting in a booth at the restaurant with Crystal beside him. Maybe this was a further step forward. Another couple from the class sat across the table from them. Two courting couples? Mack wondered. But not really. Just friends.

He had discovered earlier that Crystal was easy to establish a conversation with, and her clear voice so pleasing to hear. When he looked into her face, he saw again how beautiful she was in an elegant manner. She was special and he knew it. There was a stirring of a sweet feeling in his heart. Beginning to happen too soon? He didn't want to get involved too early, and immediately wondered if he was kidding himself. Getting involved with this lady was not a bad idea, even if it was little frightening, and even if it seemed to be happening a little early.

Ken Albright and Jan Smith across the table were in a conversation with Crystal about a Saturday college football game. Mack had seen a little of the Georgia vs. Alabama game on TV, so was able to join in after the waitress took orders. No one was an avid fan of football, but it was a subject that all could comment on.

During the meal, conversation was light-hearted on several subjects, none of them of great consequence. Crystal, Mack learned, taught high school math at a school ten miles outside of town her first year there, but she had taught several years in other parts of the state.

"Are all your kids above average?" Jan asked.

"How I wish they were. When it comes to putting off work 'til another time, they probably are. Well, I oughtn't to say that. Many are very studious and do their work on time."

"Why teach math?" Ken asked. "I never could see the point in solving meaningless equations."

Good naturedly, Crystal said, "It gets you ready for the next course, where equations become more complicated."

Mack liked her nature, not taking herself and her work too seriously. How different from what he had been years earlier, and probably still was. And Rebecca? She always took life too seriously, probably herself as well. Poor thing, traveling through life with hardly a laugh at all. Born to suffer? There had been times Mack thought so, but God did not ordain that; he believed that because he had to.

"Mack, where have you been? We've been eating and running our mouths." Crystal said.

"Was living in my memories. Sorry, but I had tuned out everything else for a couple of minutes.

Jan, in a tone of sympathy said, "You can't get rid of what you can't get rid of. Now, that's the dumbest sounding statement that can be made."

"But the easiest understood," Ken added.

Crystal commented, "Something you shouldn't have done and you knew better at the time."

Jan spoke again. "You ask God to forgive you and you know that should be the end of it, but—"

"You can't forgive yourself for being so stupid," Ken finished for her.

Crystal said, "We try to live as Christians ought to, but never seem able to completely measure up. Mack, you are the expert. Tell us why."

"And it's like Jan said, I can't get rid of what I can't get rid of. I'm working on it and will continue to work on it. Maybe being a Christian is work in progress for most of us."

"The martyrs you spoke of today—some walked to the stake and never recanted their claims that the church and what it had become were doing terrible things," Jan said. "Incredible people!"

"To me, the people who burned them are just as incredible. Unbelievably evil." Ken commented.

For a minute, they continued eating without conversation. Mack then added, "Science today claims there is no evil. It has not explained a Hitler."

Later in the afternoon, Mack recalled the conversation. There are people who had experienced life, probably at its worst, or something close to it. How little we know what others are like inside. We seldom talk about those things inside that mean a lot. Afraid of rejection if we did. What a comfortable group they are to be with.

CHAPTER TWENTY-THREE

And a few weeks later, they went to the county fair together in Ken's four-door sedan. At the fair with its rides and cotton candy, they each discarded the years that had made them adults. The girls were not to be outdone in taking the scary rides as the boys challenged them. There were squeals and shouts and plenty of laughter.

Holding hands with Crystal at first, Mack soon found himself being hugged as they went higher and higher and then dropped as fast as gravity could go. And he was hugging her in return. It was so natural and felt so exciting. Being a preacher was totally forgotten and he was doing something he and Rebecca or some other girl should have done years ago. So perfectly harmless and so perfectly delightful. Even on climbing high again, he thought of how he'd missed so much by being so doggoned proper. And as they were falling again, Crystal squeezed him even harder.

Fair prices for hot dogs weren't fair prices at all Jan pointed out as Mack was ordering them with sodas for all. Luckily and surprisingly, he found a picnic table that was just being vacated. Four adults in early maturity were soon licking off excess ketchup and mustard and enjoying the taste of something that would have been a child's delight.

Mack and Rebecca had never done anything like this that he could recall. It was one of the many regrets that had paid him brief visits during the evening of fun.

From there, it was to the agricultural exhibits. Alf met them there and took them to see his entry, a Hereford with a blue ribbon attached. He managed to get Mack aside to express his approval of the young lady he had brought. "It's time, Mack. And she's a looker, and that adds something extra. It would for me if I was at your age and single. Go for her." And added, "Take your time."

Before leaving, they chose another ride, but not one with so much excitement that would have Crystal clinging to Mack as fear overcame her. This one was fun, lots of fun and that was just right.

It was the kind of date that left Mack thinking well into the night. She was likely to burst out laughing at something that would have brought a faint smile to Rebecca's face. She sought things that added some zest to life where Rebecca would have sought retirement from activities requiring considerable involvement. Rebecca had been so lady-like and elegant before illness made her so terribly different. Mack wasn't comfortable comparing her to Crystal. They were different and that was as much as ought to be said, but it was hard to refrain from thinking how different they were.

Had illness not have destroyed her, she might have by now become all that he had hoped for. A lady under all conditions that a pastor might come across, always ready with just the right words that needed to be spoken in the difficult times. At twenty-two, she was not all she could have become, but it was at twenty-two that disease invaded her brain and no medication could stop its settling down to stay. And later, it was the disease of living-death of the brain that began at a time that was never to be determined. Her first illness was a disease of withdrawal growing out of unwarranted fears, and the second one was not detected until she began having trouble feeding herself. If ever a young adult had entered a world of diminishing possibilities . . . .

Comparing Crystal to her might be a little unfair, but it was inevitable. Was Crystal to be the one for his coming years? Was there to be anyone? For such a long time, it had been just him and God, and Jesus . . . and his work which had been, and still was his staff in his tough times of life. He, with the Lord's help, had made it through those years.

Now, was it time to consider trying again? Far from knowing he wanted to take on a companion who might become victim of a long illness. Did he want to deal with that uncertainty?

He had his trips to the coast and the mountains, his daily hikes, and his recorded music, the pleasantness of his favorite restaurants and the woodland trails to sustain him. His carpentry which included fellowship with the other men. Counseling had become a rewarding addition. Visiting hospital patients. Helping the grieving people cope with their loss. He could have gone on. It was enough to cause him to pause while the opportunity was there to do so. Do I want to court Crystal with marriage in mind? My life is so full. In my list, I didn't even include preaching. I know my life works and I'm close to being content as things are. I'm aware I have friends who think I need to get busy with the business of finding a wife. I've made it for years when things were worse. From counseling sessions, I'm learning that marriage can be less than blissful.

There was no deadline for making a decision. Crystal was fun and he would be with her in class and in eating out after church. She was probably as uncertain as he was about anything beyond their present association. This night had been special; the county fair would be closed after this week. There would be other special occasions when he might take her out. He wasn't ready to just take her out on a date. For that he would need skill in small talk, something he and Rebecca had never practiced. All their conversations had been about things of consequence, not always related to faith and religion, but things of social importance and in rare cases about politics and the corruption that frequently was a part of it. Of fashions, sports, cars, and movies they knew little, and had an interest that matched. They had, no doubt, been good people and had little interest in what others were interested in. At that time, he had been somewhat proud of that difference. Now he wished he had been more of a regular person.

But all from that period was not a failure. He had learned to speak convincingly on matters of faith; the evidence was there before him each time he preached.

Nationwide, church attendance was sliding while where he preached attendance was growing. Few eyes drifted as he spoke; he watched for that, always ready to insert a bit of humor or change his voice a bit or shift to something that should be difficult for his audience to ignore.

Finally, he was able to sleep, though no decision had been made about his future and Crystal. The last conscious thought was that she might not be in his future by her choice.

And it was first on his awakening the next morning. Sadness came with awareness that she might not want anything beyond friendship within a group. Had he made too much of what had appeared an interest in him?

It was a good day to go to the Men's Retreat. No doubt some men went to get away from their wives. He went to get away from himself. Retreat from himself? Exactly. His unhappiness had returned and he was anything but what he urged his congregation to be. As he drove, he knew that for a time he could put aside his self-condemnation for not living up to the Christian standards he talked of from the pulpit. Did other ministers see themselves falling far short of living the messages they preached? Probably, but he had not discussed this with any of those he might have. Why do we reveal so little of what we are?

Entering the place of fine breakfast aromas and the voices of men not speaking in worried tones. It was an excellent place to put behind your worries and fears of the day. Can anyone enter a place of calm voices where hot bacon and ham release their fine essences in the air, and not feel better? Fried eggs or scrambled eggs, hot buttered toast, and fresh brewed coffee. Aromas that resurrected great memories of childhood and his mother's cooking. It was as close to glory as man is likely to get short of Heaven. That was what Mack experienced on this first morning he woke up to anxiety about a relationship that had not yet developed and might never come into existence. As always, the Retreat was living up to expectations. Anxiety always had a hard time surviving within these walls. Mack suspected that most who came left their aggravations and worries at the outside entrance, and would no more consider letting them enter the restaurant than they would coming in talking in foul language about life's frustrations. This was a retreat from all that was unpleasant in life. Temporary, but what a blessing!

"When did someone hang the second shingle onto Men's Retreat?" asked the fellow who asked permission to sit at Mack's table; the restaurant was filled almost to capacity.

"Two or three weeks ago, it was," Mack answered. "It was the local garden club that thought it was reverse humor, poking a little fun at the sign above it."

It was at this point the fellow introduced himself as Clyde. And "I'm Mack," followed.

"The preacher?" When Mack indicated he was, the man continued, "I've heard a lot about you."

"Any of it good?" Mack asked in a voice with a trace of fun.

Clyde put on an expression that was overly serious and answered, "Some of it was," and they both chuckled; such was the atmosphere in the restaurant.

When their food arrived, they ate as if taking that seriously. After they finished, they sipped slowly their last cup of coffee and talked of the Yom Kippur War. Serious business, they agreed and Israel was in a fight for its life, and war was likely to continue into the next century they agreed.

When there was no further excuse for remaining after the coffee was all gone, they arose simultaneously. After shaking hands, Clyde said, "Maybe we can get together again soon." And Mack expressed a similar feeling.

At a raised platform where a checker game was usually in progress—with four chairs close by—and storytelling was often going on, a lone man sat at a small table that held a checker board. It was Friday. Mack had no pressing responsibilities that morning. On a sudden impulse, he climbed the two steps and spoke to the old gentleman who sat as if awaiting a partner.

"Sir, I'm Mack. I'm not offering to play you a few games. Before I could make three moves, you'd see how you were going to slaughter me. My dad is pretty good at the game; I've never come close to beating him except for three or four games he just allowed me to beat up on him.

"You lived through the Depression. I'd appreciate hearing how you survived. Dad has told me stories about it. I date back to 1938 and have no memories of it."

"I'm Zeke," the old man said. "Won't you sit down? I'm not half as good at the game as you seem to think I am. But I'd be happy to tell you a little about how the thirties were. Old men, universally, it's been said, love to trot out how it was when they were young, especially if there's somebody who's interested.

"I was riding on a train. There was a woman and four small children riding in the same car I was." He stopped at this point. His eyes misted as if some very difficult thing was to be talked about. Mack said nothing that might prod him to continue, believing that to be unnecessary.

When the man continued, his voice had become hoarse and shaky with emotion. "I shared, not a coach but a box car with the family. The wide door on each side was open.

"You know anything about hobos riding freights in those days?"

"It was a common way to travel, Dad said. He never did it but was aware of it."

"I got on this car in Columbia, Tennessee . . . the L and N Railroad. The family was already on it. There were other people in other cars, some even sitting on top of freight cars."

"How was it the woman and four children happened to be so desperate?"

"Mack, that'll take some telling. If you are willing to listen, I'll pass it on the best I can.

"She came from West Virginia. Her husband had first entered a coal mine at age eleven. A general flunky he was until fourteen when he'd grown enough to do a man's work; that was five years before she met him.

"They married when he was twenty-one and she was eighteen. According to her, he was heavily muscled and strong as an ox. Well qualified to drill in rock and mostly, that was what he was doing.

"You ever hear of company towns?"

"From a lady in her late eighties."

"Then you know of company stores, company doctors, company money, and company houses. The company owned her husband, body and soul, and according to her, that is not an exaggeration. He developed a cough . . . bronchitis the doctor said. When she went to the doctor and asked if it wasn't really silicosis—rock dust in the lungs—that was making him so weak and short of breath. As you could expect, she was assured it was no such thing and that he ought to be getting better soon."

"He didn't get better." Mack said as a statement of fact.

"No. Since he couldn't perform hard work, they turned him into a flunky again. Deeper and deeper the family got into debt to the company store as time went by."

"And of course he died," Mack knew this was coming.

"Yes. The company gave her thirty days to find another husband who would move in and take a job in the mine. Even put a sign in the yard to the effect that a young widow lived there."

Mack had heard horror stories growing out of company towns, but nothing to equal this.

"What I'm telling you is what she told me. Found it hard to believe then and still do."

Mack finished that part of the story for him. "So when she couldn't deliver a husband to work for the operator of the mine, she was evicted from the shack she lived in. Unbelievable!"

"Yes, but I believed her. A company deputy of the law came and evicted her.

"One man had come in response to the advertisement in the front yard. He might have married her had there only been one or two kids.

"When I rode with them all the way to Birmingham, she and the children were showing signs of slow starvation. She had a sister in New Orleans where winters were not so cold."

"Do you know what happened to her afterwards?"

"I figured somewhere along the way, her kids were placed in an orphanage and she in a poor folks home. The most unusual thing I saw in my three years drifting about the country by rail, picking up work where I could find it. If the children lived, they'd be middle age now.

"Why am I telling you, a stranger, this forty years later? Because it haunts my soul. I dreamed a dream last night, sorta mixed up, but they were in it. For the hundredth time, I've been asking myself should I have gone with them all the way to New Orleans? But I was set on going to Florida and when the opportunity to do something was there, I didn't give it serious thought. Had enough troubles of my own.

"It was a mass migration, riding the rails to wherever there might be a few days of work. The other big migration was out of the Dust Bowl.

"People can live on less food than they thought possible. Their bodies can become adjusted to a lot more cold than they thought possible. Homeless people of this day still get by as I did those days.

"I'm sixty-six and have been guessed to be in my eighties. Why didn't I stay where I grew up and deal with poverty right there? It's like I was caught up in a movement that had spread over the country, like a contagion. I was a part of something that just might offer hope. I absolutely could not stay where I was, letting the Depression do whatever it wished to do with me. I had to have some sort of control over my life, even if there was a risk of making life worse. At the time, that seemed like a mighty small risk, and it turned out that it was.

"I have so many memories of places few ever see.

"The youngest of the four children, a little girl of about four. I saw her in my dream more clearly than the others. I wonder . . . ." He could go no further as a few tears came and his voice choked up.

"Zeke, you've told a most remarkable story. I loved it even as my anger flared at the story of what amounted to slavery, a story of mankind at its worst."

After a little throat clearing, Zeke invited him to a checker game.

"If you'll go slowly, patiently explaining where I made bad moves, and what I should have done instead."

Perhaps it was because Mack had allowed him to tell all of his story without any sign of impatience, Zeke did just that. And played one more game—showing "a slow learner" how to play the game, always with two or three possible moves ahead in mind.

Zeke's story about the Great Depression would become something Mack would never forget. It dealt with a level of evil that had been beyond his ability to comprehend. He had on a number of occasions preached that Satan was real, that he could take possession of a person's soul and bring about behavior that was truly evil—that went beyond the sins that were a part of being human.

Mack knew that modern science concluded that all human behavior could be accounted for by environment acting on what had been inherited. What could be so different in the heredity and environment that could account for the owners of that coal mine being so cruel as to work a man in such conditions when he was terminally ill before thirty. And hiring a company doctor who knowingly misdiagnosed the illness. Kicking the mother and kids out of one of its look-a-like shacks. That revealed the true evil that people could sink to.

There was a clear distinction between ordinary sin of the flesh due to human weakness and an act of evil in which other lives are destroyed. Hitler and Stalin came to mind. And coal mine operators in the days before Congressional actions and John L. Lewis.

In a few weeks, he would preach on the difference in ordinary sinful acts and the truly evil.

⟨⟩

Crystal. Now that was someone that could take his mind away from the painful, somber thoughts that often assailed him. They ate out together once a week other than with classmates after church on Sunday. They hiked together in the city park a couple of times a week, not briskly, but leisurely as light conversation flowed freely and easily. One evening as they walked under the lights, she asked, "Were you always like this . . . a good listener and sometimes coming out with something rather funny? Were you and Rebecca ever as laid back as we are?"

That question revealed a little of the essence of Crystal. Many would not have asked Mack such a right-to-the-point question about his days of courtship and marriage for fear of dredging up sad memories. But there was such a warm innocence and gentle kindness in the woman that Mack took no offense at all.

"No, hon. We knew so little about how to live. She was nice, prim, and proper; I was, for a man, a nice match for that. But even in those early days of preaching, I made a conscious effort to avoid an unctuous style in my speaking. I did not want to deliver a message in the manner that I'd heard a few others do."

"That manner of speech is a real turn-off for some who may badly need to hear the message. No, Mack, you talk like regular folks, except there is a sincerity and fire in your words that cause people to listen."

There was no one coming toward them. She said, "I'll race you to the next turn." They were off. Neither was in shape for a sprint and they were both gasping for air as laughter caught up with them. A well-placed park bench caught their colliding bodies, when there was no running left in them.

When breathing would allow words to come. Crystal asked, "Mack, are we what might be called a dating couple now?"

"Some might call us that. I'd not thought about it before."

She goosed him in the ribs, a little harshly and said, "Liar," as she was getting the expected response.

When he could talk, Mack said, "Maybe I am a wee bit."

"You ever look into the future?"

"Not as much as I might if my life had been different all those years. Hope lived, but it was not much of one. What it would take was a real miracle to help her—miracles are few and far between. When a miracle finally came, her body was already in the grave.

"No, Crystal. You get into the habit of not looking at the future when your wife suffers from "the living death." You can't take on more than one day at a time.

"Sure I prepared sermons in advance, but that was about the only thing in the future that time was spent on. I took short trips to the coast and to the mountains, usually with no advance planning."

"You'd get up, check the weather, and leave an hour or so later?" she asked.

"Yes, that's how it usually was. But until right now, I never realized those trips were unplanned because I couldn't look at a future. I would just take the notion to go, and was out of there.

"You know she was going to die. You don't ask her doctor how long her Alzheimer's disease will allow her to cling to life. You are afraid he might say six months, nine at the very most. As her body clings to life, you cling to hope that something might come along that will build new brain cells. After the passage of years, I discovered her blinking reflex was gone.

"Then the coughing reflex was gone, and pneumonia took over. You steel your emotions at a level enabling you to await the day she passes. Thank you for asking the question that allowed something to burst through, as it had not before.

"Yes, Crystal, we are what I see as a definite dating couple."

"And for the time being, you are content with us like we are?" she asked.

"Yes, for now. And I'm beginning to think of the future. I can't hold that back anymore, even if I wanted to, which I don't"

"Does it become scary when you look ahead?" she asked.

"Just a teeny bit."

"Let's be content for a while with what we have now. On the way back to your pickup, let's walk slow and easy. My calves are already beginning to tighten and feel sore."

⊨⊦ ⊣⊨

Off to a good start were Mack and Crystal? Yes, but for the present time, that was as far as it went. They continued their times together. Mack poured more of his soul into this sermons. The chants of the counter-culture rang with the clarity of a bell in his mind and his heart. *Just do your own thing* was the one that scared him most.

From the pulpit on an early November Sunday, he quoted it and followed up with, "In a small town of one thousand adults, imagine that one thousand different value systems are being proclaimed as the way to go, the way to behave, the way to treat fellow humans. Be completely selfish in all decisions. Let everyone else follow his own model. You are the only person who matters. All others have the same right to behave as they please on all occasions. Civil rights will be the battle cry against tradition. Civil responsibilities, anybody? Why, only a fool would even consider such nonsense. Matters of conscience? Why, those are for our parents and grandparents. They are the ones that brought us to this kind of belief. Why, they still believe in God who wants them to do this and not do that, especially in the not do's. They ruined their lives by believing there were all kinds of fun things they oughtn't to do. Simple-minded, they believe their God created everything in the universe, including themselves. Silly folks . . . they don't realize God died in the last century. While they continue to do *the good for the community thing*, we do our own thing. Life is short and they live without fun they could be having. Ethical behavior? We are not taken in by that sort of thing. They were and look how that took the life out of living." He paused for a sip of water before continuing.

"Do you want to see this nation run by such people? Not all of this generation are like that, but the most vocal ones are, and they'll still be vocal for twenty, thirty years and more . . . as will their sons and daughters."

This was not all of the sermon, but was the heart of it. As a minister, he felt he had extra responsibilities that exceeded his personal life in importance. Crystal might be the woman he'd marry; he liked her a lot. If it was to be, he thought he'd be willing for it to happen. He asked God's guidance. This happened as the congregation sang the song of invitation. Three teenagers came forward together and his personal thoughts were gone, replaced by joy of the moment.

CHAPTER TWENTY-FOUR

L eaves had fallen. Bare limbs had a winter-time beauty in the state park where he was on a long hike. Trunks of large hardwoods, some centuries old, had a special appeal. Often he wondered at these. Weren't they used by God to communicate with man by creating a special appreciation in those who love nature? In one place, they stood patiently for their lifetime awaiting those who would come and admire and love what were the largest living things in the Southeast. Mack always felt he was in a presence that went beyond the massive towers that grew toward the heavens. There was a harmony here with animals that depended on the forest and the variety of organisms that converted the substance of fallen leaves, twigs, and limbs into support for new life. When one of the giants lay fallen in death, not many years would pass until it was also converted into nourishment for new life. In an old growth forest, all things worked together to maintain what the Lord had created as an expression of an awareness of the needs of man's heart.

It was thus that Mack arrived at his comfortable rock by the little stream that spoke to him in a lively voice of the journey it had just begun on its quest for the distant ocean. He fantasized about its tiny contribution along the way to a river, splashing its way down cascades, its thunder being the only sound that could be heard at a high fall, and on to the serenity of passing through bottom land.

The acorn he picked up had stored in it all the information needed to build a massive white oak like the one whose branches had recently dropped a blanket over the place where he sat. The acorn contained information about when and how to grow the many types of cells that would become necessary to form a giant like the one it had recently fallen from. If a host of leaf-eating insects began eating its tender new growth, it knew how to create the correct chemical messenger to release on the wind, warning neighbors that it was time to start making a natural pesticide that would repel the insects.

There are times I wonder if there is a better place to know God than in a place undisturbed by noise that is man-created. The sound of the little stream and of a breeze sifting through the thousands of needles on yonder ancient pine and the cheeping of a winter wren close by in no way disturbed the basic quietness of nature's church—mind and soul completely open to a visit from God. And sometimes I know His presence in a way I sometimes do not sense even in church. And this is one of those times that I treasure. But if I shared this from the pulpit, would my congregation understand? How I wish I knew that they could. I would that all could know the blessing of an hour in such a place as this

A time of meditation and a kind of worship not experienced in just any kind of setting had him better able to live with night-time dreams that would leave him wondering some days if he was making any progress from those horrific times of Rebecca's illness. The dreams were muddled and confused and only a few details were remembered, but they were about the "marriage that never was." That was how he had too often thought of it and never without shame. She was the one whose life began to end when barely twenty-two. He doubted if she even lived one quality day, beginning with a few days before their marriage.

He had managed to experience a life of sorts even in those days when he couldn't get a sitter. And he could think a cure of 90%, or even better, could come along any time. Her abnormal brain function produced suspicions and fears that were as emotionally devastating as a person's would be in any truly terrifying physical situation. Traditionally, people had thought that it was all in their heads, as if that was not a real problem. Mack had early recognized that to Rebecca, her fears were fully justified and real.

His morning moods were what he thought of as a hangover from those nights when the dark and obscure dreams came. By nine or ten o'clock, he had usually worked through the debris the dreams had left behind. It helped to remember that she was now well and in Heaven. The morning she was allowed to come rescue him from a miserable morning of fishing was enough to convince a rational mind that the troubling dreams were no more than a little trash left behind by the psychological storm that he had never admitted the full severity of during those years. Never admitted the severity of it because it would have been too overwhelming for him to carry on with his work. Sometimes troubles are too great to face up to if we are to go on with living. He was beginning to realize how he survived those years. It was with this thought, he established a mental landmark and could take one more big step in becoming whole. Appropriately, he thought with a smile in his heart, this point was reached in the retreat of the forest, how appropriate that was its place of arrival.

⇥ ⇤

Crystal was so different. It was at least the hundredth time Mack had acknowledged this. Frequently she laughed. It was as though she saw humor and wit where most others saw something that could do no better than draw a faint smile and a little twinkle to the eyes. One Saturday morning, Mack went to her apartment to pick her up and take her out to Alf's farm for a visit and a hike. She was watching cartoons and was in no great hurry to leave. Tom and Jerry were on.

"Mack, I watch the Roadrunner. I keep hoping that the coyote catches that smart aleck bird that outruns and outfoxes that supposedly wily animal. I don't know why I ever watch that one anymore. I know how Tom and Jerry is going to end but Jerry is so cute, I tolerate him." So there was a brief wait for this one to end. When it did, Mack teased, "You're not grown up yet."

"Why should I? Kids have Saturday morning fun. Adults have worries. A car payment due next week. Field lines that may have to be replaced before long. A squirrel has moved into the attic for the winter—the adult knows it's get it out or listen to racket in the months ahead, but a kid thinks squirrels are cute and its funny there's one up there. Why don't all of us older sorts join the kids?"

"Do your high school math classes know you watch cartoons?" Mack felt pretty sure she hadn't told them.

"They know and think it's neat."

<hr />

It had been Crystal's idea to visit Alf and Nell. "They have all those animals."

But it wasn't the animals that Crystal was so fascinated with. Alf and Nell were talkers and they spoke a language Crystal understood. No put on, no talk of the sort to try to make an impression. Down-to-earth. And conversation was a two-way street.

Mack observed they liked Crystal. In that, they were like everyone else. It was difficult to keep from making comparisons. They were two very different people. Had Rebecca not been struck down with illness, she would have been well-liked. Probably never as soon as Crystal would she make a good impression, but she would have been able to win people with her quiet reserved manner. Mack realized he was thinking like he and Crystal were going to be married and he wasn't sure that's how it was going to end up yet. He rejoined the conversation by suggesting they check out the livestock.

A brown and white horse came to meet them as they were closing the gate. It wasn't Mack the mare came to and offered a soft muzzle to be caressed.

"I love horses."

"She knew it without being told."

"What beautiful eyes you have, horsie. And cute ears." She hugged the animal's head to her upper body and face.

It was only after this that the mare showed interest in Mack by offering her head to be petted.

They walked among grazing cattle, white-faced Herefords. All of them paused to look at Mack and Crystal, then went back to grazing. Two baby ones would not let Crystal get close enough to feel the curly hair that covered their faces.

As he had a number of times before, Mack wondered if Crystal was the one. Was he ready to seriously consider another marriage. Her company was something he always enjoyed and at this point that was the extent of his feelings. To get married, a fellow needed something more than that. He was set in his ways, and for the most part, he liked those ways. Marriage would demand that some of those ways be changed.

Crystal had now found a nanny goat that would allow her to pet it. The goat's kid came to start nursing and the mama allowed Crystal to continue fondling her ears. Mack had a fine camera at home, the usual place it sat when a great subject appeared. He loved this woman. Whoa! He loved her ways with animals and people also. He had seen the looks of approval in the eyes and faces of Alf and Nell. He liked for the folks he especially liked to approve of . . . his girl? Well yes, she was his girlfriend if the friend part was emphasized sufficiently.

As for holding to his ways, he probably had too many of them and this young woman might be worth more to him than hanging on to lots of them. Am I in the early, *very* early stage of falling in love? A month ago, I had not come close to asking such a question. A month from now? Don't want to think about it. Too many questions, Preacher Man. You got too many serious things to be thinking about. A preacher has an endless supply of those. It's time you follow that advice you've been known to give others; take each day as it comes, and do with it the best you can, and tomorrow? Treat it the same way you did today.

Two days later was Thanksgiving. He had phoned Crystal the day before and had wished her a blessed Thanksgiving. She was leaving the next day for Jacksonville, Florida to visit her mother in time for the evening meal. Would stay until Saturday and return that afternoon. Mack drove to the home of his parents on Thursday. His two brothers and their families had already arrived. The four men sat in the living room as the women were finishing preparations. Kids were outside on a cold day playing with a basketball—shooting mostly, but getting some practice dribbling.

"Have you found a lady friend yet, Mack?" one of his brothers teased hopefully.

"There is a lady I've been seeing some. She is a friend in a very nice sort of way."

"You are off to a good start," his father said. "Mother says you are leaving for the coast right after dinner."

"Isn't it too cold to be going to the beach?" the other brother asked.

"It'll be six or eight degrees warmer than here. But cold enough to keep the beach bunnies in hibernation. A perfect time for a preacher to go," Mack said.

The second brother asked, "What in the world is a beach bunny?"

The brother who had first spoken answered that question. "A shapely young woman in a bikini. Bunny is a term used by Playboy. A preacher might find himself being lustful if he's on the beach on a warm day when they come out to get some sun."

Mack admitted that was the essence of it. "It's best if a preacher doesn't even give the appearance of questionable conduct."

"You never know" said the father. "Some of the church members might be on vacation in the warm months and if they find their preacher taking in the sights, it would make its way back to the gossip line."

They were soon called to dinner. The five kids had correctly anticipated the call was soon to come and had washed up and were ready to enter the dining room immediately. Mack asked God to bless the food and the members of the large family who were there. He spent more time touching on the things they had to be thankful for.

Smoked turkey from a barbeque restaurant and all the other traditional dishes were lined up on the long kitchen counter. Since this was a once-a-year celebration, plates came to the table heavily loaded. Eating this much was too serious a matter to allow conversation to hinder it a great deal.

Pecan pie was for dessert. Each of the three ladies had cooked one, using identical recipes . . . Anita Baldwin's. The kids wolfed their pie down. The adults took small bites and savored all the wonderful things the rich dessert had to offer. Sips of coffee helped slow any urge that might come to eat it hurriedly like the children did.

Mack silently thanked God for the best pie he'd ever eaten and for the mother who cooked his—she had made sure his came from the one she had baked. "Not that the ones the girls baked wouldn't be just as good as mine." This had been quietly said close to his ear, when everyone else was talking.

When the pie was eaten and the children had gone outside, Mack said, "It's been my finest Thanksgiving ever. Fourteen years ago, I was a college senior sitting at this table, never dreaming how the next thirteen years were going to be."

"Would you have married her if you had known she would already have been so seriously ill at the time of your wedding?" his father asked. Continuing he said, "Mother and I have talked about that. As parents, we've wished you could have seen into the future as you sat here that Thanksgiving. And yet it does not seem quite right, had you known, if you'd have dropped her because you had seen a future where she would never get well."

Mack answered, "I've had many years to go over and over what I might have done had I known. Would I have gone on with the courtship and ahead with the marriage? Would I have done that had I known what was in the future? I think I would have. I hope I would have."

His mother said, "Daddy and I decided what a blessing not to know what's in our future."

It was not easy when the time came to leave. "Next year, I won't leave in such a rush," he told his family. "Next year, I may have a regular life. The coast has served me well in my hours of need."

His mother asked if he might have a wife to bring next Thanksgiving.

"That has an ever growing appeal." Seeing his two brothers apparently happily married and with their children was an encouragement in that direction.

<hr>

As always, it was the pavement coming steadily toward him giving a sense of relief. Relief from what? Nothing that he could name, but that's how it always was.

The next day, he was walking the beach by nine. The ocean was dependable, always different. It was as if it were the first time, like he had not seen it before. He was glad that the thrill of seeing it anew was with him each time he came.

Clouds were low and heavy. The horizon seemed closer than ever before; the north wind greatly disturbed the sea beyond the beach, generating huge swells that would be felt as high waves on all the shores that lined the Gulf of Mexico.

The incoming surf broke with sounds like thunder, and reached high on the sea side of the great sand dune. It was a day of moving sand as torrents of water rushed back to sea before the next curling wave hurried up the dune even further than Mack thought possible. It was cold, not a good day for foot wetting, but occasionally he would be surprised as he had been by that last big one. Canvas shoes he'd worn for such small emergencies. He was not going to miss the fun of flirting with tiny disasters just so his feet would stay dry. As high as his knees, his pant legs got splashed. But his upper body and arms were heavily clad and dry.

Marine birds were out in great numbers. He never tired of watching sandpipers skillfully avoid a tumbling by being alert at all times to the irregular activity of the ocean as it crashed to shore.

Gulls squeaked and squealed as they circled and made sudden descents to outmaneuver the competition to a bit of something to eat.

Pelicans were spurred on by the cold weather in a search for food. Mack, as always, felt an uplift in his spirit, almost to the point of laughing. Were they not evidence that God had a sense of humor, those lovable, laughable birds?

Mack had no plans for the distance he might walk nor for what he wished to see. He was here and that's where he wanted to be. The sights and sounds were for immediate enjoyment, and for memories in the months and years to come.

It was a good place to view things back home as he never could have when there. Back there, all things were too close to be seen as objectively as could be from here. Was it that there was less urgency about people and problems when he was watching the ocean come to land over and over? Here he had no responsibility for anything. For this day and the morning of the morrow, he was free of any duties. It was not that he ever wished he was free of all responsibilities. He would be unhappy without those he had, but he occasionally needed time to review his life and what he wanted to do in the future, somewhat like an impartial observer might. This was as close as he could come to being that impartial observer.

There would be changes, probably some of importance. For thirteen years, his life had been shaped to a large degree by Rebecca's illnesses. Since her passing, things had gone on much as before. Crystal had, of late, added another dimension to his life, but nothing of certainty yet. So far he had a buddy for two or three times a week, a short while each time. Overall, life was pretty much the same. There was pastoral counseling, something he wanted to get into more. Changes were coming in family life that society was unfamiliar with . . . unprepared for. The counter-culture war was really getting under way.

After hours of walking in sand that offered little traction, he was tired. And hungry. The beach? He was not at all tired of it. He'd be back at it after eating, and he should be able to find a place to eat without a long search. People from the colder states of the North usually had begun arriving for the winter by this time of year. He had talked briefly to a couple he had met on the beach. They were here to escape the Minnesota cold. Compared to back home, the 55° was like a day in the spring, they had told him.

A boardwalk exit, built so as to protect the high sand dune from pedestrian caused erosion, took him to a paved area. Motels, shops, and an occasional restaurant were along each side of the coastal street. He chose the nearest restaurant which offered fresh-caught flounder as a special that noon. He ordered garden salad with Italian dressing, and a baked potato all to be served at the same time. Coffee that helped indirectly warm cold feet was the first to be served, followed immediately by warm sliced bread, crusty on the outside and soft on the inside, and a convenient dish of dipping oil. At this point, he began to feel that good luck had been with him in selecting a restaurant.

The lightly crusted fish that had been fried in a manner that didn't take up a lot of oil was a delight in taste and in texture. A freshly baked Idaho was perfect. The salad dressing must have been put together by an Italian who was a culinary expert. Fresh, warm bread was served; it was almost as if he had inhaled the first. If over-eating was a sin, he would need to spend some time on his knees. Considering his big meal of the day before, he wondered where such an appetite came from. The inward smile came; it was all the fault of the people in the kitchen. This meal went a long way in making up for some mediocre ones he sometimes had on the road. He had a long, cold walk back to his lodging to burn off much of this. Maybe there would be no extra time needed on his knees. As he slowly sipped coffee from his final refill, he thought of himself, his life, and where he was in it. He guessed that no preacher is ever satisfied with what was being accomplished in his ministry, yet he felt he was doing about as well as he should expect. Carpentry? On a few occasions, he had examined someone else's work in what he specialized in. Modesty did not allow him to boast, but there had been factual evidence of a difference.

He was not certain he was becoming happy but felt he was making some progress in that direction. There had been a time long ago when he was happy and optimistic, so he had a good idea of what it would take to arrive there. He was better, but the lingering guilt for his betrayal of his wife while she lived with her illness, was something that stood between him and an opportunity to become perfectly happy. God's forgiveness had not been a part of the problem for a long time. He could even come close to forgiving himself for the actual act itself. He could not give himself a pass on his stupidity.

He took his last sip of coffee that had not been allowed to get cold. He tipped the waitress excessively. Then he walked to the place where he had come over the dune and began the long walk back, at times too close to the crashing waves.

The ocean entertained. It always did, especially when the wind was up. He watched the swells as they came across shallow water. Sometimes he guessed correctly on which ones were to become huge breakers that came thundering far up the beach. His successes were cause for gleeful shouts and his failures for low moans of disappointment.

A preacher acting this much like a child? He knew there had to be some truth in his answer for he had said aloud, "Why not? Does some of the boy not always remain in the man? What a pity it would be if all of being a boy perished with age. But women, do they find a man who still longs to be a boy some of the time . . . do they see that as a weakness, an undesirable thing we ought to feel shame for? Somehow, I really believe there are some women, if only a few, who would find endearing a remnant of the boy in the man. Crystal might."

For close to a half hour, he stopped and allowed the ocean to take him where it pleased. He became more aware of it and less aware of himself. Far off places to the south were tropical beaches that never saw freezes blacken the greenery of forests that grew close to ocean edges. Did large whales frequent the Gulf far out to sea? Sharks swam not far off shore. Below the surface was another world where countless species lived, most as inaccessible to him as he was to them. Mysteries by the thousands existed out there. He would never know about more than a few.

Is God concerned about the welfare of those creatures who live in the deep? It's easy to imagine God sees the health of a forest as being important, but is He equally concerned about the giant beds of seaweed? Have we been so man-centered that we fail to give a place of importance to the other species that live on land and in the sea?

I guess what I'd like to be able to do is to see clearly all there is in the great world of the ocean. Oh, if only a large whale should surface and blow—the day is cold enough to make its exhaled breath quite visible. Dolphins must be swimming not far from shore, right now.

He had read that as ice ages came and went, the shoreline moved out and came back. How had this land looked at the height of the present ice age. The present ice age? It was not easy to think the twentieth century was located in an ice age until the ice caps on Antarctica and Greenland were taken into consideration.

So much of the ocean's attraction for him was not understood, but the longing for it was as real as longing to see the hills and mountains.

As he resumed his walk, he became aware of another longing. He had asked Crystal if it was all right if he phoned her this evening at her mother's home. Eight would be a convenient time for her she had said, and she'd be looking forward to it

Suddenly, he felt the loneliness of all the years of his marriage. Crystal represented the possibility of real hope. The risks that he usually felt when thinking of a woman in his life was outweighed by the anticipation of living in a house that was not empty. The memories of those years when there was no one to share good news or bad, no one to sit with and talk, Not once had he ever had some one to snuggle with. His wedding night had pierced his heart. Before marriage, he and Rebecca had never smooched. It had been something they had agreed on as being unwise and possibly sinful.

He continued walking, always aware of the sea, but became even more aware of his internal thoughts and feelings. What if he fell in love with Crystal and asked her to marry him? Would he need to confess what he had done that time when all decency had fled him?

Well, he wasn't, on this afternoon, even close to discussing marriage with Crystal. He liked her. She was a friend. And that was sufficient for now. Talking to her at eight, just the thought of it, and he was not so lonely. It was at exactly eight that he dialed the out-of-state phone number. On the first ring, the receiver was picked up and the voice he heard was the one he wanted to hear. The conversation was not very long but it told Mack much. She was awaiting his call, apparently closer to the phone than anyone else. Her voice was filled with warmth, letting him know how much she welcomed his call.

Feeling a need to return for a slow walk on the beach, he dressed warmly and went out. The clouds had cleared and the moon was beginning to rise, creating rippling flashes on the horizon. He stood for a time watching until it broke free from the ocean. A memorable sight that he wished Crystal could have shared with him.

The wind had calmed somewhat and following suit, so had the breakers. He walked without any risk of being caught by surprise and getting his feet wet. Paying scant attention to the waves, he only sought the sounds of their companionship. While the moonrise worked its magic on him, he thought of a future that might include romance and Crystal as his wife.

Do I still fear getting married again? If I didn't any at all, I'd be foolish. There will be risks—she could become sick with something serious. Not once did it cross my mind that there could be a downside before my marriage to Rebecca.

How blessed I was on that day last April when she was allowed to come and prove to me she was alive and well. Well! Dear Lord, Well! It didn't hurt my feelings that as long as she was in my presence, I out-fished Alf by a wide margin and he was as convinced as I, that we had witnessed a miracle. Lord, preachers love to talk about miracles and it sure helped that I experienced one, and life after death became a certainty.

"Lord, if my relationship with Crystal continues and moves on to another stage, please bless each of us with good health and sweet dispositions," he said aloud.

He would try to do a better job of leaving the worrying about what might happen up to the Father and the Son. It wasn't that he didn't know intellectually that this was the better way, that it was living proof of his faith. Actually, it was a measure of his faith and sometimes he didn't measure up.

He continued on, walking slowly, facing the moon, which as if by magic, was much smaller than the last time he had paid attention. On a darker night, the phosphorescence of breaking waves would have been more distinct, but it was there, first showing at one point and quickly running the full length of the wave. And the next breaker would be close behind and different enough to keep and hold his attention almost to the exclusion of everything else.

The ocean, and its ever-changing moods, drew him when he was away and drew him from his lodging early in the morning and back again after supper. Like the moon and stars, the earth and its seas were of the Lord's creation. He felt a touch of sadness for the generation only a few years younger than himself, who were hurrying thoughtlessly to the burial of the idea that there was a Creator. And what would they get in exchange? Sex without cultural restraints and free from the burden of guilt. Greed given free rein as if they would be able to take possessions with them when they breathed their last.

Tolerance for whatever it was that they were or wanted to do was fast becoming the new order. And anyone who was not tolerant of every aspect of the new culture was a bigot. And people who tried to preserve the moral code that had protected the family as a place where children could grow up whole, would be verbally attacked. They already were.

Mack felt sad where he had been at peace a few minutes before. He would do all he could do to slow the wave of counter-culture that was rolling over tradition as surely as the ocean's waves had rolled over the beach earlier that day.

But it was not only this disturbing thought that kept him awake an extra thirty minutes before sleep came. It was Crystal. What was he going to do about her? For the present, he hoped to continue as they had been doing. Let time be taken. Be not afraid. Don't make an *effort* to fall in love. If marriage eventually comes, let it be after they had lots of fun in a girl-friend, boy-friend relationship without responsibilities, something he had too much of for years.

This decision made, he easily slipped into sleep and remained in that blissful state until a quarter 'til eight. At nine fifteen, after a shower and breakfast, he walked to the beach to thank God for caring for him though the night and to bid farewell to the ocean 'til next time.

The man who drove back was a somewhat different man from the one who had driven down Thursday afternoon. If things developed between himself and Crystal, especially falling in love, he was not unwilling to think about it. The possibility was a welcome one. But he was not there yet and was in no big hurry to arrive there, or so he thought.

Three weeks later, he had a date with Crystal for supper. On arriving at her apartment, she asked him to come in for a few moments to see a small desk she had purchased. It didn't take up much space in her living room, which he estimated was about ten feet by fourteen feet; The desk was just the right size. A solid piece of maple, it was very handsome—he could see why she was proud of it.

"Now I have a place for my school work. No more will it be cluttering up my tiny bedroom." The desk's chair had a padded seat, the rest being maple.

"Beautiful piece of work. It always pays to get quality," he complimented her taste and judgement.

Her hair had been down the night of the fair. As usual in preparation for going out, she had it pinned up. He loved it that way, and on her it looked impressive. It made a handsome woman beautiful. An unfamiliar heart beat caused him to feel drawn to her even more than usual. He felt pride because he was to escort her to dinner, that is to supper; he would never get used to calling it by that fancy name like city folks did.

As they were driving away, Mack said, "I didn't realize your apartment was so small."

"It's a reflection of a teacher's pay. We have a good retirement plan compared to our regular salary. You need to be dedicated to the kids and most teachers are."

"Once I heard a school superintendent say he did not want teachers who got into the profession because it paid well. He wanted them in it because they were dedicated. That left me with a couple of questions I wanted to ask, but figured it would be useless to ask if he wanted to weed out those who wanted to earn a living."

During supper, Mack surprised himself by asking, "Would you now say we are going steady, Crystal?" He thought that had been settled before and was surprised that he was the one doing the asking.

Her eyes sparkled with mischief. "Why do you ask?"

"Well I just . . ." and left the sentence unfinished because he didn't want to admit that he wanted reassurance. "Didn't you once ask me something like that?"

"We go out quite a lot and it's pretty much on the same days of the week. So it would be accurate to say that makes us going steady." Her face was a picture of amused warmth. She was pleased that he was the one asking about the status of their relationship. She had thought she knew, but there was nothing quite like the idea of the man asking. She felt like saying she'd been wondering if he was ever going to bring up the subject, but on her list of questions she might bring up, it was far from the top. She asked, "Is there anything special you'd like Santa to bring you?" as a means of changing the subject.

"A necktie. Something in blue. What would you like?"

"Perfume. Something like musk would be nice." It was hard to keep from giggling. The stuff was said to arouse certain emotions in men. "Or another nice one is . . . ." She gave him the name of something that smelled very fragrant but did not have a naughty reputation.

He was a very proper gentleman which was proper for a minister. But there were times she wished he'd give her a brief peck on her lips. One of these days . . . but she was patient and would not hurry him beyond what he was ready for.

CHAPTER TWENTY-FIVE

Christmas came and Crystal had gone to her mother's for a few days. Mack felt lonely even though he spent the day and a night at his parents' place. Doggone it! I wish she hadn't gone off for almost a week. What in the world has gotten into me to make me feel like this?

Things had never been like this when he was dating Rebecca. He had admired her a great deal but was not so emotional in the first months of their relationship. This was happening too fast. His interest in Crystal was not based on how suitable she might be as a minister's wife. She had a sense of humor and preferred soft laughter to being overly serious. She was different and Mack thought that was a plus. He liked her and liked her a lot, he now had to confess to himself. It was a fun relationship and knowing she was a good buddy was a comfort. Knowing that she felt the same about him was a soft cushion between his loneliness and the days she was away. When he phoned her twice while she was at her mother's, she made it plain that she welcomed his calls. She called him once and his evening brightened. "Just didn't want you looking longingly at another during my absence."

"Would never consider that."

"I bet you wouldn't," she said with a hint of teasing derision in her voice.

Did she think he would, even for a moment look upon another as she obviously knew he did at her? Did he sometimes look at her with a feeling of longing so apparent? Was he beginning to be lovestruck? He wasn't sure exactly what that meant and if he would recognize it if it came his way. He was thinking of her more. Would Crystal like to go window shopping? Would she like to go back to Alf's farm? What about Valentine's Day, what would she like?

—⇥⇤—

On his way home from his parents' home, Mack stopped off for a visit with Rebecca's parents on the afternoon of the 26th. Their two other adult children had been there for Christmas Day.

"We made it through the first one since Rebecca passed on," Anne said after the initial greetings were over. "But today, it's just been Lee and me. She had really passed on years earlier. We had known that, but had not accepted it any more than you had, Mack. It wasn't over until it was over. We couldn't deny any longer what we had somehow denied until about six months before she passed on. Even then we clung to false hope."

This was Mack's third visit in the past two months.

"We know she's in Heaven. There are times I wish I could go on and be there with her. She's well now, isn't she?"

Mack knew Anne wanted to hear again of her visit and assistance with his fishing in the presence of a credible witness.

"With the awareness that her presence was with me, I was also instantly aware that she was well, that her two illnesses were no longer with her. The grossness of her toothless face was gone. She was older than the eighteen-year-old-girl I first knew—maybe mid-twenties. But her eyes were so expressive of her intelligence.

"Alf didn't see her but he was very much aware of the help I received as long as she remained with me. I was really clobbering him as long as Rebecca was there helping. In my hour of need, she was allowed to return and offer tangible evidence that she survived beyond death."

"You have been blessed, Mack," Lee said. "And yours is a blessing to us. I believe in God and His Son, and sometimes it's hard to believe. Why does God remain so silent? Why are experiences of the magnitude of yours so rare that most never have one?"

Mack responded, "The Old Testament has many stories of God telling this person and that person a variety of things. Perhaps after Jesus came and spoke for God, saying that God had told Him what to say and there were reliable witnesses who wrote down these things, God may think we have sufficient reasons for belief. If we could survey everyone, asking if any had ever had an unusual experience relating to faith and God, we might find that these events are not as rare as we may think.

"Through Jesus, God has spoken to us on a wide range of things, giving us what we need to know to establish a complete value system," Mack concluded.

"There were times toward the end when I strongly felt Rebecca's soul had already departed and gone on to Heaven. My prayers that God would heal her have been answered."

"Changing the subject, Mack, it is our hope that you will find the right woman and live a normal life. It would be doubly sad if you were afraid to try again," Anne told him.

"There *is* a woman that I take out to eat at times. We hike in the city park on pretty evenings once or twice a week. Talk on the phone. I'm just now at the point of thinking she may be in my future. It's comforting to have a friend to think about, when loneliness begins to come creeping in."

⚊╬⚊

Jesus dealt with corruption in His teachings and His actions, knowing that there was a price to be paid. Hundreds of years later, the official Christian church in Europe had become corrupt almost beyond our ability to believe. Martyrs paid the price again.

There were times Mack felt very upbeat regarding what he should do to combat evil, to change things. This was not one of those times. When beat back for a time, evil was patient while awaiting the moment when vigilance seemed unnecessary, when human foolishness proclaimed victory had been won. But victory would always be fleeting, unless it was remembered what is needed at all times to keep it won.

As much as he liked to think about Crystal, he could not let up in the time and effort to prepare sermons. He needed time to open up the door to his heart and sit silently as he awaited God's entrance—sometimes it worked better than at others, but never did it completely fail. At this point he had to admit there had been times during Rebecca's long illness that despair overwhelmed his heart. How tempting it is to see ourselves as being better than we are. How disturbing it is to see the worst of what lives within. And then he would think he had not done badly in opening up for the Lord to enter. So many times he felt certain in his spirit that he had been successful in allowing God to come in.

⚊╬⚊

In January, he preached from the second and third chapters of Genesis. The tree of knowledge of good and evil and the warnings that were given if Adam or Eve ate of its fruit. Free will had been given. Man had now been granted the right to select a course of action that could be the wrong one.

Free will makes mankind different, more so than intelligence. Adam and Eve have been faulted for introducing sin into our lineage but what they did in disobeying God was to exercise the power of free will. Modern mankind continues to use free will to make wrong decisions. But the upside is that we can and do make many good decisions. Who wants to be like a pig or cow with only heredity and environment interacting to determine our every action? God has provided us with a simple plan for dealing with our mistakes and wrongdoing.

These were notes Mack scribbled down as he planned a sermon on the events in the Garden of Eden. The first Sunday in February he preached on the subject of modern determinism and its effects on religion. "More and more people are blaming their shortcomings on someone else—particularly the people who had been an important environmental factor in their lives, primarily their parents who had bought into the popular psychology on child-rearing to prevent warping their personalities. Old-fashioned discipline, suffering the consequences of choosing bad behavior, became a no-no. Not all parents bought into the Freudian-based psychology that emphasized the possible and imagined mistakes of parents in raising their kids. Many continued to treat their developing children as if the youngsters had to take responsibility for the possible negative outcomes of exercising free will; these are the ones who are prepared for life in the real world. Whether the country can survive the leadership of those who were reared without the inconvenience of suffering from the consequences of bad decisions, remains to be seen.

"Adam blamed his sin of disobedience on the woman that God gave him."

"Isn't that just like a man?" a clear, strong voice of a woman came from the middle of the congregation. Laughter was instantaneous, dominated by sopranos.

A week later, Mack went back to Genesis and the guilt Adam and Eve felt after the free-will choice that had followed temptation. Their feeling of innocence gone, they attempted to clothe themselves with leaves. They had not been punished before, yet the feelings of guilt were there.

"To have the gift of free will, a price has to be paid when it is used foolishly. If you eat three or four candy bars in succession, you know as you are doing so that a price has to be paid; you feel yucky and have no appetite for the fried chicken which is to be served an hour later. Sad, isn't it?

"Adam and Eve knew better. They had been told better. Yet, they did it anyway. Near the very beginning, man was given free will, but the Tempter came along and told the woman there would be no negative consequences following disobedience to God's rule.

"Modern thought says there is no such thing as free will. In the real world, we struggle, may even agonize over whether to do *this* or whether to do *that*. Do we buy a new car or continue to drive the old one that has required repairs four times in the past six months? Do we take out a fifteen year mortgage to buy that new house? Then there come all kinds of moral decisions that have to be made—unchanging values make many of them automatic.

"Today we hear *Just do your own thing*, whatever you feel like *your own thing* is. It's said seriously in a total lack of concern for other people. Where this will lead if many people buy into this value system is frightening.

"Free will makes mankind unique among the creatures on earth. It sets us apart. We have a conscience, those of us who exercise a free will. If we do wrong, make a bad moral decision, we become like Adam and Eve when they tried to clothe themselves so God would not see their nakedness. Their innocence was gone, and so has it been with mankind ever since. Like Adam and Eve, we continue to use free will foolishly at times and some use free will to decide to do a downright evil act.

"But aren't you glad you have been blessed with the gift that allows you to consider and then step back from the outside pressures that may be trying to sway you, and then and then only make the best decision you are capable of."

At the sermon's end, he hoped he had communicated to the people what it was that he had tried to say. He felt inadequate, even more than usual. At lunch with Crystal, Ken, and Jan, he was somewhat reassured when they agreed that they had not looked at eating from the tree of knowledge as a sort of experiment in seeing how man would use free will that God had bestowed on them.

"It was free will that was God's final act in making mankind into man in all his complexity?" Ken asked.

Crystal said, "Perhaps more than anything else, it separates us from the animals of high intelligence."

Jan said, "Before your sermons, I'd always thought that the original sin had messed things up for every one since Adam and Eve. If only they hadn't eaten the fruit, we could all be living as if in the Garden of Eden. It would make me angry at them. Though I have made some stupid decisions that I regretted and begged God's forgiveness for, I'm glad I had the freedom to make mistakes. Some decisions I've made give me great joy." She took Ken's hand and looked into his eyes with love so plain to see, and said, "Ken has asked if I would marry him. I'm going with him to the jewelry store tomorrow after work."

Crystal in that happy manner women have in cases such as this said, "That's absolutely wonderful!!" She looked at Mack and asked, "Don't you think so, Preacher Man?" She often called him that, always with a twinkle in her green eyes. And he answered, "It is as you say, Teach," a name he'd used for her on a number of occasions when they were clowning up a bit.

The two women were now talking with each other at a rate that at least was double the rural speed limit for all vehicles. And Mack said in a jovial manner, "Another good man bites the dust and women celebrate his downfall."

Ken laughed and said, "And they never heard one word of what you just said."

"May I offer you congratulations, Ken, she's a fine woman. Later tell her I said that."

The men said nothing further. Mack tuned them out as he began to think about himself and Crystal. He wasn't there yet, but at some point in the future, was he going to be in the same predicament as Ken? Oops! That ain't the right word. Glad I didn't have my mouth in gear when I thought it. Shoulda thought, *in love like he is.* I didn't use to think in terms like I just did. Crystal has been changing me. I'm taking up some of her foolishness, which is so different from what I was with Rebecca in our days of courting.

"Mack, where were you just now?" Crystal elbowed him lightly in the ribs to get his attention. "You been in a daze thinking about Ken's good fortune?"

Mack said, "What I was thinking was more like 'Another good man has bitten the dust.'"

"Shame on you, Preacher Man," Crystal teased in return.

"Are you going to tie the marital knot for them?"

"Didn't you intend to say the martial knot? Yeah, I'll do that if asked. But Ken knows the probate judge and may want it real legal."

Ken and Jan were in such high spirits, they were giggling throughout. Ken commented when the fun settled down, "Mack has performed a number that I've witnessed and they are all working out. Maybe it's pre-martial counseling he claims he does."

"Silly!" Jan exclaimed. "You're as bad as Mack. Y'all act like teenage boys."

Mack said, "In all seriousness, I think like one at times. Maybe it's because I never was a real teenager. Back then, it was all about being serious in my thoughts. I couldn't understand why all the other fellows were not like me. I'm beginning to enjoy my new way of looking at things!!"

And indeed he was. "There are times I'm beginning to feel happy and feel sorta bad that I do. Poor Rebecca never knew happiness, even before her illness set in. Neither she nor I ever suspected that God might have a sense of humor."

Crystal said, "Mack, she might have been happy in her serenity and the absence of any tendency to be a cut-up. I knew a girl in high school who was quiet-natured and modest. Once I asked why she didn't join in the fun of lunch-table talk and laugh along with the rest of us. She told me she was happy the way she was, that I should not think she was an unhappy misfit."

"At the time you were in your teens, I bet you were happy like today. You've been through years of sadness and are coming out of it a different man who wants to enjoy life in a more light-hearted manner," Jan added.

Three very special friends. Mack knew he had too few near his own age and took a moment to express his appreciation for their help in bringing him out of his emotional doldrums.

<hr />

On Valentine's Day, he had three red roses delivered to her apartment around four-thirty. "From a not-so-secret admirer," the enclosed note said.

A little before five o'clock, his expected call came. On answering at the first ring, a voice he had come to like a lot, asked, "Do I happen to be talking to a not-so-secret admirer?"

"I hope you don't have another one," he teased. "But I could believe it if you had half a dozen."

"Thank you very much. The color is just right." She'd have loved a dozen, but understood Mack wasn't quite ready for that. Things as they are, are so very good and to be enjoyed. When this time has passed, it will be looked back on as pure treasure.

No responsibilities of marriage yet, and all the anticipation of a continuing relationship that made her heart skip a beat each time she thought of her man. Yes, he's the man of my heart. He may not know it yet, but I do, and will let him know it when I'm good and ready to tell him.

At this line of thought, she felt she was being irreverent. Irreverent to be thinking about the preacher in such a way as she had been doing. Maybe there was a more fitting word but she hadn't been able to pull up one when she realized he had been talking and was now awaiting some kind of response. "I was in the act of being giddy, or just plain silly, and didn't catch all you said."

To this he said, "I'll bet you sometimes have a student whose mind is off somewhere else as you explained an equation you had put on the chalkboard. And you'd become impatient because of the kid's inattention."

"Are you saying you are fretted with me because my mind was on nothing but the roses and the guy who sent them?"

"Now, hon, how could I possibly be fretted about that?"

━━┼·┼━━

One morning when he had finished breakfast at the Retreat, he had at least a half hour before starting toward his job. A checker game was under way. The man who had told him the story about being a hobo during the Depression had a partner. Mack asked and received permission to pull up a chair and watch.

Zeke, the fellow who had told hobo stories a few weeks earlier said, "And my checker companion is Frank, a mean checker player."

To Frank he said, "This is Brother Mack, a preacher I found out about a week after I'd told him stories about the Great Depression and my days of being a hobo and seeing the USA. One of the guys who saw us in a lengthy conversation said he hoped I'd been truthful because it was a preacher I'd been talking to. Thinking back,

I couldn't recall that I'd told a lie or stretched the truth more'n a quarter inch or so. Keep that in mind if you're gonna continue with the one you started a minute ago.

Frank remained silent until he studied the next move, and made it. "It was in the twenties, fellers; the depression had hit farmers long before it hit business and industry. Me and the wife were wearing ourselves out growing five cent cotton and fighting a losing battle against boll weevils. We called them boll devils.

"The five-day rain stands out in my memory in those days before the Great Depression, as they now call it. Like most pore folks, we had a four-room house without the hallways like you see in peoples late-model homes today. Well, the roof was old—a wood shingle one that had got real leaky.

"It was in '26 or maybe '27. I had three boys but none big enough to help on the other end of a crosscut saw. A neighbor helped me cut a fine shortleaf pine and then helped saw it into roof-shingle lengths.

"I swan, Zeke! You took advantage of me while I was running my mouth."

"Well, what'd you expect? Now put a crown on that man."

And following that, Frank jumped two of his partner's men, and on he went with the story as soon as he had gloated momentarily, "I'd never rived any shingles before, and would have loved white oak ones if I had felt I was up to the job.

"Got the two bedrooms covered before cotton started opening, and in August I'd work a while on the roof and pull corn fodder while I rested from that. After the cotton was in and hauled to the gin, there was corn to be picked and hauled to the crib. The living room and kitchen would just have to leak because the rainy season was on us."

Frank appeared to be competing adequately on the checkerboard with Zeke as the story went along. "The five-day rain me and the wife called it. Not ever a hard rain but never slacking once. We had leaks in the kitchen and living rooms like you can't believe. New leaks joined the old ones of the past summer. We ran completely out of anything to catch water in. Bowls and cooking pots and water buckets, and anything we could find, even drinking glasses.

"I had put dry stove wood in our bedroom as soon as I saw how bad it was going to be. The wife had a terrible time staying dry even as she cooked. One pot was on the stove just to catch leaking water from the roof so the fire wouldn't be put out."

Zeke ended the checker game with one winning move, and complimented Frank for a good game, which it had been from his side of the board. "He'd have clobbered me if he'd not been telling his story.

"Frank, I can just see Marie dodging about as she cooked, trying to stay dry."

"Places that hadn't been leaking would of a sudden be dripping right along with the others. Our two hound dogs could no longer sleep under the front of the house like in better times when the weather was drier.

"Marie was jumping from here to there in front of the cook stove looking up at the ceiling half the time, trying to spot where the next drop was going to hit."

Zeke's imagination was all fired up as he tried to envision the poor woman's evasive movements. "You mean to be telling us that your wife continued her rain dance as the water continued to fall after three-four days of it? Did you consider shielding her with an umbrella?"

"It was no rain dance she was doing. Finally, I remembered a poor excuse for an umbrella we had in a bedroom closet and carried it to her. Never had she given me such a smile since courtin' days."

Mack checked his watch and knew he had to be going, but he had one question for Frank. "How did you get through the rest of the winter with a sifter for a roof?"

"On hearing of our troubles, neighbors came to do emergency repairs with tar paper enough for two rooms and the porch. One who had a pecker-wood sawmill brought boards to hold it in place."

As Mack was driving to work, he considered the heart-warming ending. No doubt that part of the story was factual. He smiled. Some other parts of it may not have been exactly sticking to the facts. Those two old men, what a pair! Would there be any such men fifty or sixty years from now.

—=÷+÷=—

His camellia bush, to his surprise, opened two flowers in late February. It had not bloomed the past two seasons. Red and more beautiful than the three red roses that had been delivered to Crystal almost two weeks earlier. He clipped them, then phoned Crystal to make sure she would be home.

The woman who answered the doorbell was different from the one he had become used to seeing. It was Saturday and her clothes were casual jeans and a blouse of light blue broadcloth. The face was even more strikingly beautiful than usual. He had quickly averted his eyes from the rest of her, because she was so definitely a woman, too much of one for a preacher's eyes to linger long.

He extended the flowers to her as he said, "The first ones ever from the small plant I bought at a nursery near the coast two or three years ago." Realizing his voice was a little shaken with emotion, he said nothing more.

"Camellias! There's nothing prettier. And we were having freezing weather earlier this week."

She took scissors and cut the stems very short so she could freely float them in a shallow dish of water. Placing this on the kitchen table, she said, "They'll be my company. They'll be for me to love at breakfast." Instead of you, she was thinking.

"Crystal, I hate to hurry off, but it wouldn't look good if I stayed long."

"To whom? Not me . . . I'd love for you to visit a while. If someone from church saw you leaving right now, he'd not know whether you'd been here a minute or an hour. So what does it matter if you'd

373

been here ten minutes? If it went beyond ten, I'd be hurrying you outta here." she said as a smile turned her beauty into a radiance unlike anything he'd ever seen.

He stayed five, perhaps six minutes. Her hair pinned up like she wore it, gave her a stately look, somehow emphasizing the firm, but soft curve of her cheeks. And her eyes as she talked, never left his face. They spoke of an emotion she did not speak of as they briefly sat at her kitchen table. The conversation was all about flowers. She referred to the two African violets she had growing under a grow-light on the kitchen cabinet. And then it was back to camellias, which she'd love to have a yard full.

Mack was paying only a bit of attention to the content of her speech, mostly focusing on the rich, soft voice and every word so distinct from the others. What a teacher she must be! What a woman she is and she clearly has some degree of interest in me.

She checked her watch and said in the teasing way she so often addressed him, "It's been seven minutes since you arrived, Preacher Man, and you'd better leave while your fine reputation is intact."

Leave, he knew he had better. She was becoming more attractive faster than ever he thought she could

At home, his thoughts did not soon leave her. As he had paused at her doorway before leaving, she took his right hand in both her soft warm hands and something of importance had been exchanged. They had sometimes held hands as they walked side by side, but that had never affected him as this five or six seconds had. He had looked into the misty green eyes and the full lips as red as the flowers he'd brought, and wondered how it would be . . . . That was as far as he got. He was a preacher and she would be in his congregation the next morning. How would it be if he could forget that for a moment? He couldn't forget her, or that he was a preacher, not even for a moment. He'd done that once years ago and regret had been a daily and, too often, a nightly companion—sometimes only briefly but sometimes like an unwelcome visitor you thought would never go home.

His had become a new life these past six months. Light-hearted, as never had he been before, yet still as serious or even more so about his ministry. A year earlier, he had thought he was as certain about life after death as he was of the sun's rising each morning. Not a lot of days after Rebecca's burial, her presence for about forty-five minutes and brief image of the healed person, proved to him that she was very much alive. Over and over, he had been thankful to God for lending her to him to convince Alf and himself with real evidence that she was there to give absolute proof of life after death. Maybe God blessed him with this special miracle because he had suffered so long.

"Bad things happen to people of faith. Belief in God and in the messages of Christ do not assure any of us that tragedy and illness will not come to visit us," Concluding a sermon one Sunday, he advised his congregation, "Do something about the things you can do something about and leave the worrying to God—a motto that will improve the quality of your life. Since childhood, all have known that at some point death will come. The non-believer is left with Solomon's advice; "Eat, drink, and be merry for tomorrow you may die." But what was he left with when poor health or age has left him with the inability to follow his own advice. Awaiting death while believing you are the creation of nothing more than the end of a long string of chance events. Believing that this life is all there is or will be is far too much to be borne when life's end stares you or a loved one in the face."

He loved the sound of it, the rising and falling of the soft swishing of the April breezes in the pines along the ridge top. It was from memories of childhood. A longleaf pine stood in the back yard. It was from a time when life knew no serious or troubling moments. It was a time when fancy flowed freely. Though he had never been there, the breeze in the pine suggested far away places. He didn't know of a particular far away place, but he sensed there were such. And the breeze that made pine needles sigh would go on to others. As soon as it left the large tree in their yard, it would soon be heard again, but barely, from the timber beyond a narrow stretch of pasture. And the next stirring of a breeze would create the sound again.

Across the ridge, he walked and dreamed of far-away places he had visited. Slowly he moved through the trees that now whispered of adventure and, on this day, also of love. Briefly the image of the girl on the Mount Rainier trail revisited. Had she introduced him to a longing for a woman who resembled her. More certain of it than ever as the image of Crystal appeared in his mind. He longed to see the first one and thank her for making him aware that another such woman might be in his future. He enjoyed thinking of the possibility.

He walked away from the trees that whispered of those places of his fantasies, and down along the trail toward the small stream whose voices spoke of things he loved to ponder.

Did anyone else come to the rock and sit, like the girl on Rainier said she had done earlier? What if someone else had made the discovery of his stone by the stream-side and was using it today. It was with a small amount of relief that he found it empty, awaiting his arrival.

Some would complain of the stone's hardness that made itself aware the first thirty seconds it was sat upon. But Mack seated himself, thankful for nature's having him in mind while fashioning the shape of it during its millions of earlier years. He smiled at the absurdity of such a notion, but liked the thought anyway.

As always, the little creek made music for his ears, and he was reminded of topping a hill on his drive to the state park this day, and there before him was a large puff of a white cloud with feathery arms on three sides. It came with total unexpectedness, music of crispness and clarity and as silently as remembering a great church hymn. A curve in the road and the music was no more. And when he again found the cloud, it no longer was as it had been, and the brief music he had experienced was not continued. Of one thing, he was certain; it had never been heard by him before. Would such a visit ever be his again? Silent to his ear, but loud and clear to his mind. Not the kind of story to be told if he wished to keep whatever credibility he might have.

Crystal. He had come here to enjoy spring in his favorite forest. Again, he smiled. He had come here the better to think about her and to let his feelings for her run freely, taking him with them wherever they wished to go.

And it was to her eyes—green, soft, and warm—that his emotional state carried him. They were still as they were six months ago. Even back then, they had looked at him with warmth and genuine interest and at times a hint of amusement. Was it amusement at all? More likely a joy of living that had to express itself, no matter the circumstances of the moment.

But the eyes had changed in ways he could not exactly describe to himself. He had seen something of the expression in the eyes of young couples who came to him for pre-nuptial counseling. He had seen it in the eyes of Ken and Jan when they had come to show her engagement ring. Years ago, he had seen it in the eyes of couples on the college campus as they sat on benches under a tree and pretended to be talking of affairs academic, all the while their eyes doing the real communicating.

Was he sure that Crystal was sending a message? Pretty certain, but probably not doing it consciously. Even for a brief moment, did he express such an obvious affection for her with his eyes? No, not

Mack. He could exercise control over his emotions, and he still questioned whether he even had such strong feelings that could send such a message so that others might know what was going on behind those windows to his soul.

Yet when he would leave her at the apartment entrance after a meal out, he would drive off with a great feeling of sadness that they could not be together all the time. Being so alone during those years of Rebecca's illness had left him deeply scarred. He knew in ways not many his age could possibly know, how deeply loneliness can reach and continue its pain into the future.

Even his faith in God had not fully protected him from hurt. And that was something he had not shared, even with Maude. He had not wanted to leave himself spiritually naked for another to see how much he fell short in his faith.

Crystal had begun taking his hand in both of hers each time he was about to leave her at the apartment entrance. It was an experience he enjoyed that led to nothing further. If the guys in the Sunday School class knew that after six or seven months, they had not gotten physically further along than this, they would smile in disbelief, but Mack thought it wise and proper.

Memories of Rebecca in her illness, hallucinating about the young lady back at Mount Of Olives Church came to haunt Mack one evening after taking leave of Crystal in the manner that Rebecca had accused him of allowing. In her illness, she lived with horrors that others did not know. Her behavior mirrored what it was like inside to a person who could get by the barrier of believing it was no more than just imagined problems in her thinking, that she ought to see the same realities that the healthy mind sees. There were some who thought the illness could be overcome if the patient would just decide that they wanted to shape up and be like the rest of us.

Mack realized anew that he had not overcome all the pain that had been associated with her illness. The experience of a year ago came again to comfort him. He recalled yelling to Alf above the sound of the outboard, "Rebecca is here, and she is well!" Later, Alf had told him that the Lord had healed her on entering Heaven, "Your years of prayers have been answered!"

Mack remembered many things that day he sat on his favorite rock. Benches in the church of his childhood took no consideration of human anatomy and he would have to sit still for up to an hour at a time. His mother would pinch him if he started wiggling about on that hard flat surface.

The sounds of the little stream were just right for his next thoughts about Crystal. Her laughter knew just when to appear, never a premature giggle nor an inappropriate chuckle, always a sound of delight that lifted the spirits of those who heard.

And her diction! Never a slurred word and never a piercing sharpness, but rounded softness instead. When she read something in Sunday school class, no explanation was required and he would think how like a good teacher of poetry who just by reading it aloud made its meaning clear.

Of late, he was not as careful to avert his eyes from her body as he had trained himself to do many years earlier when looking at women. Crystal was definitely a woman. Still, he was able to not let his eyes or his thoughts linger.

Not knowing whether he was falling in love, he knew his thoughts more and more were turning to her. At times, she was a sweet presence in his heart, whether with him or miles away. He was far from ready to let her know how his feelings were ever softening toward her. Even as he sat on his comfortable rock letting his tiny creek weave its spell, he considered. Was he on a one-way track to being hopelessly in love? Maybe he should arise and leave this place before he knew for certain.

Dating Rebecca had been as different as fall is from spring. Fall was quiet beauty. Spring was an awakening—a promising of excitement. With Rebecca had come subdued feelings, not delight and a tugging in the chest where the heart's beating was something that he was very much aware of. He thought of Crystal's voice and fun-loving ways. He listened to streams's merry voice, much like Crystal's it was.

If there was a point and time when Mack knew he was in love, it was that April afternoon that he sat on his comfortable rock and listened to the tiny creek. It was not as though he was listening to a person. He knew it was just the sound in the highlands of water that had recently been born of the earth and was in the early exciting stage of journeying to the Gulf of Mexico. But it *did* seem to help Mack clarify his feelings toward Crystal.

It was not like being ready to marry her, but it was a new stage in their relationship from his point of view. He valued the time he spent with her too much to continue in the low-key manner he'd been courting her. Unless she was not enthusiastic, he'd be on the telephone more, he'd hike in the park with her more, and he'd spend more time with her in their favorite restaurants. They'd go see Maude; what a change that would be! Maude probably hadn't heard that he had been seeing someone.

But when they went, the first thing she said after introductions was, "So this is the young lady I've been hearing about—going out with our preacher. I've had her pointed out to me more'n once by one of the church ladies. She's a looker, Mack."

"You mean people have nothing better to talk about than that the preacher is seeing someone?"

"Not some small item of gossip, Mack."

"Do they generally approve or do they think it's too soon after?"

"They, that is the people who talk to me, are one hundred percent in favor." Turning to Crystal, she said, "It is said of you that you are a real down-to-earth young lady. People tell me they hope you catch him, though I can't say I wish such bad luck on you," she said as laughter filled the room. She had instantly liked the young woman.

Mack was not in any way embarrassed or made to feel uncomfortable. He had told the young woman what to expect. Maude did not disappoint.

"I'm eighty-nine and holding, Crystal. I hope I live long enough to see Mack do something about his life. He's a fine preacher, partly because he's had me standing behind him for the past few years." The eyes behind the lenses of glasses were sparkling with mischief that she was not completely able to hide. "When you address me, please call me Maude. Mack and I got on a first name basis the first day we sat and talked.

"Well-meaning church biddies sicced him on me, trying to get me to come to church."

"Did he have any success, Maude?" She already knew the answer.

"Well, not for a while, a pretty long while. But he had more brains than they did. We talked each time he came about things we had mutual interests in. He didn't come talking to me in an unctuous manner."

"You mean in that super smooth manner that sounds so artificial?" Crystal asked.

"Exactly. I can't see why they think they can win more souls that way. We had one of those years ago, one of the reasons I'd quit attending church. One time too many, I heard a phoney voice say, 'Lettuce spray,' and I became a cranky backslider and there were other reasons. I had an idea what Jesus might have said about addressing a congregation of regular speaking people in preacher-speak."

Crystal asked, "Did Mack come visiting you talking in that kind of preacher-speak?" It was obvious that she was enjoying a moment of amusement.

"Of course he didn't. He talked like regular folks. Just as he does now. He didn't preach at me or to me. We were equals. He showed interest in what I had to say. I found him to be interesting. We communicated. I invited him to come back. It went on like this for weeks so I decided I wasn't as crippled as I'd been telling I was.

381

Sure I hurt, but with the help of three of those ladies, I made it to church expecting to shock Mack.

"I never got to see as much as an eyebrow lifted in surprise. He preached on the prodigal son. A favorite sermon of mine. He wasn't preaching at me for being out of church several years. His sermons, I'd been told, were always prepared weeks in advance.

"I know Mack well now. He'd never have pressured me to come to church, even if I'd never returned. As I did him, he understood me. He was and is my friend and I know he feels I'm his.

"I've prayed that he would find a good woman and marry her."

Crystal, in a manner that was pure Crystal asked, "Maude, do you think I might be that woman?"

"Honey, you speak my kind of talk. No phoney baloney. He wouldn't have brought you to me unless you were mighty special. He thinks you might be that woman. I know him as well as he knows himself."

⚊⚌⚊

As Mack was driving her home, he listened to Crystal's opinion of Maude, "She says things I wish I could say, and gets right to the point. Her hands and probably legs and feet all crippled up. Her eyes sparkle with humor and intelligence. I like her very much. No phoney lady there. Can we go see her again?

"Would next Sunday afternoon suit you?"

"Very much if I can't talk you into taking two ladies out before then to a good meal." And of course he did.

The following Sunday morning sermon again revisited the world's most prominent atheist, Jacques Monod. It had been almost three years since he had first told his audience that the brilliant scientist who had shared in the Nobel prize had said in a newspaper interview that people have to have a value system, without which they cannot live as individuals and cannot deal with society. Monod had to have something to believe in.

"The certainty of eventual death is universal and universally drives man to seek some kind of purpose for living.

"The person who believes in God finds meaning and purpose in life, Though Monod believed in Chance, he selected something with purpose because he had to. Without it, he could not live.

"The Christian, as part of the salvation experience, will find that he no longer takes pleasure in things of the world and must give up bad behavior and bad attitudes in exchange for the peace, love, and companionship of his Lord."

Based on these sketchy thoughts, he preached a sermon that drew many compliments, even a couple of congratulatory phone calls.

Later, at Maude's house, he and Crystal listened to interesting comments on the morning's sermon.

After coffee and teacakes were served by her live-in companion, Maude complimented him.

"I liked it, Mack, liked it a lot. Everybody does have to have something to live by. A scoundrel may draw pleasure from cheating an old lady out of her savings. King Solomon evidently drew great pleasure out of lying with women, yet in his advanced years saw the vanity of having wives and concubines by the hundreds.

"There are evil people. Hitler and Stalin for example. Satan possessed? I think so.

"Enough of that sort. Let's look at Christians, real Christians. How much does it cost for a person to be one?"

"Giving up some of the things you've been doing," Mack said without giving it much thought.

"Or some of the things you've not been doing, but might in the future," Crystal added.

Then Maude interjected, "Mack, I wish you had given a bit more positive picture of being a Christian."

He had for years been receiving criticism from this remarkable woman, so he took no offense, just listened.

"It doesn't cost us a thing to become a believer. Of course we all know that it cost our Lord His life's blood when He died on the cross for our sins that we might have eternal life."

Crystal and Mack said an amen in agreement.

"Oh, if you've been a career thief or lived by cheating people out of their assets, you'd want to turn to another way of making a living. But for most, it would cause one to stop gossiping or trying to make time with a member of the opposite sex.

"Things like that might be looked on as costs by some. But they are not costs. If benefits exceed what's given up, does it really cost you something?"

"No. Call that profit," Crystal said. Mack agreed.

"If a Christian isn't receiving more benefits from being one than what he might have given up when he became a believer, he is not giving God an opportunity to pile on the benefits that are available for the asking. Like letting God's presence comfort you when you are lonely, like asking God for help in making a decision. You have over the years pointed out a long list of benefits by letting God live in you . . . letting Him be a companion. And you've done it well."

For a couple of moments, nothing further was said. Then Mack said, "You mean that this morning was a good time to point out that Christians were too often only casual partakers of all that Jesus offered us when He allowed Himself to be crucified?"

"Mack, for too much of my life, I didn't make much use of a service that was freely offered, where the Son and the Father would welcome my leaning on them. God knows that we didn't ask to be put on earth and that at times of despair, we wish we never had been born. If we will just take Their help, They'd be so pleased. Jesus came and saw what a miserable fix we were in. They understand. Feel sorry for us? I think so.

"Jesus saw people with horrible diseases and terrible afflictions. Did He know that many wished they had not been born? He healed by the hundreds. How must He and the Father have felt about mankind that They had created? Does the Lord feel disappointed that we don't let Him do things for us that He wishes we would?

"I'm old, very old, and there are times I feel I already have a foot in Heaven." She paused, grinned, and then added, "At least a big toe.

"Preachers, I think, and that includes you, Mack, tend to spend valuable time expounding on some selected verses of doctrine from the Bible," she stopped.

"And need to talk more about the big picture, not teach another Sunday School lesson from the pulpit.

"What do you think of this, Crystal?" Mack asked.

"That she is as wise as she is old, maybe very wise for one who is only 89 and holding," she answered with a twinkle of humor in her eyes.

"So you are saying, Maude, that what I need to do more of is to convey the idea that if there is going to be any worrying done in my house, it'll be up to the Lord to do the worrying?"

"And that, my dear preacher, means there'll be no worrying done. God will be pleased.

"For a very old lady, I do right well, but my pain medicine is allowing pain to start coming back."

"And it's time we went on and let you take your pain meds and lie down a while," Mack said as he and Crystal were getting up from their seats.

CHAPTER TWENTY-SIX

L ater that afternoon as they sat on a park bench under a fully leafed-out willow oak, Crystal asked, "Has she always been as frank as she was today in criticizing preachers?"

Mack laughed. "At first she was worse. Then as time went by, she conceded I was not as bad as the worst of them. From her, that was high praise. Some of her theology, if I preached it, I'd soon be run off. But there are times I feel I ought to take the risk."

A man and his wife from church came walking by, and greeted them but didn't stop.

"Mack, I'm making progress. You didn't withdraw your hand because someone we know saw us holding hands."

"I've been thinking a lot lately about us, Crystal."

"And?" She was looking into his face and eyes, as there was a touch of merriment in her expression.

"I was window shopping the other day and before I realized it, I was next door to a jewelry store." He said nothing further.

"And since you just happened to be there through no intention of your own, you decided you might just as well go inside and see what such stores sell." She said nothing further for a moment as she now looked off into the distance. "Did your curiosity get satisfied?"

"Yeah, but I don't know that being engaged is worth the sort of money they were asking," he teased back.

"Pick me up at 4:00 this coming Friday, and I'll go with you and help you decide if being engaged is worth the kind of prices they are asking. This isn't the most romantic proposal I ever heard of, but I'll accept it in the spirit it was intended."

After looking in all directions to see if there was anyone in sight that he knew, he leaned toward her as much as she did him, and gave her a light kiss on the lips. The first time this had ever happened and his heart felt a special tenderness for this young woman who had occupied so much of his thoughts lately.

"Will there be more of that in the future?"

"If I didn't plan on it, I'd not have done it then," he retorted.

"All teasing and foolishness aside, I understand your reticence about physical acts of affection. Maude explained in a phone conversation the other day that you only go to the beach during cold weather when the beach bunnies are in hibernation. You even avert your eyes from my body, and I take that as a compliment, that you found it attractive and don't seek temptation. You are a gentleman, Preacher Man, and a man to admire.

"Let's walk a little in the park. Isn't that why we came?"

During the next four days, he often wondered if he had gone one step too far. As much as he liked being in her company and as much as he thought about her in all tenderness, still . . . Yet, when he looked at the man in the mirror as he shaved, he saw the eyes of a man obviously in love, a look he'd have been hard put to describe before, but one easily recognized now. He asked the Lord for the courage he needed to enter the jeweler's come Friday afternoon.

Maude was right. He and Crystal entered the store at 4:15 and he was not scared at all. He, a preacher who advocated prayer to his flock, had followed his own advice and here he was with a slow, regular heartbeat. Crystal needed no assistance in finding the very place where pretty engagement rings rested under glass. The proprietor was with another customer, giving them time to look and quietly exchange opinions.

She found one she liked in just seconds. Mack said, "You must have slipped in here earlier this week to get a head start, but you wouldn't do any such thing. Well, which one did you pick out when you were in?"

She giggled. "I didn't admit to coming in earlier."

"But you did," he said in a tone of fondness.

She pointed as she said, "The bottom row, second from the left."

After taking time to carefully look at the rings, he asked, "That's really your pick?"

"Oh, yes, Preacher Man. I liked it on Wednesday and I like it today." A look of worry appeared on her face, "Is it too pricey?"

"My credit rating is pretty good."

She interrupted before he could continue, "Oh, I know it's a gift from a man to a woman and I feel funny asking you to buy this one, but I fell in love with it."

"Let's consider another one too. On the same row. Move to the right skipping two. How do you like that one?"

"A gorgeous solitaire! But it costs far too much."

"I told you my credit rating is good. Look at it some more, comparing to others while the gentleman continues with his customer."

"Don't need to look at any others. This is the one! If it isn't too much." In a whisper, she said, "I hope he didn't hear me. You might have been planning to bargain with him on the price."

He whispered back, "It's okay if he heard you, I think."

When the proprietor came to serve them, Crystal quickly guided him to the solitaire. She didn't notice that he removed a tiny tag from it as soon as it had been removed from its resting place in the jewelry box.

"It's a perfect fit." she said in an exclamation of excited pleasure. She walked over to a full length mirror and turned her hand one way, then another. "Any way I look at it, it's beautiful.

"It costs so much, Mack, but can we really get this one? Maybe you can . . ." her voice trailed off.

"I don't advertise it," said the proprietor, "but the list price leaves me a little wiggle room. Mr. Baldwin realized that when he made a substantial deposit last week on that ring. If you like it, he is to pay the balance today."

"I love it! Thank you, Mack!" As she squealed, she gave him a full-length hug and then a kiss that sent excitement coursing throughout his body.

The other gentleman did not raise an eyebrow in surprise. He'd seen this many times before and was busy thinking how fortunate it was for him that young men in love don't buy engagement rings during a period of sound judgement. Thirty-six years earlier, he had lived through just such a time, and the woman at home who'd have supper waiting a short while later was worth it all, many times over.

And Crystal was still so excited an hour later as she and Mack were eating at their favorite restaurant, she had not commented on how the ring, a perfect fit, just happened to be that way.

News of the engagement spread among church members like a fire in a field of broom sedge while a March wind was having a great time fanning the flames.

Mack's sermon had been planned weeks before and a good thing it had been. His usual organized self had gone off somewhere else. Whether at the church office or at home on Saturday, the telephone was ringing. Congratulations and well wishes from all, and many ladies wished to know when the big event was to be and if they could be there. It was fun. It was gratifying to know that so many cared. Maybe he was crazy, but it was too late to be considering that possibility.

It was also a hindrance to clear thinking and his thoughts resembled a logjam. Sunday, Monday, and Tuesday were busy days with church and work on houses. Wednesday, he'd already scheduled a couple of counseling sessions in the late afternoon before evening church services, but he could go to the Men's Retreat for breakfast and relaxation.

Breakfast there might not be healthy; some folks said it wasn't, including Crystal when he had told her what he ate.

He ate that calorie-filled breakfast with the delight that hot fluffy biscuits, premium bacon, and fluffy scrambled eggs can ignite. Warm fragrances mixed and mingled with the air he breathed. Coffee as he would carefully sip its complementary essence to the food. A dab of butter on a warm half biscuit that was then thickly spread with apple jelly was a great way to cap the meal. He ate the other half-biscuit prepared the same way. Now he knew he should take the forty-five minute drive to the state park and hike the four-mile loop trail.

Once at the trail head, he set off at a fast pace. Thinking was sometimes easier to get started when he was hiking because it took away some of the energy he often wasted with a variety of fanciful thoughts.

Of course, it was Crystal he needed to have a clear mind for. Should he tell her?

It had defined much of his inner life for the past ten years. The one black mark that made him a flawed man. There was all the extra effort, the intellectual energy it had taken to keep his emotions as averted as he did his eyes from the bodies of women. Years of compelling himself to not think in terms of legs and busts and waists and posterior shapes. Always dwell on faces and eyes and things that were spoken. Maybe not all monks were able to accomplish this, but he knew that many of them had and did for years. At one time, he had sought the advice of a Catholic priest, who without inquiring specifics as to why Mack came to him, gave freely of how he accomplished this with daily prayers for help. "You got to pray a lot, but you have other things you need to spend lots of time asking God's help in dealing with. I understand your problem," he said.

At the jeweler's, Crystal had planted a big kiss and big hug on him. And he felt some of what he felt those years ago when the sin was committed, when the infidelity caused him to lose respect for himself.

God had forgiven him, he was certain. But he had not and could not forgive himself for his unfaithfulness to his wife. And the young widow made emotionally helpless by her grief, he took advantage of in her weakest hour. When he could have acted to go get a chaperon, he didn't. He recalled how he let procrastination use up the time he could have acted. He recalled that at one time he thought this was an opportunity to do some pastoral counseling, not for long, but long enough to miss one opportunity to go get help.

There were other reasons he had often used to beat up on himself, but this was more than enough to rawhide a soul that had not entirely healed.

Maybe if he spilled the episode to Crystal, she would understand. Maybe she would and she might not hold it against him. Maude knew and understood, but she was not the one he was getting married to.

If he told Crystal, she would probably want to know things about the young woman. Mack couldn't imagine how he could explain how it happened that wouldn't make him look like the creep he was that night. She might lose a lot of her respect for him.

He asked God what he should do. Before long, he had a feeling that things would be okay. No decision had to be made right then. A little procrastination could be a good thing at a time like this when he didn't know what he ought to do. Anyway, he felt better. Things would work out.

He walked along the top of a ridge as he was thinking. There was enough of a breeze to stir the pines into a rising and falling of whispers. Old long-leaf pines, only an occasional grove left. They were special in their massive tall trunks, in their towering crowns of glistening needles, so long and beautiful. How easy to feel close to God in one of His great creations. How poor the man or woman who quickly looked and then turned thoughts to something that spoke not at all of their Creator.

Crystal loved nature, she said, because God created it all. In walking among trees, she felt uplifted on pausing to look up to their tops that pointed toward Heaven. Birds in flight were a never-ending source of amazement to her—how could a large flock in perfect unison suddenly change direction with no collisions? How did vultures find updrafts and sail endlessly without wasting energy? How unlike Rebecca she was.

It wasn't that Rebecca was less than Crystal as a human being. She had been, before her illness, a quiet stream that flowed in near silence, serenely beautiful. Crystal was a stream that bubbled and splashed merrily along the terrain it passed over.

Before her illness, oh, before her illness, Rebecca inspired feelings of tranquility and quietude. I loved the peace she represented. In her presence I could in silence go ahead with my meditation and often did. What a loss of such companionship that allowed me to be myself when I needed time to think through some meaningful subject I had just read.

Now Crystal, so different, will have me laughing and trying to respond with a touch of wit. I think on subjects I want to ponder far more easily when I'm not with her. But the problem is I want to be with her most of the time. A Saturday in mid-June is when she wants the wedding. There are two Saturdays that might be said to fit that category. I find myself wanting her to pick the first one, and yet feel a touch of anxiety about that being so soon. Ken told me there'll be times I'll feel very little love for her and wonder what was I ever thinking about when I bought her the ring.

Mack knew that big, important life changes can scare a person when the time draws near. Leaving home to go to college had caused anxiety for weeks before the actual leaving occurred.

Yet when his marriage to Rebecca was approaching, there had been no touch of anxiety.

If Crystal picks the first date in June, that's just a couple of days plus two weeks. Less time to wonder if I'm doing the right thing.

What if Crystal comes down with some dreadful illness or what if I do? Lord, be my helper. I need to feel more at ease about this. Help me do the right thing. Please take away such unrealistic worry. Let me know You are behind me.

With that prayer, his prenuptial doubts and fears ended and were not to seriously return.

On learning that evening at supper that Crystal had selected the earlier date, he was happy it had been settled. "I'll call Maude tomorrow to see if we can come over Saturday just before noon." Mack said.

"And take her out to eat and tell her when, but to keep it secret for a few days more?"

"I need some advice on a thing or two."

Crystal didn't ask, "Why Maude?" She had learned the lady had continued to grow in wisdom with each passing decade.

⊫═╫═⊒

After lunch they returned with Maude to her home where the first thing the elderly lady did was to give Mack an official looking document. "Mack, this is your title to the '57 Chevy Bel Air. I had an air conditioner added last week, so you two can drive on your honeymoon trip in comfort."

"I feel bad about your giving away your car, but I'm thrilled to be the one receiving it. There has never been another like it."

They talked about wedding plans. "Two weeks from today," Crystal said, "and then you'll be mine, Preacher Man."

"It'll be in church, of course." Maude suggested.

"We'd hoped to have it more private. Why not right here? You have a large enough living room for a few guests," Mack had suddenly thought of this possibility.

"No way. Not that you wouldn't be welcome. For years, you've had close to a thousand enthusiastic fans, plus a couple hundred more members who are a little on the backslidden side. Why hurt them when it will be so easy to avoid doing so?

"Let Associate Pastor Wes Madison announce it the Sunday before the wedding that everyone who wishes to show up for a brief ceremony at two o'clock?"

"That's the time we set," Crystal said. "But we do not want wedding gifts. That's one of the first things Mack insisted on. We've both been married before. Mine was very short-lived and Mack's . . . everyone knows about. We both have things from before."

"You will be having a reception? Would be a shame if you didn't."

"We were hoping to slip out and get on our way to Gatlinburg. Crystal?"

"If the wedding is at one o'clock, we could."

Maude thought two o'clock would be better. "One o'clock is too soon after lunch." So that settled that.

"Ken Albright and his wife will be making pictures for us. If others think the occasion merits it, they can bring their Polaroids or 35 millimeters and take all they care to, though I doubt many will.

"If we have a reception, I'll get a caterer to handle the refreshments." Mack said.

"A week from tomorrow, it should be announced at church." Crystal said.

For Mack, it was the busiest two weeks he had ever known. And he had thought he'd known what being busy was!

The Saturday of the next week, Maude phoned him to come over. She gave him two sets of keys to the car.

He choked up even more than on receiving the title, unable to say anything without bursting into tears. Instead of thanking her, he took the thin, frail body into his arms and placed a kiss on her cheek. Then he did break down and attempted a blubbery "Thank you!"

"It's okay, Mack. I kept the keys 'til today so I could drive to see to my friend at the nursing home. I wanted you to enjoy the car while I was still alive. I couldn't stand the thought of you driving that old pickup on your honeymoon."

There were other things during the following two weeks that he wished he had time for, but everything kept coming at him too fast. He did take time on his wedding day for breakfast at the Men's Retreat. It was there he hoped to collect his wits—as if he thought he had any left. With a wry grin breaking just a little, he wondered if Crystal would object to his coming here occasionally. Things would be different. He'd never been able to learn what marriage was like.

His bacon, eggs, toast, and grits were up to expectations, and he delighted in the care of the man in the kitchen to prepare everything to the usual high standards. Briefly, his memory turned to the horse apple cobbler he'd eaten once on his return trip from the Smokies.

It was at that restaurant he planned to stop for supper. Maybe he should be like a city feller and call it dinner. Ten miles beyond was the Holiday Inn where he'd made reservations to spend his first night with Crystal. The Saturday reservation at Gatlinburg had been reset for Sunday.

"This is your D-day, Brother Mack," a fellow from church had paused by his table.

"Won't you sit with me, Bob?"

"Thanks, yes. I've already eaten, but I'll have coffee.

"You have the look of a concerned man." His eyes sparkled with amusement while feigning sympathy. "Are your feet becoming a bit cold?"

"It makes no sense. I've been alone for so many years and couldn't ask for a better woman."

"But you are going to have to change your life quite a lot just as she will. And you had adjusted to the life you had all those years."

"Yes, and in time became pretty comfortable with it . . . a different kind of life than most have." He paused and added apple jelly to a bite of toast he was about to take. "It has nothing to do with her," he said before taking the bite he'd prepared. "She's the best there is," he added after he'd eaten the piece of jellied toast.

"Any sane man or woman will have doubts at times as the wedding day draws close. To keep one or the other from backing out at the last possible moment . . . isn't that why we have engagement rings for the woman?"

Mack laughed. "And announcements, bridal teas, and all else that precede many weddings. Too embarrassing to chicken out after these things have been done. After the whole church was informed last Sunday that Crystal and I would be getting married today—"

"You'll be awaiting her at the altar at two o'clock."

"If I fail to show, Lowell would fire me."

Bob interrupted, "You'd have to give up preaching and flee to South America." At this point, they both had a good laugh at such absurdity. Mack would be there. Suddenly a chilling thought flickered across his mind. What if the bride failed to show. "She'll be there, Mack. She'd have to give up her church and her friends. Also it would only be right that she return that fine diamond you bought her."

"It's really nonsense for me to entertain even the slightest fear of marrying."

"But, it's so natural." Bob got up, took Mack's hand and said, "Every member of your audience at church is super happy for you.

I bet fifty people have told me they are really praying that the greatest of happiness is visited on you both."

Mack lingered a while longer over a coffee refill. Bob's company and encouragement had warmed his heart, but of greater value was the fellow's complete understanding of the touch of jitters that the nearness of the wedding had brought with it. Now he could smile outwardly and did, but more important was the warm inward comfort that brought relief from any vestige of unease.

⟞⟝

It was only ten minutes before two when Maude and her live-in companion entered church. A large crowd had already gathered. Their walk down the aisle was accomplished without any unusual problems for Maude.

They seated themselves on the very first row. Maude didn't consider herself the matron of honor. That was a bit too highfaluting for her. She was a ring bearer. The ring was around her left thumb, one of the few fingers that wasn't too knotted by arthritis to easily slip the ring on.

Will Crystal object if Mack phones me as often as he has done for years? Will she allow him to come visiting on Sunday afternoons. Dear Lord, I pray that she will not be the type that tries to reshape all of the husband's social life.

Mack, you are the grandson I never had. Crystal could be the granddaughter I've only seen twice. The day my sun will finally set can't be far off. Lord, please place in the hearts of those two that I'll still have needs. Please don't let them forget.

At this point, Wes Madison, Ken Albright, and Mack entered from the side and took their places for the ceremony. Mack wore a pale blue tropical weight suit, a white shirt, and dark blue tie. His shoes were black and had been recently polished. There had been a couple of times in the past when she had gotten after him about his dull looking shoes that had only been buffed occasionally by lifting a pant leg and rubbing a shoe against the sock just above the ankle. How like a boy he was at times, and him the pastor of a large church.

But he's a fine-looking young man and has been my buddy for years. Where others failed to move me, he soon had me coming to church and he never once got after me about my backsliding ways. I'm as proud of him as if he were my grandson. God bless you, Mack.

Then the organist fired up the over-sized organ with "Here Comes the Bride." A thrill ran through the elderly body as she stood and took the three steps to the position she had been coached to stand. A glistening new cane was to be her only support during the ceremony.

Indeed, here she comes. A more lovely bride I've never seen. Eyes radiant with sweetness and joy . . . oh, how she must love him! So graceful and lovely in her tea-length wedding suit of orchid silk with flaring tulip hem and softly fitted matching jacket with its curved front and covered buttons. And medium kitten slingback heels of dyed-to-match orchid satin. True to her name, she wears delicate sparkling crystal at her ears and on her wrist. Her glossy honey blond hair is secured by a sparkling crystal comb in an elegant upsweep. She carries a bouquet of white calla lilies.

When Crystal had taken her place beside Mack, Maude concentrated her thoughts on the couple. She felt proud of her role in bringing them together on this day. She was old and experienced enough to realize she might be taking a little more credit for this happy occasion than she was due. But what if she was? Doesn't being eighty-nine and holding sometimes carry with it a privilege of being a little prideful.

When the time came, she took the large ring from her left thumb and passed it to Crystal. Mack's *ball and chain* crossed her mind as Crystal was soon placing it on Mack's finger—but it's time he had one. He needs her to remind him of the things he gets careless about and the things he may not think are important, but are. Maude was in sort of a day-dreamy state as Wes continued the ceremony. Her adopted grandchildren would be in her life. Crystal had promised they would. What a heckuva woman! And gosh! He has just kissed her, planting a dandy one on her. Bet he can feel a tingling all the way to the tips of his toes. It's high time!

The next thing she noticed was the organist was beginning the recessional. An unusual selection for this type occasion, but it was at her own request for she thought it fitting and appropriate for Mack after those long years of trials and grief.

Wes had pushed the church's wheel chair gently against the back of her knees and was soon hurrying her through the hallway that led to the Family Life Center and the reception. Ken hurried with them.

Mack and Crystal were walking down the aisle as the congregation watched and those who had been seated toward the front fell into a line that was forming behind them.

Mack was wondering about the selection of "It is Well With My Soul," for the recessional. Everything was well with his soul. Well, not quite. There was that one thing he'd thought he ought to tell Crystal about, but there had just never been a time that he felt was exactly the right time.

They were outside on a broad walk that led to the side entrance to the reception area.

Jan Albright had taken the shortcut that Ken, Wes, and Maude had used. Jan's camera became busy just as Mack and Crystal were entering. A lectern had been set up and a floor-stand microphone placed beside it. It was just before reaching these that the newly-weds stopped to greet the line of well-wishers that was forming.

A wide variety of tempting refreshments had been placed on long tables. Nearby, guests could select from a variety of drinks. Teenage girls were assisting.

Tables with chairs should be enough to accommodate all who came.

Handshakes, hugs, congratulations, and well-wishes were almost a dizzying experience for the couple. People waited patiently in line. In the many decades of existence, the church had never had a pastor who got married right there in the sanctuary. Few, if any wanted to miss any part of the event.

Somewhere, perhaps halfway though the actual reception, people were beginning to say that this was fast taking on the air of a festival.

Wes had used the public address system twice to encourage people, after meeting the bride and groom, to stay for refreshments and visit with each other in celebration of this happy occasion.

⊶⊷

They were finally on the highway when Crystal exclaimed, "It was exciting! Never would I have dreamed of a reception as warm and filled with so many good wishes. I'll save the memories the rest of my life, but I'm glad it's over."

The trunk of the car held all of their luggage and had since the night before. Ken had kept the car at his home, making it possible to keep the secret that the honeymooners would not be leaving in the old truck, which Mack had left in its usual space behind the church.

"Ken has been such a good buddy slipping off from the reception and bringing it back to park close to our exit so we could drive by the pickup on the way out and look at all the fun things some of the guys had done to Old Faithful that was going to have to be cleaned up at the first service station we came to," Mack said.

He was recalling the looks of surprise on the faces of the guilty ones as he had driven by with the window of the Bel Air down and said, "Great job, guys!"

"Cheater!" a good-natured young man called back.

But that had been thirty minutes ago, and the feeling of amusement was spent, and the moment of confession was closer. He had tried several times to talk himself out of it, but with no more success than he had been able to forgive himself over the many years of mentally beating himself up for such poor judgement when there was opportunity to do otherwise.

"You are being mighty silent, Preacher Man," she said in the light-hearted teasing manner he had come to associate with her. Affection was always present in her voice and her words. Pure Crystal, he thought.

"Just thinking. Partly, there is a bit of a letdown following such a reception."

"Of course, there is, Hon. We couldn't bear on and on such a level of excitement like that. Quiet reflective moments are necessary.

"Our marriage is ahead of us. All of it. And sometime within the next six hours or so, we will start another part of our relationship. Are you wondering how that will be?"

"I'd be a liar if I said I haven't." What he didn't say was that he had prayed to the Lord that he would avoid fouling up on that. She was the woman about whom he had worked so hard at trying to always keep intimate things off his mind when with her. Was it going to be something he could face with the ease and assurance he felt each time he stepped into the pulpit? So far, he had not been quite able to manage that level of self-confidence. So many months I've had to work at channeling such thoughts away from her and now it's morally correct to let me think of Crystal as my lover-to-be. As a pastor, I've not only had to preach sexual morality, I've tried to live it, and have done what I think God would approve of, with that one exception and the sometimes exciting memories of some aspects of it . . . all mixed up with guilt.

They passed farms with horses and cattle. And they talked of the farm they hoped to have some day. Cornfields came and whizzed by, leaving the expectation that the stalks would soon be sporting tassels, and silks on the ears that would be beginning to form.

"A farmer must gain satisfactions that no city dweller can ever experience," Crystal said.

"And experience aggravations that the city dweller doesn't have to consider. The cornfields we've been passing are at the mercy of the weather. Dry, hot weather hitting at the time that the tassels are having a hard time restraining themselves from bursting forth. Broad leaves begin to roll in on themselves during the hottest part of the day, trying to conserve moisture. Tassels appear and yield smaller quantities of pollen. The ear of corn will be small and may have a few seeds here and there on a stunted cob." Mack realized he was running on too much, but the restaurant where they were to dine was not more than an hour ahead. It was there the confession would be made. He would not wait until they were in their room at the Holiday Inn, ten miles further up the road; that was not a place to tell her something that could cause hurt feelings and disappointment in her husband.

They had been seated in a corner booth at the restaurant. Crystal had ordered roasted pork tenderloin with green beans, mashed potatoes, and house salad. Mack ordered the same. Iced tea had already been served.

They had taken a couple of forks of the salad when Mack knew it was time to confess, unless he was never to tell her.

"Crystal, there is something I did years ago that I wish I hadn't. I want to make a confession."

At this point, she excused herself to go to the ladies' room and was on her way immediately, before he had time to respond. She was gone for what seemed like five minutes. Mack wished she had waited. Getting started again would not be any easier than the first attempt.

The woman who came back to sit across from him was not the same as the one who left. Her hair had been freed to fall to her shoulders where it graced the sides of her face.

"Mack, you don't have to tell me what happened."

"Your eyes are different! They are blue!" he said, wondering how that could be. She was Crystal and yet she wasn't.

"I was there. I know how and why it happened. I was June Lamar then. I wanted to talk and you were a good listener. Finally I just wanted to be held and then things were all out of control. I'm so sorry."

"And you really are the woman who lost her husband in a mining accident." It was too shocking, too stunning to take it all in at once.

"I felt so absolutely terrible about what I had done to you and even worse for what I had done to a woman who was in a mental hospital.

"Hundreds of times I asked God to forgive me. But I've never been able to completely forgive myself.

"I hired a private detective to locate your parents and neighbors who were close friends of theirs. I met the neighbors and through them, I kept up with how Rebecca was doing. I had no intentions on you. Just thought I'd feel better if she started improving and could return to you."

Mack's emotions couldn't keep up with what he was learning. "And your name?" He asked her.

"Had my surname legally changed to my mother's maiden name and swapped the order of my given names, June Crystal became Crystal June. This was done *after* I learned she had Alzheimer's. And the green contact lenses served only as part of the disguise.

"Surgery changed the looks of my nose and to a degree the tone of my voice. I took speech therapy when I was in college thinking it would help me in teaching. Didn't want to speak in a manner that might cause kids to imitate and mock me behind my back. I decided to use some of the money I received from the mine operator for David's death.

"Once I told you I'd been only briefly married. Like it had been one that I soon decided I'd married the wrong man. I guess I ought to be sorry I caught you while being in disguise. Are you so mad at me now that you'll have our marriage annulled?"

He reached across the table and took a hand between the two of his. "I ought to be very angry for your trickery, but what I feel is as though a dark, lingering cloud has finally been lifted, and I can begin to forgive myself. No, I'll keep you, despite your scheming ways."

She came over to his side of the booth, leaned down, and was openly embracing him when they heard a distinct throat clearing. "Shall I bring your entree back in a couple of minutes?" the young waitress asked.

"No, I'll be sitting beside him in less than one second."

After they'd had time to sample the delicately seasoned tenderloin and the vegetables and had tasted hot yeast rolls, lightly buttered, Mack asked "How long has Maude known who you are?"

"Since sometime in the second week after you introduced me to her," she said. "She advised me to go for you, that it would lead to double self-forgiveness. But how did you know I'd told her?"

"Call that a smart guess."

"Are you not at all mad at me?"

"No, Teach. I'm just Play Dough in your hands. For the first time in fourteen years, I'll be totally happy when the reality of this has had time to sink in."

And Mack marveled that he was able to notice how truly remarkable the food was. But the Mack who had loved good eating in the worst of times could see no reason for not enjoying delightful food in the best of times.

"Who could have asked the organist to play that unusual recessional," he wondered aloud.

"Haven't you figured that out? It's the sort of thing only *she* would think of doing. May God bless our dear incorrigible Grandma Maude."

AUTHOR'S NOTES

Including the visit by the nursing home dog, the description of how Rebecca died is an exact description of my wife's last hours, as Alzheimer's finished the final destruction of her brain.

The story of Rebecca's visit a few days after her burial, including Mack's vastly improved catch of bass as long as she was there exactly describes my experience ten days after Janett's burial. My good friend and neighbor, Clayton M. Reid, Jr., was the fellow in the front seat and I in the rear. He commented that he "envied all the help" I was getting. When her presence was no longer felt, fishing returned to normal, the fellow in front catching more fish as before.

I am well into my third novel, *Memories from the Great Depression*. For those of you who are interested in that era, I believe you will garner from the novel some new insights. My goal is to present an engrossing reading experience that you will find informative, entertaining, and inspiring.

TO THE READER

I hope you enjoyed your reading experience with *The Lingering Cloud*. Please take a moment to rate it and if you will, send a review to Hollis Hughes at lilah_macl@yahoo.com.

You may also be interested in checking out my first novel, *Mindful of Him: Wilderness Encounter*, recently published as a second edition.

If the Lord grants me more years of good health as He has thus far, there are more books coming. My head is running over with ideas, plots, and characters.

God bless you and may you always find just around the next corner an inspiring, entertaining, and enlightening read.

ABOUT THE AUTHOR

It began before daybreak on a February morning in 1928, in a house that was well ventilated in winter's cold.

I fell in love with books at an early age because my mother, a gifted reader, carried us four kids and my father to worlds far different from our world of the 1930's.

Though I grumbled like other kids about having to go to school, I loved it, but had enough smarts not to admit it.

On graduating from high school, I found a small Methodist college that offered me room, board, and tuition in exchange for work. Early in my sophomore year, I was given work in the college library, a job I fell in love with. Because I wanted to become a thinker, for reasons I still don't understand, I spent a great deal of time reading philosophy, sometimes to the detriment of a higher GPA.

I had wanted to write since my mid-teens, but there were lots of things I wanted to do. To marry my first love as soon as I had a secure job as a teacher, and to become a school counselor because I'd been the sort of kid that surely needed one at times.

A trip to Mobile, Alabama was a time of falling in love with azaleas and camellias. Rhododendrons in North Carolina and it was love at first sight. Nothing would do but that I start growing them. But "it can't be done in the steamy, hot summers where you live," I was told. For eighteen years I marketed about twenty varieties that had been propagated and grown on my twenty-one acres of wooded property. A good many of my rhododendron plants make their home at the Birmingham Botanical Gardens, which granted me a lifetime membership with the Botanical Society.

Too many hours spent fishing and daydreaming about fishing, and I still had not written my novel. There were just too many things I loved to do.

Eventually, I became my wife's caregiver. Alzheimer's disease was destroying her brain. The once bright lights of her mind were going out . . . one at a time, never to return.

My first novel was written during the advanced stage of the disease and published years after her death.

During my eighty-fifth year, I wrote a second novel, *The Lingering Cloud,* a story I could not have told ten years earlier. What would have been difficult to write in my seventies now flows far easier. My third novel, *Memories from the Great Depression,* is becoming far different from the other stories I've read of that era (1929-1939).

And afterward? If God continues to grant me the health and the time . . . I get excited just thinking about it! It's been one heckuva ride!

Made in the USA
San Bernardino, CA
06 July 2014